Offsides

**A story of romance, rugby...
and chasing your dreams.**

PG GELDENHUYS

First published by Pieter Geldenhuys, 2021

Copyright © 2021 Pieter Geldenhuys

ISBN: 978-0-620-93990-4 (print)
ISBN: 978-0-620-93991-1 (e-book)

Cover and interior crafted with love by the team at:
www.myebook.online

To my darling Caroline.

PROLOGUE

Jimmy's dad was being a prick. It was not only unfair, but humiliating as well. A huge party was expected at their place this weekend, but now he was stuck in the car with his parents and the holier-than-thou Vanessa for a family getaway.

He loathed these weekends. The holiday house was in Bettys Bay, a small coastal town only 90 minutes from their home in Cape Town. The neighborhood in Bettys was mostly elderly and retired people, as well as families with young children. Their sleepy getaway spot is more than 50 kilometers from their friends' holiday homes in Hermanus. The sixteen-year-old wasn't allowed to go to them before he got his own car two years later. He was too old for monopoly and walks in the mountains with his family. He had better things to do during the Easter weekend of 2013.

Vanessa didn't seem to mind. A year older, she was Little Miss Perfect. Excellent grades, impeccable manners, perfect boyfriend. The more she loved this "precious time with the folks", the more irritated he became. She would go to her room to play her violin and write in her journal. He loathed her.

All of the arrangements were in place. Mom and dad, along with Vanessa, wanted to go to the holiday home for the weekend, but he pretended to have a golf game with the school team on Saturday. His best friend, Tommy, had helped him set up the cover story. He would stay with Tommy and Tommy's folks for the weekend.

They were busted. Once his mom learned that Tommy's family were out of town themselves (without him), they had no choice but to cancel the gig. The girls from Herschel, where Vanessa went to school, were coming to the party, so he suspected it was probably her who snitched on them.

Their big entry would have been something to behold. Senior kids from Bishops Diocesan College have said they'll attend the party (and bring alcohol). Even Marlene Steyn, the cute blonde that he liked, said that she would attend. The party would have been the highlight of the year. As part of his punishment, they took his phone for the weekend. He couldn't even send a WhatsApp to anyone telling them the party was off.

He brooded in the passenger seat as they drove through Gordons Bay on the coastal road. As a child, he was always scared of this road. There was a sheer drop of over 100 meters to the ocean at its highest point, but they had driven it many times. His mom used to play games like "I spy" to distract them.

However, she hasn't done it as much in the last few years. She mostly kept quiet; it wasn't that she didn't engage with them—she did that well enough—but it was like a lot of the laughter had gone out of her.

He involuntarily looked over to Vanessa and at her left hand. That's when it all changed: after Vanessa's hand.

A phone rang. His dad hadn't yet inserted the phone into the new handsfree set—which was ironic, since that was the reason why he bought the new Mercedes, instead of holding on to the 2010 model.

The 2013 had the same safety features, but with more advanced communications. Jimmy's dad grew up poor, so as a financially secure adult, he loved to buy the newest luxury car every two years. Jimmy was excited about getting his own car when he turned eighteen. He could hardly wait until then.

Jimmy's father pulled out the phone and pressed it to his ear.

Although Jimmy could not see his mom's face, he knew she was annoyed.

As if on cue, she said, "George, please don't do that now. Can't it wait?"

"It won't take long, hon." He had done it a thousand times before —she always objected, and he did what he wanted. Jimmy sometimes thought that was why his mom went off to Europe on a retreat every year: to get away from all of them for a while. Jimmy was about to reply, just to piss off his dad, the man who humiliated him. Yet his sister, who knew him too well, touched his hand condescendingly, and shook her head.

He wanted to show her where she could park her condescending smile, but she shushed him by pressing her good index finger to her lips. A bully father and a walk-over mom—he wanted to tell them all off.

Neither of them noticed the truck approaching the pass until it was too late.

J immy's new home was a dump.

That was a little harsh. It was a nicely maintained, large three-bedroom house in the center of Oudtshoorn. The housekeeper came in three days a week, and the gardener came in on weekends.

Uncle Joe drove Jimmy up from Cape Town in silence. Jimmy's scars had almost all healed; the worst damage had been done to his shoulder, which dislocated during the accident. However, even that was no longer sore. They had popped it back in while he was unconscious. Though he had very little discomfort, his thoughts were still all over the place. The quack psychiatrist said he was suffering from PTSD. What an insight. Imagine the heartbreak you would be feeling if you woke up one day to find your entire family dead, and your life had been ruined?

Uncle Joe had been great to him. He was the one who brought Jimmy home from the hospital. He spoke with the lawyers, accountants, and everyone else. He was also the one who delivered the bad news.

He was Jimmy's godfather, but he never showed much interest in Jimmy's life up to that point. Both sets of grandparents were deceased, so Uncle Joe was the only living relative. Additionally, he had no children of his own—he was always off somewhere in some exotic location, cooking for the rich and famous. Among his favorite places to visit are the Seychelles this year, Las Vegas next year, and a few memorable years in Singapore, where he traveled many times because of the direct flights. But things always seemed a bit... strained... between Uncle Joe and Jimmy's dad.

As far as Jimmy was concerned, there was no one else around. Suppose Uncle Joe didn't want to take him—what was left for him to do? Since he wouldn't go to a foster home, they were stuck together.

Uncle Joe led him to his room. It was bigger than his old room, which was not surprising. The biggest economic activity in the region is the local military base, the annual arts festival, and the ostrich farm industry.

He threw down his things and took a shower. It was already extremely hot outside, and the air conditioner was not working. No pool either—What a bummer. Although his shoulder ached a little, the cool water provided some relief.

Afterwards, he went through to the kitchen. The famous chef made him—wait for it—a peanut butter sandwich. He realized he was really hungry and gulped it down. Even the milk didn't faze him—what was he, eight? Tasted good.

Uncle Joe was in the kitchen cutting vegetables. Giving Jimmy his space.

Jimmy was not yet ready to discuss what happened to his family. He found the silence stretched, and he wanted to fill it. If he didn't, he would go bonkers.

"So, when will it all be finished? How long until we find out how much is left?"

Suddenly, Uncle Joe stopped slicing onions and looked around. He did not need to say anything.

"Is there anything left?" Jimmy had to ask. He suspected he knew the answer.

That gray eyed uncle stared at him—eyes that knew, eyes that remembered, eyes that didn't seem to judge. They were not sympathetic eyes—they were simply sad. He shrugged and turned back to the onions.

Math was pretty easy for Jimmy. Accounts, too. He was probably smart because he read so many books when he was a kid. Before he discovered sports, beer, and girls in high school. Mostly beer.

Even with minimal effort, he had received straight A's during his first few years of high school. After his grades dropped the last two years, his parents were not happy—but at least he could comprehend basic math.

They had lived above their means. The car, the house, even the furniture; everything belonged to the bank. His dad's company, which always seemed to do so well, was also highly leveraged. The idiot had signed over his life insurance policy to raise extra capital.

Jimmy knew that he was being too hard on his old man.

Back in the early 2000s, his dad had gotten carried away in the property market—that was a good time... They had a place at the fancy golf resort of Fancourt, the holiday house in Bettys, and even shared a lodge up in the Kruger game park.

Then 2007/2008 happened—he was ten years old at the time. It was the annus horribilis.

Vanessa's hand was crushed in a freak accident while his parents were getting drunk at Apres ski in the Austrian Alps. His dad traveled while his mom stayed at home and supported his sister through all the surgeries.

All property prices plunged along with the stock market crash. There was a lot more fighting, and no more overseas vacations, or Fancourt golf. No more Kruger.

His dad had lost a lot of money, but none of them knew how much. He was really angry when he wasn't allowed to go on the Bishops overseas trip at 13 years old, but it made sense now. He was still in the best private school in the country, they still lived in an awesome house, and they still had amazing cars.

But now he knew it was all a lie. His father had spent all their savings and incurred more debt to keep up appearances. Now all that was gone, and he was stuck with his underachieving uncle in Oudtshoorn.

Uncle Joe was cleaning up.

"Listen, Jimmy... I have to pop over to the restaurant. Do you want to stay here, or do you want to tag along?"

After sating his hunger, the last thing he wanted was to hang out in a restaurant. What did he want? He pondered the question for a moment. He wanted to run. Run his anger and sadness and frustration and emptiness into the ground.

He shook his head. Uncle Joe nodded and cleared the plates. "I'll bring you some dinner from the restaurant—my shift is covered, and all I need to do is check the stock take for the rest of the week. I shouldn't be gone for long."

"Whatevs."

Jimmy took out his favorite Nike Air cross-trainers. While they were great for working out in the gym, there was no Virgin Active health club in Oudtshoorn. In addition to serving as trainers, the shoes also doubled as running shoes. Like everything else he did, Jimmy was a gifted athlete. Although he had talent, he had to work hard to be at the top in the increasingly competitive environment at Bishops. In order to impress the girls, he had been pumping iron in the gym since he injured his shoulder. Running was different—though he was never going to compete in it, he liked it for the sheer pleasure of it.

His iPod had been destroyed in the crash. He assumed there was no money for a new one. After hurling a silent curse at the universe; he took to the streets of Oudtshoorn in the late afternoon light.

As he jogged, he crossed through a little ditch (there had once been a river here, now dried up in the middle of summer) and ended up on a road leading out of town. The sign to the famous Cango Caves (20 kilometers) caught his eye, and he decided this was the best possible route. After running for five kilometers, he checked his speed on his Garmin watch (top of the range), then turned around. By the time he trotted back into town, it was well after 6 pm. He felt hungry again after working up a decent sweat. Wasn't Joe's restaurant on this same road?

Instead of returning to his new home via the same road, he took a little detour—and sure enough, he saw a cluster of four restaurants on both sides of the road. The last building on the right-hand side was the

Italian restaurant. Hard to miss with a painted sign in the colors of the Italian flag.

He pushed through the open door and was bombarded with noise. Pots were clanging, people were shouting, voices were raised in conversation. It was not a large place, maybe eight tables at most, but it was packed. The predominant aroma was the familiar smell of pizza, and suddenly his mouth watered.

An assortment of pictures and paraphernalia lined the walls, and it was dimly lit, cozy, and filled with people. A glance around revealed a mixed crowd: a family with young children here, two young lovers there, and a table full of elderly German tourists.

A small bar was situated in the back, overlooking the kitchen. He could see Uncle Joe back there, scurrying around. As he crossed the bar to the kitchen, someone burst through the adjacent door, almost colliding with him. The woman skillfully shifted the two large pizzas she was clutching, and their eyes locked.

For a moment, everything seemed to slow down. Her emerald eyes locked with his. Then she winked at him, and brushed past.

Uncle Joe spotted him.

"Jimmy! Hey, sorry bud. A German tour bus rolled in and the gang needed me here. Have a seat at the bar, and I'll get you a pizza takeaway. I'll just be here for another few hours or so."

He did as instructed—and a large beer appeared before him. He looked to his left and saw the blonde with the green eyes again. "Welcome to Oudtshoorn, Joe's nephew. Here's your welcome drink."

He couldn't help himself. He defaulted to dumb-assery.

"You know the cops could close you down for this. I'm not 18 yet."

She smiled, and leaned over. "I won't tell if you won't…"

And then she was gone.

She was the only waitress at Joe's, but two cooks doubled as runners.

Jimmy had to admit, the pizza (delivered to him within fifteen minutes, warm and delicious with some avocado on the side), the service, and the general ambiance were as good as anywhere he had ever been in Cape Town. And for a Sunday night, super busy. A few people had joined him at the bar waiting for tables. It looked like Uncle Joe would be here for a while.

Despite his best efforts, he couldn't help but trail the blonde with his gaze. She wore tight blue jeans and a t-shirt that featured the restaurant's logo. Her figure was athletic yet curvy. She was tall – almost as tall as he was. It was her job to work the room, smiling, clearing plates, flirting with the Germans, and, he would presume, collecting huge tips.

Whenever he wasn't watching the blonde, he watched Uncle Joe and the two other guys performing their dizzying food-prep dance in the kitchen. Pastas, pizzas, salads—the man was unstoppable. Uncle Joe's kitchen hands were equally skilled and friendly. One guy was around Jimmy's age, and the other one in his forties.

He never heard much about Uncle Joe from his parents. Jimmy knew that Uncle Joe lived abroad for most of his life and moved back to South Africa just a couple of years ago. Even then, there had been only one visit with his father—and that had been a stilted, strained affair. There was a story there... He was suddenly quite tired and got up to leave.

He grabbed the blonde's wrist as she rushed past him; "Hey, how does it work? Do I pay you... uh... what's your name?"

Clumsy. He had better moves than this.

Again, her eyes danced, and she gave a slight chuckle.

"My name is Lauren, James. And we'll be seeing a lot of each other. And no, this one's on the house. Even the beer..." Another wink, then she disappeared through the door into the kitchen.

He waved at Uncle Joe and walked out into the cool night air. It had been a long time since he had been called James... The only one who ever called him by his full name was his mom. And she had reserved it for when she was angry with him, in later years. Which had seemed to be fairly often. Funny, though: he didn't mind Lauren using it.

His new home was a short walk away. After another shower, he lay down on his bed. Maybe this place wouldn't suck as much as he thought.

He couldn't be more wrong...

Lauren and Sally had been best friends ever since preschool. Lauren was always the tall, slightly reserved blonde to Sally's short but sassy brunette vibe. Their shared interests—the outdoors and good books—contributed to their friendship. The main difference was that while Sally was intelligent, she never really cared about academics. She was more interested in fun—and boys, eventually.

Sport was something Lauren thoroughly enjoyed, and she ended up being the captain of her age group's netball team for years. She found that she had to work harder and put in more hours than Sally to get only slightly better grades in her classes. The two of them ranked above the average for most of their high school years.

Sally's family owned an ostrich farm and several properties in town. While growing up, Sally often went on exotic overseas holidays with her wealthy parents. Though Lauren had everything she needed, there was never an excess of money. It was a frequent source of arguments in her family, and somewhere near the end of primary school, Lauren realized that her father and mother had a bad marriage.

Her mom became more disengaged over the years, and Lauren grew more resentful of her mostly absent father. The more she learned about their financial difficulties and his gambling problems, the more conflicted she felt. There were also the affairs...

Her mother did not generally confide in her, but she was not stupid. It was a time of tears and fighting, and her solution was to spend less time at home and more at Sally's.

It's good to have best friends like that. She worked her way through high school, and snide remarks from girls were few and far between. Small towns had a way of covering up sores, especially if they were discreet—and her parents were.

The result was that she had difficulty trusting boys. Although Sally sought out sexual gratification and had lost her virginity by the age of 15, Lauren stuck to chaste kissing with the captain of the rugby team. There was also a beautiful surfer on holiday, and a few other less memorable encounters. It kept her relatively safe...

But the captain of the rugby team still had feelings for her.

In many ways, Sam had been a dream come true. His family moved to Oudtshoorn the year he started high school.

Sam did not come from money either. In addition to being charming and smart, she appreciated how hard he worked. He earned the respect of others with his work ethic and for always putting the team first. He was cute, too.

But their casual relationship during high school didn't lead anywhere serious. Not for her. Perhaps she kept up her walls, perhaps their souls didn't seem to connect on that level... Perhaps they were just too young. It didn't matter how she ended things; he was devastated. As captain of the first team, he had his pick of girls, and she hoped he would get over it. However, even though he had other girlfriends, she always knew—in the way that girls do—that he wanted her back.

There he was... mostly harmless, but also a barrier to anyone else in the school who might be interested. Even though it annoyed her a bit, it made her life easier as well.

That way, she could concentrate on her sport, her friends, and her studies. As her mom never had a career, and was entirely dependent on her father, she would never be able to find the courage to leave him. Lauren was determined that would never happen to her. She would have her own career and never be dependent on a man.

She felt confident heading into her senior year of high school. Steering clear of drama at home, she locked herself in her room or was out doing sports.

She told herself she was content.

Then Jimmy Barnes walked into her life.

There was a lot of talk in town about the tragedy, and about how Joe gave up his bachelor lifestyle for the sake of his nephew. In many ways, Joe was a role model to her about how to not let life get ahead of you. Even though she had never told him about the problems at home, she always had the sense that he was well aware. His understanding on those odd occasions when she had to rush home early, or were a few minutes late, meant so much to her.

She decided to cyber-stalk the nephew. On Facebook, the profile of a popular pretty boy revealed that he lived a high-class lifestyle and was completely self-absorbed. By just perusing the profile, she decided she would like him for Joe's sake—though she knew it wouldn't be easy.

But as soon as they collided in the restaurant, she knew she was in trouble. Yes, he had arrogant energy, but in his eyes, you could also sense a kindred spirit. She easily presented him with the customer-focused Lauren every restaurant patron knew and loved. But she might have flirted just a little bit more than usual…

That night, she walked home with a slight smile on her lips. He had been watching her all night… His gaze felt like a slight electric charge on her skin the whole time. It had been delicious.

She frowned. According to his Facebook profile, he was quite the rugby player as well. This might all get frightfully complicated with Sam…

As she arrived at her front door, she brushed aside the thought and prepared to enter. The porch light was on, and she let herself in quietly.

A Meg Ryan film was playing on the TV. Her mom was asleep on the couch. A half bottle of gin was half empty on the lounge coffee table.

Her dad was away on one of his 'business trips', so she couldn't blame her mom for losing herself in the booze. It happened more and more frequently these days, and Lauren was tired of being the adult in the house.

Lauren woke her mom up and walked her to her bedroom. She helped her to bed still fully clothed, and turned off the light.

In an attempt to push the anger and disappointment to the back of her mind, she ran a cold shower. She enjoyed the cold sting of water on her skin. Once again, she was reminded of Jimmy Barnes' gaze…

2

Oudtshoorn High was a dual-medium school where the kids spoke both English and Afrikaans. Joe's dad had been English and his mom Afrikaans, but he had gone to Bishops his whole life. His Afrikaans was rusty.

In the past, Jimmy hadn't given school uniforms a thought. All South African schools, including Bishops, wear uniforms. A vague memory of him and his mom going to try on shirts now and again came to mind, but the gear always seemed to appear in his closet.

It's a funny place, Bishops. His dad had always reminded him how lucky he was to go there—and how expensive it was! He vaguely understood that many kids did not share his privilege. Within his broader group of friends, he did not know any such kids. His sister always seemed to unearth them somehow, but not from her equally privileged Herschel environment.

This was different. There was nothing wrong with the school. However, where Bishops remained a predominantly privileged white show, this school was multiracial. As he walked in with his uncle, all the questioning stares he saw were from Cape Coloureds, a racial group that appeared to be equally represented.

As a student, Jimmy didn't always get along well with his teachers.

It seems like they all picked on him the last few years, as his grades dropped. Perhaps this was an opportunity to start over. Bishops teachers, according to him, were stuck-up idiots. Perhaps people in the country had better ideas. However, their first meeting with the principal did not quite support this expectation.

His name was Fred Abrahams, and he made it clear that he was doing Jimmy a huge favor by allowing him to join their crappy school midway through the year. A speech about school values, ethos blah blah blah...

Jimmy tuned out, Fred noticed. He walked out of the office sure that he had made his first enemy. Uncle Joe didn't say a word. He might have been aware of further humiliation to come.

They went to the second-hand clothes closet and Uncle Joe proceeded to kit out Jimmy in someone else's old stuff. It fit fine, but it was second hand! The jacket looked slightly faded and Jimmy detected a stain up around the collar.

"Uncle Joe, I can't wear this. I mean... it's... stained..."

Uncle Joe nodded his head. "Absolutely. We need to get you some new school gear. Apologies, kid, I hadn't thought about that until now. Wear this for now so we can get you going, and we'll take care of some new stuff later."

First class was in session already. Uncle Joe walked with Jimmy and the principal to the doorway. Jimmy gazed through at his future classmates, and almost didn't hear Uncle Joe.

He turned to his uncle. "Sorry, Uncle Joe, what was that?"

Uncle Joe put his hand on his shoulder. Jimmy wanted to shrug it off, but if it made the old man feel better, maybe he could allow it this time. It was a firm yet gentle grip, and it was the first human contact he'd had in a while.

"Jimmy, I know it's not ideal. It's not Bishops. But I want you to remember something, son. Wherever you go, that's where you are."

He let Jimmy go. Jimmy opened the door to his new life, thinking, "What a freaking stupid thing to say."

The math teacher was a portly chap and the only available desk was right in the front. In the seconds between being welcomed by Mr. Math and sitting down, twenty pairs of eyes fixed on Jimmy. They were curious, hostile, mocking, and indifferent. Except for the one, friendly, familiar face. Jimmy sat down, thinking, *This day just got a lot better.*

It took all of his willpower to focus on the teacher in front, and not look around to take a peek at her, but he knew rule number one in attracting women: Play it cool.

So, he focused on Mr. Math, and he was pleased to note that the school might not be a crapshow after all. The problems and methods presented were on par with the higher-grade math class he had taken at Bishops. He suddenly realized he didn't know what was going on.

Jimmy had taken a general attitude of minimum effort required as he progressed into his teen years. The more his parents pushed him to apply himself, the more he slacked off. It wasn't as much a rebellion as it was a statement of intelligence. He was smart; he didn't need to work as hard as the other kids.

But he also knew, instinctively, that once the pack left you behind, it was hard to catch up. Jimmy's dad had loved to cycle the annual Cape Argus race. Jimmy had watched him go past on the bridge at Ladies Mile Road every year for as long as he could remember. When he was younger, he found the whole thing incredibly exciting.

There were people with banners that said things like "Good luck Steve!" and "Superdad", chaps who were doing a *braai* (the South African version of a barbeque) on their portable weber, ladies with pre-made sandwiches and camping chairs. It was festive, Cape Town tradition.

The only disadvantage was that the cyclists came by at great speed, usually at 50/60 kilometers an hour.

You only got a glimpse—if that—of the dad/brother/sister/mom/girlfriend/boyfriend you were supporting that day.

Over the years, once or twice Jimmy's dad would come through by himself, not in a pack. On these occasions, he was cycling at a far slower speed, and it was easier to spot him.

One day, he had explained to Jimmy how it worked;

"You see Jimmy, cycling is like life. If you go at it alone, you can go at a certain speed. But if you go with a pack... ahh, that is magic. If it's a good pack, a fast pack where the leaders are strong and share the burden of being in the front—then you can go as fast, even faster—but with half the effort, because the pack momentum drags you along."

Last year, Jimmy cycled with his dad in the Argus. Like in all things, he didn't train that hard for it, but did it to please the old man. He figured that if he didn't put too much effort in, no one (including and most importantly himself) could be too disappointed if he didn't do well. It was not a great experience. His dad was very patient—and they rode it in over five hours, where his dad would usually come in around three hours.

He was encouraging, pushing Jimmy along on some sections, riding with him on others. And Jimmy experienced the pack thing his dad talked about. Only, most of them came whizzing past them. But there was the one time... going down Blue Route, actually past the bridge where he had always waited before. That's where they found themselves in the middle of a crowd of fifty riders. His adrenaline surged, there was such velocity—and his speed crept up as the wind traction swept them along. It was glorious. Then the pack left them behind again, and being untrained, Jimmy couldn't keep up.

Afterward, he felt ashamed. Ashamed of not being prepared, not putting in his best effort, but his dad just seemed happy that they could do it together. It made him feel even worse and he opted not to ride the next year. The old man was extremely disappointed, but Jimmy felt he would go again sometime in the future. At a time when he could focus on the training. He had too many other things to do, his social life wouldn't wait. And now they would never do another ride...

He roused himself out of his reverie and opened his textbook. He was behind this pack because of the accident. He could still catch up, or he had to wait for the next pack. In school, that meant falling back a year, which was a humiliation he was not willing to face. He forgot about Lauren-with-the-eyes for the rest of the period.

The bell rang to indicate the end of class, and there she was. Hair now tied back in a tight ponytail, she looked—what was the word? Fresh-faced pretty. He realized that the previous evening she was wearing the slightest bit of make-up, while today—as per school rules —you had to keep it clean. He also realized she was beautiful, either way.

She hooked her arm into his and grabbed a tall, ginger-haired chap walking past by the shoulder. "New boy, you need a guide to survive the jungle that is Oudtshoorn High. Please allow me to introduce you to Robert, the resident carrot top, reluctant teacher's pet, and the future president of a major multinational corporation. Robby, meet James. And be nice to him—he's Joe's nephew." And with that, she let go of him, to join a couple of giggling girlfriends and be gone.

The ginger gave him a friendly, open grin. Jimmy immediately liked him. He was lanky, his ginger hair cut to the absolute limit of what was allowed (the back of their haircut was not allowed to touch their collars—it was a funny thing about Afrikaans medium schools). Jimmy could immediately sense that here was a guy who liked to push the envelope. He could relate.

"Hiya. So, you're Joe's nephew? Heard about your folks—so sorry man. Come, looks like I have been seconded to be your tour guide by the head girl. Let me walk you to the next class."

And just like that, a friendship was born. Jimmy would learn that Robby (no one called him Robert, except for Lauren, who had an annoying habit of calling everyone by their proper names) was the top academic achiever in school. He was also well-liked by everyone, including the faculty. He was friendly, helpful, and worked hard, including organizing all kinds of extracurricular activities.

Jimmy had never been much of an organizer. There always seemed to be other people willing to step up to arrange the school fundraiser, the dance committee, the sports support club. He and his mates found it easier to fall in step and focus on sports. That way, they could criticize the ones who did put themselves out there to volunteer on behalf of the student body. Being friends with Robby would eventually sweep him along.

Coming out of Accounts class (where he noticed that the teacher kept leaning on Robby for answering questions, which Robby did willingly if not enthusiastically—and hence the name, reluctant teacher's pet, now Jimmy got it) he felt a hand tap on his shoulder.

This kid was as tall as Jimmy. He was also much broader in his shoulders. There was something funny about his nose, Jimmy suspected he had probably broken it somewhere. His ears had the starting signs of wear and tear, which would eventually culminate in what they called cauliflower ears in the rugby-loving community. It was a disfigurement reserved to the most industrious of forwards, the flank. A bruiser then, and judging by the two hostile-looking lieutenants that flanked him, the leader of the pack.

There was the briefest moment of sizing up each other, but the tension was broken by Robby. "Jimmy, allow me to introduce you to the Trio of Terror. The Man with the Plan. The Pirates of Pain, the…"

"Save it for the post-match write-up, Robby," said the bruiser. He smiled, but the smile never reached his eyes, as he stuck out his hand. "I'm Sam. This is Koos and Steve. Do you play rugby?"

The handshake was not a friendly one. There was more pressure in the grip than necessary, and Jimmy reciprocated. They stood like that for a couple of seconds, then the bruiser released. "No," said Jimmy. He felt like he needed to add, "Used to. Dislocated my shoulder last year. My…" he was about to say his mom wouldn't allow him to play after that, but he knew he would lose face with these guys for such a statement. And she was gone, after all.

"I intend to start up again this year."

The one lieutenant—the short one, with a stereotypical short man attitude (must be the scrummy) said, "We'll see if you have what it takes, Soutie."

Sam nodded. "Practice starts next week. Talk to Robby here—among other things, he is our manager. He'll hook you up. In the meantime, I suggest you figure out how things work around here. See you around, Soutie."

Jimmy took note of some telltale signs. The bulging veins, the dilated pupils, the slightly over aggressive air. Sam, and the smaller mouthy one—he must be Steve—both looked like they might like the 'roids. Koos he was less sure of; he was a big boy, seemed solid, but did not have the aggro vibe. He needed to be careful here. Now he had committed himself into their world, but he knew all about alpha dogs, and backing down now would not be a good idea.

Now, Soutie (short for salty dick, a derogatory term applied for English-speaking South Africans by the Afrikaans community) was a term Jimmy had NEVER heard at Bishops. Why? Because the whole school was English.

It was such a stupid word, anyway. Because English-speaking South Africans (often, not always, Jimmy sure didn't have one) carried dual passports for Britain and South Africa, they were seen as less committed to the continent. Afrikaans people, on the other hand, had left behind their Dutch-French-German roots hundreds of years before. English speakers, therefore, have one foot in Africa, one foot in England—and their dicks hung in the salty water of the Atlantic Ocean. Charming.

But the lads left him alone for the rest of his day.

As they sat down for lunch, Robby gave Jimmy the lay of the land. "Sam and his gang are harmless—they live for rugby, but only Sam has ever been good enough to get a scholarship to Paul Roos or Gray, the top schools. They reign supreme in the area here—the high school in George across the mountains is our biggest rival, and these guys live for the annual inter-school tournament. If you can play a bit, you'll find them a very welcoming bunch." Robby saw Jimmy looking away distractedly, and he followed his eyes.

"Ah," Robby said, identifying the group of girls Jimmy was watching that went to sit down on the other end of the quad. "Word of warning though... Lauren Kinsman is a wonderful girl, and along with Sam, they are the head prefects. She thinks of him as an overprotective brother, he still hopes he can help her lose her virginity at the matric farewell dance later this year. So be careful about wading into the middle of that..."

That made sense to Jimmy. Sam and his goons reminded him of this gang back at Bishops—and it made sense that he was the head prefect and not Robby. That was just how high school hierarchies operated: the most fitting person was overlooked in favor of the sports star. It was a world where rugby was still akin to religion in many high schools. Robby didn't seem to mind though—and in later years, Jimmy would realize that it was due to the integrity of his values.

The immediate problem, however, was that Sam and the goon gang should be Jimmy's friends, but he was now on the back foot because of Lauren. He liked her too, but now it seemed like he was faced with a choice, and he didn't like it one bit.

He was right to be concerned. His arrival had upset a well-established hierarchy in the school, and trouble was brewing...

3

I t was a short walk back to Uncle Joe's place, like everywhere in this two-horse town. It was warm in the afternoons. In the arid semi-desert of the Klein Karoo, the town heated up during the day, but was pretty cold at nighttime. Especially now—April and May months were autumn, and the chill was in the air.

Jimmy's shoulder had been fine. After he dislocated it last year, he did six months of rehab in the school gym, and it felt ok. The physio, of course, advised that after a first dislocation, any major trauma or hit to it would activate a recurrence. After that, the joint would remain loose and give him quite a bit of discomfort. The alternative was a costly operation—and for sure that was not something Uncle Joe could afford now. The dislocation in the accident had left him sore for a few weeks—but now he felt ok. But it would probably not hold up to a major hit, he was sure.

He stopped in front of the house, lost in his thoughts. The smart thing to do would be not to play a contact sport like rugby, where he was liable to hurt the damn thing again. There were many other sports he could take up. Problem was, he understood social systems. You were either one of the main men in town—i.e., on the team—or not. If not, you would be a guy like Robby, who demonstrated value in different ways, particularly by working hard and acting like everyone's servant. This did not appeal to Jimmy at all. He had always been one of the "manne" (the main men)—and he would like to keep it that way. He would take his chances.

Decision made, he walked into his new home.

Uncle Joe was in the lounge, reading a book. He looked up, nodding a greeting to Jimmy. Please don't ask me how my day was, thought Jimmy. He couldn't bear the small talk. Luckily, Uncle Joe was not much of a talker either. He put down the book, being careful to insert his bookmark.

Then he walked across to the kitchen. "Hungry?"

Jimmy suddenly realized that he was. "Sure." He sat down at the highchair at the kitchen counter, but first poured himself a glass of water. He had just returned the pitcher of cold water to the fridge when Uncle Joe also took it out. He poured himself a glass. Jimmy thought to himself, *I could've asked him if he wanted water as well. Will remember to do so next time...*

Uncle Joe wasn't just making a sandwich this time. He was putting together a few fresh ingredients along with some roast chicken breasts from the fridge. In less than five minutes, Uncle Joe had concocted a good-looking plate of chicken and salad, with a side of toast. Jimmy grabbed his plate and was about to go sit in front of the TV when Uncle Joe stopped him. "Jimmy, one should never eat alone unless you can help it. When you're by yourself, happy for you to have the TV to keep you company. When we're together, we eat here, at the table."

Jimmy's folks had allowed it. They often sat together, in front of the TV not talking but watching some inane show. In his opinion, this was also eating together, but he did accept that Uncle Joe had different rules. It probably wouldn't hurt to concede this one, he would be at the restaurant most dinners, and then Jimmy could do what he wanted.

So, they sat down, and ate their first meal together.

Halfway through the chicken, Uncle Joe asked the dreaded question; "Got homework?"

At least it wasn't "How was your first day of school?"

"Uh-huh," replied Jimmy.

"Need help?"

"Nope." And that was the end of that. Great conversation, Jimmy thought.

Uncle Joe had set up a study desk for him in his room during the morning. It looked out over the garden, and Jimmy had to admit that it was thoughtful. He didn't feel like working, though. He laid down on his bed, thinking about his new life and the one he had left behind. He grabbed a bunch of his old comic books to read, but was soon drowsy and drifted off to sleep.

He woke up with a start. Dusk had settled in and he had done no homework. He decided to get stuck into it before he got distracted again—he had a lot of catching up to do.

Math was first. But the problem presented by the teacher was complex, and even by studying the textbooks, he was struggling with the concept. He decided maybe he could use Uncle Joe's help after all. Uncle Joe probably would know less about this than Jimmy, but it was worth a shot.

Problem was, his uncle had cleared out. Of course, this was every night. He was working at the restaurant. Dammit.

Jimmy had cruised through at Bishops. He had always assumed that he would get good grades, and as they started to slip, his dad had started to get tough on him. His dad was always going on about how he needed good grades to get into university, how valuable education was, how much it had helped him get ahead in life. Hmph. He still ended up bankrupt.

Jimmy knew the value of money. He knew how it made people treat you differently, whether you had it or not. He needed to get it. He wasn't quite sure how just yet… but studying hard and giving himself the option to go to university was probably a good start.

But now he was stuck, almost immediately.

What are you gonna do? Call the smartest kid in school, I suppose.

He grabbed the house phone (didn't want to waste airtime on his cellphone) and called the one number he got today. "Robby? Its Jimmy. Uh… what are you up to?"

Of course, Robby was happy to help out. His house was on the other end of town, and it was a bit of a further walk (I need a bicycle, Jimmy thought) so it took about 30min to get there. It struck Jimmy that the town was bigger than he thought. He just happened to live in one of the nicer houses in the center of town.

Robby opened his front door with a big smile, ushering Jimmy in. And he stepped into the chaos.

He ushered Jimmy to the small back garden through a tidy but small waiting room, with the kitchen on the left. Robby's mom (a tall redhead) and his dad (a whole head shorter than her, but with a chin that broke no argument) interrupted their kitchen shouting match to yell a greeting to Jimmy, then they pushed on. They almost tripped over the two Labradors chasing each other before settling in by the *braai*, where Robby's brother and sister were discussing the best way to prepare the meat.

Robby's sister, Jess, immediately started to flirt with Jimmy. She was cute but slightly pudgy, so Jimmy decided to try to ignore her, which would prove to be a disastrous strategy. Ben, the older brother (Robby had said he was studying at the local police college) was putting some meat on the *braai* and grunted a greeting. The Labradors were chasing each other all over the small garden.

"Don't mind the chaos, bud," said Robby. They sat down on the bench in the corner, after he told Jess to go find them a cola (she happily obliged, smiling at Jimmy).

Jimmy thought this whole perfect family scene would make him miss his family, but it didn't. Rather, he felt angry, and he didn't know why. Jess (even though she was nothing like Vanessa) irritated him right from the get-go. He put on his best charming fake smile, though, and tried to shrug it off.

"Nah it's fine," he replied. "Listen, I was wondering…do you guys have, like, after-school study groups or something? I am a bit behind, and was wondering if there was a way to catch up…maybe join yours?"

Robby blinked, then laughed. "That's hilarious. We do, but they are more like tutor groups that parents sign their kids up for. You came to the right place, as I run just such a group."

"How does it work?"

"We meet twice a week…let's see, today is Monday, so Wednesday afternoon at three we meet. I charge R50 per kid per session to the parents—it's great pocket money. But in your case...um...."

Moment of silence.

"You know what, you're gonna be my guest. New kid privilege invoked!"

"Thanks, Robby. That would be amazing. But is there any way I could steal a bit of your time tonight? I'm way behind...I brought my books..."

His new best friend studied him thoughtfully. "Pushy sucker, aren't you. I'll make you a deal—I think you're probably a smartie. So sure, I'll get you up to speed. If you're up for it, tomorrow night too. But then you help me run the tutor groups, by way of paying me back. Deal?"

Jimmy was struck, somewhere in the back of his mind, by the simplicity of the construct. Robby had just taken a potentially humiliating situation and turned it into a win-win.

In the front of his mind, however, he merely said, "Sure." He intended to not honor the promise. When he had what he needed and was caught up, he wouldn't need to help Robby.

Their colas came, and Jimmy took out his books.

They were all caught up by the time the grumpy older brother served dinner. They all sat down around the kitchen table. The easy camaraderie and the aggressive yet warm banter, led by Robby's parents, made for a great evening.

It was after 11 pm when he arrived home and he was surprised to see Uncle Joe still up, in his regular easy chair, reading his book.

Uncle Joe put down the book, (a lengthy tome, the collective musings of Winston Churchill) and studied Jimmy. Jimmy realized he didn't let his uncle know where he was or who he was with. He waited for the admonishment to come, but his uncle simply said, "Did you eat?"

The question caught him by surprise. "Yes..."

Uncle Joe nodded. "Ok. I brought some pasta back from the restaurant. You can have it for lunch tomorrow."

And with that, he stood up. "See you tomorrow, sport. I'll be at the restaurant until after lunch. If you want anything special for dinner, come by and we'll cook it up together."

As Jimmy took a shower, his mind was filled with all the events that occurred during the day. Once his head hit the pillow, however, his body shut down completely. Math problems and blondes with green eyes filled his dreams...

4

J immy was introduced to the rugby squad on Thursday. He was given a friendly reception into the locker room, but when the drill began, all kid gloves came off.

Jimmy played forward. He had played flank and in earlier years, hooker. His bulk had not kept up with his height, and he was now considered lanky. He had started to trail behind the pack in the competitive world of Bishops Rugby. He could only make the second team in his penultimate year of high school.

He had hoped his speed and ball skills would gain him a spot in the team now that he was a senior; but truthfully, he had feared that he would not be picked. It had weighed on him in the first few months of the year before his accident, but then it became a moot point.

This, however, was not Bishops. The school had only two senior teams, not four, and the competition was much smaller than at his old school, where kids from all over were recruited.

It was true that he wasn't as fit as he usually would be, but he was confident that he could catch up. But he would have a rude awakening. He really struggled to keep up during the first set of drills. Sam and company took pleasure in seeing him suffer.

After that, he did better in skills drills, as he had good ball sense.

His passing and kicking, as well as jumping in the lineout, were also up to par.

But there was clearly a brief to tackle him hard. After about 20 minutes of feeling like all the love (or lack thereof) was directed at him, he felt like complaining to the coach. He didn't. Snitches get stitches—and he knew he had to take the pain. He had to protect his shoulder though, and he was worried that the coach would notice.

Finally, the punishment ended and they were assembled by the coach. He gave the usual rah-rah of a big season ahead, and said that he would post the teams for Saturday's game in the morning. Everyone needed to be ready for a call-up.

Jimmy viewed it as a partial success. Although the lads were warming to him and he even got a few smiles at the end, Sam remained aloof. Must be the Lauren thing. A little caution was needed here...

She mostly ignored him at school. He tried to chat to her a few times and, although she was always very friendly, she never lingered to chat. At the restaurant, she was always flying by to her tables, even if he was hanging by the bar for a pizza (there were no more beers on the house).

He couldn't figure it out. He had always been popular with girls. As long as he had lived (up until now), he could pick and choose from the bunch. His sister always was critical. She reckoned he had it too easy, and because he never chased after them, he ended up with the wrong kind of girls.

He lost his virginity to a senior at the Bishops sister school, Herschel, a year ago. She took him upstairs at a house party and showed him the ropes. She helped him put on the condom and afterwards they shared a cigarette. He had coughed, not used to the strong flavor. She was not mean about it, and reassured him that he had been great. He was sure that she knew it was his first time, even though he didn't admit to it.

Looking back, he didn't remember how hot she was. Just how everything was just amazing exploration, and how experienced she seemed. It didn't matter that later his mates had a dig at him for riding

29

the school bicycle. He remembered she was kind. And maybe a little sad.

Then there was Lauren. It was hard for him to tell if she liked him or not. She was not flirting with him; not giving him anything to work with.

He discussed this with Robby on Friday, and his new best friend chuckled. "Ah, my son. So much to learn. Shall we go and consult with the oracle?"

Jimmy was bemused. The what?

The Oracle turned out to be Robby's annoying kid sister, Jess. She was upset when she realized the object of her affections had a crush on someone else. She bounced back in typical teenage fashion, and quickly shifted into a role as relationship expert.

"Then what makes her tick, you doofus? Girls fall all over you so easily that you haven't taken the time to consider what she likes. This is one quality chick. Smart, pretty... the guy that gets her needs to be at the top of his game. And don't think it'll be soon. If she ever gets married, it won't be until she's in her late thirties, when she'll have already reached the zenith of professional success and be able to resume a lucrative consulting career once the kids are in school."

All this from a 15-year-old. Jimmy was slightly bemused but also impressed. The life plan that Jess had just articulated might be Lauren's... but it could well be Jess's, too.

"Ok, smartass. What do you suggest? How do I know what she likes?"

Jess smiled. "I could find out for a fee..."

That's when, for the first time, Jimmy realized he had zero cash.

He had not discussed it with his uncle. His parents always gave him ample pocket money in the past, and he had been expected to do a minimum of chores. He had to keep his room tidy, take out the trash (he often forgot to do even that), and wash the cars on the weekends (rarely). It had been mostly a free ride, and now it was over.

Before Uncle Joe set off for the evening shift at the restaurant on Friday, Jimmy broached the subject. Well, he kind of just barged into the room with, "Uncle Joe, what are we going to do about pocket money?"

The obligatory book came down, and Uncle Joe looked at him with a slight smile. "Yes, what? I'm open to suggestions."

"Well… um… my folks used to give me R200 a week for random expenses…"

"And what would you do in return for this allowance?" asked Uncle Joe.

"Mow the lawn. Wash the cars. Take out the trash. Stuff like that."

"Ah, I see. Well, I only have one car… and the lawn isn't very big. I like to do that myself every other weekend. But I'll tell you what, sport. I'll pay you R50 per week to take out the trash, R50 to wash my car, and R100 if you come to sweep out the kitchen in the restaurant Tuesday-Friday after the lunch rush."

It didn't sound like too much work, but there was a contractual sound to it that Jimmy was unfamiliar with.

"So, if I forget to take out the trash every day? Like one day I just forget? Do I still get a pro-rata payment on the trash?"

Uncle Joe laughed again. "Pro-rata? I like that. You're gonna make a great accountant. Nope, this is an all-or-nothing gig. You miss a day taking out the trash, you either forfeit payment for the week, or you make it up to me."

"How would I make it up?"

"By coming in to sweep the floor after dinner is done and everyone's gone home…"

"That's ridiculous! I'm still at school. That would be way too late!"

"Then I suggest you don't forget to take out the trash…"

Jimmy wasn't sure what to make of the exchange. He had easily reneged on his rich Cape Town allowance, but it felt like Uncle Joe was going to be a bit more rigid on holding him accountable.

He pushed it to the back of his mind. Next Saturday morning, he'll be playing on the second team and reserve for the first team.

He was eager to show them what he had.

5

The second-stringers played the warm-up game to the main event. This game was against the Military Academy kids—and boy, they were a tough bunch. The annual inter-schools later in the year, would be against Outeniqua High School from George. The matchup with the Military kids was going to be a good measure of their ability.

Especially in small towns, rugby was super popular- and important-in South Africa. It was like the movies portray American Football in Texas high schools. As a rule, parents stood by the sidelines of the field supporting their children. Your social status was determined by your place in the sporting hierarchy, and the captain of the first team was king. So, every second team player always ended up that: a second.

Seven of the second-stringers warmed the bench after they had been beaten up for 80 minutes. And Jimmy would find himself among this crew.

There was another deep, dark underbelly to high school rugby. At a school such as Bishops, kids are recruited into high school. The first team was generally regarded—and had to perform—as one of the top school teams in the country. The pressure was huge. This invariably meant there was a mostly unspoken, but thriving, steroid culture among high school superstars.

It was not uncommon to face off with a six-foot 17-year-old who looked like The Rock's more intimidating brother. It seemed that it would be less of an issue in small town Oudtshoorn, but Jimmy had been wrong. As he looked across the field, he reconsidered. Those were some big boys...

Whether they were on the 'roids or not, they were not very bright. They were strong, somewhat skilled—but then, so was Jimmy's team.

The guys played with conviction, and everyone took the whole thing very seriously. There was a lack of coherent strategy though. Mike was quick as lightning but had no ball sense; so, when he got the ball and a gap, he would score. There was only one problem: he never caught it.

Jimmy played his heart out upfront. The team captain—one of Sam's lieutenants; Koos, otherwise known as the Hulk—was playing on the coach's instructions to get the ball out to the backline. Once there, they could get it into Mike's hands as fast as possible. Everyone seemed to be hoping that Mike would be the silver bullet, but then the other team knew it, too, and tackled him relentlessly.

At halftime, they were down by 10 points, and things looked bleak. Despite catching the ball and scoring once, Mike had failed to get it every other time he was in the gap. Each drop led to turnovers, and losing possession.

Jimmy had been paying attention, and when they huddled for halftime, Koos was blabbing about keeping it tight and then running it wide. That was the silliest bunch of generalist idiocy that Jimmy had ever heard. He decided to cut in.

"Koos, why don't we try something different? We know Mike tends to drop the ball. They're also marking him the whole time."

"Hey, new kid, you might think—"

"No, wait, listen to me. Why don't we switch it around? Why don't we rather use Mike as an attack missile on their line, then use our forwards to mop up?"

Koos, and the others, were suddenly interested. Even Mike perked up, less offended. "What do you mean, Jimmy?"

"Well, you switch in closer to the scrum. When their flyhalf gets the ball, you shoot up and tackle the hell out of him. You're bigger than

33

him and fast enough to catch him with the ball almost every time. He spills it, he holds onto it, whatever… boom, turnover, and then we can drive up with our forwards."

His teammates nodded in agreement. "Sure, but that would only work a couple of times, then they'll be wise to us," Koos tried to reassert his authority.

"Right. At that point, they'll stop using the fly half and let the scrum-half kick or run. He's not that good, so maybe the flyhalf will pass it along to the next guy as quickly as possible because he doesn't want to get it. Either way, we have the advantage."

"Let's try it," said Koos.

And they did. And it was glorious.

In the first play, the opposition gets the ball, forms a ruck, the ball pops out, and gets to the flyhalf—along with Mike.

BOOM! Ball spills out. Koos is at hand to gather, and sprints through for a try.

The other team is shocked, while Jimmy and the guys high five each other.

In the second play, Jimmy's team has the ball. Instead of passing it to Mike, their scrummy does a decent job of an up-and-under, and this time their fullback is there to catch it. Only he doesn't, because Mike is coming at him like an angry steam train. The ball spills out of his hands while he is distracted. In that moment, one of Jimmy's center teammates gathers it and scores!

Tables are turned.

While they're behind the posts, the other team has a team chat. In the next play, they keep it super close behind the forwards. This doesn't work; Jimmy and his mates work super hard to keep the forwards back, so eventually, they have to move the ball. And BOOM! It's Mike's turn to take the flyhalf.

It was a spectacular turnaround. They ended up winning by 15 points, and Mike and Koos were the team heroes. The spectators on the side of the field treated them like heroes too. Jimmy was initially miffed that the other two seemed to get all the credit. But he was quickly mollified when Koos pulled him closer and screamed to the stands, "This is the guy! The new kid knows how to read the game!!!"

It felt good. He was aware of Lauren sitting in the stands, smiling at him. He was also aware of Sam, who was warming up for the main game, being about the only one who wasn't smiling.

Uncle Joe was there. He was chatting to a friend, but he turned to Jimmy and lifted his cap in a salute. Jimmy was struck by the fact that his dad had never come to any of his games. His old man had always been away. Jimmy had always reminded his friends that his dad had international commitments, so that was ok. He suddenly realized how nice it was to have someone at the side of the field.

Jimmy didn't get picked as a reserve for the first team game. Koos and Mike were, which was kind of stupid. They were exhausted from all the graft they put in the previous game.

Jimmy watched from the stands, and he could tell where the team was going wrong. While the Academy guys were no more talented, they had put in the work. They knew that Sam was the star player. He was big, quick, and was known for sneaky runs off the back of the scrum. They were ready for him, and their equally big and quick flanker marked him carefully.

It was unimaginative stuff, and the first team ended up losing by a whisker. Afterward—and for the rest of the week—it was whispered in the hallways, on the field, and even among the parents; "They didn't change their tactics. Maybe if that new kid was playing…"

Uncle Joe invited the whole team (the victorious second team, that is) to the restaurant for an early pizza (before the main crowd came in, of course) and there was great camaraderie. Sure, they were the second-stringers, but they had won! Uncle Joe did take Jimmy aside and dropped his voice; "Well done, bud. You made a big difference today. I know most of the glory has gone to these two guys, but remember, you can accomplish almost anything in life if you don't mind who gets the credit. Enjoy the moment!"

6

O n Monday, Jimmy smelled trouble when he suddenly received lots of smiles and high fives in the hallway. Koos had been going around telling everyone that it was Jimmy who made the difference. Koos had turned out to be a big, honest, and friendly mate, but he wasn't too bright. If he was, he would know he was burying Jimmy by making too much of him. He was the new fresh flavor, and maybe he could save their ailing first team. Lauren also congratulated him on the win, and even lingered a little bit in the hallway to chat with him. Jimmy would've enjoyed his moment of triumph more, if he didn't see Sam stomping away in the background, like a bear with a thorn in his paw.

He wasn't looking forward to Tuesday practice.

When he arrived home that afternoon, he saw a note from Uncle Joe on the fridge: "Come around to the restaurant around 10 pm tonight. I'll make you a pizza before you start cleaning up."

Dammit. He had forgotten to take out the trash in the morning... from hero to zero...

The dinner time crowd was thinning out when he got there. Lauren wasn't working, disappointingly, but he was cheered up by the sudden attention the other waitress, Vicky, was paying him.

Vicky was out of school for a couple of years. She was quite saucy. She flirted outrageously with the customers, she wore quite a tight top (she had great breasts) and she was careful to apply the right make-up —which meant she looked like a knockout most nights. She didn't work every night, so she and Lauren seemed to pivot on shifts and were hardly ever there at the same time. Jimmy also suspected they didn't like each other much.

Vicky… Well, if this had been Cape Town, she wouldn't have been a Herschel girl. His mom would have said there was a certain lack of breeding. Jimmy had judged his mom for this language in the past. People weren't horses! The phrase came to mind when the hot older girl was suddenly very attentive to Jimmy.

Jimmy was sitting at the bar waiting for his pizza, when she came up to him, leaning in real close. So close, that her breast was pressing against his arm. He made no effort to pull it away… this was glorious!

"So, Jimmy, I hear you were the mastermind behind Team Losers' Saturday miracle?"

"Umm… yeah…." He had conflicting emotions. He was feeling a tightening in his pants because of that breast, but he was also mildly repulsed by her breath. She had laid into the garlic earlier that evening.

She smiled, and leaned in even closer, and whispered; "I hear you have the hots for Little Miss Perfect. But I'm going to keep an eye on you. When you make it to the big time, there's a little tradition here…"

"Hey! Vicks! Leave my nephew alone and go cash up!" yelled Joe, bringing the pizza.

She gave him a wink. "To be continued, whizz kid…"

Jimmy smiled to himself. He was back on his game. But his good mood was ruined when he looked at Uncle Joe, who just shook his head in a firm "no".

He ate his pizza, and by the time that was done, the restaurant was empty. Uncle Joe showed him to the kitchen sink filled with plates and glasses, and to where the mop and bucket was.

He kept on reminding himself as he packed the dishwasher and contemplated the grimy floor: Focus on getting money. To pay off Jess. To get the goods on Lauren. Eyes on the prize…

He almost missed school the next day.

7

It was hard to keep awake in most of the classes. This didn't endear him to any of his teachers. He had managed to take out the trash before school. He wasn't about to make that mistake again.

Things were back to normal after all the Monday backslapping. Lauren ignored him, Sam was edgy, Robby was supportive and his new best friend Koos sat with them at breaktime. Jimmy felt like he was starting to find his rhythm. At rugby practice that afternoon, he resolved to work a bit harder than usual to try to win Sam over.

It seemed to work, as well. The more tackles he made, the more Sam and crew thawed. That kid Steve being the exception—he remained a nasty piece of work, and Jimmy was sure they would never be friends. He was also grateful that the coach didn't make more of a fuss over him. After the weekend, he didn't need the attention. But he was aware that his suggestions were listened to quite attentively by everyone—and it did give him quite a bit of an ego boost.

His shoulder was hurting a bit afterward, which he supposed was normal. He had again been careful to avoid heavy direct contact. He lead with his other side—and he was wondering if anyone noticed. He had taken one big hit there, but he had deflected enough, and it had held. He considered telling the coach, but he knew it might impact his ability to play the next week, and he wanted things to keep on track.

There was no going to the restaurant Tuesday. He was exhausted, and after a quick sandwich and getting his homework done, he was asleep.

Wednesday could not have started better. He went for an early morning run, which set up his day in the right way. Sorted out the trash, kicked ass in math class (Jimmy could do numbers—but Robby was amazing at this stuff, and helped him a lot to catch up). Then, at breaktime, Lauren approached him.

"So… I didn't see you at the restaurant last night."

He met her green eyes, and something passed between them. "Missed me?"

It was SO the wrong thing to say. Whatever was there, faded. "No. Just wondered, you don't strike me as someone who likes to cook for themselves."

She was about to leave and he knew he had somehow messed this up, and he tried to save the situation. As she turned, he grabbed her arm.

"What I meant was… I would have liked to come. To see you."

This made her hesitate, she didn't turn back yet but she was listening.

"But it was a hectic day… chores, school, practice. And you're right—I can't cook. I made a sandwich and passed out."

She turned back to him, and he knew he had somehow come back from the dead here.

"You should ask your uncle to show you. He's the best—I would love to be able to make food like he does one day," she said.

He smelled an opportunity. "Well maybe one day I could ask him for a lesson—and you could come around, and we make it a group class."

She smiled, and it was glorious. "I'd like that."

He couldn't stop grinning for the rest of the day.

Rugby practice was rough, but he enjoyed it. Building camaraderie with the team was great. He proceeded to ace most of his homework that evening, and had a pizza at the restaurant for dinner. Steve was there, but they didn't greet each other. Asshole. Besides, he was enjoying attention of a different kind. Vicky came to grab orders right next to where he sat. She was pretty overt about standing real close, and casually putting her hands on his shoulders, or accidentally rubbing her breasts against him as she turned. He enjoyed it. Innocent fun, right? It wasn't like he was doing anything. When the restaurant emptied, she lingered a little bit.

He had brought some of his math problems with him. He was mulling over an equation and a half-eaten pizza when she sat down and asked him, "So you seem pretty smart, huh? Going to be a rocket scientist?"

He laughed. "Yeah, maybe. Probably not. My dad always wanted me to study something solid for business like a commercial degree, or accounting. Both my parents went to university, so they always thought education was very important."

She leaned in, putting her hand on his thigh. "Couldn't agree more. Depends on what kind of education you are after, I suppose."

He gulped. Talking about rockets, his pants were suddenly about to launch. She glanced down and gave him a knowing look.

"I am about to cash up, sugar. My apartment is around the corner. So, if you wanted to…"

This was going to be the best night of his life. He was about to reply when Uncle Joe shouted from the kitchen, "Vicky! Cash up, table six is waiting for you!"

She glided away to table six, where Steve and his parents were waiting for their bill. Jimmy's eyes lingered on the way her tight jeans showed off her rear. Uncle Joe came up and said, "I'm done for the night, champ. Let's walk home together for a change."

Uncle Joe was really cockblocking his game.

They walked in the cool night air—it was just after 10 pm, and Jimmy had to admit it was quite pleasant.

"Do you like her?" asked his uncle.

The question caught him off-guard, especially as he wasn't sure who his uncle was referring to. Lauren or Vicky? How does he answer this one? Maybe he could go generic.

"Sure, she's great."

"Would you date her?"

This one was harder. He had had a couple of girlfriends back in Cape Town—but he and his friends had always argued about the definition of dating. He decided to go there.

"What does that mean, Uncle Joe? Dating somebody? I mean it's not a term we use these days anymore."

He had never really dated 'seriously'. Because he was one of the cool rugby guys, and his folks had money, the girls were always available. He never found it hard to attract them, kiss them, fondle some breasts, and even a couple of times more than that. There were also a few times he was outright rejected by girls that he liked. And he defaulted into girls that were clearly into him—but they were often not the right girls, he supposed. It was complicated.

"It isn't? Hmm." Uncle Joe walked for a minute, still musing on the term dating, and then responded, "It means different things to different people—without further qualifying it with a word like 'exclusively'. I kind of think that is implied; most women think when a guy is regularly kissing (or doing even more stuff) with her, then they are dating. And that means he isn't doing it with someone else. But I've also known a lot of guys who think dating is something you do with multiple partners."

He chuckled to himself. "That's kind of why I'm back in Oudtshoorn, bud. I would also like to date someone. And I mean exclusively."

This completely caught Jimmy by surprise. He knew Uncle Joe was in his late thirties, still single and never married. Doesn't look to be gay, pretty good shape, seems to have social skills, and is a ninja in the kitchen. He hadn't considered the question why Uncle Joe was not attached—and now they were talking about dating. It was weird.

Uncle Joe pressed on; "So for me, I guess, dating would be picking someone—then being with her for as long as it made sense to either evolve the relationship or end it."

They were almost at their front door.

"And that goes to my question: Do you want to be with her, and only her, for as long as it makes sense to either evolve it or end it?"

The person that came to mind was Lauren. Yes, he liked her. And he wanted to be with her. It didn't seem like she wanted to be with him, though, and Vicky was putting it all out there…

"I would like to be with her, yes."

His Uncle nodded and opened the front door.

"Then I recommend you don't mess it up by messing around."

And they were clear. He would steer clear of temptation and keep his eyes on the prize.

8

The problem is, she also clearly had her eyes on him. He tried making small talk with Lauren at school the next day. She shut him down, six-love.

He made his move at the first break. She was sitting with a few of her friends, and, emboldened by her friendly behavior the previous day, he walked up.

"Hi Lauren."

She looked up, and there was nothing friendly about the look she gave him. Her whole crew seemed outright hostile. What the hell was going on here?

"Yeah?" She didn't get up.

"I was wondering… could I speak to you alone for a moment?" He had to isolate the target, or he was dead in the water. He realized it had been an amateur move, but he had been overconfident after yesterday.

The bitchy brunette to her left confirmed. "We're kind of busy here, JIMMY. I'm sure there's nothing you need from Lauren that you couldn't get at the restaurant."

Ah ha. They dismissed him, and he had to slink away with his tail between his legs. Somehow his flirting with Vicky had gotten back to

Lauren and her gang, and he hadn't even done anything! It felt very unfair.

It must have been that asshole, Steve. Jimmy was sure he also had the hots for Vicky – but she had blown him off and flirted with Jimmy instead. This was his revenge.

What was he supposed to do now?

Robby gave him the lowdown and confirmed. "Yeah, it's all over the school. People are taking bets on who you gonna shag first: easy Vic or untouchable Lauren. Not many people are taking odds on Lauren... she's a famous virgin, while Vic had been through half the first team."

"This town is nuts!" fumed Jimmy. "I haven't even been here a week, and..."

"Yeah bud, but it's obvious you're into Lauren. And Sam is into her. And she might be into you. But you avoid her the whole week and flirt with Vicky instead. This is a small town, and people love to gossip..."

Robby sighed and held out an olive branch. "My suggestion? Steer clear of Vicky, give Lauren a chance to cool off, and find a way to demonstrate value."

"What do you mean?"

"Bud, you're not bad looking and you might be the main man on campus after Saturday's rugby game. A win will get you into the panties of half the willing girls in school who only care about who is most popular. But a girl like Lauren—you need to find your angle."

"I thought your genius socially connected kid sister was going to help with that."

"At a price, as I recall," sighed Robby. "She's going to do well one day. Keep your nose clean till the end of the week, then maybe you can get the scoop on Lauren, and proceed with a strategy."

Jimmy togged up for Thursday practice, the last before the weekend game, with a weight on his shoulders. He didn't have a good practice and didn't bother to go to the restaurant. He wasn't surprised when, on Friday, he wasn't picked for the first team. He made the reserves, though. On the flip side, Sam was again warming to him—

obviously because he no longer considered him a threat for Lauren's affections. This place WAS nuts!

9

There were fewer fireworks in the second team this time around. They easily won their game; the word was that the second-stringers from Monument High were pretty average, but the first team had a really strong lineup.

And it proved to be so. He was glad to have had an easy game sitting on the bench. Sam and the troops fronted manfully, but it was one of those days where things just weren't going well for them.

From the sidelines, Jimmy could see what was wrong. After the previous week's showing, they put Mike in the firsts and tried to use him as a human wrecking ball in the same way.

The problem was, this team stood deeper—and both their scrumhalf and flyhalf were big boys, so Mike's effectiveness was curtailed. He even got blown up a couple of times for late tackles, and that led to the loss of points and penalties.

Koos was also on the bench. Just before halftime, Jimmy asked him, "What's up with Sam? He's having an awful game."

Koos pointed at the opposition scrumhalf. "See that kid? The showy blonde dude? He was a lifeguard in Herold's Bay last summer—and he was all over Lauren's Facebook account. You know how Sam is about Lauren—at the time, they were kind of/sort of dating—but then it looked like this guy was wading into Sam's turf. Lauren dismissed it as saying they were just friends, but Sam is still convinced they had a thing."

Now it made sense. Sam was spending way too much time going after the scrummy. The other team was baiting him too, and his focus on the kid opened all kinds of gaps for the others around them. Just before halftime, the scrumhalf pulled in Sam, even though he was supposed to mark the other flank. He did a short pass to the flank, who strolled through a gap as wide as Newlands Stadium entrance for a soft try. Suddenly the team was in trouble.

In the changing room, the coach was furious. "Sam, get your head outta your ass! Those guys are playing you like a fiddle—and if you don't quit it, we'll lose this game."

Jimmy felt a sudden sense of impending doom. And yep, there it was.

"Barnes, you have a head on your shoulders. From the sidelines, are there any plays that you think we should go with? Anything we are missing? These guys are being outplayed on strategy. Any ideas?"

Jimmy was trapped between seeming stupid and contributing something. Groaning inwardly, he went for option two. He knew that this would put him into Sam's bad books for a while to come. But he had to front up.

"Well, look—the thing with Mike coming up quickly? That doesn't work when the other team lies as deep as they are. They figured out that he has weak hands," and at that, he apologetically looked at Mike, who just shrugged in resignation. He continued, "They keep on putting up and unders to him. That scrumhalf has a killer boot."

"Also, he's got killer looks," Steve said, to snickers from the rest of the team and Sam going bright red. Jimmy swore he was about to blow his top. This was not helpful!

"Ok let's stay on this, Barnes. It isn't working. What should we do, then?"

"We keep the ball in hand. We have better forwards—just play it close, keep possession. Their backs are deep, so if we can make small breaks through the first tackle around the scrums, we can build up real

momentum before we hit the next line. I would use Mike as a dummy."
As he said it, he instinctively knew it was the right move.

"Show me," said the coach.

Right after halftime, they played into the new strategy. They kept
the ball off the kickoff, played it real close for a few rounds—and Sam
seemed more focused, keeping at the strategy. In the 12th phase, Mike
shot up as first received. The show pony scrumhalf went out of position to block him, then Sam dummied and slipped through. He was
blocked by the second tacklers—but he was a big boy, and it took three
of them to take him down.

High fives all around, rinse, repeat. Mike as a dummy again; same
story. They made good ground and were close now.

If it isn't broke, don't fix it. On the third iteration, the scrummy
kept his eye on Sam—and completely missed the pass to Mike, who
this time DID take the quick ball (and held onto it!) and was straight
through for a try. The conversion was good, and suddenly they were
back in it.

Jimmy breathed a sigh of relief. He didn't want to be the teacher's
pet. At the same time, his input had seemed valuable, and Sam was
now playing to the strategy. They might even win this one! The crowd
was in good spirits, and Jimmy would have loved to play. He would,
however, take it as a net win if the team won with his help off the field.
And by the last quarter of the game, they were ahead by five points.
Could they be lucky again?

It wasn't to be. There was a maul that collapsed. As the whistle
blew, Jimmy could see Sam was one of the last to get up. The show
pony, seeing that the referee's attention was elsewhere, gave Sam a
slight shove that left him sprawling again. Sam thundered to his feet
and swung a massive right hook at the scrummy. He was quick,
though, and Sam's fist hardly touched him. He went down like an
Argentinian soccer player at the height of his acting powers.

The referee DID see this—and that was a yellow card for Sam,
which meant that, for the next 10 minutes, their team would be 14
men playing against 15.

Sam came to sit down dejectedly. The coach walked over. Jimmy pretended to keep on watching the game, but he still overheard. All the reserves did.

"I expect more from my team captain. You're out for the rest of the game. When the 10 minutes are up, I'm subbing you out."

The coach turned to Jimmy. "Time to see if you can do the same for us on the big stage, kid."

It was a very long 10 minutes. Their team was getting creamed out there. They were without their captain and one man down. Meanwhile, the show pony had miraculously recovered from the punch, and was running, kicking, and generally wreaking havoc.

Off the pitch, Sam was sitting quietly. Jimmy didn't dare to look over there, but he could sense those eyes on him, spearing him. And he was once again faced with an impossible choice: If he went out there and didn't do his best, he would lose an opportunity to entrench himself. He had to admit, he did like glory, so that felt like a bad option. If he gave his all and rocked out, the situation with Sam would be even worse.

Which way to go? Screw it. He suddenly decided he might be the new kid, but Sam had dug his own grave.

They were six points behind with 10 minutes to go when he ran onto the field.

His next problem was the de facto captain was Steve, Sam's lieutenant n. And his loyalty was with Sam above else. "New kid—do your job, block the scrummy but keep an eye on the flyhalf—and the rest of us will do ours. The first team is different from seconds."

It was a lot harder—more physical, and Jimmy took a few beatings in the first minutes. He fell badly on his shoulder, but it held. Sore as hell though!

And that scrumhalf sure was slippery. Jimmy did manage to block him in next lineout—but he was playing decoy, and the flank on the blindside slipped past Steve and was tackled out just before the line. They were in deep trouble!

They won their lineout and started a maul. Unfortunately for Jimmy, he lost his footing. The maul collapsed, and that led to a penalty. If he got this over, it would be a nine-point lead with three minutes on the clock—impossible to catch up.

There was an audible gasp from the stands (the home crowd was loving their hero, and he rarely missed) when the ball shaved the uprights. There were only a couple of minutes left, and they still had a chance.

As they walked up to the quarter line for the drop-in kick, Jimmy walked next to Steve. "Steve, I know it's not my place…"

He could tell the other kid didn't want to hear it. But he was also sure that the need to win might overrule petty rivalry. He was right. "Have an idea?" asked Steve.

Even a thick 17-year-old can sometimes see the bigger picture. Thanking the gods, Jimmy told him.

And it was glorious.

They hoisted the kick way high. Mike and the other wing shot up out of position and closed down the first receiver. He managed to get away a weak pass, and then the second receiver knocked on with Mike in his face. Turnover ball, recycled quick, Mike moved down to the end of the field.

They spun it wide for the first time in the game, confusing the hell out of the opposition. The kids scrambled to cover Mike as he shot up at speed. But at the last minute, he passed to Steve, who went down in the tackle. Quick recycle, the ball to the scrumhalf. He hoofed it laterally to the other side of the field—and there were Jimmy and Mike, who had run all the way across! Jimmy gathered the kick (he had pretty good hands) and then put Mike away with only one defender in sight. Jimmy stayed close (man that kid was quick) and Mike passed the ball back to him just before the line, when they were sure the defender had committed. Jimmy slid over the line and knew it was golden. Score!

The team celebrated—a trifle too prematurely, but what the hell. It was an angle kick from the right side, just like the other team had just missed. But going from a day when nothing went right to a day when all went their way—the kick was good, the ball flew over the uprights.

They would go home victorious. All the reserves ran up to high five them - even Sam was joyful. And the coach was going nuts. It was great!!! Jimmy couldn't believe he had thought about giving it up. His mom, if she was still alive, would have been concerned about his throbbing shoulder—but what the hell, a man's gotta live.

The team bus was festive on the one-hour drive back to Oudt-shoorn. Jimmy finally felt completely accepted. He had played two games, been victorious in both, and they loved him.

He was still apprehensive about Sam, who sat quietly in the corner for most of the journey. As they drove into Oudtshoorn, Sam suddenly got up and grabbed the mic from the front.

"I owe all of you an apology. I was pigheaded today, and I let that kid get into my head. It almost cost us the game. Luckily it didn't. Coach, you made the right call there—and Jimmy, we are so glad to have you with us. What a rock star move. Three cheers for Jimmy!"

The bus erupted in cheering. Sam walked over, to shake Jimmy's hand. Man, that felt good. Jimmy truly felt like he had turned the corner. Sam held onto his hand for a moment longer than was quite normal and leaned in; "Good to have you onboard, sport. Looking forward to playing with you next weekend."

"That means a lot to me. Thanks, Sam." They both smiled, and Sam walked away.

Jimmy sat down, still drunk on the juice of recognition and cama-raderie. If he was paying more attention, he would have noticed that Sam's smile never quite reached his eyes…

10

M ore good news when he arrived home. There was pocket money of R200 waiting for him in an envelope. Happy days and a score! The first thing he did was high tail it down to Robby's place.

They were having a late afternoon *braai*. Shouting, laughter, the smell of *boerewors* (a type of South African sausage) and onions. What a day! The family had already heard about their away victory, and over lunch, he regaled them with the play-by-play from the game.

After they ate, he approached Jess. "So, I wanted to know…"

"If a deal can be made, for some inside info." She laughed. "I knew you didn't come straight over here just to hang out with my brother." She leaned in. "And I got some info for you—and just because you are the new school hero, I'm even going to let you have it for free. This time."

He was half glad and halfway irritated. He had just spent the last week busting his ass on chores, and now that hadn't seemed necessary. But then again… if he didn't have to pay Jess anything, maybe he had some money to spend on Lauren.

"Ok go. I'm listening."

Jess took out a notebook. "In preparation for this meeting, I did some asking, took careful notes, and I was sure to be discreet and not let up that I had interested parties."

Then she rolled her eyes. "As if. She knows you have been asking about her—and I wouldn't be surprised if some of these were not carefully planted morsels by her minions."

"Get on with it Jess…"

"The lady in question likes to watch nature channels to relax. Discovery, National Geographic, that kind of stuff. She is into nature and animals."

"Brilliant! There's this Cango Wildlife Ranch place in town that looks amazing, I could take her."

Jess held up her hand. "Hold your horses bud. Into animals—in nature. Not in captivity, and she is always petitioning to close that place, which is a glorified zoo."

"Oh." He dodged a bullet there.

"Nope, you want to go birdwatching—or take her to a true animal conservancy kind of place. Word on the street is that she is dying to go to Addo National Park."

"Where's that?"

"400 kilometers away. So, no biggie." And Jess gave him a sweet smile.

"Ok, that's a bit out of my range, I reckon. What else?"

"She's vegetarian. For health and moral reasons. But she isn't a princess about it, and she has been noted to get stuck into a steak or a piece of chicken at a *braai* so as not to offend the hosts. But you would do well to try to observe her preference."

"This is good stuff, Jess." He was making some of his own notes.

"Finally, the lady has a pretty spotless dating record. She had a brief but not so serious fling with the lovestruck Sam. There are rumors of the surfer at Herold's Bay—I assume you made his acquittance in your game today."

"Yep." He was still hurting.

Jess continued; "So far, she has a reasonably high popularity/sports/good looks bar. It might only be because of the talent on offer, and also because most nerdy kids don't approach her. I think it is silly of them, because she is quite cerebral, and they might be in with a chance. Intelligence is sexy."

He closed his book. "Ha-ha. Where did you come from using words like 'cerebral'?"

She laughed. "Because I'm dang smart, you fool. Hang out with this family and you will be too. Maybe one day you'll be smart like us and realize I'm the woman of your dreams."

"From God's mouth to your ears, kid." He ruffled her hair and thought to himself, *I am warming to her.*

"Jess, how do I play this? She's still miffed because of the flirting with Vicky, so what do I do to get past that?"

Jess, of course, knew how.

11

He was on top of the world. Mr. Popular. Even the teachers were cutting him some slack. Sam and his friends, if not falling all over themselves to be his best mates, were deferentially friendly. Even to the point that Sam had now quit the hostile stares whenever he chatted to Lauren.

She was a harder sell. Not impressed with his newfound rugby hero status, he still received chilly treatment on Monday. But he had some cash in pocket, some inside info from Jess, and he used it well.

After an after-school shopping trip, he did his chores and home-work, went for a loosener run in the late afternoon, and then cruised into the restaurant for an early dinner. He had confided his strategy to Uncle Joe, who seemed supportive of his initiative. Uncle Joe, as he now was finding, once more had a few nuggets of wisdom for him:

"Be sure that, whatever you are doing, it is sincere. And that you can keep it up. Many people try to be something they're not to impress the other, and it always backfires."

And the second nugget:

"Timing is everything, bud. But I'll help to set you up for success."

Jimmy mused on timing. Even though his dad had always done well in life (well, right up to the point where he was completely bankrupt when they died) he always seemed to be slightly unlucky. Jimmy remembered a few business deals that went south—and particularly the big real estate crash of 2008. His dad must have said it a million times: "I had the right idea, just the wrong timing."

Uncle Joe was also fond of quoting Gary Player, the famous golfer: "The more I practice, the luckier I get." It was just after lunch, and Jimmy put down the plate he was cleaning. "I remember when I was younger, Jimmy," continued his uncle. "Your dad and I were both always very good at doing things on the fly—we were inventive, and we often got away with things because we could think on our feet. Once I started in the restaurant business, though…"

He was lost in his thoughts for a second. Jimmy prompted him, "The restaurant business? You mean all those fancy restaurants you worked in?"

"Yeah. I have had a pretty good run. But for good food, you need good ingredients. And time. And the right tools. And you need to combine them well. And for that, you need to plan. Planning is key."

"What does this have to do with me winning over Lauren?"

"Well, let's map it out…"

UNCLE JOE PLAY BY PLAY

PHASE 1:

Arrive at the restaurant before she starts her shift. Sit at the bar doing homework, so that when she arrives, she sees you there. Be friendly but not overeager. Focus on your work. She will wonder if you are there for her or the food. She will be 95% sure you are there for her but make her wonder a little. The whole evening be yourself, but strike a boundary. At some point she will want to strike up a conversation. Apologize but be firm that you would love to speak to her at the end of the night, right now you need to finish your work.

PHASE 2:

As things wind down toward the end of the evening, she will approach you, puzzled at your restraint. After all, you should be chasing her. Lauren is a good girl and doesn't play games. She is still a girl, and her mind will go nuts trying to figure out what's going on now that you have slightly shifted your behavior. Do you still like her? Did something more happen with Vicky? She might even build up a case against you and be even more aggro when you finally talk. This might work in your favor, as you can completely diffuse her with your trump move. Don't be a dick about it, though. Be gracious, authentic, and generous, i.e., it must be a no expectations move.

PHASE 3:

She sits down. She's cashed-up, actually quite agitated, and she asks you—to make small conversation—about the weekend game. Don't get into it, she isn't interested, she is just going for context. Speak your truth. You loved it, it's great to feel a sense of acceptance and to have helped the team win. Be vulnerable—as the new kid, it's hard, but you are lucky that sport has given you the gift to make friends quickly. Don't overdo it. Gratitude is sexy, but too much will seem insincere.

She'll thaw and steer the conversation to things she likes. Nature, cooking. Ask questions. Be interested. And then, when you sense it's a good time to cut the conversation short (always be first—don't run out of things to say and let her say goodbye), pull out your ace in the hole. Give her the book: the second-hand Nat Geo special edition focusing on the best photographic shots of the Serengeti animals 2010. It might have cost you most of your weekly allowance—but it will be worth it.

Then don't push your luck. She will be a little bit unsure—so again, be truthful. You asked around, found out what she liked, and went looking for it. An effort is sexy, women want to know that their suitor is willing to work for it.

At this point, pack it up, and start to leave. Ask her if she's ok to go home by herself—she will reply she has a car/her dad is picking her up. Either way, offer to walk her to the car. Easy choice if it's the old man, but if it's her car, open the door for her, and say goodnight. Don't lean in for a kiss, don't linger, don't push it. You're in there, kid; now let her come to you.

He went back into the restaurant, deciding tonight he would wait for Uncle Joe. It wasn't long, and they walked home together.

"And?"

"It was perfect, Uncle Joe! You called it almost to the exact detail! How did you know how this would go? You do know women!"

"Only recently, my boy. I spent too much time in my life not understanding them. Women are complicated creatures, and they are not. But let's face facts. You can fool a woman for a short time with tricks, but if you want to have any shot at a real relationship, sincerity is the key. You were great tonight!"

"Yeah. It was hard, though... I really wanted to kiss her there at the end..."

"And she might have allowed it. But then afterward she would have been angry at herself, she would have questioned your intentions, and you might have taken two steps back. Timing is everything..."

"So, what's next?"

"Well, she'll avoid you tomorrow. She'll try to figure all this out. Stay courteous, give her space. When she's ready, she'll approach. At that point, maybe invite her along to a public event. This is the key thing before we lean in with the cooking lesson..."

Uncle Joe sure knew a lot about women. Which made Jimmy wonder—why was he still single?

It was a long time before he fell asleep, thinking of those green eyes...

W omen were strange. She avoided him the next day at school, as Uncle Joe predicted. He didn't push it—he had other things to worry about.

Sam was cooking up something.

Jess slipped him a note during the break, and it simply read: "Come by the house this afternoon. There's trouble afoot for you."

He was disquieted and went straight home with Robby after school.

On the way, he broached the subject.

"Robby, am I missing something? There was a weird vibe at school today again from Sam—he was super friendly, but it just felt like he was... I dunno..."

"Trying too hard?" Robby chuckled. "Well, maybe you're not as thick as my sister says. Sam is a bit of an idiot, but he's not sneaky. He hates your guts, but he's trying hard to make you believe differently."

"Why?"

"Come on, dude. You stole the limelight on Saturday at the game..."

"Now hold on, he blew it himself. I didn't..."

"No, you didn't cause the blowout. Not directly. But we've been over this. You're playing nice with Lauren, and this other guy on the field gave him an outlet for his jealousy and anger. Things go wrong for him and he gets sent off. To add insult to injury, the dude that he is angry with walks on to replace him, plays the hero and fixes his mess."

Robby shook his head. "He is team captain—but now, even his actual position is under threat."

"No, it isn't. I'm blindside flank, he plays openside."

"Sure. But our number eight is as good as he is and could easily slot into openside. And Koos has also had a helluva two games and could be brought in. It would be unusual for the coach to drop him, but if you keep on impressing and he keeps on acting like an idiot around you... Results are important bud, and right now you are the new flavor in town."

"Shit," thought Jimmy, as they arrived at the house. "So, he is feeling super threatened. Why then is he being all chummy-chummy?"

"Come on in, and Jess will give you the scoop, I'm sure."

Jess delivered.

"My friend Gina gets her hair done by this totally gay dude called Victor. Victor's boyfriend lives with his sister, who does the house cleaning for Sam's family on Mondays and Fridays, and she was doing Sam's room and he had left his computer on, and he was researching shoulder dislocations."

"Might just be that he is worried about me," suggested Jimmy without conviction.

"Victor's boyfriend's sister also heard him speak on the phone to his sidekick Steve, and he was pretty clear that his problems would all be gone by next week."

Smiling at school, upset at home, and researching shoulder dislocations. Jimmy tried to figure it out—if he dislocated his shoulder again, he would be out for the rest of the season—maybe for good. They had this Saturday's game against a team that they should easily beat. It was an away game. The next weekend was the big Intervarsity game. Surely if Sam was going to get him dropped from the team, he wouldn't do it at the big game—would he? He would do it away from the home ground, so as not to make a martyr out of Jimmy.

Maybe he was overthinking it. Only he knew he wasn't. He had a target on his back.

Robby was philosophical. "Just quit bud. Don't play—or if you play, just play the seconds. That puts you off his radar. If you have a bad shoulder, the smart money says don't play rugby. Lauren doesn't care, and I'm sure you could be a swell tennis or cricket player too."

Rugby was king. Jimmy, with awesome clarity, knew that he wasn't about to give it up. Last year, after the injury at Bishops, he had felt it less because of the highly competitive environment. He knew, deep down, that he could make the first team again. But he would need to work a lot harder than he was used to. He just wasn't wired that way. He had kind of made peace with not being the star any more.

But now it was back in his life. He was suddenly a god among men at this new school. He wasn't about to sacrifice his newfound status because the school bully had a crush on a girl. No way.

"No Robby. I'm going to take him out of commission first."

His friend frowned. "What do you mean?"

"Now that I know what his play is—I'll just figure out a way to take him out first. Get him to break something/dislocate something."

"Whoa there, dude. You can't be serious. That's… Well, that's just not right."

"But he plans to hurt me?"

"We don't know that, Jimmy."

"Robby, my dad loved to study the history of South Africa. You know, one of his favorite stories was of the Great Anglo-Boer War of 1899. When the mighty British Empire was taken on by the tiny Transvaal Republic. What a lot of people forget about that war is that the Transvaal commandos started the war by invading the KZN territories of the British."

Robby seemed impressed by Jimmy's grasp of history.

"Yes! The world's smallest republic invaded arguably the greatest empire in the world!"

"And why?" asked Jimmy. "Because if you know there's going to be a fight, it's better to get in the first punch."

Robby nodded. "I see your mind's made up, bud. It is a few days to the game, so sleep on it. You might win the fight—but lose a whole lot more in the process."

He stewed over it the whole week—things were awkward at practice, Lauren kept on avoiding him all through Tuesday—and it didn't help that Uncle Joe was out of town the whole week. He had gone to Cape Town to oversee some final stuff with the estate.

Jimmy was fixing himself a ham sandwich for dinner when he heard Uncle Joe's car pull up. It was late Tuesday evening.

He came in and plopped down on the couch. Jimmy needed to talk to him about the whole Sam rugby thing. It seemed like a bad time, though. Uncle Joe looked exhausted. And... sad? Jimmy made two sandwiches and brought them through to the lounge, where they ate in silence.

Jimmy was desperate to know what had gone on with the estate. For once in his life, he managed to put a guard in front of his mouth, and he waited for his uncle.

Eventually, Uncle Joe pushed aside the plate, and he looked at Jimmy. His eyes were red-rimmed. "Can I tell you when things went bad between your dad and me?"

Jimmy was floored. Did he want to know? There was a lot of stuff here—but would it be... he didn't... but all he said was "Sure."

Uncle Joe had a faraway look in his eyes.

"You never knew your grandfather. You're named after him, you know. He was a helluva guy—personable, a charmer, and a hustler. Which was probably why we never had any money. Drove our mom nuts—but they scraped it together to raise us, and when things changed in this country, we were both set up with a good chance for a future with decent education."

"Your dad was ambitious. Go to university. Get the degree. Marry the prom queen. Status, networks, and recognition were important to him. Probably why he put you in Bishops—we went to a no-name school in the middle of nowhere, and it left a deep impression on both of us. But we went in different ways."

Jimmy knew this part. The school had been Elgin High. His dad had told a few stories of that time, but they were not joyful.

Uncle Joe continued, "Your dad was four years older. So, by the time I finished high school, he had already finished studying and was working. I suppose your granddad was underwhelmed by me. I chose not to go to university but started working as a waiter at the local steakhouse."

"Parents should never have favorites—but they do. And I was your grandfather's. I didn't want it, but he loved me. He loved my free spirit, he loved my lack of pretenses, and no matter what your dad did, he would always be second—even though he was older. I think the old man put too much pressure on him to get a degree, to succeed. And with me, he could just dote."

"Thing is, the more your dad reached, the worse their relationship became. Your dad gets a great job—your grandfather doesn't acknowledge. He gets a promotion. Buys a fancy car. Dates the varsity queen. Whatever. The old man never really showed much validation."

Uncle Joe poured himself a large whiskey. He didn't normally drink that much, and Jimmy had spotted the bottle of good Scotch on the shelf before. It was clearly kept for special occasions – or times of need.

"I was away when he became sick. You were quite young—and it happened quickly. Six months from the diagnosis, he was gone. It was lung cancer—and lung cancer is a bastard. I came back from France and spent six months supporting our mom. Your father-well, he was busy making a name for himself in the business world. I always thought he could have slowed down a bit more to spend more time with the old man right at the end. I suppose we all make our choices."

Uncle Joe sighed. "When he passed, he didn't leave a will. Mom inherited the estate—what was left of it, I suppose, which wasn't much. She didn't last long after that either. She loved your grandfather to bits, and I suppose she died of a broken heart, just two years later."

"Things went bad between us because of the watch. The goddamn watch."

He paused. "Man, it feels horrible telling you about this."

Jimmy nodded. "I know my dad was a bastard sometimes, Uncle Joe. Go on, I think I know where this is going."

"Your grandfather loved that watch, son. Wore it everywhere. Just before he passed, he gave it to me. It was a vintage Rolex—a gift from a grateful client when he was young. As I said, we didn't have much—but, he had that watch."

"After his funeral, your dad came up to me. And asked for the watch. We all deal with grief in different ways I suppose—but I took offense to his actions. We had a big fight, right there by the gravesite. He was going on about birthright, being the oldest, he should get the watch, yada-yada... pretty sure it helped push our mom into an early grave."

Uncle Joe took a long sip. "I was sad. And angry. But it was horrible, the whole thing was horrible, so I gave him the damn watch. Told him to keep it and stick it up where the sun doesn't shine. And I told him we were through. That he wouldn't be seeing me after that."

Jimmy sighed. "My dad never wore the watch, Uncle Joe. He kept it in the safe, and sometimes I would find him in his study looking at it. My mom had told me a version of this story. I knew it was part of the reason for the rift between you, but never the full details."

Uncle Joe put the drink down and went to stand by the window. "Such a pity. I would've worn that thing every day of my life. And yesterday, it was auctioned off to the highest bidder. It fetched R100 000, I will have you know."

He came to Jimmy and rested on his haunches. "Now, I am sorry about the rift it caused. I do care that the watch is now gone, and I do care that your dad was petty about it. But I can only take responsibility for my own actions, and I should have let it go. He was what he was—it's funny how we grew up in the same house but ended up so different."

He looked into Jimmy's eyes for a second, then stood up to leave. "It's been a rough couple of days—but now it's done. I'm going to bed."

He was so angry. Angry at his parents for deserting him. Angry at his father for pissing everything away. Angry at the ragged school clothes he was now wearing, at Lauren for making him jump through hoops for her attention, at Sam and his gang for being such assholes.

He didn't sleep well that night—or any night for the rest of the week.

Wednesday morning at school, things blew up even further.

It was Steve again. They were changing for PT in the third period, and he saw a couple of the kids sniggering on the other side of the locker room. They were clearly sharing a joke at his expense, and weaselly-faced Steve was in the middle of it. Jimmy stomped over there, only in his socks and his jocks, and confronted them.

"Got something to say to me, assholes? Say it to my face!"

Steve was a lot smaller kid than Jimmy, but he was a tough little shit. He was from the "wrong side of the tracks" as his parents would describe it, and he stood up, eyes twinkling. The other two kids backed off a little bit—it was all a bit different when Sam wasn't around, and he was on a different class schedule that day.

"I was just thinking, new kid. How did you ever manage to stay in Bishops, if you can't even afford proper socks?"

Jimmy looked down, and mortified, he realized that there was a tear on the heel of the right sock (they were gray and also from the used cupboard). Shame gave way quickly to anger.

He grabbed Steve by the front of his vest and pushed him up against the locker door with so much force that the weasel's teeth clacked.

"Listen here, asshole. I am having a really, really shitty week—so maybe you should find something better to do than checking out my wardrobe. Or I might just need to rearrange yours. Do we understand each other?"

Steve nodded; the wind taken out of his sails.

Jimmy let him go and turned to walk back to his side of the locker. But Steve wasn't done with him. "Let me know if you need to borrow any socks, bud. We keep a charity bag at home."

It was too much. He swung with a big right haymaker—and completely missed Steve, who was lightning quick and ducked under his fist. He ended up connecting with Dougie—one of the other conspirators, and a usually unassuming nerd. Worse, Dougie wore glasses—which were sent flying and shattered on the floor.

Uncle Joe came to meet him in the principal's office, an hour later.

They drove home in silence. The school nurse had to treat Dougie for a bloody nose, he would miss practice that afternoon—and he would need to pay for the glasses, which would take two weeks' worth of chores. That also meant no money to spring a surprise second date on Lauren! It was a horrible—horrible—day.

Uncle Joe heated some lasagna for lunch, and they sat down. Jimmy had been in a couple of scuffles back at Bishops—he had a temper, but it was never as serious as this. And once or twice that his parents were notified, his dad never even knew about it. He was always away on business, so his mom would end up sorting it out with the school.

He was in unfamiliar territory here, and decided to lead with offense.

"I didn't mean to strike that kid, Uncle Joe. The punch was meant for that weasel Steve."

"What did he do to merit such a reaction, Jimmy?"

"He called me poor."

Uncle Joe chewed on this for a second. Then, as they finished their food, he cleared the plates and beckoned Jimmy to come with him to the lounge.

They sat down, and Uncle Joe grabbed a book from the shelf.

"It's completely up to you, son. But this book changed my life. Read it when the mood strikes you—and if you want to make notes in the margins, please do so."

He handed it over. It was called "The Seven Habits of Highly Effective People", by an author called Stephen Covey. Jimmy had seen it in the bookshelf—but had not paid much attention, his father had always scoffed at "self-help" books.

Jimmy felt his anger rise again. "That's it? That's your parenting style? To tell me to go read a book? Aren't you going to give me a speech? Tell me to be the better man? Tell me sticks and stones can break my bones, but words can never hurt me? Tell me that it's not so bad to be called poor, because hey, we are!"

Uncle Joe regarded him. "Well, you already know the answers. You can either be angry, or you can be curious, Jimmy. Right now, you are very angry—and I get it. There's a lot to be angry about. When you're ready to not be angry—become curious. Read the book. And then we'll talk. I have stuff at the restaurant I need to take care of. We'll talk some more later."

The book would remain unread for a while. Things were about to go from bad to worse for Jimmy.

Lauren knew she had to say something. Vicky and Lauren never worked the same shifts at the restaurant after things turned sour between them. Lauren had always wondered why the older girl was so mean to her. Lauren had started at the restaurant after Vicky, and their shifts overlapped regularly at the start. But then guests would start to consciously prefer to sit at Laurens table. So, Vicky became jealous. Her trash mouth almost got her fired by Joe, but she pleaded with him and so he let her stay on. He relented and split their shifts, so they never worked together. Then guests would start to understand who was on when, and more people would show up on the nights Lauren worked.

Lauren was meticulous with her cash-ups, to the point where she double-checked opening floats against the previous night's closing balance. And that's when she started to notice a discrepancy on the opening register balance. It was never more than a couple of hundred Rands. She realized someone was skimming off floats. The only person it could be, other than her and Uncle Joe, was Vicky. She didn't want to be a snitch, but she needed to do something. She decided to confront Vicky the next day, on Thursday afternoon.

She arrived just as they were setting up for the dinner crowd... and the whole kitchen was gossiping about Uncle Joe's hot date.

She took Vicky aside, trying to keep it civil.

It didn't go well. Vicky tore into her for being a goodie-two-shoes princess, accused her of being jealous because of Jimmy, accused her of being a snob. Lauren couldn't comprehend the meanness of such a person, but she kept her cool.

"Vicky, I need to go to Uncle Joe with this. He needs to know."

"You little bitch. Well, you'll get your wish. I quit. I hope you don't have plans this evening, because you are going to have to cover my shift." She took off her apron and threw it on the table. "Tell him whatever you want."

She walked up to Lauren, and got in her face. Lauren stood her ground, and Vicky hissed, "You'll be sorry about this. Guaranteed."

And she stormed out.

Lauren put on the apron, and took over the prep work. She hated to do this, but the boss needed to know. So, she called him, and he popped in on his way to pick up his date. She told him what happened. He nodded, thanked her for her honesty—and she offered to take up Vicky's shifts in the short term.

That should have been that. But Vicky's parting words kept ringing in her ears...

———

Thursday morning was not a good day for Jimmy. Lauren was now officially not talking to him. She blew him off when he tried to chat to her in the hallway—and in fact, word had gotten around that he had hit Dougie, who was well-liked and generally harmless. Robby, to his credit, didn't leave him completely socially isolated. Koos, however, took a wide berth.

By the time he arrived at Thursday practice, he was ready to kill. And it played right into Sam's hands.

It was scrum practice. The forwards were slamming into each other and the tackle machine. Jimmy was going at it. Hells bells, even though his shoulder was really hurting. What made it worse is the coach, who had until this point been a big fan of his, also treated him like persona non grata.

Part of him wanted to quit right there. Especially with loathsome Steve laughing behind his back, over there by the backs. But he wasn't going to give them the satisfaction. Sam wasn't exactly picking on him —but even the forced friendliness had evaporated.

The final humiliation happened with the team announcement after practice. Jimmy was left in the second-team—Coach, sensing the vibes, thought it best to leave him out of the first team with Steve and Sam. Dammit, he should've expected this—but it still felt unfair.

He stomped home, took a shower, slapped on some shorts and his favorite t-shirt, and noticed a note on the fridge. "I'm not working tonight, Jimmy. I'm off on a date and might be back quite late. I left some lasagna in the fridge for you."

He felt incredibly alone. Even his uncle wasn't there when he needed him the most! He sat down, hair still wet from the shower, looking at the drinks cabinet.

Jimmy and his mates had had fun starting to experiment with alcohol when they were about fifteen. It had been easy to get their hands on some of their parents' brandy, his dad had a lot of booze left over from parties at the house. It had always been easy for a half bottle of brandy to disappear. He and his mates would have sneaky drinks in the park or at home a lot.

Uncle Joe only kept the good stuff, though. It was twelve or eighteen-year-old whiskey and craft beers. And Jimmy knew that he would notice if something went missing.

Right now, though, he didn't give a shit. On a base level, he remembered this was something his dad sometimes did when he was deeply upset. He would just sit by himself, swigging back the drinks until he would go to bed. He would never become paralytically drunk —and as far as Jimmy knew, he didn't drink like that when they were out and about. But at home, sometimes…

Tonight, he wanted to escape. To dial back all the crap from last week. So, he grabbed the 12-year-old and poured himself a neat double. It was like fire down his throat, and he took another. And then another.

A pleasant warmth spread through him, and he sank down in front of the TV. He would probably regret this later. It was obvious that the bottle had taken a hit. Maybe he would dilute it with some water. But surely Uncle Joe would notice?

He was flicking through channels, letting the numbness set in, when there was a knock on the door.

He walked to open it, slightly unsteady. Maybe it was Lauren? Could he hope?

It wasn't.

Vicky had a pizza in one hand, a bottle of red wine in the other. She was wearing a tight white top, and, from the clear outlines of her nipples, nothing underneath. She smiled at him, and asked, "You gonna invite me in, sport? I've brought pizza…"

Taken by surprise, he managed a brief nod. She breezed past him to the kitchen. She quickly found the opener, popped the bottle of wine and poured them each a glass.

"I heard you were having a rough time at school, sugar. And I thought I would come over and cheer you up. Let's sit down."

She didn't wait for him, and her skirt crept up her thigh as she sat down. He knew he shouldn't start something here. But he was happy for the company, and just one glass couldn't hurt, could it? He took it from her hand, and took a deep swallow. It didn't taste great—he had not developed a taste for wine yet. But the second try was better. His head felt nice and fuzzy, and getting fuzzier.

She was smiling and sipping her wine. She had grabbed the remote and was casually flipping through channels, until she found the music channel. She put on some deep house and turned the volume down, then turned to him. Man, she was hot! He felt like he had to say something. "It's Thursday night - shouldn't you be working?"

She laughed and opened the pizza box. "Oh, you haven't heard? I have parted ways with the ol' Italian joint. I've decided to spread my wings and leave town. Time for this girl to go check out life in the big city!"

He watched her take out a slice of pizza. Her lips were bright red, and she held his eyes while she took a bite. "Hmm…" The way she said it even felt sexy! Then she held out the same slice for him to have a bite. He leaned in, and steadied himself with his left hand on the couch. Whether by accident or design, she moved her leg slightly, and he felt it brush his hand.

"So… umm… what are you going to do now?" His mind was racing.

She sat back, breaking contact. He immediately wanted her to be closer again. But hold on… what about Lauren? He felt it difficult to focus.

"I have a friend in Cape Town—there's loads of waitressing jobs there, she works at one of the spots in the Waterfront and I can crash at her pad until I get myself set up. I plan to leave tomorrow."

"That's cool, I guess. Won't you miss it here?" She leaned forward for another bit of pizza, those breasts straining against her blouse! If she was leaving tomorrow… if something were to happen… no one would know?

She laughed. "Seize the moment, you know? There is an opportunity for me now. It might not come again." She leaned forward again and put his hand on her thigh – at the very point where her skirt had hiked up to. It was like an electric shock through his body, and he took another big sip of wine – but he left his hand there.

Her eyes twinkled, and she licked her lips. "We have to seize our chances, right?"

He nodded, and it felt like his hand had a life of its own. She held his eyes as it crept beneath her skirt, and made its way down… down… She sighed. "Baby, this move is long overdue."

"Which move… are we talking about…" he managed. She was completely wet down there. And his pants were about to explode!

"The move where we are home alone for the night, and you send me off in style."

She suddenly stood up and left him in the lurch. She looked around. "Which way is your bedroom?"

For a moment, he thought of Lauren. And the conversation with his uncle. And how bad this was. But then she pulled him up, and kissed him. Her tongue in his mouth, and her hand massaging his crotch. He shouldn't… he musn't…

"Your bedroom?" He nodded, and let her lead him out of the dining room.

They got to the door of his room, and he tried one last time: "Vicky, I don't think…"

She took off her top. Her breasts were glorious. She managed to open the door with one hand, while the other found its way inside of his shorts. "No one will ever know, sugar…"

He had lost all control.

"Vicky…"

"Hush." Then she pushed him onto the bed.

He had had a couple of sexual encounters before—but this was next level.

"Oh God," he exclaimed. She had taken off his pants, and had taken him into her mouth.

He came so quickly it was embarrassing.

She jumped up to go to the bathroom—and he heard her spit. She came back, only wearing her panties. "Can I borrow your shirt, sport? It's pretty cold tonight and it's gonna be a while before you are back in action."

She didn't wait for his answer but grabbed the shirt he had been wearing. Breakdancing Darth Vader sure looked a lot better on her.

"This'll do." She was almost naked, in his room, in his shirt. Then she went back to bed. "If I know guys, you probably want to take a nap. That's ok bud… just as long as we do round two when you wake up, and I get my turn…"

"I'm pretty sure I could be ready sooner than that…" he said. She tilted her head, and lay down next to him. "Let's see," and she gently ran her fingers across his groin. "Wow. Look at that," she murmured.

She fumbled for something by the bed, and produced a condom. Where did she get that? "On second thought, let's skip the foreplay. Lay still while I put this thing on."

He could only watch her as she skillfully ripped open the plastic, and rolled the condom onto him. Then she stood up, and slid off her panties.

"Lets' see what you got, sugar…"

She got on top of him, and slipped him into her. He just lay there, a jumble of alcohol, desire and teenage stupidity rendering him incapable of speech. She started a slow gyration, her eyes closed. This time, he managed to contain himself. She went faster and faster… and then she started to moan. Soft yelps at first. Then louder and louder.

He realized that it was a good thing he was drunk. And had come once already. Otherwise, this would also have been a very short session. As it was, he could hold on until she came… and then she came again… and she was so loud that he almost had time to wonder if the neighbors could hear… and then he didn't know anything anymore…

After he finally spent himself, she slipped off him. "Well done, sport. I am going to be sure to give you a glowing review…" She snuggled into his arm. And within moments, she was snoring. He looked at this glorious creature, and counted his lucky stars. And then he promptly passed out.

When he woke up, she was gone. The house was quiet and he looked at his watch, it was way after 3 am. He listened and he could hear Uncle Joe snoring in the other room.

He felt a combination of intense guilt and drained elation.

What a night!

The next morning, before he set off for school, they had a quick breakfast together. He had a bit of a headache—but not as much as he might have expected. A few glasses of water helped!

Good thing, too, as his uncle was in a chatty mood.

"See you had company last night," he said, cocking his head at the empty wine bottle and two glasses that were still on the kitchen counter.

Jimmy was tucking into a bowl of cereal. Should he tell Uncle Joe it was Vicky? Knowing he didn't approve? How else to explain the wine? Stupid, stupid. Had he looked at his drinks cabinet and noticed the knock in the whiskey? "Yep. Vicky came by to say goodbye; heard she had quit at the restaurant and was leaving town."

Uncle Joe snorted. "Quit? That's what she told you? That girl is trouble, Jimmy. I told you to steer clear."

"I couldn't be rude, Uncle Joe. Besides, I'm kinda short of friends right now, and she was here when I needed company."

"You didn't need to be drinking. You're not yet 18."

"Sure. But like I said—she brought the bottle, I was happy to have her here, and then she left."

Uncle Joe's eyes arched—and it was clear that he wasn't taken in by the lie. Not one bit.

"All right. Hope you're not throwing away a good thing here bud. Eat up and get to school."

He emptied the trash, jumped in the shower, and felt like a million bucks. He had slept with an incredibly hot older chick with no conse-quences, it didn't seem like he was found out for drinking. In fact, his uncle was incredibly cool about the whole thing. He would still turn this sucker around!

He mucked around for a bit before he set off to school—the sun was out, and he couldn't find his Oakleys. Finally, giving up on the shades, he resigned himself to looking for them when he came back—probably they fell on the floor in the lounge or something.

And he was on a roll! Someone slipped him a note in the fourth period—and it was from Lauren. He glanced back, and she gave him a brief smile. He didn't dare read the note—the teacher was razor sharp at this kind of stuff, and he couldn't take more humiliation.

The first thing he did when the bell rang was read it.

The note read: "I heard what happened with Dougie, but only heard the full story yesterday afternoon—about your folks' estate. I'm sorry—if you need to talk, walk me home after school. Lauren."

Man, it was a miracle! Voluptuous Vicky was skipping town and he was pretty sure no one, especially Lauren, would ever know about their little rendezvous. And now she was reaching out to him. Things were turning around.

More good news—the coach called him in just before the end of the second break.

"I still think you are bad news, Barnes. You have an attitude problem you need to fix. But both Steve and Sam came to me to apolo-gize for their bad behavior. They pleaded that you be allowed to play this weekend. It is the big game, and we need all the help we can get. For the school's sake."

Jimmy couldn't stop smiling. "Sure Coach! I'll give it my 100%!"

"Top man. We have the big pre-game rally tonight in the school hall. Be ready, the Big Brag is huge fun, and the first team is the main event."

Jimmy had to stop short of pinching himself. As he came out of the coach's office, Sam and Steve were waiting for him. He approached them with slight hesitation. There were a lot of students hanging in the background. They were expecting some kind of show, and he clenched his jaw. If these guys wanted a show, they would get it.

But Sam completely took the wind out his sails. "Jimmy. Steve wants to say something."

Jimmy turned his attention from Sam to Steve. The other kid also looked a bit defensive, and the vibe he gave off was he would rather be somewhere else. But then he softened his stance and even smiled. "Hey look. I was just having a go, you know? I'm sorry. I didn't realize what was going on with you this week. It's gotta be tough." He stuck out his hand.

"I know I can be an asshole. If we're gonna win some games together, please just take me with a pinch of salt going forward? Teammate?"

Everyone was watching. The apology seemed slightly insincere—but at the same time, it was an apology. And things were going well. Jimmy felt he still needed to be careful, but for now, he was happy to make peace.

They shook, and Sam clapped them both on the shoulders with what seemed genuine pleasure. "Good! Remember we're not each other's enemy. This weekend, it's those guys from George we have to beat. Eyes on the prize gentlemen."

And with that, they were off. The bell rang, last period flew by… and Lauren was waiting for him outside the main gate of the school.

It was about a 10 minute walk to her house—and, remembering his manners, he offered to carry her backpack. She laughed, and he liked the sound of it. "My, what old school good manners you have. No, I'm fine, thanks. But I do appreciate the offer."

They walked in silence for a couple of minutes. Then they started up simultaneously, "I…" "You…"

That laugh again. Then she said, "Ok you go first."

"You know you have me twisted in 100 different directions, Lauren."

She nodded, as if to herself.

Emboldened, he continued, "I like you. I think you know that by now. And I do think you might like me, too."

"Maybe…" she smiled.

Then she spoke up. "I'm not one for games, Jimmy. But I am careful. Especially of good-looking boys with fast words and big egos. And

I judge you a lot to be one of those… no matter how cute your ass is…"

He started at that saucy comment. It was almost crude—not lady-like at all. Maybe this chick had a bit of a wild side after all.

"Look, all I ask is don't judge a book by its cover. I'm trying hard to fit in—but it's also a political minefield at this school, what with your ex making it clear that you are off-limits."

"Sam doesn't own me. And we hardly even dated. But yes, I can see your point. And I haven't tried to make trouble for you."

They had reached her front door. "Trouble has a way of finding me, Lauren."

She lowered her eyes and murmured, "Looks like it. You're bad news. My mother told me I should stay away from you."

He couldn't quite hear what she said next and stepped in closer. "What was that?"

Then she fixed those green pupils on him and lifted her lips to his. "I said… sometimes I like to do things that my mom would disapprove of…"

He wanted to kiss her. So bad. Her lips parted slightly…

But then he stepped back and cleared his throat. She blinked surprised and off-balance.

"Will I see you tonight? At the Big Brag?"

She recovered quickly. "Of course. The whole school will be there. Wouldn't miss it… just don't let your ego get too far in your way…"

He walked home, a happy man. Uncle Joe would be proud—he kept his cool and didn't push.

Life was good!

The upward curve continued with the Big Brag that evening. High schools all over South Africa had a tradition to celebrate the different teams participating in the big weekend inter-schools derby. In their case, Outeniqua High in George were their arch-rivals.

The kids worked themselves up into a frenzy as the different teams were introduced onto the stage. First the junior teams for rugby, squash, netball, and hockey. Moving up to the more senior teams—and every first team that went up to their theme song. The Hockey Boys first team went up on Queen "I want it all". The girls had "Girls just wanna have fun". The squash team (who always lost; Jimmy heard) had "We're not gonna take it".

And then, when it was the time for the first team, as tradition had had it for decades in Afrikaans schools all over South Africa—they walked up to "Eye of the Tiger" from the Rocky movies. Bishops had had their own rituals, but there was something about the raw small-time emotion at play here. It really got to Jimmy. When he walked up, he was pumped!

Finally, a sense of belonging. And to crown things off, Lauren was elected the "Champagne Girl"—she who would pose for the pics and pop the champagne to signal the start of the game tomorrow. HIS girl, he thought—and it was confirmed when she blew him a kiss just before they walked off stage.

He was on top of the world.

The Big Brag ended at 8 pm, and although the rest of the team wanted to go grab a pizza, the coach admonished them to go straight home. He had a big day ahead.

Jimmy decided to go to the restaurant anyway. He was way too alert to go to sleep—and anyway, he had a hunch.

It paid off. Lauren was there with her girlfriends. She was the captain of the netball team, and the usual suspects were surrounding her. The reception, when he walked in, was far less chilly. Not warm enough for them to invite him to sit down—but there was lots of friendly ribbing, and by the time he went to go take his usual spot at the bar, Uncle Joe had popped the usual Hawaiian down for him.

"I'd say eat up and hurry home, sport. Big day tomorrow, and I'm sure you didn't get much sleep last night."

Jimmy looked up sharply at the comment, but Uncle Joe's gaze remained guileless. Did he know? How did he know?

"Looks like you are in the good books again over there, though," said his uncle. "Lucked out, I guess."

Jimmy nodded and wolfed down the pizza. "Yep. Sometimes we get lucky."

Uncle Joe left Jimmy to his own thoughts—he felt guilty about Vicky today, as much as he loved last night. It wasn't as if he and Lauren were together—I mean, they were getting closer, but they weren't an item. So, he shouldn't feel guilty. Should he? What would she do if she knew?

He pushed it to the back of his mind. Vicky was gone, and their little encounter would stay their secret.

Lauren and the girls were paying their bill and getting up to leave. He finished his pizza and followed them out the door.

"Lauren?"

She turned and waved to the girls. "Be right there, ladies. Just want to see what this fine young gentleman has to say."

The car was parked across the road. The two of them stood outside of the restaurant, and he realized he didn't know exactly what he wanted to say to her. He had felt so confident this afternoon and had felt on top of the world at the Big Brag, but now her mere presence had him tongue-tied again.

"I wanted to say... that... I hope that after the game tomorrow..."

And then she interrupted him in the best possible way. She stepped up and kissed him.

She tasted like... peaches. He felt her hand touch the back of his neck—then her lips parted, and he felt her tongue gently probing his. Somewhere in the distance, he could hear whooping and cheering.

It was only seconds—then they broke, she blew him a kiss, ran across the street, and jumped in the car with the other girls.

He walked home deep in thought.

Things were finally going his way.

He wished he could quiet the voice inside his head, and just enjoy it.

13

Superstitions are funny things. Jimmy had never indulged in them. It was, however, a well-known fact that some of the top sportsmen and women in the world were deeply married to their rituals. They could easily be put off their game by something breaking in their pre-game set-up.

He woke up and was filled with a sense of foreboding. He tried to shrug it off and thought he would go for a very mild run, to get his mojo back. The sun was already out, and he looked for his favorite Darth Vader T. In the lounge, in his room—he couldn't find the damn thing. Come to think of it—Vicky had worn it when they had sex. Did she still have the T? He hoped not… he loved that shirt.

He went for his run, but felt unsettled. When he came back, he rummaged through the laundry, but couldn't find it there. Realized he didn't even have Vicky's phone number. Uncle Joe would have it, for sure. But he was embarrassed to ask him. He would get it later from someone else at the restaurant.

The game was a home game this year, and they were only scheduled to play later in the morning, so he had lots of time. Still, as a first-team player, he was expected to show up and support all the other teams. And truthfully, he was excited about supporting Lauren in her netball game.

So, he put on his school gear, packed his togs and uniform for the game. Uncle Joe had eschewed a big breakfast in favor of a steamy bowl of oats, with some banana and topped with cinnamon. "No bacon and egg for you today son. This will give you the right energy for the big game."

They ate in companionable silence.

As he was wrapping up and getting ready to leave, Jimmy asked "Will you come to watch the game, Uncle Joe?"

"Wouldn't miss it for the world."

Jimmy mused that his father had missed plenty of games over the years. But that was in the past—Uncle Joe was turning out to be a great cheerleader, he had the world at his feet and today was going to be his day.

Still, that nagging feeling.

"Uncle Joe, did you ever play? Rugby? I mean, my old man didn't seem to care much... which I always found surprising, as he was so crazy about the game when he was a young man. I mean I saw all the pictures."

Uncle Joe set down the plates and took a moment to answer. "He was a great player. But he was always doing it for your grandfathers' approval. Problem was, Granddad would show up, get angry, then leave before the game was done. Afterward, he only had criticism for your dad. I was a bit younger and saw this play out—so I just decided to not play at all. Didn't seem like it was worth it."

Jimmy had never heard this before. "But all the trophies—the awards?"

"He hated it. But it was what he thought he needed to do to be the big man on campus. And give credit where credit is due. It worked. In a place like Stellenbosch, being the main man in terms of rugby carries a lot of currency. I always wondered if he even liked most of the people he was hanging with, having said that. But he did succeed in his goal."

Uncle Joe sat down again. "Jimmy, your dad was many things. And some of his traits were less than admirable. But I have to give it to him

—he was always 100% committed in everything that he did. Even if he didn't like it, if it needs to get done, he would give it his all. You gotta respect that."

Jimmy reflected on this on the way to school. It had always irritated him how his father brought up his past, how hard things were, how lucky Jimmy was... blah blah blah. It always felt like not giving 100% was a small act of rebellion against that constant pushing.

Where did that leave him today? 100% probably meant not protecting the shoulder—he still had to be careful. And so far, he could use his brains not his brawns to add value. No, he would be ok firing only on a few cylinders.

He met up with Koos and Robby at the sports grounds. The lower age group teams had started to do their match-ups, and the grounds were abuzz with activity. There would be a total of twelve rugby matches today—there were three teams in the lower two age groups, and four teams in the senior category. There was also netball going on. The hockey and squash teams played yesterday (and won!).

They walked on over to the netball courts, and he was pleased to see Lauren and her crew also cheering. They were flushed with excitement and egging on the juniors. He thought of going over to say hi—but he couldn't catch her eye, and he thought he would wait till he could find her alone later.

Sam, Steve and the rugby crew showed up, and then they all cruised together like a big gang. Sam was still very much the alpha—and initially, Jimmy thought there was trouble between them again. Sam was highly agitated, avoided Jimmy and walked around like someone had stolen his lunch again. As if reading his thoughts, Robby commented: "Don't mind Sam, Jimmy. This is his second year on the first team. Last year he was younger than most of the guys, and the team got bashed in the final. So, he takes this very seriously—he is always wound up before a big game, and this is the biggest one of his life so far."

Jimmy supposed it was a big deal—he was, to a degree, quite jealous. Sam really cared about the game, the team, and for him, the sky would feel like it was falling down if they didn't make it today. How did he feel? Rugby and the game provided a path toward popularity, but he had to admit he couldn't really give two shits if they won or lost. As long as he came out of it looking good, he would be ok. There were surely more important things than just the game. He wasn't his father.

The first netball team came out for their game. Lauren looked amazing out there—she had such gorgeous legs, and she was pretty quick around the court too. She was the main goalie and one of the tallest girls on the team. He noticed a few times when she could have easily scored, but rather let one of the other girls take the shot. A few times they missed—but it didn't matter, they were always well ahead. Lucky that—if it was him, he would rather have made sure of the points.

As they came off the court, laughing and high fiving, she gave him a wink. "Your turn, sport!"

Game time approached swiftly. The second team was getting whipped out there—Koos was captaining, but the opposition looked more organized, and fitter. Jimmy only halfway paid attention—but he could tell what was wrong. Mike was having an absolute shocker, and not only knocked almost every single ball that came his way, but he also missed a bunch of tackles. Jimmy thought the coach should rather take him off and sub him. But by the time they went into the change rooms to prepare for their game, the seconds had started their second half—and Mike was still playing.

Jimmy was putting on his shoes when he broke a shoelace. "Dammit!"

"Don't read too much into it, sport," said Steve. "I used to think that was bad luck—now I just think it's bad shoes. Here are some extra laces."

Jimmy relaced his shoe, but Steve's comments stuck with him. Was it a cleverly layered insult? Bad shoes? Was he messing with his head? Bad luck?

He tried to dismiss it but as they started their warmups, he still felt off. Sam was completely in the zone—he had a crazed look in his eyes.

The only good thing out of all this was that all that nonsense about setting him up for a shoulder injury was in the past. It was more important to win this game. Wasn't it?

Anyway, he had to focus on his own game time. He was playing blindside flank again, and the word on the street was that his opposite number was big—and quick. He was lined up to play for the Border team, which was the provincial representation side. So, the kid would have a lot to prove today.

But so did Jimmy.

They huddled and discussed their strategy. The other team was known for having a really good lineout, so they decided to keep the ball in play as much as possible. Also, their inside center James Adams, as well as the flanker Rob More, were tipped to be provincials—so Jimmy and Steve were allocated to mark those two danger men.

Coach did his best Al Pacino impersonation and gave them a pretty rousing speech. This was the biggest day of their lives so far, and Jimmy was sure he quoted Gladiator ("What we do in life, echoes in eternity"), Rudy ("No one comes into our house and pushes us around"), and even Forrest Gump, God help us ("Life's like a box of chocolates").

Still, the team was pretty fired up.

When they finally walked out onto the field, Jimmy was ready to go to war.

The two teams lined up, the champagne girls between them. Jimmy did a double-take: Lauren was dressed in a knee-length white dress, her hair hanging to her shoulders and with the slightest bit of make-up. She looked incredible and completely outshone the other team's girl. First points go to us, he thought. And that's my girl!

A rousing rendition from the crowds of the school anthems, and then it was game time. As they lined up to receive the first kick, Jimmy heard his name shouted from the side. He looked over to the other side of the field, where all the cars were parked for tailgating—and there, sitting on the hood of a bakkie, was Vicky.

"Good luck champ! Rooting for you!"

Jimmy was swamped by mixed emotions—she looked super hot, cleavage hanging out and legs up to here—but in kind of a trashy way. He couldn't help comparing her to Lauren, who looked like an angel. Why was she still here? He thought she had left town? She wasn't an alumnus of the school either... and in the back of his mind, there was a disquieting thought that suddenly reared, previously unexamined.

What did she mean when she said she would give him a great review? Who would be asking?

Distracted, he wasn't quite ready when the ball came to him off the kickoff. He thought he had it, but then that flank Rob More charged into him. He fumbled it, the other team secured the ball and surged forward. The resulting ruck led to a penalty, and they scored the first points within a minute. Horrible start.

As they waited under the poles, Sam hissed, "Get your head out of your ass, Jimmy. This is the big game. Forget about the girls and focus on this!"

Girls? What did Sam know? Why did he...

But there was no time. They went back to the halfway line, and now they had to chase.

Then there was no time to think about his romantic troubles. The other team was strong, fast, well-drilled—and that flank was a nightmare. Jimmy had his hands full; they used Rob to draw in the defense, and it was working. He slipped through Jimmy's tackle, forcing Steve to come in and bring him down. Rob offloaded to the flyhalf, who then drew in his man and brought in the center James. And presto—the dude glided through a gap as wide as a barnyard door to score the first try of the game, just ten minutes in.

They gathered under the poles again, waiting for the conversion kick. Sam was livid. "Guys, I know how these guys roll. We have to stop Rob More in his tracks, and we can't commit extra guys to do it. Barnes, if you're carrying an injury and can't do the job, tell us now, and we'll get the coach to sub you."

There it was. And it all became crystal clear to Jimmy. There was only one way he walked away from this game without being the weak link. He had to put his body on the line to cover the opposing flank. They had talked about this in the pre-game sessions—but looking back now, he was too distracted by all the other stuff going on in his life. He hadn't realized the implication.

He looked at Sam, who took a moment from looking frighteningly angry to smile at him. Sam cared about winning—but he clearly cared slightly more about eliminating his opposition. He was setting Jimmy up for pain! Jimmy cursed his stupidity—there was nothing he could do but go full in. And that meant putting his shoulder at risk.

The next 20 minutes were brutal. They managed to contain the opposition this time—but Rob More was a pest. They varied the strategy a couple of times—but Jimmy needed to put in at least five big hits on him during that period. It was exhausting, the guy was big, strong, and tough as nails. On the last hit, he twisted around the tackle, and they went down onto Jimmy's bad shoulder. Ouch! But it held this time, and Rob spilled the ball in the process, resulting in another scrum. He held out his hand to help Jimmy up. As they rose, the dude said, "You're bringing it, bud. Heard you might be a weakness in the team—but not seeing it so far."

As the set for the scrum, Jimmy mulled over Rob's words. He would be a weakness? Because he was only recently brought into the first team? Or more likely, they also knew about his bad shoulder… and the only way they would know that was if somehow it leaked to their camp. Sam!

It was a good scrum, and they managed to move the ball up-field a few times. Sam was the main carrier off the back of the mauls, and now it was Jimmy's job to be a decoy runner. This meant he was pummeled by Rob a few times, while Sam and Steve actually made good ground. The move was rounded off with Steve breaking through the line for their first try. The conversion was also good, and that meant they were back in the game.

The whistle blew for halftime. Jimmy was livid—he was hurting like hell, and Sam and Steve were scooping up all the glory. He glanced over to the side of the field where he had spotted Vicky—and thankfully, she was no longer to be seen. There was at least that to be thankful for.

As they ran through to the changerooms, Lauren waved at him with a dazzling smile. This cheered him up a little bit. He still had a score to settle with Sam, and his good mood evaporated as soon as they entered the change room.

"You guys are holding your own out there. We discussed this before—we have the weapons to take these guys, but we have to contain their star players," the coach repeated.

"Sam, you and Steve are looking good running the formation out there. However, they will rework their defense, so we need to go to plan B. That means we switch to the blindside for the first 20 minutes. Barnes, you look like you are taking some strain out there. Are you still good to give it 100% for the second half?"

Jimmy didn't appreciate being singled out like this—but he couldn't afford to show his bad temper to the coach. "I'm fine, coach. Bring it."

"Ok good. Let's go out there and finish this."

The plan was a good one. The only hitch was, now the action had moved away from Jimmy. Rob More was still in his face—but his role changed, and his primary responsibility now was to run angle support off the ball. He realized that he was getting tired and getting to the breakdowns too slowly. And his shoulder hurt like hell.

But they made some good progress, and with five minutes left on the clock, he was hanging on. They managed to trade scores, but they were still trailing by three—which meant they needed to score a try to win it. And the good news was the other side was also slowing down.

The opportunity came with a couple of minutes to go. They worked it down the blindside again—and Jimmy realized that Rob More had drifted to the other side to block Sam, which left Jimmy wide open. Steve saw it too—and hoisted a kick!

It flew perfectly, and Jimmy, unmarked, charged through their line. The kick bounced once -and into his hands. He beelined it for the try line, only 10 meters out—and through the surge of adrenaline, he heard someone on his tail. He couldn't dare look back and charged for the line.

Three paces out, he felt a crunching tackle get him from behind. But he had enough momentum to get one leg out of the tackler's arms, and it was enough to get him... almost there...

He came down just short of the line, but as per the rules of the game, he could stretch with the ball. He had it in his left hand, and managed to stretch... over the line... just... and as he grounded the ball, he felt a secondary tackler fall on him—his outstretched arm exposed...

POP.

They say time does slow down. The roar of the crowd, the weight of the opposing player on him, the excruciating pain as his shoulder left the socket... in that order. He could hear the referee consulting with the linesman, blowing his whistle to award the try. He could hear the crowd going nuts, then going quiet. Then the medics were there, the doctor - painkiller, hold your shoulder like this, hold on let's see if we can—and then the click pop as the doc pulled it back into position.

Taping his arm close to his shoulder, the pain now quite intense—but as the team played out the final moments, he walked off the field with the doc to a standing ovation. Images of delirious happiness as only schoolboy rugby can generate, they loved him.

There was one exception.

Lauren stood silently; her mouth set in a tight line. She was holding a package in her hand.

Somewhere, among the pain and the delirium and the joy and everything else, Jimmy was absolutely, 100% convinced that he knew what was in that package. And who had given it to her...

She came to see him. After.

After the team had all come to congratulate him. After the crazy celebrations in the locker room—Sam and Steve the ringleaders, and everyone acknowledging that Jimmy had been the star of the show. His two enemies were happy—they had won the game, and with the added bonus that Jimmy would not be playing again that season, if ever. He would need at least six months of rehabilitation from the injury. Talk about a win-win.

After they had all gone off to Joe's to celebrate. He declined, knowing Lauren would be there, and unable to handle talking to her. He went home instead, painfully unwrapping the shoulder—and took a hot shower. Uncle Joe offered to come home to help him—but he said he would be ok. After all, it wasn't the first time. He knew what to do.

After he lay down on his bed for a while, staring at the ceiling. Monday, he would be a hero, not a zero. He would be able to trade off this for a few weeks in terms of popularity—but after that, he would slip back into being someone who used to play. He knew how it worked.

It was early evening when she knocked on his door. She looked pretty, dressed in her standard work jeans-and-black shirt combo.

They looked at each other for a bit.

"Congratulations on the win," she finally said.

"Thanks. Look, Lauren…"

She shook her head. "I don't want to cry, Jimmy. I knew it was a bad idea to start falling for you…"

She took the package out of her purse. She handed it to him. He didn't need to look. He knew what it was.

"I don't know what's worse, Jimmy. The fact that you did that… or the fact that she came up to me, surrounded by all the girlfriends, and handed me this… shirt…"

"Lauren, I was in a really bad place, and…"

"And she came to comfort you. Yeah. You know, she's been comforting a few guys around this town. She knows how to pick her moment."

Her green eyes were flashing with anger now, and he could feel a sudden surge of fury build in him as well. Before he could speak, she continued, "You know what she said to me? You know what? She said, I believe you are the lady in our new hero's life. Lucky girl. Could you do me a favor? He let me borrow his favorite shirt Thursday—and I'm leaving town today, so maybe you could just give it back to him?"

"Lauren…"

"So now I like this guy. I had just kissed this guy. And then the town slut comes up, and proclaims to everyone listening that you slept with her the same day as you kissed me?"

"It wasn't…"

"Does it matter? You romance me, and at the first possible opportunity, you sleep with the town bicycle. How do you think that makes me feel?"

Before he knew it, his cheek was stinging. She had slapped him with all the force she could muster. And that's when he lost his cool.

Her eyes were still blazing, and her hand came up for another slap. But he grabbed her wrist, and pulled her close.

"Ok, fine, judge me if you will. But you were giving me the cold shoulder - and just for the record, yes, I did sleep with her. And it was great. And she was wearing this shirt when I was doing it. But, so what? We weren't together. I was in pain, and you were playing games. And what's more—she left in the middle of the night and had no reason to take my shirt. So, ask the question—why would she do that?"

"You're hurting me, Jimmy."

He realized he was still holding her by the wrist. He let go, and she stepped back, rubbing it.

But he was still angry, and the words poured out.

"You think you're so fucking perfect. Little Miss Champagne Queen. Let me tell you, I know girls like you. You're judging me—but you don't stop to think, isn't it strange that this happened today? You string along with poor Sam even though he has no chance—and guys like me are just the collateral damage. Actions have consequences, I know that. But this is what happened - I won't play rugby again, maybe ever—and that's on me, but Sam set it up so I would be vulnerable today. Pretty sure he put Vicky up to this move as well. And it comes back to you. Sure, be angry—but go be angry somewhere else. I can't deal with this shit anymore."

Her eyes flashed, and her mouth curled in a sneer.

"It's never anyone else's fault, is it Jimmy? You think Sam would do all this—hurt me, hurt you, almost throw a rugby game, the one thing he cares about most in the world - just to mess with you? You're not that special, you know. Just another entitled asshole who thinks the world owes him something. Just another asshole who uses women and blames others when he gets called on it."

He studied her for a second.

"Leave me alone, Lauren. Today was supposed to be a good day— a great day. You and your crew and your politics and your small-time bullshit can all go fuck yourselves. I am going to do my thing, and also get out of this town as quickly as possible. Now go away."

He turned his back on her and went inside.

14

"Hurry up with those Margaritas, bud. Ladies are hungry!" shouted Jimmy. Robby grinned and furiously rolled a few more pizzas. It was quite something to watch him at work—he was almost as good as Joe at this point, even though it's been only three months since he started in the kitchen.

Jimmy grabbed the drinks for table three, double-checked that he had enough glasses (they were a table of five), and hustled over there. It was old Mr. De Jager and his family—Jimmy had come to know them as regulars; every Thursday night they did a family outing. The kids were relatively well behaved, and he always tipped the same – R200, no matter what the bill.

"Here you go, folks," as he put down the two colas and the three wine glasses. The elder De Jager boy had recently turned 18 (he was in Jimmy's class) and he was now allowed to legally have a drink with the old man.

"How's the shoulder, son?" asked Mr. De Jager, perpetuating their weekly ritual.

"All good, sir. I might still need to have an op, but rehab is almost finished and it feels pretty good now."

"Hmmm… maybe you can come to play for the local club side next year. Our under 20's always need someone."

Jimmy shook his head. "Don't think so. My playing days are over, I think. Excuse me, I will be back in five to take your order."

And with that, he hustled back to the kitchen to pick up said Margheritas for table two, which was the two old ducks from the local retirement village. They always had two Margaritas and shared a sparkling water, and did not tip. He didn't mind. They were easy clients, didn't stay long and occasionally they brought him some home-baked *beskuit* – South African rusks. He and Uncle Joe reckoned it was some of the best home *baked beskuit* they ever had.

He had his shoulder out of a sling about a month after the game. Uncle Joe had had little sympathy for his Lauren situation. He knew that he was being held in not a small amount of judgment by his uncle. Not because he said anything—but Jimmy knew.

Things had been weird at school. He had become a divisive figure— it turns out a lot of other kids could see - and overhear—when Vicky came to sit down and gave Lauren the shirt. There were a bunch of rumors—gossip is universal—around Lauren, Sam, Jimmy, and Vicky. It was counterbalanced by the goodwill and sympathy he had from every-one. Everyone loves a winner, even those who were angry at him "two-timing" Lauren with Vicky. Lauren avoided him like the plague. Even though he was desperately sorry about the way he treated her, he knew there was no way back from this. So, he made peace with it—sort of.

He knuckled down and did something constructive—concentrated on his studies. He spent about a week feeling sorry for himself, but then Uncle Joe put it into perspective.

"Ok, so you can't be the star of the school team. And you lost the girl. But the girl is all your own fault, and as for the rugby… many kids will never have a moment of glory. You got yours—and the biggest thing you need to do now is remember that the worst thing for you would be if that was the highlight of your life. There are many other glorious things to look forward to—if you let yourself."

There was a practical result for Uncle Joe, as well. As it turns out, he had fired Vicky for stealing from the cash register. It now made sense to Jimmy—she had decided to get revenge on Uncle Joe by way of Jimmy, and it was probable that the whole thing had nothing to do with Sam. But because of the way Jimmy had treated Lauren, and she knew he would be around the restaurant because of his uncle—she had also quit.

Uncle Joe was, therefore, briefly without enough waiters. But then Robby, of all people, decided to step up for some extra cash. He even roped in little sister Jess to help—but that only worked till the end of the school holidays, Jess had way too big a social schedule and had to bring down her shifts. At which point Robby and Uncle Joe roped Jimmy in.

And now they had settled into quite an easy and rewarding rhythm. When Uncle Joe's regular kitchen hand quit to move to Cape Town, Robby stepped up to help in the kitchen even though he made less—and partly because Jimmy suggested they share the tips with the kitchen team.

It had been a big change. He was not heavily into the social aspect —he knew that the last days of school were supposed to be treasured. But outside of Koos (who had turned out to be a loyal and wonderful friend), he was only really close to Robby. Sam and Steve seemed to no longer be buddies, either. Jimmy wondered about that, but was glad he no longer needed to engage in the rugby politics. One upside, that.

Sam had ended up making the Border provincial team for Craven Week, the premier school tournament. He had played a blinder—and was awarded a junior contract to play with the Western Province team.

Lauren had withdrawn into herself—he was told she was heavily focused on her grades; she had been admitted to study at Stellenbosch, and Jimmy knew how important it was to her.

To a degree, he felt sorry for her. She had been grumpy as hell these last months—she didn't look well; she had lost some weight and she wasn't looking after herself. He felt somewhat responsible—but, as Uncle Joe put it, everyone also takes responsibility for themselves. He wishes he could get it together to apologize to her—but somehow, he never had the opportunity or courage to do so.

So school was not a glorious ride into the sunset—but he was doing relatively well academically, and he was enjoying the restaurant and his friendship with Robby and his family.

As spring turned to summer and the Karoo heat cranked up, thoughts also went to the final school exams—and what happens after.

In his past life, Jimmy had always talked with his buddies about a backpacking trip around South East Asia. First, go to Plettenberg Bay for the matric rage—then hop on a plane to Thailand and go bum around the islands, learn how to scuba—that kind of thing. But those friends had all but disappeared now—he was no longer a Bishops boy. Those friendships seemed tied to membership of that club.

Besides, for both the rage and the trip to Thailand, he needed quite a bit of money. He had saved quite a bit since he started at the restaurant. Now, seeing as it was his money, he wondered if it was well spent going boozing on the beach. Besides, Robby was not interested in any of that stuff—so who would he go with?

There was also university to consider. Jimmy had, with all the other drama in his life, missed the application deadline. So, he had to think about other options. If not university… what then? Uncle Joe suggested he might take a year to figure things out, then go to university once he knew what he wanted. And he would need to save up if he wanted to go to Stellenbosch. The place was expensive.

The last tables paid their bills and left satisfied customers. Uncle Joe came over to Jimmy as he was cashing up—and put his hand on Jimmy's shoulder. "Good night, son. I'm proud of how far you have come."

Jimmy nodded. "Thanks for sticking with me, Uncle Joe."

Even with his uncle owning the joint, Jimmy was almost fired a dozen times in the first month. He was surly (still pissed at the world after the game), didn't get on well with the rest of the staff, and inaccurate. He would have quit after day one—but his uncle sat him down and laid down the law.

"Look, I'm not letting you walk away from this. Get your shit together. Being a waiter is some of the best people training you will ever have. You have talent, kid, but you also need to park the attitude, take responsibility for your actions, and bring your A-game. You can quit, sure. But I need help here, and if you can't be it, then you need to do the chores at home without pocket money, because I'm going to have to hire someone else."

So, he stayed. And, after a few weeks, he started to get the order right. As he found the flow of things, customers started warming to him. He started to build relationships. He even found it in himself to say he was sorry once in a while.

Having Robby there was a massive help. It was as if Robby had adopted Jimmy as a personal project. His natural way of being in the world was in stark contrast with Jimmy's anxious inner struggle (I don't care what people think! I do care what people think!). Many nights, as they were mopping up and laughing about the night's stories, Robby inadvertently shared his views on life with Jimmy.

And lucky for Jimmy, he learned how to pay attention.

Like this one: "Jimmy, you're super smart. And sometimes you like to talk down to people. Thing is, people don't care how much you know until they know how much you care. If you're going to be a know-it-all wiseass most of the time, you're not going to make many friends. Show people—show the clients—that you give a shit about them, and they will open up to you."

Or, after he received a horrible talking-to by Mr. De Jager, back before they became best buds.

"Have you ever stopped to think what's going on for him, bud? Sure, he was crabby tonight—but he isn't usually. And sure, the food might have been off and your service shitty, but he didn't need to react so aggressively. Nah, I'm sure if you dug a little, you would find out that he was just lashing out because of something else that's going on for him. Sometimes it is ok to park our ego."

Funny enough, Jimmy mused, he did get to the bottom of it. Mrs. De Jager had recently heard she had cancer, and they were all going through a lot of stress as a family. Once Jimmy showed empathy, Mr. De Jager became a completely different man. And he showed empathy simply by not saying anything. He knew she loved their ice cream dessert, and habitually gave her an extra scoop every time. It was a small thing—but she noticed, as did her husband. And that gesture went a helluva long way.

One evening, at Robby's place, Jimmy was surprised to find that

Sam had also been invited. But Robby calmed him down as he was about to walk out. "Jimmy, just listen to what the man has to say. I promise you it'll be worth it."

Robby's parents were an easygoing bunch, and gave them all a beer. Then Sam and Jimmy went to go stand in the corner of the garden, the others giving them space.

"Jimmy, I wanted to clear things with you. Before we all go our separate ways."

Jimmy had his guard up. But he nodded. "Go on."

"What you need to understand is the pressure. My dad never made it to the Springboks. And he wants me to go all the way. My house... it's hectic." He looked away. "And when you came to town, everyone went nuts. Wanted me to do something about you, you were going to get in my way according to them."

"Who is everyone?" Jimmy asked.

"My family. My friends. Steve, especially."

"So, you decided to take me out by telling the opposition about my shoulder."

Sam looked ashamed. "Steve and I talked about that. But it was one step too far. I told him to drop it. He didn't. Later, I found out that he told the other team. And now we're no longer friends. That shit isn't cool."

Jimmy looked at the large boy as they sipped their beers. He seemed sincere.

Sam continued, "And I don't care if you believe me right now. But I had to tell you. For me. I'm sorry you were hurt. I'm sorry that things are bad between you and Lauren. I have finally let go of her. And I wish you two could patch things up. But that would be up to you."

A few months ago, Jimmy would not be able to let go of his anger. But with Uncle Joe, Robby, and the books he was reading, it felt like he was getting a better handle on himself.

"Thank you, Sam. I suppose I get it. The pressure. Needing to be the alpha. Parents can be... challenging." And as he said it, a whole lot came up for him.

Sam stuck out his large hand. "Truce? I know we will probably never be friends, but at least we can be... friendly?"

Jimmy took it, and they shook. "You never know, hey?"

Robby joined them. "This is very good, chaps. Glad you guys are patching things up. Now let's go grab some chicken kebabs."

As Jimmy got better at the people thing, and he spent more and more time at either the restaurant or at Robby's place. When neither of them were working an evening, they invariably had dinner at Robby's. Jimmy almost failed to notice, at the start, that his uncle spent less and less time at home in the evenings. Jimmy started to read on the nights he wasn't working—starting with the Seven Habits book. And there was a lot of good stuff in there, practical advice around taking responsibility for yourself and having a vision for your life. It really helped him, and the demons in his head started to talk in slightly softer tones...

He could therefore be glad for Uncle Joe when Melissa came into their life.

She rarely came round the restaurant—but they were seen around town, hanging out. It was about two weeks after the game when she came round to their house for a meal, and Uncle Joe introduced her to Jimmy.

She was an attractive lady—no looker for sure, not like Lauren. She was quite petite, with jet-black hair and very fair skin. Her dark eyes, however, spoke of lots of lived experience and hidden pain. Jimmy reckoned she couldn't have been far from Uncle Joe's age—and it turns out she was 35 (because Uncle Joe baked her a cheesecake, and Jimmy helped decorate the candles). She was divorced, worked as a data analyst at the local military base, loved good food (where did she put it, he sometimes wondered), and ran marathons for fun.

They seemed perfectly matched. It was interesting—Jimmy had never really asked too much about Uncle Joe's travels, he seemed to keep it private. But with Melissa, the conversation often reverted to international references. Lucky Jimmy had been to a few places with his folks, so he could kind of relate. But these two had been everywhere!

Melissa had always traveled for fun—it sounded like her husband had had some kind of important job that took him all over the world, and she sometimes joined him. But then, and this was not spoken of but Jimmy could read between the lines, he found someone else and she divorced him. After that, she still traveled for holidays—and she and Uncle Joe spoke of walking the Camino, skiing in Austria, river rafting in Colorado… amazing adventures, some that they had both done, others that they described in great whimsical detail.

And they talked about food. When she visited, they would spend all their time in the kitchen. That was part of the reason Jimmy started to spend so much time at the restaurant, and at Robby's. He could tell he was the third wheel in a beautiful dance between two people that had waited a long time to find each other. The only downside, he missed out on the chow! The stuff Uncle Joe cooked up at the restaurant was great feed, but the dishes they sometimes conjured in their modest kitchen… It was like watching a high-end cooking show.

He did ask, once. And Uncle Joe just shrugged it off. "I worked in great restaurants all over the world, bud. I learned a few tricks."

At that point, Jimmy decided to properly Google Uncle Joe. And he was astounded by the results. Uncle Joe's picture popped up dozens of times, at different restaurants on five continents. It seemed he never stayed at the same place for more than a few years—but where he worked was invariably the best restaurant in town. When it wasn't an exclusive island resort in the Bahamas it was the top private ski lodge in the Three Valleys. Words like "acclaimed" and "Michelin Star" came up a lot. Jimmy had to google what a Michelin Star was—and it occurred to him that his uncle used to be a big deal.

One evening, as they sat by themselves on the porch, one month before his 18th birthday, his uncle opened the whiskey. Jimmy had never refilled it—and his uncle must know that half of it had been consumed in the "Vicky" incident"—but he didn't say a thing.

They sipped in contented silence, then Jimmy asked, "Uncle Joe, why? Why come back here? It doesn't seem like opening Joe's does justice to… well, all the other places were these rock star locations and best in the world restaurants. And this is…well…"

"Oudtshoorn? Ha-ha Jimmy. Quite right, I suppose it might seem strange to you."

He seemed lost in his thoughts for a moment.

"You know, our father I've spoken about a few times. Love him or hate him, he had some interesting lessons to impart. And the one thing he told me, back in my early twenties once I had started traveling so much, was Joe, *a rolling stone doesn't gather any moss*. Now that was good advice, but I didn't listen to it. When you keep on moving, it's hard to settle down. And by settling down, it's not buying a house, getting a cat. Its relationships. In my life, there was my fair share of women—but none of them stuck, because I suppose I was a rolling stone. And when you're a rolling stone, you don't attract any moss."

"Ok…"

"Yeah, so at some point, I realized I wanted to meet someone. Settle down. Have some kids and get a dog. And I could do that anywhere in the world—but there's something about South Africa, Jimmy. Something about our people. Our DNA. People here are real—this is home, and you will just struggle to connect meaningfully with anyone else. South Africa has such a complex history, it is woven into us—the kindness, the anger, the excitement, the anxiety—it's all part of who we are."

"I realized that to not stay alone, I needed to come back. Put down some roots. Create the kind of environment that would attract the right kind of lady. And Cape Town wasn't it—it's still too European, too fast, too cosmopolitan. No, I wanted the country. And Oudtshoorn is a perfect fit. It's a big town with a cool cultural scene, this side of the mountains is desert but a 40 minute ride over the pass and I can go surfing at Herold's Bay. It's a great spot, and I found the restaurant for sale—it used to be a burger joint before, but Ol' Man Higgins didn't care too much for it, and I could buy the premises for a song."

"So, I opened a restaurant, built a community, and had a couple of years of fun. It was always sad that I couldn't patch things up with your old man, but that was more his choice than mine. There were a few ladies in this town that showed interest. But I didn't indulge it—you gotta be patient sometimes. But the day Melissa moved here, I moved like lightning. It's like an avocado—you gotta be patient, but when the time is ripe, you gotta move fast, or miss your opportunity."

Jimmy chewed on this—lots of pearls of wisdom in it, and he was still struggling with the idea that one would leave the jet-set lifestyle, the fame and fortune for a life of relative obscurity. But, he supposed if he looked at his uncle now with Melissa—yeah, he got it. With a pang of regret, his thoughts invariably led back to Lauren. And he knew he couldn't just leave things the way they were.

He mustered up the courage to go see her a few weeks later. He was a bundle of nerves as he walked over to their house. He hoped that she was home—and he hoped that she would answer the door herself.

As it turned out, it was her mother. He had never met her before—but she was as Lauren described her. Tall, and with the same flashing green eyes. They were currently in full force as she glared at him. "What can I do for you?"

"Umm… hello Ms. Kinsman… My name is Jimmy Barnes. I wondered if I could speak to Lauren?"

"I know who you are. And I know how badly you treated Lauren. She's not home. Goodbye."

She was about to close the door on his face, but he stuck his foot in the doorway—jamming her effort. "Ms. Kinsman—with all due respect. I know she's home. And I would just like to talk to her. Could you ask her if she could just… give me a minute?"

Jimmy knew that he was probably barking up the wrong tree with this approach—and it was supported by her reaction, which was even less friendly.

Luckily, there was a voice from behind her. "It's ok mom. I'll speak to him."

Lauren came forward. She was dressed in a loose-fitting jersey and jeans, with her hair pulled back in a ponytail. It was a no-effort look, but she still looked great to him. Tired, but great.

"Let's take a walk, Jimmy. I'll be back in a bit, mom."

They walked in silence for a few minutes. Two blocks down from her house were the dip down to the river. There was a small footpath that he often ran on that snaked along the river… and they walked down there.

"Lauren, I'm sorry." It felt like an inadequate apology. But he thought he would just start simply.

She kept her eyes forward, but replied, "Go on."

"I'm sorry for what I said—I… I didn't know about…"

She spun round to face him. "Didn't know about what?"

He was slightly taken aback. The fire, and anger, was back in her eyes. "I just meant that... well, I heard..."

"About my folks. Yes, well done Jimmy. My mom kicked my dad out. Not only was I humiliated at the inter-schools by you, but my mom... after years of just turning a blind eye... finally decided to call my dad on his bullshit. So yes, you know... along with everyone else. God, it's been the most horrible year."

He wanted to put his arms around her. He reached out, but she recoiled from him. "Don't touch me!"

He lamely dropped his arm. She seemed to soften, and they stopped by a bench next to the river. "I'm sorry Jimmy. I don't... I mean... ah hell. Let's sit down here for a second. I'm so tired... all the time..."

They sat down.

She seemed to collect her thoughts. "My mom has known for years about my dad and the other women. He hid it well, but women know. Too many long trips on the road, too many lame excuses. He is a cheat... and a liar. And I'm so torn. I'm super proud of her for finally standing up for herself. But it's also been massively humiliating, and a part of me was just wondering if she couldn't just stick out another year. Till I leave this town and it doesn't matter. But I feel horrible for even thinking that."

She faced him, and her eyes had started tearing again. She wiped them with the back of her hand. "And there I go again. I liked you— and I know we weren't technically together, but we were kind of dating... and the timing of it was just so horrible. It felt so... intentional to hurt me. I never did anything to her to deserve that. Or to you."

He felt the need to respond, but he sensed she wasn't finished.

"I had no right. But I had hoped... I had hoped that you would be different." She shrugged helplessly. "But you aren't. You're just another horny boy. And I suppose it's on me. So, I'm sorry for the way I acted as well. I... could've handled it better."

The words hung in the air for a few moments.

He had so much he wanted to say to her.

He wanted to tell her about his parents. How he knew how she felt

—that he always suspected his dad was the same. How he felt humiliated when his father disrespected his mother in front of others. The disparaging remarks, the jibes, and the way she just always took it. He wanted to tell her that he knew it was wrong, and he knew he would find things to be different, but he learned the lesson of disrespecting women from his parents. As a popular rugby player with family money, the girls in the southern suburbs never made him believe any different.

He wanted to tell her that he was piecing together a better way now. To treat himself, to treat others, to treat women. That between Uncle Joe and Robby and his family he was learning a different set of values, and a different way to be. And he knew that it was late in the day and maybe he was still an asshole and maybe things would never be good between them again but maybe they could be friends and maybe they could still... still what?

What he ended up saying was, "What are you going to do now? You and your mom? I mean... are they divorcing or..."

She sighed, and her shoulders slumped. "He's moved to Cape Town. Staying in his flat there, doing God knows what. I think we're ok... my mom cries a lot; she never really had any control of the money. That's one reason she took so long to walk away."

"I will never let myself get into a situation like that! I'm going to Stellenbosch, and I will have my own career, and be independent, and no man will ever treat me like that!"

There was an "ever again" that hung at the end of that sentence. He prodded, "So you're ok."

"Yes, Jimmy, we're ok. My grandma has some money—that's a whole different story, I don't even want to get into her and my mom's stuff. But she'll help. Financially. But I'm out of here in two months. Exams finish, and then I'm off."

"Where will you go for the summer?"

For the first time, she smiled.

"I'm going to go soak up the sun, Jimmy. Going to leave all these troubles behind. I'm going to Thailand."

And so, it would begin for Jimmy. The Thailand obsession.

He knew that he probably blew it with Lauren. And he knew that he didn't have the money or the prospects. But he also knew that he had to try.

Problem was, Oudtshoorn was pretty dead this time of year—and he was never going to make enough money in tips to get a ticket over there, let alone pocket money. He could ask his uncle for a loan—but he would feel guilty doing that, so he needed to find a different way.

He had other things to worry about first, though. Like finals exams. Lauren mostly disappeared from view as school ended and everyone went into high study mode. He cut short his shifts at the restaurant to focus on studies. As a result, he was confident he would do pretty well.

He also knew he wanted to go to Thailand. He had R4000 saved up—but he needed ten.

The answer came from an unexpected source.

They were hanging out at Robby's place. The restaurant was closed on Sunday nights, and the family was having its usual crazy *braai* vibe. It was the end of November; exams were almost over—and Jimmy was confident he had done pretty well.

"You reckon you aced it, huh?" asked Robby.

"Aced is a strong word. But I feel pretty good about the exam—physics has always been a strong suit, chemistry not so much," replied Jimmy. "Now it's just wait and see. The English exam is the last one to come up, but I reckon there's not much more we can do to prepare for that one."

"Roger that." Robby prodded the sausage on the grill and was rewarded with a sizzle from the coals. "Almost done." He turned to Jimmy.

"And your application to Stellenbosch University?"

"Not next year, hey. There are student scholarships, and I reckon I could waiter there as well to make up the difference. But I am going to take a year off first, to save some money. Uncle Joe said he would help as well. So yeah…waiting on that too, I hear it's hard to find a decent place to stay."

Robby nodded. "Yeah. I have already been accepted into

Helshoogte residence—but my dad applied at the start of the year, and him being an old boy, they already approved it. So that will be fun."

Jimmy heard the slight inflection in Robby's tone as he said it. He knew his friend well enough by now to realize that going to study was just all part of the plan—and somewhere deep down, Robby was unsure how much of it was what he wanted and how much of it was what his dad wanted.

In Jimmy's case, he didn't feel the timing was right. His parents had always stressed a good education. He knew that by getting a degree he would have a better chance of a good career and a good salary. So, he supposed it really was about the security of money. Robby had applied to be a business major—and he got in, which spoke to his grades. Jimmy had heard that Lauren was also going and planning to study to be a doctor. As for him... he didn't know what he should study. And he knew he needed to figure that out first. He pushed the thought aside.

"What about the holidays, Robby? Final exams are done next week —are you still planning to work the whole summer?"

"Hell yeah. This is the first year my dad will let me run the food truck by myself. Two months on the beach in Buffels Bay; it's a great deal. Pretty ladies, surfing in the mornings—and I can pay half of next year's tuition with that money."

"What about the job in the kitchen at Max's in Franschhoek?"

Robby scowled. "That guy strung me along for months—then he gave the job to someone else last minute. Let me know in that French accent that he dropped me! I know he's your uncle's buddy and all, but... Oh well. He's one of the best chefs in the country, and it would have been a great opportunity. Hey, cowboys don't cry. The food truck is a great gig." He took the sausages off the grill and put on some steaks.

Jimmy remembered when Max Devine came to eat at Uncle Joe's place. Max and Joe were old friends, it seems, from days working together in the South of France. There had been some friendly ribbing, specifically around the type of fare that Uncle Joe was now dishing up—and Max lingered after the other guests had left.

It had been a memorable night. Uncle Joe had allowed Jimmy and Robby to stick around as he and Max caught up with a beer late that night—and the stories they told! They skirted around some of the details, but more than a decade prior, they had been quite a bachelor pair in Nice. They were lyrical about the fresh ingredients available, and the quality of the wines.

Jimmy's dad had always taken a view that the European wines, especially the French, were highly overrated and South Africa produced stuff equally good. He was therefore intrigued when Uncle Joe and Max delved into the merits of a Burgundy Chardonnay, an actual Bordeaux Blend, and some other cultivars they had not even heard of.

At the end of the night, Max had indicated to both of them that they just needed to call him up if they ever felt like a change of scenery. Uncle Joe didn't mind, either. And Robby had taken him up on the offer—calling him not barely a week later. And Max had promised that he would have a summer job for Robby in his kitchen.

"Ah, it's a pity. Hmm… I never did call him. He seemed to like me as his server—do you think it's too late to still get a hold of him?"

Robby shrugged and turned the steaks. "Worth a try. Want the number? Still have it."

"Sure. What have I got to lose?"

"Well… weren't you hellbent to go to Thailand this summer, work in a bar on the beach, and chase Lauren?"

Jimmy smiled. "I could still do that. The tips at Max's as a waiter would be ridiculous—so if I play my cards right, I could be done there by mid-Jan… and then I could go find her. It might not be the two-month backpacking extravaganza I was hoping for, but this could work too."

"Or you could just keep on working, save up for your studies, and chase her when she comes back."

Jimmy frowned. "I could. I should… but I dunno, Robby. No time like the present, right."

"Roger that. In the meantime, steaks are ready. Let's eat."

"Yes, of course, I remember you, Jimmy," said Max Devine.

Jimmy breathed a sigh of relief and pressed on. "Thanks for taking my call, Mr. Devine. I'm finishing up high school at the end of the month, and I was wondering…"

"Your uncle already gave me a buzz last week; told me you might be calling. I do have a couple of vacancies available—and my restaurant is very different from the pizza joint. But I liked your style and am willing to give you a go."

"That's amazing! Uh… so how do I…"

"You need to come down here straight after finals. That means next Monday at the end of November. Remember, training starts immediately. You shadow for about a week, then we get you working as a runner. As soon as you're ready, you get a shot at being a waiter."

"Thank you so much, Mr. Devine. I won't let you down."

"Count on it. See you in a week."

Before Uncle Joe drove Jimmy down to Franschhoek, he had a final dinner with the Robby crew. And then there was only one last thing to do.

It was late, but Lauren was still up—packing.

They stood on her porch. Things were still awkward between them —but there was a slight softening to her shoulders and energy, which encouraged him.

"Just came to say goodbye. I'm off to Franschhoek for a summer job."

"I heard. It will be a great learning experience, I'm sure." She suddenly gave him a dazzling smile. "You know, I'm kinda proud of you. I still hate you. But you're much less of an asshole than when I first met you."

He laughed. "Yeah, still an asshole though. Figuring things out, I suppose. Where are you heading this summer?"

"A few of us are going to stay at my dad's place in Natures Valley for a week or so—then I hop on a plane to Thailand with a couple of girlfriends. One of the girls has a friend who runs a hotel on Koh Tau main beach, and we can get jobs there. So that's the plan—go to the island, get some massages on the beach, have some girl fun."

He made a mental note. "Sounds good. You know, I also, at some point, was going to go to Thailand this holiday. But the friends I was going with…"

"No longer friends? Yeah, I know how that goes. Out of sight out of mind, as they say." She paused. "But who knows? Maybe you make enough cash to still make it over there. I don't plan to come back until the second week of university. The first week is all silly networking stuff anyway."

She took a notebook out of her pocket and scribbled down something. "This is the name of the hotel we're going to. If you do manage to come over—look me up."

"I will, Lauren. I…"

"I still don't forgive you. After the year I've had. You, my parents splitting." She shook her head, then looked up with a touch of sadness.

"But I will try to forget. So maybe we can be friends, right? Will you come to Stellenbosch?"

He hid his disappointment. "Sure. Friends. And yeah, I'm planning to apply… maybe only a year later, though."

"You're taking a gap year? Never understood that, myself. But I can respect it if you need to. Anyway… hope to see you… new year, new beginnings, right?"

She kissed him on the cheek and disappeared back into the house.

On the way to Franschhoek two days later, Uncle Joe was his usual silent but direct self. Jimmy had run into some obstacles in the last couple of days, and he hadn't told Uncle Joe yet…

He decided to bounce his love life with Uncle Joe, who laughed.

"She was right, Jimmy boy. You've come a long way from teenage rivalries, dislocated shoulder bones, and wallowing in your anger. I do think you've grown up a lot this year."

"Yeah, but you're not answering my question. Do I use the money from the job for Thailand, or do I save it all for Stellenbosch?"

"Well, how much do you need? I can help with tuition fees, you know. You are, of course, assuming you're going to make a million bucks up front. You might need to govern your expectations."

"Waiters earn a fortune at these fine dining spots! We used to go there all the time with my folks, and the bill, and tips, were enormous."

"But you're going to shadow first, then be a runner, and only then a waiter. Might take a whole month before you get to step up. Might not get a chance the whole season."

Jimmy was dismayed. "I didn't... I mean he said, but I had assumed that..."

"Never assume bud. Makes an ASS out of U and ME. But enough popcorn wisdom. Max will train you well. You'll earn enough as a runner to pay the bills."

"Bills?"

"Sure. You need to stay somewhere, right? Need to eat? Need to get to work?"

"I guess... I haven't thought about it."

"Where will you be staying? Yeah, I figured. Don't worry, I got you covered. Melissa has a friend who happens to have a garden shed in the back. It's modest but functional, and within walking distance from Max's restaurant. You'll feel right at home."

Jimmy realized he had never asked how much the job paid. Or thought about what his expenses would be. He had worked solely on the assumption of big tips straight to his pocket.

Uncle Joe also circled back to the elephant in the room. "So did Stellenbosch accept your application?"

Jimmy couldn't look him in the eye. "I missed the application deadlines. They said I should reapply a year later."

Uncle Joe said nothing. Jimmy forged on; "It's not such a bad thing. I'll be able to make more cash waitering, and catch up later..."

Uncle Joe nodded. "I could have taken more of a firm hand here— but I don't want you to go study and not be motivated. You must want it. Do you?"

"Sure. I mean, a degree is a road to wealth and success, isn't it?"

"So why did you not make sure you got in?"

"Well, I don't know. I figured... all those entitled rich kids, maybe it's not... I mean... My world is different now. Now that I..."

"Now that you're not one of them?" Uncle Joe looked at him. "You've grown a lot this year, Jimmy, but you still put too much value in money. It's a vehicle to serve your goals. Once it owns you, you're in trouble."

"So what? I'll work hard at the restaurant. I need to get myself to a better spot before I go there, otherwise Lauren won't want to be with me. I wouldn't be able to compete."

"You should give Lauren more credit, son. She's not about the money. She just wants someone to be good to her. And that he knows what he wants."

"I know what I want. I need more money."

Uncle Joe smiled. "Ok then. You'll learn. But in the meantime, let's talk about that money."

They were passing through the picturesque Robertson wine valley, and Uncle Joe said another thing that hit home for Jimmy: "You always need to run the numbers in your head, kid. You did well at accounting. But that was book learning. I opened a few restaurants in my life. They take a while to get going—but in the meantime, you have to pay rent, have staff, buy equipment…"

Jimmy nodded. He understood profit and loss. As if reading his mind, Uncle Joe pressed on; "Profit is income minus expenses. But never forget about cash. For example, what happens when we get to Franschhoek and you want to rent the place from Melissa's friend? She might want a month/two months' worth of rent upfront. And you're not getting paid by the restaurant for at least a couple of weeks. So, you need some upfront cash—that's usually called capital—to get you going."

It was funny. They had talked about it in accounting class, but that had all been theoretical. Suddenly Jimmy felt the reality of it.

"I have some savings to carry me through, Uncle Joe. I think I'll be ok."

"No probs. I'll let you do your thing. If you need a loan, shout. I'm just a phone call away."

Jimmy had been to Franschhoek many times before, mostly on Sunday lunches with the folks. He couldn't remember ever coming in from this side though. After leaving the Breede River Valley and cutting through the town of Villiersdorp and past the Theewaterskloof dam, they went up the Franschhoek pass. It was quite pretty, and as they popped out the top, Uncle Joe pulled over at a viewpoint.

The Franschhoek valley was spread out below them, with the hamlet of the "French Corner" right below.

"Pretty, isn't it? When the early French Huguenots settled back here in the late 1600s, they thought that they had discovered a piece of home. It attracts hundreds of thousands of tourists every year, for wine tasting, fine dining, and festivals. And Max is among the elite of that crew."

Jimmy had a good feeling about this. The mountains hugged the village on both sides, with the vineyards sloping up in the shadows.

He didn't know much about wine as yet. Uncle Joe served a limited range at the restaurant, and he mostly had worked with limited know-how there. He was sure that would change here.

As if reading his mind, Uncle Joe murmured, "Kind of regret keeping it simple at Joe's when it came to beverages. I could have prepared you better for what's coming."

And those were prophetic words.

The room was simple enough. It had an en-suite bathroom with a shower (no bath), and a small kitchenette. But it was at the back of a voluminous garden with a lovely pool. Melissa's friend Sue was a retired chef herself and spent most of her time traveling. The rent was super reasonable, but part of the reason was that she expected Jimmy to feed and walk the dog—a 10-year-old staffie called Booster. Booster and Jimmy warmed to each other immediately—his folks were never big on dogs, but Jimmy had always wanted one. This would work out fine.

It amused Jimmy how much Sue fawned over Uncle Joe. She turned into a bit of a giggly school girl when he introduced himself, and then fell all over herself inviting him to dinner. He graciously accepted, and the three of them enjoyed a lovely meal on her terrace. Jimmy was not sure how she put it all together. She did an amazing little lime-infused raw fish starter, and a fillet steak with a béarnaise sauce cooked to perfection. Uncle Joe obliged with an approving "hmms" and "oohs" as she went about her business, earning them radiant smiles of delight.

The desert was a crème brulee, and again she nailed it. The

conversation, of course, was also around food, where Jimmy was a bit lost most of the night. But it was clear that, in her mind, Uncle Joe was a bit of a food rock star. This was funny because when Jimmy googled her, it appeared that she was one of the most famous female chefs in the country. Heady company indeed.

It was late, and Jimmy offered to help with the dishes but was shooed off. "You go get a good night's sleep, son," she said. "We don't eat like this every night—next time there will be less to do, then you can help out. Rather go rest—Max is a slave driver, and tomorrow's your first day."

"Sue, that was magnificent," said Joe. "As good as I remember it, and I am so flattered that you went to all this trouble."

Her smile made her look 10 years younger. "Max said you chaps came to eat at the old joint when you were just young bucks—and he was kind enough to remind me what you had. And how much you enjoyed it. So, I thought I'd dust off the old apron…"

"Well, I'll be sure to thank him. I am sleeping at his place tonight; I'm heading over there now."

She winked. "I'm sure you guys won't be going to bed soon. Lots to catch up on."

And with that, they went their separate ways. Sue to clean up, Jimmy to his new (and very comfortable) three-quarter bed, and Uncle Joe to catch up with Jimmy's new patron.

F or Lauren, the initial excitement of being on the island wore off very quickly.

Koh Tao was a tropical island and a study in contradictions. It was spectacularly beautiful from a distance, but completely built up with scuba shops and hotels up close. There were lovely little alcoves that you could get lost in, but the main drag of Sairee Beach felt like one constant rave party.

Sally and Jen, her companions, loved it. Away from the conservative bubble of Oudtshoorn, Sally let loose. Jen, Sally's older sister by two years, would be going for her third year in Stellenbosch. This was not her first rodeo on the islands, and she navigated their way to Koh Tao, which was something Lauren was extremely grateful for. Their arrival in Bangkok was a shock to the senses, and it wasn't super straightforward getting the ferry. There were lots of hustlers trying to get their attention, it was crazy.

Lauren, of course, had heard all the stories of Thailand, and Bangkok in particular. She had hung out with Jen many times during her visits home. Part of the reason that this trip could take place at all, was that Jen was smart enough not to tell their conservative parents all the hard details. About the ladyboys, the seediness, the constant harassment—it was a wild place. They stayed only one night, and then they took the first bus down to the ferry and the islands.

Lauren wondered what the other passengers thought of the three of them. On the trip over, they had played the game which animal they most associated with. Lauren felt she was the giraffe—overly tall her whole life. The other girls guffawed at that, and Jen dismissed it out of hand. "You are a tall drink of water, blondie. The boys on the island are going to swarm around you." Jen thought of herself as a leopard, always stalking. Lauren suspected that she was not quite sure what she was stalking though. Girls? Boys? It wasn't clear. She wore her hair in a crew cut and Lauren thought she was pretty but quite masculine. Sally, of course, thought of herself as the fun-loving rabbit. She loved the boys, and they adored her.

So, Jen was the leader, Lauren was the striking one, and Sally was the sexy one. And they had high hopes of making a big splash in Thailand.

Problem was that their room for three was the size of a room for one. They were not quite prepared for how modest the staff quarters at the hotel were. The hotel, if you could call it that, was a one-star dive getting the budget scuba business off the main beach. That meant the charges were light, and the pay for personnel even lighter. Sally and Lauren were hired as housekeeping staff, with a vague promise to move to the bar (where the good tips were made) should something open up.

They dealt in different ways. It was Jen's second season at the hotel, and she had already transitioned to being one of the scuba instructors. She was pretty good at it too. Lauren also wanted to do her course, and as staff, they did get a significant discount as one of the perks. So that, at least, was a benefit. She was therefore ok with the housekeeping work. It was fairly monotonous and structured. She suspected she was getting hit on less doing this than if she was at the bar.

Sally, on the other hand, made the transition in a flash. Literally. They had been there five seconds when she hooked up with the head barman, a charming lout called George. He was a white Rasta from Birmingham, and unlike anything Lauren had ever seen. Sally started working the bar after week one, and the entire hotel would be entertained for the rest of the season with the occasional nuclear level shouting matches between her and George. From being in control, the much older George (Lauren suspected he was in his late twenties) was quickly spun around Sally's little pinky. She was in her element, and all the attention she received from the boys at the bar... Well, that was part of the reason George lost his cool so often.

Lauren didn't mind. While Jen stayed in the water and Sally grabbed most of the attention upfront, Lauren could stay in the shadows. This suited her just fine, for the moment.

After two weeks, Lauren found that she had the flat mostly to herself. Jen would sleep at the flat only intermittently (every few weeks she picked a new tourist as a plaything—said tourist usually stayed in nicer digs and there needed to be no commitment). Sally moved out by week two to stay with George.

So, Lauren found herself with plenty of alone time. Once word got around the hotel (and the island, she supposed) that she was a virgin and she planned to keep it that way, the boys also left her mostly alone. She had to fend off the occasional overture, but it usually came from one of the resident Casanovas off a bet with his mates. She gently but firmly sent them all on their way, and she was grateful for the general energy of the place. Everyone was smoking too much weed to get overly handsy.

So, she had lots of time to think.

About her dad. About her future. And... and she hated that he got into her head all the time... about Jimmy.

She was pretty sure that you didn't need to have this many emotional scars by the age of 18. She knew she could count herself lucky to not have suffered sexual assault (she always suspected there was something there for Sally, but she never confided anything upfront), but still. Her philandering father, her accepting mother...

And the fact that so much of her father she saw in Jimmy. That there was much good in him that could shine through was for sure. Jimmy was, however, also a child in many other aspects. Sleeping with Vicky was just a reflection of not taking responsibility for the consequences of his actions. She couldn't get past that. She knew that she had had no right to be that angry, but she had vested so much hope onto him.

Which was weird. She had lain awake many nights trying to self-analyze. While her friends were on the beach sending light balloons into the sky, making love, and smoking weed, she sat alone on their porch. Reflecting on why she couldn't choose a nice guy.

"Because nice guys are boring," she admitted to herself. Her biggest problem had always been boredom. She had learned at an early age that her peer groups did not share her passion for reading. The girls that she would hang out with for all of her high school career would always be more interested in boys, fashion, and celebrities than issues facing the world.

The nice guys that would shyly approach her once they hit puberty were all too vanilla. Some of them, the nerdier ones, were interesting to talk to. They usually got into their own way because of their lack of social skills, and their lack of confidence saw them self-destruct. None of those friendships lasted or turned into anything more. The attractive boys liked her, but it was always apparent it was for the way she looked and nothing more.

Sam had been interesting initially. They had been each other's first official boyfriend and girlfriend, and the first boy she ever kissed. She did smile at that memory—it was awkward and bad, but he did get better at it. But then Sam started to become arrogant and self-involved when the rugby season started. He was smart, but he received so much attention because of his sporting skills. It went to his head a little. He never cheated on her as far as she knew, but he became less interesting to her. So, she broke it off.

He never stopped chasing her after that, which she must admit she enjoyed. Even when he had other girlfriends all through high school, he would give her a lot of attention. And she supposed it was nice to have that. Especially because of the way she saw her dad treat her mother.

Oh, the therapy she would need, she mused. She always saw people go to the shrink in the American movies, but it wasn't something broadly done in a town called Oudtshoorn. There was something wrong with you if you went to a psychiatrist.

And then there was that summer with Rob More. The ruckus that caused with Sam… again, she smiled. Rob was keen, and they kissed once on the beach in Hermanus that summer. But he was another popular pretty boy, and they ended up hanging out as friends. Sam's family holidayed somewhere else, but he did come through to visit a couple of times. And she could sense there would be trouble with Rob.

Things had come to a head the last week of summer when Sam again came to visit. They were all hanging out on the beach in the late afternoon. A friendly volleyball game quickly turned competitive, and then downright nasty. Sam dunked a ball straight into Rob's pretty face. They went at each other pretty hard after that. It was the ancient ritual of two head bulls clashing horns. As protocol demanded, they were quickly only to be separated by their minions.

It was such a boy thing. They did not beat each other up, which she supposed would have been a more satisfying result for her. Why did she feel that way? On what level did she want boys to fight over her? Or did she like the violence? It was a dark part of herself that she was frightful to explore—she disliked manipulative behavior in others, but she was sure the incident was orchestrated by her, if only subconsciously.

Either way, the fight was more of a fizzle than a fire. There was some rough grabbing, and then the combatants were pulled apart to their corners. Threats were leveled and posturing observed, but then everyone could go home with their pride and egos intact. Boys.

Later, when the teams squared off in the rugby game, she was aware of the underlying tension. She had not heard from Rob in a while—so when he called her it had been a surprise. What he said to her even more so; "Lauren, I hear you have a new guy in your life. And that he'll be my direct opponent on Saturday."

"Rob, you know I don't care about rugby. But I will come to watch this weekend to watch him wipe the floor with you guys," she said playfully.

"Yeah, it must be interesting to be on that side with your two fans in the same team. Works for us, that jealous ex of yours might self-destruct you guys so we don't have to do too much of the work."

"You just focus on your own game, Rob More. And we'll see who's left standing at the end of it."

"Roger that, L. I hear your man has a bad shoulder and an even worse habit for older women—I won't rough him up too much unless you ask me to."

The last comment sat with her all through the game. She could now tell that Jimmy was protecting his left shoulder a bit in the way he went into tackles. And she was worried for him. Rob could only have known that if someone from their team had told them. And that person was most likely Sam… but she didn't want to believe that.

And then the whole business with Vicky. She, Sally and the rest of the girls were watching the game 20 minutes from time and things were tight when the slut came up to them. She didn't ask to sit down—just pushed the plastic bag into Lauren's hands, and told her what it was loud enough for the other girls to hear.

Even now, Lauren felt her anger rise. She tried to put it in the past —but the girl was just so… so… cruel!

Lauren couldn't comprehend the meanness of such a person. That was the night Vicky went off and seduced Jimmy, the same week as Lauren, overcome with guilt about what had happened to Vicky (even though she knew she would do it again, it's just not right to steal from someone who is being good to you) had started to open up to Jimmy.

Men were stupid. Men? Boys? But she supposed he was vulnerable too—and they all thought with their "other" heads anyway. That's what her mom always said. And she hated that the whole thing rein-forced that whole concept.

She had stalked Vicky on Facebook after it all happened—and she had landed on her feet in Cape Town, and was probably dipping her hands into the cash register of the steak restaurant at the V&A Water-front. One day, she would get her comeuppance, Lauren thought. One day.

In the meantime, she eventually earned her scuba license as part of the job. Jen was their instructor, of course, and she found that during the course she got to know George (who had qualified already but came along for the ride a lot of the time) and Jen a whole lot better. Along with Sally, the friendship between them started to deepen, and Lauren found herself coming out of her shell. She loved the deep ocean stillness of scuba—being down there was like a whole different world, and on good days it was the most incredibly serene experience.

It was during this time, about a month after they had arrived, that she met Charles.

He was Canadian—and he joined them for a couple of scuba dives toward the end of December, just before the new year. He was island hopping with some friends—and his buddy Chris was the current apple of Jen's eye.

It all felt very natural. Charles was 24 and he seemed to have a world of wisdom. They were paired up for a dive—and it happened to be a day of 20 meter visibility all around. Chumphon Pinnacle was famous for the possibility of seeing whale sharks, and they did get lucky. Seeing the massive sharks gently make their way was possibly the most amazing experience of her life thus far. Charles squeezed her hand underwater, and she felt deeply happy for the first time in ages.

No words needed to be said between them when they got back on the boat. She felt incredibly connected to him. On the way back, they started talking. And then they went for drinks. And dinner. Charles was charming, interesting, and had amazing travel stories.

That night, after the scuba crew party, he walked her back to her room. He didn't even try to kiss her, even though she wanted him to. The next day was a repeat—scuba, party, walk.

By the third night, she kissed him, and after that they were insepa-rable. She let him sleep over a few times—but it was as if he sensed she was sexually inexperienced, and he didn't push. He seemed content to do all the other things that didn't go below the belt. She was thankful for that.

She could feel herself wanting him more and more every day, though. She did want to know what the other girls were on about. She had brought herself to orgasm before, she wasn't a complete nun—but she wondered what it would be like. To be with him, in that way.

As they slipped into January, and their time on the island sped toward a close, she decided that she would give her virginity to him. The only thing holding her back was that he remained a mystery. Whenever they talked about home or family, he was always vague. She couldn't quite figure out what he did for a living, or when he was going to go back to doing that. Chris had long gone from the island at that point, and Charles seemed content to hang around. He would just read books on the beach until her shift ended, then spend the evenings with her.

She didn't mind. She was in love, maybe, and happy, and things were pretty much perfect.

Then, Jen decided to go home. She was being called back to do some exam rewrites. Even though it was mid-January, she needed to leave.

They had a massive party to say goodbye, and Sally and Lauren went to the bus to see her off to the ferry. It would be a long slog back.

Fate is a fickle thing. At the ferry, Jen suddenly became paranoid that she had forgotten her passport. She didn't have it in her travel wallet. They opended her backpack to find it.

One of the things that popped out of the bottom of her backpack was a wooden statue of Buddha. It was a pretty piece, the size of a soccer ball.

"What's this doing in here?" Jen remarked. "Did one of you…"

Sally nodded. "Ja, Chris asked me to pop it in your backpack as a surprise gift from him. He told me not to say anything. He wanted it to be a surprise when you arrived home."

Jens' face darkened. "Sally, you idiot. Don't you watch the movies?"

They were standing on the sidewalk, passengers milling around them as ferries came and went. Realization dawned on Lauren. At the same time, she became acutely aware of many Thai policemen standing around on the docks.

"Put it back in your bag, Jen. Now!" said Lauren, under her breath.

Jen had been standing with the statue in her hands, fuming at her sister. She snapped out of the daze and put it back in her bag. "I need to get on this ferry or I'll miss my flight."

Lauren was thinking quickly. "Ok, give me that thing. I'll… I'll…"

"Throw it in the ocean!" piped up Sally. "It's probably filled with drugs, right? From Chris?"

"Keep your voice down, Sally!" hissed Jen. "Listen, I am going to call you when I get off on the other side and in signal. Should be in about two hours. Let me know that you guys are ok."

Lauren grabbed the statue and tucked it into her smaller backpack, and pushed Jen onto the ferry. She was carrying an object that potentially could get them all thrown into a Thai prison. She saw a movie once where this happened—and the girls were sentenced to death!

At the same time, she needed to be sure. If Chris was a drug dealer…. Then maybe so was Charles…

It was the longest taxi ride of her life. Sally was a mess, but thankfully, they reached the hotel, and their room without incident.

Once in the room, Lauren set to work on the statue. She went to go find a hammer in the general maintenance cupboard. And yep, a couple of swings did it. It was filled with white powder. She was pretty sure it wasn't sugar.

"It's drugs, it's coke, oh God we are so screwed…"

Sally was deteriorating rapidly. It made it hard for Lauren to think.

"I mean… he said it was just a beautiful gift…"

"Sally, I love you. But if that package was sniffed out in Bangkok, Jen would have been stuck in a prison here for a long time. They take drug trafficking very seriously in this country."

Sally's hysterics were building. "They catch us with this, we'll go to jail. Forever!"

At that moment, there was a knock on the door. Lauren was still trying to gather her thoughts, she thought she might see a way out. There was another knock, quite insistent. She was scared to death it might be Charles or Chris, but then a voice said, "Open up, girls. It's George. Sal, we need to start our shift."

"Sally, stay put. You're a mess. I'll go speak to him—tell him you've got the flu or something."

She went to the door and opened it a crack. George was impatient —and confused why she wasn't letting him in. "L, what's up? Sally ok?"

"She's fine George—we both might be coming down with a bug or something. So, I don't want you to come in, you might catch it…"

They both heard the toilet flush, and a feeling of dread came over Lauren. "George, just one second. I just need to go check."

She closed the door again and reached Sally, who was on her hands and knees in the bathroom, wiping the floor. There were four empty plastic bags strewn around the base of the toilet.

"Sally, oh no. What did you do?"

"I confiscated the drugs, Lauren. We couldn't be caught with them here."

Lauren sat down on the toilet, in a daze. "Sally…"

"What? What did I do wrong now?"

"Sally, what happens when they come looking for their drugs? With a street value of hundreds of thousands of Rands? What happens when we tell them we flushed it down the toilet."

Sally stood for a second. Then her shoulders slumped even further. "Oh, shit oh, shit… but it's Chris. He wouldn't hurt me… us…"

"You don't know that. We don't know them at all. And we don't know who they are working for. They might not do anything to us. But drug dealers are bad people. We need to think."

"I'm so sorry I didn't know, I didn't…"

Lauren shook her head. "It's done. Chris—and maybe Charles as well—don't give a damn about us. And I don't have time to feel sad or feel betrayed, or whatever. I don't know where those two are. But if they had eyes on us at the ferry terminal, they'd know the package didn't fly. And they'll come looking."

"What do we do?"

"We get the hell off this island. It will take Jen 24 hours to get home. I'm not sure how these things work, but they probably have someone at the other side who is going to lift the statue out of her backpack. If it's not there, they will come looking for us."

"Oh, this is bad, it's so bad…"

"Stop whining, Sally. These guys are bastards." And Lauren reflected; it all made sense now. The vague answers from Charles around what they did. The sometimes absences off the island, where they were also going off to do things that were never fully explained. She desperately wanted to believe Charles wasn't in on it. Deep down, however, she knew she had been played. It was probably his plan to eventually use her as a mule as well.

"Sally pack your bags. I'm going to go ask George if we can do a private charter of the hotel boat—it's late already, but he could get us to Koh Samui at least. It's a bigger island with more ferries. So, get ready."

Sally nodded and started to put her things together. Lauren headed back to the door, where George was still waiting, visibly irritated. "L, this is not cool. What is up…"

"George. Shut up and listen. If you care about Sally—and me—at all, we need your help right now."

"Ok… but I thought you were sick."

"No. Much worse. Come in, and I'll tell you."

God bless him, George turned out to be a rock. It took him five seconds to understand their predicament. "Ok, I'll get you out of here later tonight on the boat. But I can't do it right now. There's no one to cover the bar, and it would arouse suspicion if I wasn't there and the boat was missing. I might not only lose my job, but they'll throw me in jail too. No, we gotta do it later, after the bar closes."

Lauren nodded. "Ok, that makes sense. And you could get us to the mainland?"

"Yeah, but maybe better to get you to Koh Samui. We'll see how far the gas takes us; the boats are only made for local scuba trips. It has the range, though."

"Thanks so much, George. You are a champ."

"The two of you can go hole out in my flat. Here's the key. I'll cover for Sal at the bar, and I'll come and find you around midnight. Don't go anywhere or do anything."

They packed quickly, locked the door behind them. George lived in a cottage on the other side of the resort, and they walked across without being seen. Most people were still out on the beach at dusk, as the fires flared up.

His place was pretty messy, thought Lauren. But right now, she was just grateful for a spot to hide out in. She checked the clock, and when they hit about two hours after Jen left, the phone rang.

"Jen? You ok?"

"Yeah kinda. I have my stuff—but I had a look inside my backpack when they handed it out of luggage, and things just aren't quite right. Pretty sure someone was looking around in there. What was in the Buddha thing?"

"It was Coke, Jen. Sally flushed it down the toilet."

"What!?"

"Yeah. It's gone. We're pretty scared over here. We already talked to George—he's going to get us off the island tonight."

There was silence on the other end. "Ok, that sounds good. George. Yeah, he seems legit. I'm already on the bus that goes straight to Bangkok airport, so pretty sure I'm in the clear. I will check my luggage again before I check it in though... This is nuts. Stay safe girls."

The hours dragged by; the waiting seemed endless. Sally fell asleep on George's bed and slept fitfully.

Nothing in Lauren's young life had quite prepared her for all this. She prayed, for the first time in a long time. And then the scariest thought of all found purchase in the back of her mind: Could they trust George?

16

I t had been 24 hours since Jimmy left Cape Town.
It was a direct flight to Bangkok from Johannesburg after a connection from Cape Town. He arranged with a tour company at the airport for the bus and ferry tickets down to Koh Tao. A succession of taxis, buses, and finally the ferry ensued. When he saw the tropical outline of the island, his heart started to beat quicker.

It had been almost two months since he last saw her—but what a ride. Uncle Joe's predictions all came true. Fine dining with Max was like stepping into a different world of details, flavors and presentation. The training has been intense, but he took to this world like a natural. It was not just how the food looked or the wine tasted. It was how the waitering staff presented it. There was poetry just in describing a roasted turnip with a cream glaze that had taken hours to prepare.

He loved it. For the whole of December, once training had finished, he worked as a runner. And they shared in the generous tips the waiters received. He found himself saving up plenty in no time at all.

They needed extra hands on deck for the New Year's Eve party—and when one of the regular waiters left after a heated argument with Max, Jimmy had his chance.

Max was difficult. As affable as he was outside of the kitchen, inside he was a tyrant. But Jimmy managed to work with him just fine —oh he didn't escape the tirades either, but he learned his lessons, and he would never make the same mistake twice.

New Year's Eve was a heaving night—the restaurant had been packed, and the meal menu was pre-arranged and paid for by the guests at a significant premium. It was an elevation of chaos and proper baptism of fire for Jimmy. But when the last guests left at 4 am, and the team sat down to cash out, Jimmy realized he had made enough in tips in one night to probably afford that ticket to Thailand.

But his foot was now in the door. And there were also varsity fees to consider. So, he stayed—and bused tables—and worked hard. He made friends and even received the occasional begrudging nod of respect from Max. In the evenings, when he didn't join the rest for a *braai* or social at the local pub, he would surf the net. And Facebook delivered increasingly disquieting news.

As far as he could tell, Lauren had met someone. Charles had started to pop up into her pictures increasingly—it was mostly Sally posting, but it was clear a gang of sorts had formed on the island.

Jimmy was faced with a conundrum. Chase her to the islands, where she might be desperately unhappy to see him. Or not. He could go fight for her. This chap didn't seem South African and was probably just a summer romance. But what if he wasn't?

It drove Jimmy to distraction as January wore on. By the third week, Max sat him down.

"You started like a house on fire, Jimmy. But since last week you haven't been on your A-game. Do you need a break?"

"Say what? We're still in season, Max."

"Yeah, but that idiot waiter whose place you took came and apologized in style. So, I've decided to bring him back. You're welcome to stay on as long as you like—but I do know, from your uncle, that you also have someplace to be and something to do."

"You know about Lauren?"

"Jimmy, I would have to be deaf and stupid not to know. It's all you've been talking about with the team the last two weeks. You would do us all a huge favor if you jumped on that plane."

"Max. Thank you. I didn't want to drop you… I'm so grateful for this opportunity."

"And you can come back when you want. You're good. But I'm happy to let you go for now."

Jimmy hugged his patron, who shooed him off. "I had my adventures, Jimmy. So, should you. Go get her."

And so, 72 hours later, he set foot on Koh Tao.

It was an overload of people, sounds and senses on the ferry. He pushed through the crowds—and for a moment, thought he saw Sally. But then she was gone in the throng. He made his way to the taxi ranks.

The ride to the hotel was short and pretty, crossing over a small hill before the main beach revealed itself. It didn't look that large, more like a small alcove surrounded by little hotels. But it was spectacular! He had pre-booked a room without telling Lauren. Uncle Joe had helped him, without a credit card Jimmy couldn't make any booking online. He would need to fix that soon.

Problem was, they didn't have his reservation. After a bit of confusing to and fro, he realized the cab driver had taken him to the wrong hotel. There were two, and this was one of the smaller beach areas on the island. He was slightly irritated, but mollified with a free cocktail. A while later another taxi arrived, and this one had him to where he needed to be.

The girl at reception was super helpful. She was a Thai local and spoke perfect English. He had to convince her to tell him which room they were in, but she relented when he told her his story. After he threw down his backpack in his room, he found theirs. There was no answer there though—and he realized it was still only later afternoon, they might be out and about or even out on a scuba boat.

He would just need to be a little bit more patient, even though he was busting to see her. He decided to go for a walk and maybe get a drink on the main beach, and on the way, he passed the hotel bar. The barman (he also looked familiar, from Sally's Facebook) was busy setting up. Joe thought of approaching him, he probably knew where they were.

He was also concerned that Lauren might not be that happy about being surprised by his presence—especially if she had a new guy. Knowing her, it would probably be wise to give her a heads-up that he was here. This is something he should have done via Facebook before he came. But he had a romantic notion of sweeping her off her feet on arrival, which now just seemed like a stupid idea. If he told the white Rasta, he might point him in the right direction—or at the least give them a heads-up that he was here.

The chap was quite busy. Patrons were starting to sit down, and it did seem like he was short of a hand as he hustled to help everybody.

Jimmy finally caught his attention. "Beer please."

"You got it, mate," and it appeared moments later. "Anything else?"

"Yeah. Do you know the South African girls, Lauren and Sally, or maybe Sally's sister Jen? Looking for them—I'm a friend from home."

The dude hesitated, then asked, "I might. Who's asking?"

Jimmy extended his hand, "I'm Jimmy."

White Rasta looked at the hand, then took it. "I'm George. Jimmy, huh? I've heard about you."

Before Jimmy could answer, white Rasta was called away to help another customer—and Jimmy realized they wouldn't have another chance to chat, as things really started to hop.

He put down some money, and got up to leave when George came over and quickly said,

"Dude, we'll chat later. But you might have to wait until tomorrow to see them—Jen and Lauren have gone to another island with their boyfriends tonight, but they should be back tomorrow."

Jimmy's face fell, and the Rasta actually seemed sympathetic.

"Sorry, bro. I know that's not what you wanted to hear. Suggest you go get an early night, shake off the jetlag—and then see how you make out tomorrow."

Now thoroughly depressed, Jimmy went for a walk on the beach. He seriously considered getting well drunk by himself. Then he reminded himself what had happened the last time he did that, and if he had any chance with Lauren, he was better off staying sober.

So, he went for a meal at one of the beautiful restaurants on the beach and took a dip in the warm Indian Ocean waters. The sunset was spectacular, the food cheap, Asian and tasty, and the beer cold. He could imagine how easy it would be to fall in love here.

Dammit.

Disconsolate, he trundled back to the hotel after dinner. The bar was closing up—the action was moving to the clubbier spots or the bars right on the beach, there seemed to be a couple that had a regular stream of fire workers entertaining the crowds.

As he passed, he could see George was deep in conversation with two guys. It was dark so Jimmy couldn't make out their faces, but they looked a lot like the pictures of the guys Lauren had been hanging out with. But that wouldn't make sense—George had said they were off the island with the girls.

Maybe George had lied to him? He decided to go check their room again.

No luck there, though. The door was still closed and there was no answer. He decided to go back to the bar and chat with George. Problem was, it was completely deserted.

Jimmy stood at odds with himself for a moment. Something felt very off here… but at the same time, maybe it was just the jetlag. He was dead tired, and maybe he would feel better about everything in the morning.

Having decided a good night's sleep is the answer, he went to his room.

I t was after 10 pm when George came back to their room. They were both quite anxious. Lauren, thankfully, was distracted by needing to calm down Sally.

"Ok ladies. The boat is ready and fueled up. Get your stuff and let's go. I'm going to run you over to Koh Samui, and then you can get the ferry from there. A mate of mine has a hotel on that side and I'll drop you right off the beach, so it shouldn't be a problem."

Sally calmed down at this, and Lauren was also comforted. "Thank you so much, George. You're a lifesaver. Did you see the guys at all?"

George shook his head. "Nah, they have been AWOL the whole night. I think we're clear. Listen, the boat isn't in front of the hotel though. It was used by clients who went clubbing so it's docked at the main terminal. I just need to go get it, then I'll bring it down and pick you up on the beach here. Think you should stay out of sight. If you walk to the end of the beach, it's pretty deserted. No one will see you there, and just wait for me. All cool?"

Lauren paused. "Couldn't we just come to you to the main terminal?"

George shook his head. "This time of night, they can be finicky about who gets in—they are officially closed. I know the night security guy. He would believe me if I said I'm just bringing it back. But it would be tougher to explain your presence."

It seemed thin to Lauren. She had never known anyone on this island to be particularly conscious of security protocols. But did they have a choice? George was already helping them out. Or was he?

He sensed her hesitation and said, "Listen, L, if you don't want to do this, I'm cool. You can stay here the night and rather take the first ferry out in the morning."

Sally liked this idea. "Yes Lauren, maybe it's better we go in the morning huh?"

Lauren shook her head. "No. Better we go tonight. We need to get outta here. But George, take my phone and send Sally a text when you are on your way. We'll go down to meet you. We don't want to hang on the beach too long."

"Sure," he said and put the phone in his board shorts. "Be ready. It should take about half an hour."

He left, and Lauren and Sally sat in silence for a moment. They were jarred out of their reverie by Sally's phone ringing.

"Don't answer it, Sal! It might be one of the guys!"

Sally looked down at the phone. "Nah, it's Julie from reception. She might just be checking in. It would be better to talk to her?"

"Let me do it," said Lauren, and grabbed the phone.

"Hi, it's Lauren," she answered.

"Lauren, it's Julie. Sally wasn't at work tonight—and I was just checking in on behalf of the manager whether she is ok."

"She's fine Julie—suddenly came down with a tummy bug. Should be ok tomorrow. Thanks for checking in."

"Ok cool. That's probably why she didn't answer the door. I had those good-looking boyfriends of yours come round also asking after her."

"Thanks. Yes, we're laying low for the night. Really appreciate your call. See you tomorrow?" and she felt like a heel for the lie. They would be long gone by morning.

"Sure. Lauren, there was also someone here looking for you."

A chill went down Lauren's spine. "Really? Who?"

"He asked me not to say anything. That I shouldn't spoil the surprise. Sorry I said anything."

"Julie, you're freaking me out."

"Sorry! All I will say is he was eager to find you. Hopefully a nice surprise in the morning. Bye!"

And with that, the line went dead.

"Shit." Lauren stared at the phone. She looked at her watch. Fifteen minutes had passed since George had left. Another five minutes, and they should head down to the far side of the beach.

She was only 18, for Pete's sake. She didn't have the experience to deal with this. Going with George seemed like a bad idea, staying here seemed like a worse idea. They could probably haul ass to one of the other hotels in the area. But it was a small island and then they would still need to go get the ferry in the morning. And someone was already looking for them? Same people who had been into Jen's backpack?

"Let's go, Sal."

The hotel was dead quiet, it was after 11 pm. They saw no one as they walked down to the beach—but to the left, there was still lots of activity. There were a few stragglers, mostly couples making out and drunk guys walking back. They made their way down to the far side of the beach, numb with fear. But they went unnoticed.

At the end of the beach, there was a small pier at the far side with a few boats on it. There was still no sign of a boat coming in. It was a full moon so there was plenty of ambient light. She felt they were quite exposed. They were the only ones around with backpacks on.

Where was George? Thirty minutes dragged on to forty minutes. She was getting more and more anxious.

"Good evening ladies," said a familiar voice behind them.

Cold terror gripped Lauren. Sally was frozen with fear, as the two men came round to face them. Charles and Chris looked like always: t-shirts, board shorts, barefoot. Charles bore the same easy smile that she had fallen in love (lust?) with. But there was something about them. An underlying tightness to their shoulders? Their eyes, glittering like wolves in the moonlight.

She was very, very afraid.

"Cat got your tongue?" Charles continued. "Been looking for you all night. Heard from George Sal came down with a tummy bug and you were tending her. Couldn't quite believe it… swore you went to the ferry just this afternoon to see off Jen."

"Charles, listen…"

Like lightning, he slapped her. The shock was as intense as the pain. She had never been slapped before in her life, and indignation mingled with terror.

"I'm speaking, love." He said conversationally. "You have something of ours. Only it wasn't in your room. We checked. All that was there… was the shell…"

He leaned in closer. "Please tell me, Lauren, that we are guessing wrong. Please tell me that you didn't flush a hundred thou of poor snow down the toilet."

She met his eyes. They were crazy eyes. She was amazed at how different he looked. Not at all like the boy she had been spending all this time with. This was a man. A scary, evil man.

"It's all gone, Charles. Every last gram. And damn you for doing that to us. Jen could have gone to jail. You are a monster."

He smiled. "You watch too many movies, Luv. But it's all water under the bridge. The only problem, now, is that I need to recoup that money, or things will go badly for you. And me." He stepped in even closer. "Any ideas on how to do that?"

Chris had his hand on Sally's shoulder, but she suddenly broke free, and bolted for the nearest pathway to the hotel. She was quite fast and started to shout for help. But Chris caught up and brought her down. Her cries were muffled, and Lauren heard a dull 'thunk'. Then she was silent.

"That was very stupid of Sal. Hope you'll learn a lesson from that. Now, when we take you girls back to our place, people will just think she's a drunk girlfriend Chris is taking home. I can do the same with you… or you can come quietly."

Lauren felt trapped and anxious for Sally. George was clearly in on it, and there would be no rescue by boat. She could probably get away from Charles—but Sally was unconscious, and she couldn't leave her with these creeps. She didn't have a choice.

But what would they do with them once they had them at their place? He wanted to get his money back. How could they help?

Even in her heightened state of anxiety, the options presented themselves. They might want to sell them into captivity. Those stories went round regularly. Sex slaves to some Arab sheik? Or would they hold them for ransom and want their parents to pay? Or something even worse?

He put his hand on her arm. She slapped it away. "Don't touch me! Ever again. I'll come along… but just don't touch me."

He studied her for a moment. Then he grabbed her by both shoulders and threw her to the sand. "On second thought, we have time."

He got on top of her, pinning her down. He had his hand on her mouth and prevented her from screaming. She could feel him becoming erect, and his breath (oh God it was still minty—but now it just filled her with loathing and fear) on her face.

"I've been waiting a while for this. Let's have some fun first. Then we will talk about the next steps."

"Charles! Don't! Sal said she's a virgin. She will fetch more that way," Chris said. "Let's go, man. Let's take them to the man and be done with it. Time's up on the island anyway."

Charles seemed like an animal. His pupils were dilated, his breathing shallow. Her fear was making him even more aroused… and for a moment she thought he would ignore his friend.

Then he pulled himself back. She could feel the tension easing from him. The erection was still very present, and he was still on top of her.

"Lucky Chrissie boy makes sense. I want you bad, L. But I want to not have my balls cut off even more. Someone else is going to have the pleasure of your vagina. Over and over again…"

He slowly got up off her. "Play along, and this might all end up ok for you. You might even enjoy it."

She knew she had to do something. She would come back for Sally. But she needed to make a run for it—otherwise, they would both wake up in a very bad place.

He extended his hand, and she took it. As he hauled her up, she used the momentum to throw herself forward, slamming into him. He lost his footing and fell backward into the sand. She turned and sprinted away from him, toward the lights.

She would have made it, too. But it was dark, and she tripped over a piece of driftwood. She scrambled up, but she felt him tackle her from behind. Then she knew she was done for. She swung around, clawing at his face, but he slapped her again. "Bitch! This time I'll..."

And then something slammed into him, lifting him off her.

She sat up, in a daze. Her eyes were slightly teared up from the slap, so she could only make out the other person now on top of Charles, pummeling him.

Her vision cleared. The lithe young man stood up from Charles's now inert body. She only had time to register surprise for a second. "Jimmy?"

"Hi, Lauren. Are you ok?"

"Jimmy, oh shit. I'm so glad to see you... I... Jimmy! Behind you!"

He swung around just in time, as Chris came charging up, a knife in his hand. Jimmy stepped aside a second too late, and she saw the knife slice his arm, a shallow cut opening up.

Jimmy stepped back, staying between Chris and Lauren.

"This has nothing to do with you man," said Chris, waving the knife. "Walk away."

Jimmy sized him up. He was athletic—and quick. Jimmy felt blood on his arm, but it wasn't a deep cut, and his movement felt fine. But the other guy had a knife, and that put him at a disadvantage. Also, he didn't know how long it would be 1-on-1... the other one was starting to moan and stir.

What he also noticed was the inert body of what he assumed was Sally. She was lying on the sand behind the dude with the knife. Lauren behind him, Sally at risk over there. This was bad.

He made a decision.

"Lauren, go for help. I'll fend this guy off."

"No. I'm not leaving you," she said.

He kept his eyes on Chris. "Please go. Bring help. I'll keep these guys at bay."

They didn't get that far. Suddenly, Sally jumped up from the beach —she must have faked being unconscious. She came up behind Chris, and pummeled him with her fists from behind, shrieking in fury just like a woman scorned.

Chris turned on her, slashing his knife. She stepped back out of range, and the momentary distraction was welcome.

Jimmy had picked up the piece of driftwood from the beach, and as Chris turned around, he wacked him through the face with it. The drug dealer went down like a ton of bricks, and stayed there.

Sally immediately started to cry. "Lauren... Jimmy? What..."

Lauren looked at her best friend, and the boy that had just flown halfway across the world to rescue her. Then she flew into his arms, and buried her head in his shoulder, and started sobbing uncontrollably.

Jimmy held her, stroking her hair. She couldn't even make out what he was saying. She just knew that the sound of his voice and the feel of his strong arms around her. That was all she needed.

"Jimmy, it's so horrible. What are we going to do?"

"First things first." He let her go, walked over to the mumbling Charles. He hit him over the head with the piece of wood for a second time. This time he stayed still.

"Now, I think we should call the police. And then we need to have a drink."

———

Getting the baddies locked up took longer than they had expected. Lauren had some first aid training and tied up Jimmy's arm with a scarf. It was a shallow cut.

Of more concern were the two men -they had no rope to tie them up with, and they had heavy knocks so they didn't know when they would be awake. Sally went down to the nearest hotel reception to call the police—but it still felt like ages before they arrived. Jimmy let go of Lauren, gathered the knife and the piece of driftwood, and kept vigil over their assailants.

Help came from an unexpected quadrant when George showed up. He also looked roughed up. Lauren felt ashamed when he explained that he had been ambushed by the two at the ferry. He had not told them, but they had guessed what he was going to do. They had locked him in the boat's hold, and it took him a while to break loose. George ran back to the hotel to find some rope, and they managed to secure the two men.

With George there, things were resolved more quickly. By the time the police arrived Chris and Charles had woken up, apparently just with a slight concussion each. The police took the plastic bags from their room as evidence as well as the remains of the Buddha. They took them away in cuffs, and assured Lauren that they would have no more trouble.

Later, they sat at the bar, throwing back a couple of tequilas to calm the nerves (George opened up for them, even though it was 3 am). Lauren contemplated the crew.

Sally, beautiful soft sexy now withdrawn Sally. She seemed to have added some lines to her face in the last 24 hours. George had his arm around her, and the two of them, even in this moment of anxiety and uncertainty, seemed closer than ever.

Jimmy, sitting next to her. Once things had calmed down, she had withdrawn from his embrace. Now he kept his distance, respectfully.

"Jimmy, that was some timing. How did you even know where to find us?"

"I'm just sorry I didn't get here sooner, Lauren. It was the weirdest thing—I went back to my room, but I couldn't sleep. Eventually, I decided to come back down to the beach. Probably jetlag. So, I just sat on the beach in front of the hotel, enjoying the silence." He scratched his head.

"Then the two guys came running past me. I heard a snatch of conversation. Something like "Bitches gonna pay". I am ashamed to say I just ignored them at first. Figured there must be all kinds of nonsense going on here. But then I thought I had recognized the one —and the accent sounded American? Canadian?" He shrugged and frowned.

"It was only a minute or so I suppose. Then I decided to go after them in the same direction, just to see what they were up to. Even if it wasn't you, it might be some other girls, and I couldn't just turn away if there was trouble. And that's when I came onto your whole scene."

Lauren reached over, taking his hand. "Well, I am so glad you did. You are officially our hero."

George and Sally walked over to them. Sally took Lauren aside, and they came back moments later. Sally and George walked off, leaving Lauren and Jimmy alone at the bar.

"What now?" Jimmy asked.

She played with her cocktail, not looking at him. "I'm homeless. Our old room is a police crime scene, and Sally is staying with George tonight."

"You can crash in my room, Lauren. I'll sleep on the couch."

She looked up at him. He held her gaze for a long moment.

Then she put her hand to his face, and pulled him closer. "Offer accepted. And no one is sleeping on the couch."

They went back to his room. Jimmy had come here with so much to say, but now, none of it seemed necessary. It was like they had both grown up overnight.

They stood for a second after she put down her bag. Then she looked at him with those clear green eyes of hers… and she took his hand, leading him to the bed.

Later—after—she started to sob in his arms. She had been nervous but eager, and he tried to keep control. But he felt too great a need. He had felt himself push through her resistance, and came almost right away. He knew he loved her, and he knew that he had wanted to make her first time special. But his body had different ideas. And now, as she was turned into him, he kissed her salty tears.

"Are you ok?" he asked, and immediately knew how stupid he sounded.

"I will be," she replied. "Jimmy… that was my first time…"

"I know."

"I liked it… I really wanted you. I mean, I'm glad we did it. But…"

"You didn't have an orgasm?"

"No. I don't think so. I liked it… but I…"

"I'm sorry." He kissed her lips, feeling awful. "Believe it or not, Lauren, I'm not that experienced either. I think there's a lot to this that one must figure out…"

As if the dawn broke, she smiled at him. Her tears dry, a twinkle came back into her eyes.

"Well, Mr. Barnes. Practice makes perfect." She turned him on his back, mounting him. Her face framed by her locks, cascading down to her perfect breasts—and he felt himself immediately erect again. "Let's see if you can do better on the second round."

And he did.

18

They were inseparable for the next couple of weeks. Sally stayed on the island with George. Lauren and Jimmy decided to go hop from island to island and spend some time exploring the mainland. They headed across to Krabi and Koh Phi Phi, back to the mainland, and bused from Bangkok to Chiang Mai.

They talked. They listened. They ate pad thai, they swam in the turquoise waters, they hiked the jungles. They shared their fears, their dreams, their hopes. They fell deeply and irrevocably in love. And they made love—sometimes gently, sometimes with great urgency, and they discovered pleasure as neither ever knew it before.

And then it was over.

They flew home on separate airlines as per the tickets they had booked—but they landed a few hours apart. Uncle Joe was there to take them back to Oudtshoorn.

The University term had already started, and Lauren rushed back to Stellenbosch to fall in with the latter half of freshers' week. For Jimmy, it was harder. He went back to Max's and fell into his old routines, and didn't see much of her for the next two weeks.

She was so excited about going to Stellenbosch. He felt intimidated. He would make some money as a waiter, reapply for the following year... it should be fine, right?

He was fooling himself.

Lauren found the environment at the hostel quite daunting. Stellenbosch girls' hostels each had their own identity, and Erica was one of the "cool" ones. She immediately realized that she had been the smartest girl in class in high school. But here she was just another of 100 smart girls. Some of them as tall or taller than she is, many she thought were much prettier, and quite a few that made her feel plain dumb.

There were also girls she didn't much care for. They usually came from wealthy parents, held incredibly elitist world views, and were not tolerant of dissent. They were, luckily, in a minority. There was a mix of English and Afrikaans girls. There was also a small but vocal minority of colored and black girls that had neither language as a first language. It made for a heady mix of opinions and cultures.

She threw herself headfirst into her courses, joined the netball program, and became involved with the debate team and (at Jimmy's suggestion) the wine tasting society. It was a lot—and she and Jimmy had to squeeze out time to see each other. Jimmy was busy most weekends, so he would visit in the week. He couldn't sleep in the dorm with her, but he crashed with Robby, who had a room at the mens res Helshoogte. Robby, of course, was already running the tuck shop at the residence for extra cash, and doing some side hustles for sandwich deliveries.

Some weekends she would go to him. They would hike the mountains, go wine tasting, or he would cook her incredible meals in his small kitchen. Franschhoek, after all, was only 20 kilometers away from Stellenbosch. But she mostly had him only in the mornings. Weekends were his busiest time, and he would often be hectic from 11 am onwards.

She was still very much in love with Jimmy. But she had to admit it was hard. She was missing out on a lot of social stuff because she spent the weekends with him. She wished he could take more time off. But he was insistent that he needed to save, and she supported the cause. They were already thinking of what he would study when he came the next year, and it was exciting planning that with him.

Now, sitting in the library, preparing for the first-term exam on Biology, a secret smile came across her lips. She was reading up on the anatomy of a female—and her thoughts involuntarily went to thoughts of Jimmy, and the things he could do to her with his mouth… She felt herself immediately distracted. She was saved by her phone.

The text came from the wine society. She had all but forgotten about the wine tour that afternoon. They were going to go visit the Jamieson estate. It was her dorm mate Lee texting to ask where she was.

She shoved her books into her backpack and rushed out toward the center parking lot.

Her regular crew were waiting for her. They were about 10 in the minibus, and it was a mixed bag. Once she had walked Lee down off her thunderous indignation at being made to wait, they settled into their familiar bantering rhythm on their way to Jamieson, a mere 20 minutes' drive. Lee was briefly angry because they had a personal invitation from the farm owner, and being late was bad form.

Lee, of course, was the card. She was the first person Lauren clicked with when they arrived. Because Lauren arrived late to campus, Lee had taken it upon herself (after a thorough interrogation as to Lauren's suitability as new best friend material) to introduce her to all the possible boys that Lee felt were viable prospects.

She was mortified when Lauren declared herself in love and unavailable. She did not let that deter her, and she started a campaign to find a more suitable mate than Jimmy, who she dismissed out of hand. She was from Johannesburg and had a "serious" boyfriend who worked for a big investment firm. She did, however, make it quite clear that she was open to a "casual encounter" or two.

This casual attitude toward commitment initially pressed all the wrong buttons with Lauren. But Lee was irrepressible, and quite consistent. She was fiercely loyal to the Johannesburg boyfriend, and it seems like they had an understanding. Both were happy to have a bit of fun on the side. They had an agreement that if anything happened that was an actual threat to their relationship, they would be honest with each other about ending it.

Lee was also a very deliberate classist. She was very clear that she needed to marry the same-of or up. The boyfriend, therefore, had, like her, attended a swanky private school in Johannesburg, and the families were aligned in the suitability of their eventual union. It all felt very Middle Ages to Lauren. It would not be her last encounter with the social politics of the privileged. This also meant that Jimmy, in her mind, was simply not good enough. She called him "the waiter."

Their motley crew (a nerd, two overweight girls from Cape Town, the class clown, the mandatory in-the-closet gay dude, and of course Lauren and Lee) made their way up the winding road to Jamieson. Lee was the center of attention along with Solly, the clown. Lauren noticed that Lee was dressed in a flimsy low-cut blouse. It showed off her splendid breasts. This was a clear indicator that the game was afoot. It was way too chilly at this time of an autumn day for that dress code. It was clear to Lauren that there was more on offer than just the award-winning wine at Jamieson.

They arrived at the estate. The sweeping driveway led into resplendent lawns looking out over a tranquil lake, flanked by weeping willows. The wine tasting room had a terrace built up over the lake. Here they were greeted by possibly the most beautiful man Lauren had ever seen.

"His name is Jacques Jardine," Lee whispered, as they approached him, waiting in the cellar door. "Heir to the estate and he will soon be mine." And she giggled.

Throughout the next couple of hours, Lauren would learn from her companions all the relevant facts. His dark good looks and lustrous black curls stemmed from his mother's Italian heritage, while his athletic build could be attributed to his father. Jacques had a faint British accent, and she would learn he had grown up in the south of England. They had moved to South Africa and bought this farm when he was a teenager.

Lauren felt tremendously drawn to him. But she immediately felt guilty, as if that was a betrayal of Jimmy. She could not help

PG GELDENHUYS

comparing them. Jimmy was fast becoming an expert on wine and food. Jacques, however, had... breeding. As her mom would say. She was mortified to even think about it. He acted and spoke like an aristocrat.

And he was completely oblivious to her. Oh, he treated them all with equal attention and warm respect. The time flew by as they tasted everything from the acidic whites to the deep throaty reds. She was usually quite good about not going overboard at tastings, but today she suddenly felt quite tipsy. This emboldened her a little, and she found herself asking, "So Jacques, are you going to take over the estate soon?"

He focused those impossibly dark brown eyes on her, and she felt herself blushing. Idiot! That was probably a question he got all the time! But he smiled and replied, "That is the plan. But my father had no intention to retire anytime soon. He loves everything about making wine—it has been a lifelong dream for him. I have my own dreams, and I would like to pursue them first, I suppose."

"And what are those dreams?" Shut up, Lauren! What are you doing?

"Travel. Work in different countries. Do something extraordinary. Create, play, discover. Make love under the moonlight." At this last comment, he held her eyes for a second. Then he turned his gaze to the rest and concluded, "And if the road brings me back here, then so be it."

Their visit concluded with a heartfelt thank you from Lee to their host. He returned the compliment, and thanked them for choosing Jamieson for a visit from their club.

"And friends, please come and support us at the wine festival on the weekend. We will have a stand at the town hall, and Friday afternoon is the best time to come. Saturday quickly turns into a rowdy party! Most students see it as a drunken opportunity for hooking up. Please come visit earlier, when true wine lovers are welcome!" And again, he looked directly at Lauren as he said it.

Later, as they drove back, Lee gave her no end of stick. Her friend's friendly banter had a slight edge to it.

"That was offside, L. Jacques Jardine might be the future father of

142

my children, but now, like star crossed lovers foiled by a deceptive Delilah, you have come between our nascent romance."

"Lee. I have a boyfriend. And Jacques mostly ignored me."

Lee turned to the rest of the slightly inebriated crowd and asked for group input. "Am I wrong, ladies and gentlemen, in my assessment? That he was very much taken by our resident head girl? That last comment? The heat was turned up so high I felt like I needed a shower. And he practically begged you to come to see him at the festival."

There was general assent that Lauren had made a strong impression on Jacques Jardine. The conversation proceeded to what might happen next. After all, the heir to the Jamieson estate was a final-year student and was rumored to be off to Oxford the following year. He was to further his studies on a Rhodes Scholarship.

This gave Lauren even more pause. The Rhodes Scholarship was something she had heard of before. The competition was said to be ridiculous.

She told herself that she was not interested in Jacques Jardine at all. But she would like to know more about the Rhodes Scholarship, so if she were to run into him on campus, she would ask him. Yes, that's it. No harm in just asking for some information.

But then, the gang decided to take up his invitation to the festival on Friday. There was consensus that she had to be there. She first said no; she had told Jimmy she would come through to have dinner with him on Friday. But she had her arm twisted—and mostly, she had to admit to herself, because she wanted to see Jacques again. Lee was very persuasive. Yes, Jimmy was Lauren's main course, but maybe she could have a look at the appetizers... She made Lauren laugh; she was completely irreverent!

And yet, when she came home, she saw a text from Jimmy. Wishing her goodnight, telling her how much he loved her. And where it usually gave her a warm feeling of love and belonging, now she felt... anxiety...

She didn't sleep at all that night.

The next day, in class, she also felt distracted. A short chat with Jimmy in the morning didn't make her feel any better. He was his usual cheerful self, and looking forward to her visit on the weekend. He was disappointed she was only coming through on Saturday morning, but he also understood that she wanted to go with her friends to the festival. His total trust and lack of jealousy made her feel even worse.

As Friday rolled around, and they finished class, she went home. She was normally careful about her appearance. That evening, she took extra care with her outfit. Tight jeans to accentuate her legs, a blue t-shirt that she knew showed off her curves, and she let her hair fall to her shoulders. A quick application of some light lipstick and she was ready. Ready for what?

She pushed the uneasy thought to the back of her mind, checked her phone (thankful there was no text from Jimmy), and went off to meet the others.

The Stellenbosch town hall was half full when they arrived there at 5 pm. The festival would continue till 9 pm. After collecting their wine glasses, they decided to make the rounds.

"We'll get to your admirer L," said Lee. "But we mustn't look too eager. Let's go hang out at his neighboring stand, the folks of Morgenster. They have great olive oil."

Lauren rolled her eyes. She had to admit that her heart quickened when she caught a glimpse of Jacques where he was entertaining a steady stream of rapt wine lovers. And she was not pleased when she saw his helper at the stand: a ridiculously attractive redhead.

So, they visited Morgenster, to his right. Lourensford, to his left. They crisscrossed in front of his range of vision a couple of times, and she felt irritated that he didn't seem to notice them. She knew it was irrational—he was super busy, with a steady stream of adoring fans. She snuck frequent glances their way, and noticed how the redhead would frequently touch his arm, or hand. Despite herself, she felt sharp pangs of jealousy, and as a result of this distracted irritation, stopped paying attention to how much she was tasting.

Around 7 pm it became crowded, and Lee decided on an intervention. She grabbed Lauren by the hand, and they worked their way to the front of the crowd that was now jostling for some of the good stuff from Jamieson. Lauren found herself grateful for Lauren's strong steadying hand. She felt quite tipsy!

"Ah!" said Jacques when he saw them, his eyes lighting up with genuine pleasure. "The lovely Lauren and Lee. Ladies, give me a moment while I finish up with this gentleman, then I will give you my full attention."

He duly re-engaged in a friendly debate with the old chap that was swirling the Cabernet—something to do with the merits of south-facing slopes for the ripening of the grapes. The redhead poured them some Sauvignon Blanc in the meantime, and Lauren could swear she had an amused look in her eyes. She leaned over, and in a low voice said, "You're the folks from the wine tasting club. The rest of your gang has already been here. He's been waiting for you to show up. I'll take care of this guy, so you can grab him."

And she skillfully grabbed the bottle of Cabernet from Jacques, inserting herself between him and the old gent. The customer, initially taken aback by having his conversation broken, was immediately molli-fied by a flirty smile from the female replacement, and re-engaged.

Jacques winked at Lauren. "So, ladies. You're familiar with the Sauvignon Blanc Ellie just poured you. But I opened up a special little something in anticipation of your arrival. Try this. It's the family reserve Shiraz, and this particular vintage is spectacular."

It was. He continued chatting with them about the wine, giving attention to both of them. Lauren was sure his eyes lingered with her longer than with Lee. Then he said something which put her off balance;

"To me, wine is like making love. Better to gently, slowly, lovingly caress the wine. Give it a chance to breathe—let your rhythm sync, let your body chemistry react to it… now that's magic."

His eyes were playful, challenging. He wanted her to react indig-nantly—probably thought she was some prude Afrikaans girl and a virgin. It wouldn't be disloyal to Jimmy if she did a bit of harmless flirting, right? She rose to the bait.

"It's easy to talk, Jacques. But talk is cheap. Most boys gulp it down —they don't have the patience to coax out the flavors, to get the wine to grab them. They rush through it, trying to get to the pleasure of inebriation…"

And she felt herself touching his arm. Lee had disappeared, but she didn't care. He leaned in a bit more, holding her eyes, and whispered, "But you are talking about boys, Lauren. Men take their time. They are patient. They know the pleasure is worth the wait."

A hot flush started to creep up her cheeks. God, she was drunk. She loved Jimmy, but this boy… this man… he was just so sexy! She still had her hand on his arm, and he felt hot under her touch. Their faces were drifting closer together…

"Lauren?"

It was as if she had been dunked in an ice-cold bath. She snapped back her hand and turned to Jimmy.

She stood there, cheeks flushed, her hand snapping away from Jacques's arm as if stung. Jacques straightened up behind her.

He studied them for a moment. His eyes locked on Lauren, and she couldn't bear what she saw in them. Then he focused on Jacques and said, "You."

"Small world, isn't it?" said Jacques Jardine. And Lauren suddenly realized there was another layer here… something that she didn't understand.

"Let's go, Lauren." And Jimmy took her by the hand, leading her out of the town hall, quite forcefully.

It was close to 9 pm now. There were a lot of inebriated students around, and she found herself suddenly dead sober, and aware of all the leery looks and even lewder comments. Dammit dammit dammit! He steered her out of there, not looking at her.

They finally burst through the front door and walked away from the entrance up Plein Street. He still wasn't saying anything… so she tugged at him to stop. Finally, he faced her.

The look on his face was more than she could bear. It would have been ok if there was sadness… or anger… but his eyes were just cold. Ice-cold.

"Jimmy…"

"Lauren, I'm sorry. I thought I would surprise you by coming through tonight. But it was a mistake."

"No, it wasn't! I was just hanging out with my friends… I'm glad you came…." But she knew she didn't deliver the lie. "Please don't go," she changed tack. "I'm done with this party. Let's go grab a coffee."

He put his hands in his pockets. "I'll walk you back to your dorm, Lauren. But then I think it's better if we catch up over breakfast."

It was a long, silent walk. He was patient with her, she needed him to steady her along the way. She was a jumble of emotions, but she was too drunk to think what to say. He saw her to her front door. There was no kiss goodnight.

She went back to her room, but even a hot shower couldn't stop her head from spinning. Finally, she felt nauseated, and she only just made it to the toilet to throw up.

That made her feel better. But only physically.

She drifted off to sleep, her dominant thought: "I really screwed up tonight…"

19

The next morning, he came to pick her up, and they headed off to their favorite local coffee shop. They sat down, ordered their cappuccinos, and uncomfortable silence settled around them like a musty old blanket.

She broke the deadlock.

"Jimmy... I wanted to explain..."

He nodded; his eyes still cold. She hated that!

"Last night... I was a bit tipsy... and you might have misunderstood what..."

"What you were doing? Flirting with that guy? What did I misunderstand?"

She felt herself going to old offense by way of defense positions. She tried to curb herself. "No, I mean I was flirting with him... I was a bit drunk..."

"So, you were drunk and flirting. Classy."

She felt the anger rise. "Look, I'm trying here. It's not as if you have a spotless history here."

"What? Getting drunk or flirting?"

She ignored the obvious danger of this direction, her instincts screaming back down. Unfortunately, her temper again got the better of her.

"Both! Both, you prick! At least I didn't sleep with the dude."

"But you were thinking about it. And let me tell you, you have poor taste as well."

And the accusation hung between them. He saw her truth, and she looked away. "It was just… harmless fun…"

He took her hand, and she was glad for it. "No, it wasn't, Lauren."

She couldn't look him in the eye. He knew her—at this point, he knew her soul.

"What do you want me to say, Jimmy? So, he paid me some attention, I was flattered. But it stopped there."

"Only because I arrived here, and you weren't expecting me."

"Look, either you trust me, or you don't." He started to pull his hand away, but she gripped even firmer. "I won't cheat on you. I love you."

He sighed. "I know. I love you too. But things are starting to change between us, Lauren. This world of yours… I'm not a part of it…"

"That's all your own bullshit, Jimmy. You will be, you said so yourself."

"Well, yeah, but a lot can happen in a year."

She leaned back, letting go of his hand. "So, what now? I get a bit tipsy, flirt with some guy, and you are questioning our relationship?"

"Well, yeah. You're my girl. You should act like it. Especially with someone like that. Family money, Lauren. Don't fall for it."

"What do you mean, someone like that? Is there something I don't know about? Maybe you have a problem because he's rich? Money is your hang-up, not mine." She couldn't stop herself, and she knew the last comment would strike home. His insecurities were surfacing again, it made her so mad.

He put his hand through his hair. "Look, Lauren. I don't want to feel this way. But you can't brush it away. You like that guy. You were enjoying flirting with that guy. That guy is a rich asshole… but there is something there that attracted you. And I don't want to be the jealous boyfriend, not here, going nuts, going all possessive. I've seen that movie too—and I don't want to become that."

"So, what now?" she asked.

"Now… now… I suppose we take a break. I don't know… I don't want to lose you, but maybe you should… I don't know… actually see other people?"

"Are you serious, Jimmy? You're actually breaking up with me? What about our plans? You coming to Stellenbosch, then we could be together?" She suddenly felt desperate.

He had a resolute look on his face. "I think I am. I am happy. So, are you? I don't even know if I want to come here anymore. I would still need to work to get by, we would still hardly be able to spend time together. And this rich, entitled world you are starting to live in. I don't know."

She suddenly felt terror, deep in her throat. "Jimmy, please don't do this. I don't care about money and status. Never have. I just want you."

"What we have is special, Lauren. But I don't know… we're still so young. And I don't want you to have any regrets."

She narrowed her eyes. "You mean you don't want to have any regrets. What is it you're not telling me, Jimmy?"

He shook his head, and put some cash down to pay for the coffee.

"I love you, Lauren. But trust me. This is the best thing for us right now."

Then he walked away.

20

I t had been an awful week for Jimmy. And it had started so well. He was making incredible progress at Max's. The head waiter was moving on to a summer job in Europe, and although Max's would be closed for most of the winter, Max had implied that Jimmy would be tried for the winter. If he did well, the position would be his for the next summer.

Jimmy, admittedly, started to enjoy his lunch stints in the kitchen more and more. But the money as a waiter was incredibly good. He wanted to save up, so he could put himself through university.

And a big part of the reason for that was Lauren. Although the last few months had been incredible, he felt guilty she was spending all of her time with him. There was this incredible social life as a student that she was probably missing out on, and he didn't want to be the reason she didn't have the full experience. No, he would join her next year, and that would solve the problem.

But in the meantime, he was aware that their worlds were drifting apart. He had made friends with the locals in Franschhoek, who were mostly career hospitality folk: waiters, managers at the hotels, etc. It was a pretty good deal, and he was having a lot of fun. The money was good, he enjoyed the interaction with the clients, and he was clear on saving money to join the university circuit the following year.

Over time, Max had become more than a mentor. He was a genius with food, but a horror with staff. He was very much self-aware, though, and outside of work, he was an enormously personable and charismatic fellow.

And he was full of life's wisdom. His ample gut and friendly smile spoke of 52 years lived well, and he had war stories from all corners of the world.

He had many theories: "So, observe, young Jimmy, the new receptionist at the hotel, Sabine. She is young, beautiful, unattached. And all the young men are swarming in competition. She is loving the attention, but it is causing trouble at the hotel. The owner wants her—but she doesn't want him. She is more interested in the marketing manager, and why not? Better fit in beauty and age. But now, she has been inserted into the system. What do you think will happen? The system dictates that the marketing manager will now be forced out. Even though the owner has no chance, his ego will not allow for this dalliance." And of course, Max was right. The system drove the behavior.

Max's words eventually struck too close to home for Jimmy. It was another of those late-night beers, but now Lauren had joined them. They had had a great night, and she had excused herself to go to the bathroom.

Max had asked, casually, "So you are joining her in Stellenbosch next year?"

"That's the plan," smiled Jimmy.

"And in the meantime, all the thousands of young men that are there? Those already studying, educated, in the same social circles… are they leaving her alone for you?"

Jimmy frowned at this. "She has always gotten a lot of attention. But I trust her, she wouldn't…"

"No, no, Jimmy," said Max. "It is not a matter of trust. Of course, you can trust her not to cheat with her body. But she is young, as are you. What about the mind? The mind will be curious. The mind will wonder."

"Wonder what?" Jimmy felt himself becoming irritable.

"Wonder if she is missing something. If she should be having a relationship with a boy that is not around, when there are many boys from the same system that want her." They saw her coming back, and Max finished, "The system will drive the behavior."

For Jimmy, he was constantly reminded that it was a road he had thought was his destiny. And that the friends she made were different from his world now. She was coming into her own. She was vivacious, smart and beautiful. When they were together, especially with her friends, he was aware how many admiring looks she received. He also understood that most of the guys probably had a lot of daddies' monies behind them.

One of the biggest lessons of being a waiter was humility. Jimmy had earned his stripes at Joe's in Oudtshoorn, and most clients were cool there. However, there was also the occasional asshole.

In Franschhoek, given that it was fine dining, the clientele was more international. This came with its own set of challenges, as a French, Dutch and German client all had similar but vastly different ways of expressing either approval or negative feedback. Fortunately, Max had seen it all before, and the training for the first month was crucial. Jimmy now also saw the wisdom in starting someone as a runner. He had learned a lot during that time, without the pressure of delivering on the food quality.

The price point was quite restrictive. Max's worked on a set food and wine pairing menu of five-courses at just over R1000, extras excluded. This meant it was not in the ballpark for most locals. It was better suited to people with Euros or Dollars to spend.

Occasionally, though, a local table came through. Anniversaries, family gatherings, and quite often, a first date. The latter was usually some 20-something guy from the local elite winemakers. The girls were usually quite pretty but not necessarily from the same stock. They were generally easily impressed by the rich food, decadent wines, and above all the price tag of the meal.

Jimmy felt mixed feelings. Jealousy for the power and trappings that the money could buy—and disgust at their behavior. Especially because a lot of them hadn't earned it. Daddy's money!

It was Tuesday when they were treated by just such a spectacle. It was a table of four. Jimmy had to admit, they made for a striking group. The guys were confident and casually elegant—one a darker Italian-looking type (although his accent was decidedly British) and the other a broad-shouldered giant with a mop of blonde hair. Jimmy recognized the big guy as Chean Burger. He had recently been called up to the national rugby team, and he was generally seen as the next big thing and possible future captain.

His buddy seemed to be the leader of this pack though. The girls were the required mix of style and beauty, their make-up perfect, their outfits autumn demure but still showing enough flesh to keep interest. He thought he recognized one of the girls, but he couldn't quite place her. She was very well put together, but her make-up didn't quite conceal her abundance of freckles. Freckles...

They were courteous to Jimmy in the way that he was accustomed to. Some clients liked to chit chat with their server, but this lot was having too much fun in each other's company, and his primary purpose was to stay present to make sure the courses kept moving and the glasses filled.

The Italian guy's date kept giving Jimmy looks, and not the flirty kind. She had a quizzical look on her freckled face... and a sixth sense told Jimmy trouble was brewing. While he was clearing the third course, she suddenly asked him, "Did you use to play rugby for Bishops?"

This question suddenly perked the interest of the giant, who inspected him a bit closer. He now had the whole table's attention. "Um... yes... but that was a couple of years ago?"

She snapped her fingers. "I knew it was you! Jimmy Barnes... you were going to be the next big thing. Then the shoulder... and then your parents..." She paused, and then said, "I'm so sorry."

"Sure. I... listen, it's good to see you, but..."

"You don't remember me at all, do you?" Her companions were now visibly intrigued.

"I... umm..."

"Don't worry. We never really did talk much. You can go now."

And with that, he was dismissed. However, there was a look in her eye, something evolving from the quick-lived empathy for losing his parents, which he did not like at all.

He went up to his buddy Jason, who was waiting on the next course for his table to come up at the kitchen.

"Jase, we have a code red I think."

Jason loved the military speak as applied to kitchen crises. He was also quite gay, and his flair for the dramatic came to the fore. "Another lass who wants to get in your pants, pretty boy? When will you just come over to my side and we can desist with all that unwanted attention?"

"Dude, this is serious. There's a girl at the table that knows me, but I don't know her. I get the feeling that I pissed her off somewhere in my past, and the rest of the night is going to be tricky. Can we do a switch?"

"Sure, buddy boy. After this course, we can do the deed. Just let me get out this glazed duck, and then we take a minute."

Jimmy took the moment to get the next course out to one of his other tables. Before he could switch out with the now available Jason, he was called over by Freckles and her gang.

"Waiter, we have another question for you."

This was going to be painful.

He dutifully stood by their table, and now British Accent had the mic.

"We were having a bit of a debate, and we were wondering if you could resolve it for us."

"Sure. Could I just bring out the next course, then we could…"?

Accent put his hand up. "Only take a minute. Here's the choice," and he theatrically swept his hand over the restaurant.

"If you had to choose between buying this restaurant, or buying the property it is housed in, what would you do?"

Jimmy couldn't find the angle in the question. But he was pretty sure he was being set up for some kind of humiliation. It was in the way the girls were stifling giggles.

He had thought about it, from long conversations with Max (who paid ridiculous rental fees to the hotel owner). "It would depend on the numbers, I suppose. The property is prime high street real estate, but the restaurant is the main attraction. I would buy the restaurant, if I could lock in the chef and owner on the short term."

"Told you!" said the rugby player, and Accent handed over a R100 note, clearly having lost some kind of bet. Accent turned to Jimmy; "You did call the restaurant, Chean. But now, Jimmy, what would you do if you couldn't lock in the chef? Would you still buy it?"

Where was this going?

"Only if I could find someone equally as good to run it," he replied. Accent nodded and turned to his companion; "Looks like you also lost your bet, Margaux. He is not that dumb."

She pursed her lips. "Yep, becoming poor must have smarted him up quite a bit."

Jimmy flushed under his collar. He still had no idea who she was... Margaux? Didn't ring a bell...

"If that is all for now, I'll get back to your order?"

Accent chuckled. "That's all for now. Run along."

The condescending tone from him was worse than the slight from the girlfriend—but they had already dismissed him. He walked to the back, and said to Jason, "Could you cover the rest of my tables for the night? I need to get out of here."

"Max will be pissed."

He took off his apron and handed it to Jason; "Let him. I need to get some air. See you later."

Later he was in the Elephant and Barrel, the local watering hole. And Jimmy was on his fourth beer, waiting for Jason when the group from before walked in. Before he could turn his back to them, Freckles spotted him.

"Hey! Waiter. Yeah, you! You dissed us. I am going to write the worst review that restaurant has ever seen..."

They were all pretty drunk, but then he was getting there too. He didn't feel like engaging in this, so he tried to push past out of the bar.

No such luck. Accent grabbed him by the shoulder and leaned in.

"Don't mind her, mate. She's a wannabee too. But that's why she'll suck my cock all night long. Because she's a wannabee. You're at least working, picking yourself up. I admire that."

Jimmy tried to shake loose. "I'm not your mate. And I don't really care if she's sucking your cock or not."

Accent didn't let go. His grip was firm, and as Jimmy looked into his eyes, he was struck that this one seemed dead sober. "I suppose not. She knows you from before. When you were like us. And you treated her best friend really bad."

"I really don't remember her. And I don't know you. Now let go of me, asshole."

Accent let go, then said, "You might want to be nicer to me, bud. It's in your best interests."

"Excuse me?"

"See, Jimmy boy, we are coming in. This is prime space, and we now own the building. Max had his chance to sell. But he wanted his freedom. So now he will have it—completely. But you... you're the rising star. So, you might move into his slot. Depends on how bad you want it, of course..." and he suggestively pointed at his cock.

Jimmy couldn't believe this prick. He felt ready to take a swing at him, when he felt Jason's hand on his shoulder. "Don't, Jimmy. Please don't. I'm here as well—this might be my job too."

Then Accent broke into a broad smile. "Just kidding about the blowjob, mate. But I like the fact that you were thinking about it."

And then they moved on, leaving Jimmy to walk home with a mind full of troubling thoughts.

In the morning, coming in to prep for lunch, Max let him have it.

"How dare you walk out on a table like that? Jesu Cristo Jimmy, I taught you better than that!"

Jimmy rubbed his temples. He didn't want to get into it, but hey.

"Max, what's happening with the restaurant?"

Max was taken aback. "What do you mean?"

The guy at that table... said some things..."

Max blinked, then sat down. "I thought he looked familiar. He's one of our new owners; his old man has bought the building. And yes, they have given me notice on the lease."

"But they can't do that!"

"Unfortunately, Jimmy my boy, they sure can. They are within their contractual rights as the new owner—I will be out of here by the end of next month."

"And then? Surely we can take another location—maybe just off the high street?"

"Sure, we can, Jimmy. Sure, we can. But being a chef in a top restaurant and owning one are two different things, I found. I put my life savings into this place. It takes a while to get going, overheads are high, and winters are quiet. I will not start over."

Jimmy pondered this. "So, what are you going to do?"

Max smiled. "I think I'll do what your uncle did. The quiet life, in a hamlet somewhere. I might even go back to Europe. Some of my old contacts there are wanting me to come back for their summer. One last hurrah in the bright lights, before I follow Joe into ignominy."

And Max brightened up. "Listen, maybe you could come with me? You have learned much, and in the Michelin Star restaurants of France... ah, my boy, you could become a star..."

Jimmy laughed. "Ah, Max. It sounds tempting, for sure. But I want to go to Stellenbosch, study, and be with Lauren."

"Jimmy my boy, young love is grand. But there is so much in the world to experience... and your talent is for food. Stellenbosch would be next year, right? In the meantime, why don't you come on an adventure with Old Max?"

Jimmy had had this argument with Max before. "Yes, I love the restaurant business... but I want to own it one day. I want to be a businessman."

"Because you will have money, and then everyone will love you?" The accusation struck home for Jimmy, but he didn't take the bait.

"Max, I have my reasons. Please respect those."

Max stood up. "For those reasons, I would suggest you either learn to suck it up from those rich assholes or start looking for alternatives. This ride is almost over. My offer stands... There will also be rich assholes where I am going, but they often have a bit more class."

He didn't say anything to Lauren... but he wanted to talk to her the whole week, but she had seemed a bit distant. He finally decided to swap out his Friday shift and jump on the bus through to Stellenbosch. She was attending the wine fair, and she always wanted him to hang out a bit more with her mates.

He dropped his gear at Robby's (who was hanging out in the res bar, as was his usual Friday night post-rugby game deal) and rushed to the fair.

When he saw Lauren, he had two immediately conflicting realizations.

She was completely and utterly flirting with the handsome guy behind the wine tasting counter.

And that guy was going to be his new boss.

Their fights had always been spirited, she reflected. The first one, back in high school, was a precursor for things to come. Lauren and Jimmy were both strong-willed and independent and in their young lives, they had not yet learned the true value of compromise.

So, they constantly fought. Their insecurities, needs and unhindered impulses often put them at odds with each other.

But the fundamentals were there. They had experienced a lot together, and Jimmy understood her scars around her father, and she had a sense of his disappointments around his father.

The worst thing, therefore, was that it didn't end with a big fight. He had been so... calm. And she felt like there had been more there, but he wouldn't say a thing.

She felt bad about Jacques. She was also certain that any jealousy Jimmy had was just him projecting his own stuff on her. He was, after all, the one who had cheated before. She refused to accept the breakup.

But it was as if a switch had been turned off in Jimmy. He went back to Franschhoek on the weekend, and she didn't see him again for a while. He insisted that he was very busy with work, but he didn't return her calls or texts. Exams came around, and even though she was distraught, she managed to get stuck in.

In the meantime, Jacques Jardine had come calling. He was sending her texts—just harmless things around wine and art, subjects that she enjoyed. She told herself that there was nothing wrong with it, just harmless chatter—but the tone changed subtly, and she found herself enjoying it. She saw him socially and he always seemed to be at the same parties. They even had a few coffees, mostly to talk about the Rhodes Scholarship and what it took to get it. This encouraged her to study even harder. Lee was all for it. Finally Lauren was dating in her actual range, according to Lee's math.

She still felt she had a boyfriend, and even though she was battering him with text messages, he didn't respond. Lee told her to wake up and smell the roses (and jump on the winemaker).

So, she finally jumped started Lee's car and went to see Jimmy.

He was not at home; it was later afternoon on a Thursday.

She went around to Max's, and found that completely closed as well. She was stunned by this. Max's was an institution! She asked at the hotel reception, and the lady there was surprised that she didn't know.

Max's had closed over two weeks prior. A new restaurant was going to come into his place, run by the hotel's new owners. It would be a second Jardine, named after the flagship restaurant on the family estate in Stellenbosch. Suddenly a lot of other things made sense!

She finally managed to get Jason on the line. Jimmy's best mate, as far as she knew. And he was none the friendlier either.

"You broke his heart, Lauren."

"But I didn't do anything!" She had to fight back the tears.

"Ah, sweetie. He knew that. But you wanted to. There was a whole world that you were yearning to be a part of. Jimmy was reminded that that world was now forever out of his reach. The rich and powerful are their own breed. I suppose you were just too much of a reminder to Jimmy of all that. He needed to find another way in life."

"But he didn't give me a chance…"

"To do what? To insist that you wanted only him? That he was enough? Lauren, for God's sake. You're 18. He's just turned 19, and…"

She dropped the phone. She just realized that the day of the wine tasting… the day it all went wrong… the day she was so distracted by Jacques Jardine…

That had been Jimmy's birthday.

———

It didn't take long. Jacques Jardine. He was suddenly at the hotel every second day, planning renovations for when they took over. Jimmy took stock of his rival.

From what Jimmy could see, the guy was a class-A asshole. He turned on the charm easily enough, and it worked on winning over the staff at the hotel. There was no sign of the guy that made a point of embarrassing Jimmy when they first met. Jimmy kept his council. Nobody was interested in his view, they wanted to pander to the new boss. He thankfully did not come into the restaurant after they had served notice. He also did not make Jimmy any offers of employment. And Jimmy was not about to go and beg for a job.

The last few weeks before closure, turned in to a blur. Max had decided to move back to Europe, already with a position secured. After Jimmy had seen Lauren with Jacques, he had felt… not defeated… maybe deflated. He knew, from personal experience, the type of girls that were impressed with wealth and family connections. And although Lauren was not one of those, she had high aspirations for herself.

It was hard to compete. He investigated the rich winemaker son, and had to admit: he was accomplished. Born with the silver spoon, he was still a provincial tennis player, and had consistently won the Rector's award for best student in his class. He was even well documented as leading the many charitable endeavors of the family estate.

And he, Jimmy, was just a waiter. Even if he made it to Stellenbosch the next year, he would at best have to work his way up in the world. By the time he managed to make something of himself, Lauren would be long gone, with someone like Jacques. Like someone who Jimmy used to be.

A part of him wanted to wake up from this faulty self-loathing. He knew that there was more to him—more to them—but there was no doubting the way she had looked at Jacques. He felt like he needed to fight for her all over again..

But they were so busy, and she was distant and uneasy, and finally good old Max came up with the ultimate cliché: "Jimmy, she has only had you. She does not know. She does not know how good you are to her. She must… go out there and scratch the itch, you know. If you love someone, you must set them free…"

"Max, if you say that she will come back to you, otherwise she was never yours to begin with, I'm going to slap you hard."

Max guffawed and had another long sip of his whiskey. "Ah, the young love. You must end it, Jimmy. And then come with me, to the South of France."

"Are you still serious about that?"

"Of course. You are young, beautiful. I am old, experienced. Together we can conquer all the ladies in France. You can be my… how shall we say… my pointer bird?"

"What the hell are you talking about, Max?"

"Ah, with my experience, and your good looks and youth… we could have so much fun in the season. I will promise you; you will have more young French ladies than your heart can desire, and you will forget all about this one…"

Jimmy shook his head. "Max, I love her…"

"So? She loves you. But you are too young. Leave her. If the fates are aligned, your paths will cross again. And I am serious, Jimmy. I can give you a great opportunity: one of the top restaurants in France. It is waiting for us!"

As summer turned to autumn in the Winelands, Jimmy realized he had only bad options. There was not much solid work now that the season was over—he would not have enough for studies after all. Lauren… Lauren was slipping away from him…

"Maybe I do want to come, Max. What about a work visa? It is Europe, and…"

"Pah! I will take care of it, do not worry. This is wonderful!" Max clapped his hands with glee. One more roll of the dice… and how glorious it would be…"

And so it was. Jimmy called Lauren the day before their flight was set to depart—but her phone went straight to voicemail, as it mostly did these days.

Funny how something so good could wither and die so quickly.

But new horizons awaited.

21

Saint-Paul-de-Vence was one of the oldest icons on the French Riviera. A medieval town nestled on top of the hills above fabled Nice, it's one of those places that is the backdrop for many a romantic novel. Cobblestone narrow streets, rustic little boutique shops, aging locals sitting on their balconies and observing the tourist throng. Never mind the glorious sunsets observed from terraced restaurants overlooking the valleys below.

At the entrance of this hilltop town is a world-famous restaurant by the name of La Colombe d'Or. Jimmy had heard of La Colombe in Cape Town, but Max had assured him there was no connection.

Jimmy had to admit, though, that Max had made good on his word. They had barely landed at Nice airport before a reunion of sorts was organized at a local bistro. It did seem like Max had many friends in this part of the world. The promised positions at La Colombe were courtesy of a vivacious woman in her mid-thirties called Chetaine. She was the hotel manager, and, as far as Jimmy could make out, there had been more than a friendship between her and Max in the past. It was all slightly odd and very French. Chetaine seemed to be together with another one of this crew called Stefan, but everyone was cool with her employing Max in the kitchen. And, of course, Jimmy as a runner.

Jimmy was initially peeved to take a step back. He spoke no French, and he realized it was back to square one. Jimmy would only learn later that it was a mix of timing, luck and connections that set his life on this trajectory. Uncle Joe was also well respected in these parts, and between him and Max, Jimmy seemed to have the backing of some serious players. A job as a runner at La Colombe was one of the most coveted in the business. He would only later really appreciate the enormity of the opportunity.

It was also a matter of timing. May was still pre-season for the South of France. Things would only really pick up in a month. All the establishments that thrived on the summer tourist business were just getting ready for the influx. As such, Jimmy had about a month to get his act together.

There were three distinct aspects to this learning curve. Max morphed into a bit of a monster (even more so than back in Franschhoek) in the kitchen. Chetaine vacillated between fits of enormous temper and extremely friendly invasion of his physical space. Moreover, French as a language was a tricky business.

Max, he would discover, was simply adapting to a more Mediterranean way of doing things. Which implied lots of emotional shouting, emoting and tantrums. He also quickly forgave minor slights and embraced a flow of exciting conflict. Everyone adjusted to this vibe, and Max sat him down after the first week to explain things

"Lean into it, Jimmy. These people lead with passion, demand perfection. They take offense easily, they forgive, they forget, they move on. You will find your rhythm."

And he did. He found that he did three things that helped him find more than his rhythm—these things helped him discover true joy.

1. Learn French. Find a tutor, spend time each night studying simple books, and speak it as much as possible. It was amazing how far he would get in a month.
2. Stop taking offense, go with the flow, and give as good as you get. His French improved and he came to understand the flow of the kitchen and the waiters. He could anticipate

the behavior of the regular patrons and tourists. He even started to have some fun.

3. Instead of withdrawing from Chetaine, he leaned in. Boy did he lean in…

It was late one night, and they were at the bar. He poured her favorite Scotch, an 18-year-old Talisker Scotch Whiskey. For him, he had acquired a taste for Cognac… it had been part of his journey, having been exposed to mostly inferior quality in what constituted brandy in South Africa.

She was in a good mood tonight. She always looked terrific, and he could not help but compare her with Lauren. Lauren, with natural and youthful beauty, never needed to go to too much trouble. She would only occasionally dress up.

Chetaine, on the other hand, was a whirlwind of Coco Chanel, cashmere blouses and miniskirts that showed off her legs. She smoked Gauloises, and mentally he would often mock her for being too stereo-typical. She also made smoking seem goddamn sexy.

He had declined her previous invites to stay and share a drink. He might be young, but her intentions were clear. And he had maintained that it might be incredibly bad for his job prospects. Until Max, once again, offered some sage advice, earlier in the day.

"She is a carnivore, my young acolyte. She will devour you eventu-ally—and she will spit you out. You can hold out, or you can enjoy being eaten. I surely did."

"But that would be weird… I mean, you were together… Stefan…"

"Do not worry about me. I would surely like to have another spin on the Chetaine merry go round, it is surely worth it. But you are in her sights now. And do not worry about Stefan… their relationship is very French."

And so, here they were. Enjoying a private drink in a dark bar with only the outside lights illuminating their consort. Her hand resting gently on his knee as she tells him about her day. The story of another ridiculous customer request coinciding with her hand drifting further up his leg… a slight squeal when she finds the fullness of him.

And the smell of her, when she whispers in his ear to come up to her room…

And it was oh so interesting. While making love with Lauren had been exploration, discovering new heights together, and truly making love… with Chetaine, it was a wild, physical, immersive rollercoaster. She had a full body, soft and yielding. But she had the confidence of experience, and her lust was intensified by his hesitation. She used her gifts to their full potential and introduced him with her mouth, and her thighs, and her hands… to new ways of being, new ways of doing, new ways of losing yourself.

It was safe to say that she had him hooked after that. He tried hard to play it cool—but he would sleep in her bed most nights. It did bother him that she went off to Nice sometimes, and he knew she was with Stefan. But not enough to stop.

And in the process, he learned about women. And French. And food. And the restaurant business. He was completely and utterly in her power, and she was teaching him all she knew.

As the months ticked by, Jimmy was still a runner. He did fill in for the waiters during emergencies, and the money was adequate to his needs. He was not saving or making what he would like—but then again, the intoxication of life with Chetaine ruled all other considerations.

He also made best friends with Stan, one of the dishwashers. Stan was a Kiwi, and despite the ridiculously long hair (always in a ponytail) and the unruly beard, he was a gas. He was a soft-spoken but funny guy, and he did remind Jimmy of home. He was also quite a bit older, closer to Max in age than to Jimmy—but in terms of physique, it was clear that he was in much better shape than Max.

He was also a hell of a touch rugby player. One of their favorite pastimes was to go play on the school fields in neighboring Vence. Jimmy was used to playing on the beach, but the beaches in Nice and Cannes didn't allow for the space one enjoyed on the other side of the world. Stan was lightning quick, and elusive. He and Jimmy, along with Squidge, an Aussie mate of theirs who also worked in the village, took great joy to constantly beating the local Frenchies. There was constant banter around the prospects of their respective teams in the world cup the following year. It was one reminder of the joy that might still be had from going home.

One evening, Jimmy found Stan in a wistful mood.

"Who's that, Stan?"

"My wife and two babies. Miss them, mate."

Jimmy almost choked on his beer. "You're married? With small babies?"

Stan nodded. "Yep. I know it might seem… odd… but my wife has been amazing."

"I mean… I just figured…"

"That I'm just a drifter, living the nomadic life? Would love to mate. Nah, this has been such a wonderful break from the real world. You know, I've been non-stop since high school—and work has been hectic. Great, but hectic. I've also been with my wife forever before we got married. I never really had an opportunity to travel and be someone else for a while. This was that chance."

Jimmy sensed that Stan wanted to say more. But he put the family pictures away and smiled at his young friend. "Jimmy, it's been a blast. But I think it's time to go home. My batteries are recharged, and to be honest, I think I'm over washing these fucking dishes."

Jimmy chuckled. "I thought you loved that shit…"

"I do. Repetitive. Precise. But allows you to be in your own head, and think about life for a while. I sound like a song. But all good things, my friend…"

"Assuming you won't be going back to washing dishes back home, then."

"No. Back to my calling, I suppose."

"Which is?"

Stan just smiled. He swirled his drink and said, "You know Jimmy, you are very good at this job. Maybe one day we could open a restaurant together. A Kiwi and a Saffer, serving the best of French cuisine."

"Can Max come too?" said Jimmy, pointing at the snoring older man, who had the delightful habit of taking power naps at incredibly odd times.

Stan laughed. "Of course. He would be the third partner. You would entertain the guests, Max would cook… and I would not wash dishes." He guffawed at his own joke, and to Jimmy, this was just another of many such conversations of future dreams between drifters of no means.

And so, Stan was the first to leave the restaurant that season. They decided to do a big going away party for him after hours. The drinks and revelry went far into the night, and crossed over into the next morning.

They sat on the ramparts of Saint-Paul-de-Vence, drinking champagne out of the bottle. It was Jimmy, Max and Stan. Chetaine had bowed out earlier to go to bed, but with a saucy reminder for Jimmy not to take too long.

This was one night he was happy to rather spend with his friends.

As they watched the sun come up in the distance, Jimmy asked, "Stan, you're about to get on that plane. It's time for you to solve the great mystery of Stan Davis's actual job. You've been so evasive about your life back home. Put us out of our misery."

Stan chuckled and took another swig of champagne. "This has been a great summer, Jimmy. Just what the doctor ordered. The only person I think that had more fun than I did was you, mate. You and that... temptress..."

Jimmy chuckled. "It has been good for me too, bud. And you are a good-looking fellow under that mess of a beard, I am sure. But you are still ignoring my question, sir. What is your deal?"

"Yeah?" Stan stroked his beard. "Suppose it will have to come off now. Back to reality."

"Stan!" sighed Jimmy. "You're not going to tell me, are you..."

Max, who had been sitting quite bleary-eyed, suddenly burst out laughing. "I can't believe you pulled it off, Stan. I was sworn to secrecy, but I can't believe Chetaine never said anything to you either, Jimmy. It is hilarious."

Stan sighed, as Jimmy asked, "What are you talking about, Max. What..."

Max suddenly grabbed Stan. "Hiding in plain sight, my friend. Look at the shoulders, look at the speed. Look at his eyes. And I'll tell you another thing- his surname isn't Davis, either."

Jimmy was still confused. Stan turned to him and smiled. He did look familiar... he did...

"Holy shit. Stan... you're... you're..."

When he got over the initial indignation of being kept in the dark by both Max and Chetaine, Jimmy had to admit it was pretty funny. And would make a helluva story. In the meantime, Chetaine made it up to him. And how...

And then, devastatingly, the summer was over.

They were sitting at a café by the harbor when she turned to him and said, "I will miss you, Jimmy..."

He loved the way she pronounced his name, and leaned over to kiss her. But she stopped him with her finger on his lips.

"Stefan has asked me to go with him to the Alps for the season. He owns a chalet in Courchevel—and he wants me to run it for him."

Jimmy considered this information. "Ok..."

She smiled, and took a long drag of her cigarette.

"He has also asked me to consider marriage."

Jimmy almost choked on his beer. "But... I mean... what about us..."

"Mon Cherie, this was a beautiful moment for me. And for you. But it is now over. I am not getting any younger—and Stefan wants to take care of me. I will miss you..." and she leaned in... "and I will miss that part of you that has driven me to many nights of ecstasy..."

She leaned back, put out her cigarette, and got up to leave.

"But you are still just a boy. You will be a glorious man... and maybe one day the girl will come back into your life when you are both ready..."

"Lauren? I don't think so."

She nodded. "As the winds blow." And then, she was gone.

Later, Max was once again on hand with timely—and ultimately crucial—advice.

"You have taken some great lessons this summer, my young protégé. You are ready to be released on the culinary scene of France

—and its young ladies. The wonderful Chetaine has helped heal your heart, as she once did it for me. That is her gift, I think."

"You didn't tell me this, Max."

"Oh yes… when I met her, some 10 years ago, when I was in my late forties and quite devastated after divorce… and she was, as now, somewhere in her late thirties…"

They both laughed at that. Her age was the mystery of the ages, and she would never reveal it.

"It was a glorious summer. Much like the one you just experienced. But my mistake was pining for her too long after. What I would have done if I was younger… what you WILL do… is go reap the rewards of your sexual experience. And distribute this gift to the willing young lasses of Europe this coming winter."

"Where? The summer is finishing, where shall we go?"

"Ah, my young friend. We will go to Austria, of course!"

22

Lauren had fallen for Jacques Jardine. He professed ignorance of the fact that her boyfriend had worked at the restaurant he bought. Her instinct told her there was more to the story, but without contact with Jimmy to verify, she decided to let it lie. Jacques was a scoundrel, with a reputation among the girls. He was a persistent scoundrel, though. When he asked her to the intervarsity dance, she had run out of excuses.

Lee had brought her into her world of privilege, and was very supportive of a possible union with Jacques Jardine. Lauren kept pushing back. Here was a glamorous world of champagne, beautiful clothes and exotic holidays that was hard to say no to. She convinced herself that it was all harmless fun. But, bit by bit, she got sucked in.

It was the big annual social event in Stellenbosch: the yearly derby between Stellenbosch and their arch-rivals Ikeys was the highlight of the sporting year. Generally, Stellenbosch held the edge in the big rugby game. She had to reflect that this would have been a path Jimmy might have been on, if things had been different.

The evening of the game was the ball. It was a glorious affair. The crème-de-la-crème of the Stellenbosch student community dressed up in their finest evening dresses and rented tuxedos to dance, drink and laugh the night away.

And she was impressed by the company Jacques kept. He was Stellenbosch elite, and, although not a rugby player (he excelled in golf and tennis, and had been the varsity champ in both) he was regularly out with all the players from the first team. He also kept company with the student council members. At his wine farm, she started to attend parties he invited her to. There she was also exposed to that elevated crowd. Jacques also introduced her to another very exclusive group: The various heirs to the vast wine estates of the region.

It was heady stuff. She took great care (with Lee's help) to look her best for the big ball—and the dress (she borrowed) fit her perfectly. It was emerald green and hugged her figure, and she was well aware that Jacques did not take his eyes off her the whole night. Which was something, as the current varsity queen was at their table. The other dates of the first team players were all stunners. They were mostly older and more experienced, and they all treated her with more than a little bit of condescension.

It was awful—but luckily, she was quickly swept away from the table by Jacques, and then he revealed his next talent; he was an amazing dancer. She had been taught some basic ballroom dancing techniques by her mom at school, but this guy was at the next level.

She was used to boys that could dance—but it was always in the one-dimensional two-step fashion that was the norm in Afrikaans schools. Jacques, on the other hand, knew the tango, the salsa, the rumba... and his gentle but firm lead had her dizzy from all the twirling.

She eventually begged for a break, and he led her out to the porch for some fresh air.

She wanted him to kiss her then. They simply chatted, though, and he told her about his aspirations. How he knew he was expected to run the farm one day—but in the meantime, he wanted to live a big life, have a career, travel abroad...

He was smart and ambitious. He seemed to really be interested in her. He was interested in her dreams, her ambitions too. He saw beyond her good looks to the intellectual person inside—and she found tremendously drawn to him. The next morning, she told her delighted mother about him. And, of course, Lee was all for it. Everyone was enthused. Why was she resisting? Because of Jimmy? Jimmy was gone, somewhere in France… maybe it was time to move on. Think about the rest of her life.

And she found herself wondering what that life would be like if she could share it with Jacques.

It was the beginning for them.

Kitzbuhel was the jewel in the crown of the Austrian region of Tyrol. A town steeped in history in tradition, it was in many ways the Alpine counterpart to Saint-Paul-de-Vence, attracting attention and celebrities through its myriad winter activities, and its most famous downhill ski race. It was glamorous, old school beautiful… and for the seasonal workers, a paradise of opportunity.

The Sporthotel Reisch was, by all accounts, the premier property to stay at in Kitzbuhel. Sure, it was only four stars—but it was smack bang in the middle of town, and was known to host, on an annual basis, both Arnold Schwarzenegger and Bernie Ecclestone, the famous boss of F1 Racing. Both men like to attend the annual Hahnenkamm downhill ski event in late January—it was one of the highlights of the European skiing season, and Kitzbuehel became a beehive of activity for the week of the event.

For Jimmy and Max, it was a continuation of their partnership. But now, it started to feel like a more equal one. Max the head chef, Jimmy the maître d at the restaurant.

Things in Austria were different than in France. Here, Jimmy did not feel his lack of German-made any significant difference—the clientele and the staff were international, English was widely spoken, and the experience was a learning curve in a different way.

In France, food was about pleasure and taking the time. There was a languid opulence to every meal, and the clientele expected it so.

In Austria, in the adrenaline-fueled environment of the ski season, the speed at which the clients hurtled down the mountains was a perfect metaphor for what happened in the kitchen and on the floor. Service was fast, food was delicious but uncomplicated, and clients—especially the Germans—were unforgiving.

Jimmy thrived. The work felt simple and rewarding. The times they did have off Max introduced him to snowboarding and it was as if a whole new universe had opened up for him.

Just after their season kicked off, one of the waiters abruptly resigned. In a flash of inspiration, Jimmy called Robby. Delighted with the opportunity, as he had two months to kill in his summer vacation, Robby joined him in the resort as a waiter.

Man, it was fun. Max sat the two of them down early in the season, with two primary points of advice. One regarding women, and one regarding money.

And there were many women. For the first few months of the season, Jimmy followed (once again) the advice about women. He avoided romantic entanglements with what was known as "Season-aires". These were the young people, like himself, who flocked to the resorts for the winters to indulge in a few months of fun, work, and play. They came from all over Europe, the Antipodeans, and even a few lost souls from the Americas. And they partied hard, exchanged sexual partners throughout the season, and indulged in a fair bit of "Smalltown" drama.

The simpler approach, Max had advised, was to be the winter dream fulfillment for yet another young, beautiful, and transient client. They came in groups of girlfriends, were sometimes the adult daughter of a tycoon, and even sometimes a single traveler who zeroed in on him. The rule was to indulge in flirting for four days—Saturday to Wednesday—and then enjoy two nights of exquisite lovemaking before they, regrettably, jumped on the Saturday transfer back out of town.

This recipe was mostly foolproof. The occasional silly girl got it into her head to want to stay in the resort to be with him—or, on one memorable occasion, popped back up a week later and announced her intention to stay. Jimmy managed to maneuver himself out of both situations.

Robby kept his nose clean, though. He fell for Gretha, a lovely girl from Denmark, almost immediately after arrival. Jimmy often joked

that he was equally in love with Gretha's custom Bluetooth earphones
—Robby couldn't stop talking about them. The two of them had a lot
of fun over the next two months poking fun at Jimmy for his adventures. When they weren't doing that, they spent hours plotting how
they could start an import business from Denmark into South Africa.

The deadline for submission for the new year at Stellenbosch
passed. He did not give it much thought. He was, for the first time
since his parents died, carefree. He partied a lot. It was a culture in the
village, and his tolerance level for alcohol made him a bit of a legend.
He could show up for work shaking off the hangover quite easily. This
this was perfectly acceptable. He was generous in buying drinks, which
made him even more friends.

Robby did not volunteer info on Lauren and Jimmy preferred not
to ask. It was, however, inevitable that it would come up, with Gretha
asking questions about their life back in South Africa. Lauren was still
with the asshole—and happy, as it turned out. Drinking, snowboarding,
other women... These distractions helped Jimmy not to think
about her.

Valentine's day changed that. Robby had, during the season, made
some noises about Jimmy coming back, and helping him start a business in Stellenbosch. Jimmy, Max, Robby and the boys followed an
ancient restaurant tradition where all the seasonairs played all night
Poker on Valentine's Day. It had been a year since Thailand ... and
Jimmy could not, even with whiskey and gambling, put Lauren out of
his mind.

More news from home started to put thoughts of going back in
motion.

Uncle Joe was engaged, and was getting married in a few months.
The wedding would be a reunion of sorts. Jimmy knew he had to be
there. But he was sure, Lauren would also be there—she and her
mother were independently close with Joe.

Was he ready to see her again? Especially if she was with the rich
a-hole? And what would he do? If he had to admit it to himself, he was
still in love with her. But what did he have to offer her? He had missed
the deadline to go to Stellenbosch again. Truthfully, he was more interested in the business opportunity Robby was talking about. Could he

compete with Jacques Jardine? Did he want to? If that was her taste in men, her judgment... but then again, who was he to say? It was not if he hadn't made mistakes.

Jimmy honestly did not know the answer—but when Max announced that he, too, was invited, Jimmy's mind was made up. They would all head home for the celebration. With the Euros he had amassed after the last couple of seasons, he could probably return home in a blaze of glory. It started to feel like a fun project: go back, be awesome, make Lauren remember what she was missing.

He would need a new suit.

Her mother was smitten with Jacques. This caused Lauren no end of embarrassment. The way she fawned all over him smacked of social climber desperation. To her credit, she had quit the heavy drinking since she had left Lauren's father. And she was doing some correspondence courses to get a job. She had even patched up her tricky relationship with Lauren's grandma.

Lauren wondered how much of that had shaped her behavior. Her mother had been the local beauty as a youngster, but she had not aged well. The travails of her marriage, combined with the ignominy of going back to work in her late thirties... it had left a mark. She lacked both grace and charm. It was sweet of her to go to trouble with her physical appearance when she met Jacques for the first time. Still, Lauren found herself dreading the day their families would meet.

Which they would. Jacques seemed more committed than ever. In the autumn of 2015, after almost a year of dating, they had a difficult conversation. He knew she was committed to her studies, but Oxford and the Rhodes Scholarship beckoned. He would be gone for a year—but he was devoted to her, and wanted the same.

They were sitting at Java Café, a popular coffee shop on Stellenbosch's famed Church Street. Their table on the curbside offered a view of the bustle of tourists, locals, students, and shopkeepers. It was a favorite.

"Are you sure, Jacques? I mean, it is a whole year... and it is

Oxford. Don't you want to be… free?" she asked. "I mean, I know of other couples where they… I dunno… took a break?"

He took her hand.

"I could not bear to be without you, my love. Come with me! We will conquer Oxford together!"

She smiled. She did adore him. He was only her second lover, after Jimmy. And while their lovemaking was less passionate, she had to acknowledge his skill and willingness to please. But more importantly, the reputation which had preceded him—the womanizing, the awful treatment of people of certain race groups—she had not seen any of it. Only kindness, and generosity. He lived in a different world, and he had opened it up to her.

Part of it was international travel. Jacques seemed to hop on a plane to some exotic location as easy as some others would drive out to Hermanus. And he had started to take her along. Only in the last year, there was a weekend in Botswana, a week trip to Buenos Aires as part of watching the Springboks play, and, with his family, a week in the Seychelles this last summer.

She wanted to believe it would be a good idea.

"Jacques, my own studies are important to me. I have always wanted to qualify, and not end up like my mom. You know this. I don't want to hold you back, and I need to see it through."

He chuckled. "I could never steamroller you into seeing things my way, love. Ok. We try long distance. I leave mid-June and will be back for the September break, for my parents' wedding anniversary. And of course, you will be my date."

"Speaking of weddings, I received an invitation to Joe's nuptials in Oudtshoorn." She grimaced. "My mom is so excited; it's going to be the social event of the year."

He laughed. "Your mom is harmless. And sweet. No, of course we'll go. That was a big part of high school for you—would love to meet some of your old crowd."

"Jacques, Jimmy might be there…"

The smile did not leave his face, although she did see a shift in his eyes.

"Look, I also have exes. But I know how big a role in your life he played. If you don't want to be there, we don't need to go. At the same time, I think life moved on, you know? Hopefully, he has grown up since then, and there won't be any issues. I'm ok."

That wasn't what she was afraid of. Of Jacques, or Jimmy.

She was afraid of what she might do…

―――――

Robby came to fetch them at the airport, and set off on a road trip to Oudtshoorn. Robby had gone home a couple of weeks earlier to start varsity. For all three of them, the road trip was also a trip down memory lane. First, to Franschhoek to drink and revel with those that were still left from the old Max's crew.

Jimmy's hard-drinking Austrian antics meant he could drink a lot of them under the table—and, among men in South Africa, the next day he would receive much applause for his masculine drinking ability.

Max was properly hungover, so Jimmy drove them the rest of the way, and they crossed over the mountains into the Klein Karoo and finally to Oudtshoorn.

Uncle Joe had insisted they stay with him. Max, eternally wise, had suggested this was more decency than common sense. They hired a house in town, close enough to be fully present and supportive for the run-up to the wedding, but far enough to give him and Melissa their space.

It was one of those village weddings. Over 300 people were invited (Uncle Joe, wisely, electing to not insult any of his regular patrons). But there was also a surprising number of folks from across the globe. They were culinary giants, and they came from France, Italy, Australia, New Zealand and Argentina. They arrived early and left late, and Jimmy found himself once again in the intoxicating international mix of people that he had left behind in Europe—but now in his old hometown.

It was a week-long festival. The wedding would be on the Saturday, and they had received special dispensation to have the ceremony inside of the fabled Cango Caves, with the reception just down the road. The ancient limestone caves were one of South Africa's true natural treasures. Jimmy could think of no better place to see his uncle finally settle down.

Jimmy, along with Max, was asked to be Uncle Joe's groomsmen. He was, therefore, almost too busy at the ceremony to notice her arrival.

Almost.

They arrived quietly and sat at the back. But there was no way Jimmy could miss her. She looked different—still her, but somehow more glamorous. Her hair was done very prettily, and she wore a blue shawl over her shoulders that simply drew attention to her elegant frame. Their eyes met briefly across the room, and then she looked away. His gaze drifted to the man beside her. Even across a crowded room of 300 people, he detected the same look he remembered from his humiliation in Franschhoek. A look of studied superiority.

He forced himself back to the present, and his duties as groomsman. Uncle Joe was no nervous wreck, rather he seemed wondrously serene. Even more so when Melissa walked down the aisle. In a fitting bit of theater given the dramatic setting, surrounded by stalactites and stalagmites and with some of the world's best acoustics, they had lined up a local tenor to bust out some tunes.

Nothing like an elegantly beautiful bride, O solo Mio and a well-lit cave to juice up a wedding, thought Jimmy.

The reception was held on a farm down the road from the caves. Mid-April was too cold for an outside party, so a massive Marquee had been erected. Jimmy, who had some knowledge of the cost of things, was taken aback by the expenses incurred. The food was first class, the bar was open, and the live band was amazing.

Max cleared up the mystery, over cocktails. "Your uncle has money, Jimmy. He never flashes it—but he has lived a modest life while doing extraordinary (and highly paid) work. Still, I believe the bride also contributed her share. She comes from old money, from the days of the Oudtshoorn ostrich barons."

"Max, he made me go to the school second-hand inventory for clothes when I first moved here. It was humiliating."

Max clapped him on the back. "Worked, didn't it? Got that entitled monkey off your back. Now let's go for another drink, and line up for some photos."

After the photos, they went straight to the reception. He was, of course, nowhere near Lauren's table. He was also nervous about being asked to say some words, but he pulled off a tribute to the happy couple. When the dance floor opened, Lauren and Jacques were some of the first ones on it. Jimmy, watching from the bar, had to admit that Jacques Jardine had some moves.

It was quite late before he had a chance to speak to her.

He was standing outside, chatting to some of the old crew, when she approached him.

"Can we talk?"

"Sure." His heart still skipped a beat seeing her up close. She looked amazing—but, he thought, in his brand-new expensive Boss suit, so did he. They walked away from the others and stood by one of the bonfires that were blazing for warmth.

After a few moments of nervous silence, he asked, "How have you been?"

"Good. Good." She ruefully shook her head. "I mean great."

"School?"

"Killing it. It's hard work—but enjoying it."

"Still want to go find a cure for cancer?"

She smiled. "Sure. Although these days, it feels to me like there's a whole bunch of new offenders to worry about. TB, Ebola, all kinds of nonsense. But yes… I still want to save the world."

"And…" he tilted his head to the tent.

"Jacques? Yes, it's going well. What about you? Are you…?"

"No. Nobody in my life right now."

For a moment, her eyes revealed that she was… relieved? Then it was gone. Her next question confirmed to Jimmy that she had kept tabs on him. "I heard bits and pieces from Robby and your uncle… the French Riviera, the ski resort in Austria… it all sounds impossibly glamorous…"

He smiled. He was glad that she had kept track. If she saw the crappy little rooms they stayed in, she would be less impressed. "In a way, it was. It was also hard work. But I am glad. Glad I had the opportunity this last year. And I suppose, in a way, I have you to thank."

She stiffened. "You didn't even give me a chance to talk to you, Jimmy. You just left. I wanted to… clear things up…"

He shrugged, as, out of the corner of his eye, he saw Jacques Jardine approaching. "Things were pretty clear. Hello, Jacques."

"Barnes." He put his arms around Lauren and held Jimmy's gaze. "It's cold out here. Want to go back inside, Sweetpea? They are playing our song."

She nodded, and with one last look at Jimmy, they went back inside.

Jimmy stood by himself for a while by the fire. The fucking song was Summer of 69.

The conversation left him unsatisfied. He understood that he still had feelings for her—and clearly, she still felt something for him. What to do?

And suddenly, Robby was there.

"Fanning old flames, bud?"

"You know me too well bud. But she is with the prick. What should I do?"

"She's in with the Stellenbosch elite, my friend. She was good-looking before—now she's added a layer of sophisticated class. Hate the guy if you want, but he has opened some doors for her. Including the Rhodes Scholarship." Robby's eyes reflected a sly glint.

"The only way to win her back, buddy, is to come to Stellenbosch. And not as a student—let's become all-conquering entrepreneurs."

"Don't you have to study, bud?"

"Sure. But if I play part-time and you rock out full-time, we might just be able to start something big. You are the triumphant returning French/Austrian restaurant man. I have a few ideas, and connections…"

"Ok. Let's get shitfaced, but tomorrow, let's talk."

23

R obby was entrenched in various ventures, including running the hostel tuck shop. Helshoogte had over 300 boys in residence. It was a gold mine, and Robby had upped the game from pies and chips to gourmet sandwiches, crepes, and even the odd Bitterballen.

His endeavors had been noticed by a final-year commerce student called Ben Katz. Ben was a serial entrepreneur, and even as a student, he had a dozen different projects going. From trading in second-hand books, to reselling furniture and even running an occasional late-night illegal liquor store out of his residence room, he was always looking for an angle.

The angle, he explained to Robby, was catering. There were at least a dozen dances at the Stellenbosch town hall during the third quarter of the year—and they were, generally, catered by outside companies.

"The problem, Robby my boy, is that the food is always shite. I have gone to a lot of these over the years, and just because we are students, doesn't mean they should serve us crap."

"So, you want to get those catering contracts?"

"Yes! You know the restaurant game. Let's get a few dozen waiters, hire some competent kitchen staff, and go after those events for the spring. With you running the kitchen, and me running the books, we would make out like a house on fire."

And so, they did. Ben did the research and went out to talk to all the different house committees that organized the dances. He got them the deals.

Robby, in between his studies, recruited the staff and worked out the menus. He also figured out what they would need in terms of cutlery, crockery, and the rest. It was a massive learning curve, and they got it horribly wrong even on their first event. Not enough ventilation in the kitchen, food came out cold, and they ran out of glasses.

But Robby was unperturbed, and on the next one, they did better. And even better on the one after that.

Their first year, they broke even. When Jimmy was saying goodbye to Chetaine in France, Robby was figuring out where to store all the supplies for the summer, and bitterly regretting how little he had to show for all the hard work for the year.

But again, Ben was optimistic. He was moving out of the residence and into a flat uptown—he had finished his degree, but was going to stick around campus for another year. He continued his various activities—both legal and illegal.

Ben didn't want to stay involved with the business—he was happy to front the capital, but he wanted Robby and a partner to run the business, with a handsome profit share.

"He is quite a character, Jimmy. And this year, we should make some real money. But my studies are suffering, and I have a couple of other two side projects. It would be worth your while. Help a brother out, and help me run this thing for the next six months?"

Max was going back to France for one last hurrah. Although Jimmy was tempted to join him again, he was aware that another season in France could not possibly compare with the time he had. He had a backup plan in his mind... but Lauren was in Stellenbosch, and he now knew he had to go there and be close to her. He didn't have much of a plan beyond that...

But it was enough reason for him to consider it.

It turned out to be a great idea. Jimmy didn't warm to Ben—he felt he was too smooth, too fast-talking. But Robby didn't seem to share his reservations. Once they flung themselves into the maelstrom of catering to the Stellenbosch student body… there was no turning back.

They worked their asses off. They had a company credit card; they each earned a small salary and they had a blast. Profit share would be the end of varsity season, and according to Robby, who also did the books, they would do well.

It was an interesting experience for Jimmy. As maître d in France, he had become used to being accorded with a level of deference by the customers. Maybe because it was such an iconic and popular restaurant, maybe because he held a degree of power in the sense of who was allowed to the diner last minute. Maybe just because the price point and level of the clientele were of that nature, similar to what he had experienced working at Max's.

Catering for academics and students, however, was a whole different ball game. He was mostly treated as being invisible, and that would have been fine in itself. What irked him was the rough arrogance in both groups. In terms of the students, it stemmed from their mostly white upper-class privilege—and with the academic body, an intellectual snobbery that permeated their every interaction.

It fed into his demons—knowing that, in a different life, he would be one of those privileged assholes. And being both glad he wasn't, and envious that he wasn't. Some nights, as he and Robby had a drink (or three) after all had been said and done and they had packed up the last of their equipment and stocks… they reflected on the absurdity of it all.

Robby could party—but it wasn't a habit with him. When they weren't working, he liked to unwind with a good book—which, in his case, was business, tech and futurist non-fiction. They shared a flat on the outskirts of town, and with Robby's influence, Jimmy found himself reading the books when Robby was done. They had great conversations, and Jimmy found that he was inspired by Robby's clear view of the future.

Robby was always working on a business plan to import those earbuds. He was constantly Skyping with Gretha from Denmark—they had decided to just be friends after their hot summer, but they seemed to enjoy working on this dream together.

"Another 18 months here to finish the degree, bud. By that time, one of these business plans must lead to something. I'm sure of it."

"You are a hustler, that's for sure. Robby, don't you think you're spreading yourself too thin?"

"Maybe. But hey, what's the worst that could happen? Only one life, right?"

Jimmy was inspired. His plan was still to come back to Stellenbosch as a student. The only problem was: He would be a junior, a first year student to Robby and Lauren's third-year status. They would be gone a year later, and he would still have a few to go. Maybe he had missed the boat already? Couldn't he learn more from all these other books that Robby was reading? Maybe he should follow Robby's example, and look for more side hustles.

A further complication was Lauren. He had reached out to her when he arrived in town, and they had had a coffee. It was, however, super awkward. She asked to meet him at a spot on the way out of town, and he was sure it was so she wouldn't be seen by gossipers.

She was uncomfortable the whole time. He tried to put her at ease, and he couldn't figure out what the problem was.

Finally, he said, "L, we're just two old friends having a coffee. Why are you so on edge?"

He was rewarded with the old Lauren smile, and she relaxed. "We both know that's not true, Jimmy."

"So, you still have feelings for me."

"Of course. But I'm with Jacques now."

"The guy is not what you think he is, Lauren."

And now the old Lauren anger flashed back. "I know he can be... arrogant sometimes. But mostly he is incredibly courteous to everyone, and he has ambition. And direction."

It was his turn to be incensed. "What? Not like me?"

"I didn't say that. It's just... he has a plan for his life, and he wants me to be a part of it."

"And what's your plan, Lauren? After you finish your degree here, what will you do?"

He could tell the question hit a nerve. She looked away for a while, then said, without meeting his eyes, "It's important to plan, right? But maybe it's also ok to change those plans if the right opportunity comes along..."

He waited, but she said no more about it. Then she turned the tables on him.

"And you, Jimmy? Do you have a plan?"

"Sure. We started a business, and hopefully it will do well. I hope to enroll for my commerce degree here next year."

He thought she would be glad about this news. But her eyes just clouded over further. "I hope you aren't coming here for me."

"No," he said a bit too quickly. "I want to come here for me—get that degree my old man was always on about, run the business, then eventually get rich."

"Why just get rich? Don't you want to make a difference in the world?" This was her old track and familiar territory. They had had this argument before.

"Sure. But can't I do both?"

"I guess. But motivation is important. Jacques and I want to go out into the world... after studies, we could really go help people, you know?"

"Just be sure he isn't just telling you what he thinks you want to hear, Lauren." He knew it was a mistake as soon as she said it.

She called for the bill, but he insisted on paying it.

After that, she ignored his calls.

Eventually, he decided to throw himself into the company, and the work.

It was the night of the Intervarsity Ball, late July. They had catered the 300 people event in the town hall—and, of course, Lauren was there. Once again resplendent in an elegant black dress, and as ever, with Jacques by her side.

There was no way to avoid them, of course. It was a busy night, they had a better than usual budget, and a bigger than average crowd.

They had brought in a few extra hands, and Jimmy and Robby found themselves spinning. But this is where they liked to live, and it was only toward the end of the evening that he took a breather. Deserts had been served and almost everyone was on the dance floor.

This was the last big event they had booked—after Intervarsity, there were one or two small gigs, but this was it for the varsity season. The profits were looking good but not as good as they had hoped. Maybe they could pick things up with some work outside of the student contacts.

Over the last 18 months, Jimmy had also occasionally run into Sam. At the restaurant in Franschhoek, in Oudtshoorn at Uncle Joe's wedding... and around Stellenbosch. Sam was also enrolled there, although he didn't do much studying.

Their relationship had warmed considerably since school days. Sam's career was going well, but he was always interested in Jimmy's adventures.

They now stood talking at the door to the kitchen, while Jimmy kept an eye on things.

"Jimmy, I tell you, you have the life man. All these awesome places... all the people you met..."

"You have no idea, Sam. It's been great. But you also have it good. A full rugby scholarship to study here and you are starting to make the Stormers junior team. I read the news. Well done bud."

Sam shook his head. "I do love it, Jimmy. The game, I mean. It's my destiny, I suppose. But sometimes I wish I had your options."

"It's funny, isn't it? You want my life; I wouldn't mind yours." Jimmy looked over the dancefloor, and Sam followed his gaze.

"Lauren? I would let it go, man. Small town dudes like us can't compete with a guy like Jacques Jardine."

"Thanks for that, Sam. Oh, and here she comes."

Her cheeks were flushed, and he wondered whether it was from the dancing or too much champagne. Her eyes were steady though, and her voice didn't slur. The dancing, then. He had to admit, she looked amazing.

"Hello boys. Is this weird?"

"Nah," they both said, and burst out laughing. "L, always good to see you," said Sam. "But I need to get back to my date." And he disappeared.

Lauren turned to Jimmy, and said, "Jacques is having a few shots with his buddies. He is off to Oxford next week."

"So?"

"Dance with me." Her eyes were inviting. Maybe she had had a few after all?

Jimmy shook his head, old emotions stirring. "A, I am working. B, I've seen you move. The Stellenbosch scene has taught you some moves I can't match."

She smiled that old smile and took his hand. She cast down her eyes and said softly, "Please, Jimmy. Please…"

This was different from the last time they spoke. "What's up, Lauren?"

"Jimmy, I'm going with him. To Oxford."

That did take him by surprise.

"What about your studies here? I mean… are they allowing you to transfer…?"

"No, of course not. I'll come back and continue in a year. But Jacques wants me with him—it might be a grand adventure. I'll take a year off, we'll go see Europe for a few weeks, then I could maybe… I don't know, get a job while…"

He looked her in the eyes. "Get a job as a waitress? In Oxford? Sure."

"Jimmy, I don't want you to think…"

"Think that you're full of shit? All that talk of never being your mother—of having your own career, of not being dependent on a guy? Out the window the moment the first charming… and rich… dude comes along and asks you to give it all up."

She let go of his hand. "Jimmy, that's not fair. You wouldn't understand!" Some of the old fire came back into her eyes.

He straightened up. "Lauren, why tell me? We're ancient history. Look, I need to work."

Her eyes filled with tears. "I don't know. I just… wanted you to know…"

"If you are asking me to tell you that I think this is a good move, you know my answer. Why are you tethering yourself to him?"

"I'll come back to finish in a couple of years. I'm young. There's no rush. After Oxford, Jacques wants us to go volunteer with the Red Cross. Make a difference, you know."

She had definitely had a few, and for once, Jimmy was the dead sober one. Which gave him a lot of clarity. "Instead of finishing your studies, and making a real impact?"

"I don't need you judging me, Jimmy."

"Then why tell me?" he asked again.

She shrugged and looked away. "I don't know. I saw you here... and..."

"You know what I think? I think you know you're making a mistake. But somehow, telling me, provoking a fight, can help you justify it to yourself. I might not have Jacques's money, or education, or a fucking Rhodes Scholarship... but I know that I'm not a fraud."

"This was a mistake," she said. And her eyes glimmered with uncharacteristic tears. He wanted nothing more than to comfort her, but as he reached out, she shrugged away from him. Then she turned and ran into the crowd.

He stared after her for a moment, then went to the back. He busied himself with the admin of the evening. When he came out, later, the place had emptied as they were packing up.

Robby came up to him around 1 am. "I saw you talking to Lauren."

"Yep."

"Want to talk about it?"

"No."

"Want to go get absolutely unbelievably shitfaced?"

Robby always had the best ideas.

———

The hangover, of course, was even bigger than they expected. What made it worse, though, was a hard knock on their flat door.

It was Ben, and he was pissed.

"You two assholes left the van unlocked last night!" he screamed.

"Hold on Ben," said Robby. "Pretty sure it's all good… locked up in the garage…"

Ben was pacing the room. "Take a shower, you two numbnuts. And then let's talk, it smells like a shebeen in here!"

Once they had cleaned themselves up and popped a couple of painkillers, the three of them sat down over a cup of coffee. Robby had gone down to the garage with Ben. They confirmed that the company van with all their supplies and catering equipment was missing.

They assured him they had left it safely locked. He was convinced they had gotten drunk and left it out in the open somewhere. The argument went nowhere… but at the end of it, their patron stormed out, and they were suddenly left with the realization that there was no van, no equipment, and no jobs.

"Shit, Jimmy. What a horrible 24 hours."

Jimmy took a deep swig of a glass of water. "Something feels off here, Robby. Outside of one or two smallish jobs, we don't have any further gigs booked, right?"

"Right…"

"After tonight, Ben was going to reconcile the books, pay us our share of the profit, and then put the equipment in storage until next year, right?"

"Yeah…"

"But all that stuff was insured, right?"

"I think so."

"So what if he arranged for the van and equipment to be stolen? I bet you he sold it to some shady character for dirt cheap, and now he's also claiming the insurance money."

"Jimmy, that's a bit of a stretch… I mean, I know you don't like Ben much, but…"

Jimmy wrinkled his nose. "Smells funny, Rob. He doesn't need to do profit share, he can claim the insurance, he walks away blaming us for negligence. Too neat."

Robby sighed and put on his shoes. "Sure. But how do we prove it? And to what point? I mean, either way, we're never working with this guy again."

Jimmy thought about it. He was pissed, but his buddy had a point. "Justice, I guess. Bastard shouldn't get away with it."

"Jimmy, my boy, his karma will catch him."

"Screw Karma." Jimmy was sure they had been done in—he always knew Ben was shifty. But the problem was, there was no way to prove it. They had no contract for their share of the profits, either.

Robby stood up and yawned. "In the meantime, I still need to get back to my studies for the final stretch. I feel bad—I got you into this, and we did get paid—but this is an awful end to our first business venture."

This gave Jimmy pause. "Our first business venture?"

"Sure. This was a bust—and there's a lesson there about contracts and partners, I'm sure. But don't you want to do it again? We'll be older and smarter."

Jimmy laughed. His mood was improving and his hangover was evaporating. "I guess. When did you think we'll do this?"

"With my brains and your mouth, bud. We'll take over the world. Just you wait and see. But let me finish my studies first. And I want to see where the earbuds thing goes. Gretha and I are close to finishing the business plan. But what about you, bud? Since your incentive for coming here is gone—where will you go now? Back to Europe?"

"Robby, my man… seeing as the girl I used to love has sold out, and I just worked my ass off for three months for very little payoff? Europe was fun, but now, I might just do something completely different."

"And what, pray tell, might that be?"

"My friend, glad you asked. I'm going to New Zealand."

S tan had kept in touch. Jimmy had to admit he was flattered having such an illustrious mate. At the wedding, people had scarcely believed him, until he showed them pictures.

The thing was, Stan was inspiring. Jimmy read his tweets and followed his career. Stan was one of the most disciplined people Jimmy had ever met. Even more so after he was back home and living his "actual" life. But there was something to be said for the way he just took a break from the spotlight.

The mystery, of course, was why Stan kept insisting he come to Christchurch. They had been great mates… but Jimmy suspected Stan had an ulterior motive, but he couldn't quite figure out what it was. Still, he was flattered, and Stan had also promised to take care of visas and paperwork if he came over.

So, in the first week of August 2015, Jimmy boarded a plane to Christchurch. He grabbed a Kiwi Experience backpacker bus and did a two-week tour down to Christchurch. It was glorious fun. Along the way, he skydived in Nelson with some British girls, did his first bungee jump in Queenstown, hiked a glacier, and had as much fun as his best nights in Austria or France. Once again, a combination of alcohol and horny backpackers helped him to forget about Lauren for a while.

It was late in the evening, mid-August 2015 when he rocked up at the bus station in Christchurch. While the other backpackers were being picked up by backpacker vans, his mate was waiting for him. The car was a sponsored German car, and that, unfortunately, gave the game away. He was surrounded by autograph seekers, and he dutifully signed away while waving at Jimmy.

"That's your ride?" exclaimed one of his newfound friends from the bus, a Brit called Dudley. "Dude, you've been holding out on us!"

Jimmy shrugged. "Hey, he likes his privacy."

Fred, a Canadian who had drunk him under the table twice in the last two weeks, asked, "What's the deal? Who is that guy?"

Dudley laughed. "Fred, you are truly a Philistine. That, my friend, like the sign on his sponsored car says—is Stan Wilson, the world's best rugby player, and the All-Blacks' scrum-half."

It was quite something. As it turned out, Stan was married with kids—his two months sabbatical in France was a time out from what was a life of enormous joy, but also a pleasure. Jimmy was welcomed into their home with open arms by Grace, Stan's wife. But Jimmy also sensed the tension around two small children and knew that he would have to be looking for his own digs pretty shortly.

Stan made good on his word. As a mega-celeb, and close to a demi-god in New Zealand, people fell all over themselves to help him out. A friend's flat was duly arranged (an ex-All-Black who was away playing rugby in Japan for the season, and his dog needed looking after). So, Jimmy found himself at a swanky pad in a great suburb of Christchurch, and his only real responsibility was to make sure that Rufus, the Golden Retriever, was fed and had regular walks. Good deal.

And, of course, a job. They had the talk over dinner the night before he moved out. For some reason, Stan loved to go eat pizza at a local pizza joint called Il Leone. The place was never busy but the pizzas were decent. He sure had a healthy appetite, and it was the third time they had come here since Jimmy had arrived. They were working their way through dinner when Stan spoke his mind.

"So, you don't want to be a waiter or a cook again? No more restaurant for you?" asked Stan, between mouthfuls.

Jimmy took a moment to admire how Grace skillfully handled both kids—they were only a year apart, and dinner was both early and messy when they went out like this. Maybe that was why they liked the place. There were not that many other patrons this early to bother.

"Yeah, I don't know. Hated the way the last gig panned out—it was my first 'entrepreneurial' venture, and we worked our asses off just to get shafted. If I am going to work for someone again, I might want to try something different."

"Like what? What else are you good at?"

"Good question. Numbers? I was a pretty ace at math and accounts in school. Pretty good at customer service as well, from being a waiter. What does that qualify me for?"

Stan Wilson laughed and had another sip of wine. He liked the good stuff, but never went past one glass on a weeknight. He sat back and looked around the place. "I bet you could do well beating this place into shape."

Jimmy looked around with a critical eye, and he suspected this was the reason Stan insisted he come to New Zealand. About 10 tables, the walls were busy with memorabilia and it had that slightly rustic (read dirty) look about it. The toilets were not that clean either. "With quite a bit of work, I suppose. It has good bones."

Stan laughed. "That it does. Been coming here since I was a kid. Since the old man retired and his kids gave it over to others to run, the standard has gone down. Pity." Then he shifted his attention back to the task at hand.

"Ok mate. You don't give me a lot to work on. I'm going to hook you up with my agent. He's going to find something for you to do."

The something turned out to be a job in the All Blacks Pty Ltd Merchandising department. One of the biggest brands in the world, the All Blacks had been the world champions for four years. They were hot favorites to win the Rugby World Cup, only a month or so away.

Stan was going to be pivotal in that quest along with the gladiatorial and talismanic captain Richie McCaw. Shirts, caps, mugs, flags… it was flying off the shelves, and not just in New Zealand, but internationally.

Jimmy worked as a gofer for the trade relations manager Mick. That meant he fetched stuff. Coffee, cars, people. He also drove Mick around to all his appointments, sometimes sat in to take notes.

Stan flew off with the team to England and started their march to another title. Jimmy felt time flying by. Mick was an asshole, but he was Jimmy's kind of an asshole and they got along really well. Mick was initially irritated that he had a South African kid who was a friend of Stan Wilson's. Jimmy's work ethic and proactive thinking impressed him quickly though. Pretty soon Jimmy had a desk and a computer, where he started to help with recording orders, doing contracts, and making appointments.

A begrudging appointment turned into a very productive relation-ship. And Mick had game. He knew how to read people, he did his homework, he was an ace at closing a deal. But he was horrible at admin, and Jimmy quickly became indispensable to him.

Jimmy actually enjoyed the work. It was office work for the most part—but the numbers had beauty to them. Each line item to each region with each margin told a story, and he found himself completely absorbed into the process.

Therefore he was completely taken by surprise when his cell phone (yes, he now had a cell phone) rang to hear Stan's voice.

"Hey my favorite Saffer," said Stan.

"Hey, bud. Wow, it's going well over there. I see we are playing you in the semi-finals on the weekend!"

"And you pretty much don't have a chance, mate. But it will still be a cracker of a game, we'll have to work for it."

Stan was right. Even though Jimmy loved the last few months in New Zealand, it was a horrible time to be a South African rugby supporter. South Africa, historically one of the world's best teams, had had a so-so last few seasons. That meant the coach, Heyneke Meyer, was under increasing pressure and started to make mistakes in team selection and playing style. It was a story as old as time, but the team had fallen to their greatest low in this world cup by being beaten, in extra time, by lowly Japan. A team who had never beaten anyone. Ever. But their wily coach Eddie Jones had caught the South African Springboks napping, arrogant and unprepared. It was a historic moment for Japan, an absolute low for South Africa.

But it had been a pool stages game—and South Africa managed to win all their other matches, beating Wales in a tight semi-final. Now, it was a face-off against the favorites and still unbeaten All Blacks. And no one was giving them a chance.

The Kiwis were generally very good about this kind of thing. Jimmy had taken quite a bit of ribbing from Mick and the crew at the office. With the big match coming up, the excitement was at a fever pitch. Jimmy always hoped the Springboks could pull off an upset— but he was also aware of how messy the politics and infighting was back home. The Kiwis were a tight, focused, and classy outfit. And they had Stan Wilson.

"Stan, are you calling me to give me shit? I've had enough from the lads over here."

"Au contraire, my young apprentice. This is an invitation. Come watch the World Cup Semi-final, maybe even the final. Be my guest."

Jimmy almost dropped the phone. "What are you talking about? You're halfway around the world... and... and..."

"Jimmy, this is my last season with the All Blacks. Win or lose, I am retiring after this tournament. Grace is flying up to come to be with me. The coach is allowing all the spouses to come for the last week. But I get two tickets—and she only needs one. Kids are too small to come. Still, they'll be staying with grandma and grandpa."

"Stan, I mean... that would be epic." It would be. Watching South Africa against the All Blacks in a World Cup Semi-final was every South African Schoolboys' ultimate dream. Well, maybe a World Cup Final. His dad had watched SA's famous victory at Ellis Park in 1995, 20 years ago...

He snapped back to reality. "I have a job! Mick. Commitments. You guys are killing it, you have no idea how busy we are..."

"I talked to Mick. He says as long as you take your laptop and put in a few hours each day, he's happy for you to come over. As long as you come back... you've impressed the hell out of him."

"Umm… well, I suppose then… hell yeah! I would love to! Absolutely love it!"

And that was the wonderful thing about being mates with Stan Wilson.

With Mick's begrudging blessing ("You SAFFER pissant kids have all the luck!") and the jeers and cheers from the rest, he jumped on the plane with Grace and some of the other All Black WAGS (Wives and Girlfriends). They were a jolly bunch, and the almost 24-hour journey went by quickly. Jimmy made himself useful by carting along luggage, sorting out lost tickets, and making nice. He became the WAG mascot, and he was thankful that the overnight revelry on the plane did not turn flirtier.

London was curiously muted in terms of World Cup fever. Back in Christchurch, it was the main topic of conversation. In England, where soccer reigned supreme and the England rugby team had ignominiously been knocked out in the group stages, people seemed not very interested.

That was, of course, until one arrived at the All Blacks' hotel in West Kensington. Then you knew there was a craze going on. There were hundreds of fans lurking outside the grounds hoping for a peek of their heroes.

Jimmy had met some of the players before, of course. They were an amazing group of guys. Jimmy would always be a patriot, and a lover and supporter of the Springboks. It had to be said, though, that this was a special bunch. Richie McCaw and Stan were the two superstars—but they were both humble and approachable off the field, liked to have a beer with the boys, and treated everyone with respect.

It was especially hard not to like Richie McCaw. He was an absolute bastard and menace on the field, and now, thinking back on their time in France, Jimmy understood why Stan would always come to his defense. Off the field, a consummate gentleman and professional. The best player of his generation, some said.

Jimmy found himself in two minds on the day of the final. They did not get to see the players that morning, as the coach had them fully focused on the task at hand. Jimmy put on his Springbok supporter's jersey, but felt, for the first time in his life, a conflict around the jersey.

He knew he would always be a South African supporter. He didn't know any of those guys, they were not playing well and it was hard to face up to the friendly ribbing from the All Blacks. They gave him stick for everything from playing style, the ridiculous racial politics that persisted and the overall dilution of what used to be a strong playing rivalry.

On the other hand, these Kiwis had taken him in. They were enormously gracious (if a touch condescending) and their star player was one of his best friends.

He decided to leave the WAGS behind. At breakfast, they all gave him a lot of stick about his jersey, but it was mostly in good cheer. Still, there was the serious business of war for a World Cup to attend to. He also felt like he needed to go find his own tribe.

The game was only due to start at 4 pm at the iconic stadium of Twickenham. Jimmy had heard there was going to be a large contingent of South African supporters at the game. Some of them who had flown in on tours, but a good many were now permanent residents in England. They were mostly white South Africans that did not like the way the country was being run in the post-apartheid era, and had decided to look for more Caucasian-friendly environments.

The famous London subway system (the "tube") seemed like a good idea. And he had heard there were a good many bars down in Richmond, the closest subway station to Twickenham. Around 11 am, he jumped on the tube at West Kensington, and what followed was like a build-up of excitement.

There were eight stops between West Kensington and Richmond. There were the normal unsmiling subway faces on the semi-deserted train for the first minute, but all hell broke loose when they stopped at Barons Court. This was an area that was rife with expats from South Africa and the Antipodeans. Instantly, the train was filled with fans in green and gold and black. A couple of minutes later, at Hammersmith, which was another big junction, the tube filled to the brim. It was only 11.30 am, but beers were being cracked open, singing was breaking out and a lot of "Duane Vermeulen is going to take you guys down!" was heard.

Jimmy soaked it all in. It all felt slightly odd—the Springbok supporters were, by and large, a homogenous group of large men and petite women. But beyond that, they were very much in the mold of the lurking giants that were all over the Stellenbosch campus. Or the more country and English language-challenged bunch from Oudtshoorn. And there were even those that represented the British-influenced sophisticates from Bishops and the Cape Town southern suburbs.

It was his tribe, and it wasn't. His time in France, Austria, and New Zealand had changed him, he realized. He felt himself observing but not being part, and not quite knowing how to engage… and then a huge blond guy stuck a beer in his hand, and pulled him into their group. They were a bunch of lads that lived together in a common dig in Earls Court. They were not much older than him, but they were all accountants, teachers, and techies that had decided to spend their twenties and make their careers in London. They were fun, they were jovial, and he found himself relaxing and leaning into the easy camaraderie of sports lovers.

He decided to go with the truth—and his new friends, by the time they hit Richmond and piled out of the train, were all equally delighted to be hanging out with the main enemy's South African friend, but also quite livid about his divided loyalties. Their merry band got stuck into the Angel and Crown, a traditional English pub a few minutes from the station. The place was already going nuts with supporters from all sides. On the third beer (chased down with a shot of tequila) the whole place was alternately singing the South African national anthem and demonstrating the Haka. Huge masses of alcohol were consumed.

It was a great warm-up—and they decided to take the walk up to the stadium to find their seats around 2.30 pm. The flow of people had already started—and suddenly, Jimmy heard a familiar voice!

"Jimmy?"

He turned around—it was Sam!

"Sam! Wow! What are you doing here?" He hugged his old rival. Was it possible that he had grown even bigger in the last few months? He was now a giant—and pure muscle. Jimmy had seen his parents at their school games, so he recognized his dad.

"My dad put together a group of supporters for the game, Jimmy. We have had about 40 guys here since last week—it's been so much fun. Come, walk with us."

Jimmy's new gang had stopped to wait, and the guys now shouted. "Jimmy, it's cool. Catch you after the game. We recognize Sam the man. Hang out with your other celebrity friends." And the singing drunken band continued on their way... never to be seen again.

They started walking, Sam's dad preoccupied with a conversation with someone else who looked vaguely familiar. Jimmy had a look at their group—and he realized he was in the company of a whole bunch of players from the previous generation. He thought he recognized Rob Louw, Michael du Plessis. He knew he recognized Danie Gerber! Wow, this was incredible—these were some of the Springbok legends.

"This is quite a tour group, Sam."

"Yeah. It's quite something—some of these guys have seen it all, Jimmy. I feel quite privileged to have come along."

Jimmy looked at Sam. "And the pressure?"

Sam sighed. "Of course. Things are happening for me. I do love it, but…"

Jimmy nodded. "I've been reading about you in the papers. You've got some game time with the Stormers Franchise this year, impressing a few pundits. Some people are saying you were unlucky not to make the Springbok squad for the tournament."

Sam nodded. "Including my dad. But look, I'm only 20 still. Duane Vermeulen, Francois Louw, Heinrich Brussow—all guys that are still in the mix ahead of me in the loosies, not to mention Kolisi. Nah, small steps. But I think I'll get there."

Jimmy smiled. "I think you will, bud. Maybe the next cycle. Man, what do you think about today's game?"

Sam countered with another question. "I know you keep your stuff private, Jimmy—but I saw your uncle a few weeks ago, and he told me you have been hanging out with Stan Wilson and the All Blacks? Honestly, WTF?"

"Yeah, now that is a great story. Whoa, there's the stadium!"

Twickenham is majestic. One of the world's iconic old rugby stadiums, it was a fortress for the Roses, the English national team. Their fortunes, like the Springboks, had waned after several years at the very top in the mid-2000s… and there were sure to be heads to roll after this disastrous World Cup. Fans and administrators are not very forgiving, no matter what the country. Jimmy felt for the coach—but they took the credit when things went well, they took the fall when they weren't. That was the game.

Today, however, the grande dame of English Rugby played host to the age-old rivalry between Springbok and All Black. Jimmy said goodbye to Sam and his group as they went to their separate seating areas. This time, it was with a firm commitment to regroup later at a restaurant in Hammersmith, where they were staying.

He reunited with the WAGS and felt the nervousness settle in on him. His heart hoped that the Springboks could overcome their recent troubles and the humiliation of the loss to Japan. But his head spoke more clearly, especially given what he knew about the All Black team. They had everything going for them—momentum, skill, experience, talent. But the most important thing was humility. They respected the jersey and the process. Walking with Sam and overhearing the talk among South Africa's yesteryear legends, there was still a disquieting arrogance among his own. As if there was a divine right to victory and excellence, without giving thought to the realities of the modern game.

His fears proved to be quite correct. For 55 or so tense minutes, well into the second half, the Springboks competed and even led with a brutal but unimaginative style of rugby, where they forced the All Blacks back, holding onto the ball and eked out points. But there was always an inevitability to the flow as if it was all holding back a massive wave… and it was just a matter of time before it spilled over. And, of course, watching from the stands, surrounded by Kiwis, it was with equal dismay and delight that Jimmy watched Stan Wilson slot all the important kicks to draw his team ahead—and hold on to an agonizingly close 20-18 win.

With the final whistle, the Kiwis around him breathed a sigh of relief and were equally differential in congratulating him- as a proxy for the entire nation of South Africa—on a tight game and renewed pride.

Still, he was glad to leave them to their delirious celebrating. He made his way, albeit slowly, to Hammersmith. The queues were long and a mixture of dejected green jerseys and loud and boisterous All Black ones, with a smattering of neutral supporters thrown in.

He soaked it all in. He shared the dismay—but then again, he was not surprised, and he felt imminently privileged to be there at all. He anchored that feeling as he was crowded into the train from Richmond, and was glad to step out onto the platform some 20 minutes later.

The restaurant in Hammersmith where Sam and his gang were congregating, was the William Morris, located just outside of the station. It was another old British pub, and it was packed to the rafters.

With difficulty, he made his way to the bar and ordered a beer. The place was heaving, but given the average size of the crowd in Sam's group, it was hard to miss them. The barman told him to go upstairs to the private area, they had booked that off.

The tour group was in a dejected space. Their numbers had dwindled from the group that had been walking up to the rugby. Sam was there, but also subdued. Rugby supporters, especially South African ones, took losses like these very seriously. Most of the tour group had gone back to the hotel to nurse their wounds, Sam said. They would bounce back tomorrow, there was still a week left in the tour. Now, much like 1999, they would watch the Springboks compete for third place against Argentina, while other teams contested the big show.

Jimmy and Sam shared a quiet drink when his phone buzzed. He had a look at his WhatsApp—and smiled.

"What's so funny?" asked Sam.

"Bud, I have been invited to dinner. And it feels kind of ironic. It's good to see you, but this party is pretty much a downer."

"Stick around, Jimmy. You'll be glad you did."

It was a strange thing, energy. Maybe it was the twinkle in Sam's eye. Maybe it was just a sort of sixth sense. But suddenly, the air in the room changed, and Jimmy knew.

He turned around, and there she was.

25

L auren wasn't quite sure when she had lost herself. It was a slow seduction. It was not Jacques's ability in bed, which was significant (but somehow still fell short of her lovemaking with Jimmy—she told herself it was because he had been her first love). No, it was the slow seduction of power, and status, and the opportunities those presented.

She had set off in her first year full of high intentions of independence, a professional career, and a life of significance. She maintained her high grades for both those first two years. But slowly, a second life revealed itself to her. It was the life of the Stellenbosch elite. The women were smart, beautiful, and educated. They also rarely worked, preferring to fade into professional obscurity by their late twenties and focus on raising broad-shouldered boys and precocious girls.

The men would study law, accounting, and business. They would go do articles, work for big firms, eking their way in the world. By the time they hit their late twenties or early thirties, however, they would gravitate back to the family business. Whether that be working in one of the many blue-chip Afrikaner controlled wine distribution companies, returning to the actual family estate to run it, or some of the various other national companies headquartered in the valley... they would settle down with their beautiful talented wives. Then they would start the transition of power from their fathers, who would start to spend more time at the holiday house on the cliffs in Hermanus. And the cycle would continue.

The wives were expected to turn a blind eye to roving eyes and marital indiscretions—as long as these were done in brothels in the city (Cape Town) or on trips abroad. For observing this unspoken code of discretion, the men were expected to keep it tidy close to home, treat their wives with respect and deference in public, and no one aired their dirty laundry.

Jacques had, with his typical wit and dry humor, and a touch of cynicism told her these tales and opened her eyes to the world he inhabited. He felt like a kindred spirit—determined to make his own way in the world, not be another cliché in the valley, and he wanted her to join his journey. In their one and a half years at Stellenbosch, she met the most powerful men and women (and their sons and daughters) in the region. Academics, businessmen, sportsmen. Their heirs apparent and the women that would marry them.

And yet, because Jacques held this belief and shared it, they considered themselves outsiders. Rebels to the flow and they would play the game, but only until it was time. He wanted to leave the insular thoughts and confines of Stellenbosch—and go make a difference. She was attracted to his talent and his work ethic, and it was no surprise when he did receive the Rhodes Scholarship. By this time, she had also known that she did not want to let him go on this adventure alone. After all, was it not their adventure?

The first snag was transferring to Oxford. While her grades had been exemplary, they were not good enough to merit her own scholarship. She applied for a transfer, but this too, was denied. Her specific field of bio-genetics was a highly competitive cluster in Oxford and they simply had no space for her.

So, she had been left with a choice—stay and finish, or go with Jacques and defer her studies. The way he sold the adventure... just seemed incredibly romantic and filled with purpose. The University assured her that would not be a problem. So finally, she made her choice. Jacques was ecstatic.

She was, of course, aware of Jimmy's presence on campus those last months. Especially the night of the dance—she could see him working the circuit, and she was so proud of him in a way. She also felt the strong need to explain herself. That she was the same person, just making some new decisions.

His reaction had not surprised her, but it still hurt. It was as if she wanted that judgment from him. As if it was a judgment she held against herself, and no one else was calling her on it. Which was the truth, she supposed. Her Stellenbosch friends, she realized, all were completely overcome with jealousy. They all were dating men like Jacques—and they all felt that she was well on her way to living the dream. Lee, her mother... they were all for it.

The dream, of course, was the two kids and the home on a wine farm. But she was convinced that would not be them. After a year helping solve malnutrition in third world countries, they would go live and work in London, Dubai, New York. She would complete her studies at a top school somewhere and do ground-breaking medical research, and he would work for one of the top firms on Fleet Street, Wall Street, or Hong Kong Island.

The adventure started out well, too. The first couple of months they settled into a small flat in Oxford. They took a few days to explore London, and on the weekend, they would hire a car and go tripping around England, visiting Land's End, the Lake District, and historic places like Stonehenge. It was all glorious fun at the beginning.

But it changed quickly. Jacques threw himself into his studies and quickly assimilated into the crowd of Rhodes Scholars from all over the world. Lauren could not help but feel intimidated by these highly accomplished talents. And introducing herself as "the girlfriend that did not complete her studies, currently sitting around in the flat waiting for Jacques" got old quickly.

Oxford itself was not interested in co-opting her until a spot opened up... and it seemed increasingly unlikely. She considered wait-ressing to keep busy—but Jacques flatly refused.

"I will look after you, L. I do not want my girlfriend to be serving these pompous Englishman- they get drunk like everyone else, and I would hate to punch some idiot in the face for pinching your ass."

So that idea was let go. She didn't like that Jacques now had a certain power of money over her. She had limited savings but it really didn't go far in the UK, and she tried to suppress her resentment at not having control over her own finances. She was allowed some credits at Stellenbosch through correspondence learning. However, she missed the physical interaction of the classroom, and she still had to go back for the main courses.

Jacques was having the time of his life. They slipped into a routine where she would cook him dinner most nights (like a dutiful house-wife). She watched stupid British soap operas like Coronation Street, and she felt herself start to dumb down and become whiney. They started to have occasional arguments, mostly around the same theme—she would like to go out and work, but he could provide for her, and they spun around without resolution.

She was saved by her new best friend, Daniella.

Now Daniella, as Italians go, did not fit the stereotypical model. She was neither luscious nor loud, neither tall nor glamorous. She was short, plain, and blonde. And she had the thickest glasses Lauren had ever seen.

She was a Rhodes Scholar from Rome, a geneticist, and as far as Lauren was concerned, a total rock star. There were a few women in the Rhodes Scholars crowd—but, Lauren found, the others were all dismissive and judgmental of Lauren, and a bit too involved in their own ambitions.

Daniella was different. She was both kind and forthright, and she instinctively understood Lauren. That beyond the physical beauty and the consequent presupposed trophy girlfriend status, there was a frus-trating talent that needed an outlet.

She was, in that way, smart people often were, prone to bad verbal communication. As in saying things that were offensive without knowing it, and sometimes being too honest. But Lauren liked that about her. And the feeling was mutual.

It happened at one of the Rhodes Scholar mixers, six weeks after their arrival. Lauren had drifted away from the main conversation. She was out on the porch of the hotel when Daniella approached her.

"How do you spend your days, Bella?"

Lauren was taken aback. Up to that point, she had hardly spoken to Daniella. The other girls had made it clear that they all thought her to be a dyke. Was she hitting on her?

"I take long walks... I read, I guess... Why do you ask?"

Daniella put her hand on Lauren's arm, and it made her start. "I am not... as the Americans say... hitting on you if that is your concern. I am merely interested, for my own reasons."

The hand fell away, and they looked at each other for a moment. "What reasons are those?"

"Curiosity. You seem out of place. Things that are out of place intrigue me. Like a chromosome that creates a small body with big feet."

Lauren laughed. "I have never heard that before. But yes, I suppose..."

She felt herself open up to Daniella. It was the first person since she had arrived that seemed really interested in her. She talked of her boredom, her frustration, and her mixed feelings about the Oxford adventure.

Daniella listened patiently. And, when Lauren had vomited her life story to completion, she waded in with an unexpected response—and offer:

"I am a geneticist, Lauren. I like to study how bodies are constructed down to their molecular level. I would like to study you—see how we can grow you, adapt you to this hostile environment. And I would like to study you in relation to your environment as we inject new variables."

It was kind of creepy. Still, Lauren was amused. "Ok, I'll bite. Study me? How?"

"By putting you to work."

The next day, she found herself employed as Daniella Liprini's research assistant.

It was amazing- genetic studies at a Doctoral level. For September, Lauren became completely immersed in subject matters that were above her understanding. She took up the challenge and found herself loving it. She was aware that she was occupying a role that was meant for some actual Oxford Undergraduate. She was truly thankful that Daniella was probably breaking the rules somewhere.

On the other hand, it became clear that Daniella was something special. The faculty let her go about her business. As Lauren got to know her, she came to understand that she was neither a lesbian nor a weirdo. She was simply what people would describe on the spectrum, i.e., hints of autism, but socially functioning if not an adept. And her work was next level! She was fully engaged in a thesis exploring the underlying vulnerability of the human genome to strains of flu transmitted from animals. There was talk—lots of it—that she would receive even further grants if Oxford could convince her to stay on after her Masters.

So, Lauren became her confidant and acolyte. Daniella was on a generous grant, and she paid Lauren a handsome salary (under the table, of course). Lauren was technically on a prolonged tourist visa. The hours were long, the tasks demanding, the rewards elusive. But she loved it!

Jacques was not supportive at all. He started to find her to not be at home ready with a warm meal some nights. She would sometimes be up reading or working after he wanted to go to bed. They started to argue. He was concerned that the faculty would inevitably find out she was working illegally, and it would reflect badly on him.

It didn't help, she mused, that he was not performing well in his studies. His submissions had not been well received so far. He was not attaining the same academic heights as his Rhodes Scholar peers. She had also seen him up some nights, livid at what he perceived were injustices around his professors 'losing' his submissions, and being penalized for the late entries. A pattern started to emerge of Jacques believing the world was against him… and he began to change.

As September melded into October, things came to a head.

It was another late Friday night with Daniella, excitedly pulling apart prior research on the novel Coronavirus over endless expressos. But the real kicker was, just before she left, Daniella pushed an envelope into her hand.

"What's this?" she asked.

"It's a transfer application. I spoke to some people about you,

Bella. And you might find if you now applied for your Stellenbosch credits to be accepted here, they might be more... accepting."

Lauren opened the envelope, disbelieving. "But I was told... I couldn't..."

"Ah it's all such SHIT!" said Daniella, waving her hands in an uncharacteristic dramatic style. "This place trades on a very shaky mix of former glory and current performance. Do not get me wrong—it is still one of the best schools in the world, but they know they need to produce content and leaders regularly or lose their standing. I am one of those people—so, they listen to me."

"Daniella... thank you... but I can hardly afford..."

"All taken care of, my dear. As long as you sell your soul to me, of course." She laughed. That was the one thing that got to Lauren—Daniella's laugh was like a witch's cackle. Luckily, it was an infrequent occurrence.

"What do you mean?"

"I mean, they will give you credit—and waive your class fees. As long as you pass your subjects with honors, and... I deliver the thesis on time."

Lauren shook her head. "Daniella... this is too much. I mean, I can't..."

"Pooh. Can't what? You follow that boy here—he does nothing for you. Treats you like his exotic house pet. No, you are better than that. We are women of the future. We must be bold! We must excel! I did not know if coming here was a good idea for me... but now, I know that part of my purpose is to make sure you fulfill your potential."

She sat down, in a daze. "I don't know what to say."

Daniella smiled and patted her hand. "Say Grazi, and go to that awful boyfriend of yours. Maybe you can celebrate in style. I will see you on Monday, ok? Now go enjoy the weekend, your team might even win that game you are all obsessing about!"

She arrived home well after midnight. She was delighted to see that Jacques was still awake. He was under tremendous pressure. His first round of exams had proved tougher than expected, and for the first time in his life, his grades fell short of his expectations.

She threw her coat over the couch and kissed him on the head. He murmured a greeting, fixated on something on his computer screen.

"Jacques? I have something big to tell you. I think it will be good for us."

In a way that happened more often these days, he appeared not to have heard, and said, "My parents are considering offers for the farm."

"Oh." She knew that his folks planned for him to come back and run it one day… so this was different.

"My father hurt his back again. My mother wants him to take it easy… and there are some buyers." He looked up at her, a question in his eyes.

Since they had come to Oxford, this had come up before.

"They are manipulating you, Jacques. We have our own plans, remember?"

He stood up and started pacing their tiny apartment. "I know. But it would be a disaster if they sold. The wine industry is doing incredibly well, and there are good offers on the table."

"So let them sell it. It frees you to do what you want, right?" She felt herself pushing now. Danger signals told her to stop, but she ignored them.

He stopped pacing and faced her. He had an ugly scowl on his face. This, also, had become more frequent over the last months. "This experience has not been all I had hoped for. I'm starting to think it's a good idea to go back when this semester is done."

"And not finish!?" She was amazed at this.

"I am in danger of not qualifying to proceed anyway."

She needed to be careful here. "You really are thinking of going back?"

"Well yes. I could go run the farm—you could go back and finish your studies, and we could…"

"Be like every other Stellenbosch couple? I thought we rejected all that."

"Sure. But things change, don't they?"

Lauren had heard him speak in this way before, especially of late. The Jacques Jardine that she had fallen in love with—the confident, assured if a somewhat entitled heir to a vineyard empire—had whittled away here in Oxford. Away from the sycophants that fawned over his every word, surrounded by people as talented and accomplished as he was—he had diminished, not grown. Until now, she hadn't taken him seriously.

She had to admit that spending all the time with Daniella had become a bit of an escape. The petulant whining has become a more regular fixture of their interactions—and with that, their intimacy had become less. With every substandard test result or moderator criticism, he became broodier and more frustrated. He also became more jealous of her time, and that, strangely, started to push her away.

His next words reinforced that feeling.

"And I don't like you spending so much time with that dyke. I know it's your 'job'…" She hated the way he always said it in a way that detracted from the work she was doing. It was as if the fact that she was being paid under the table made it any less valid. It was a subtle but consistent slur that he employed of late, and she decided enough was enough.

"Jacques, I followed you to England. I did not take any work that could be seen as beneath the girlfriend of the great Jacques Jardine. But seriously? I am helping probably the next woman to win a Nobel Prize for science to further her work! What could possibly be more rewarding than that?"

"Don't you get it, L? She is fucking with you. Fucking with us. That little bitch is running her own little experiment on us, like rats in a cage. Keep you busy with the so-called work, while undermining me with the faculty. Oh yes—I also know people, and she has been whispering in some ears that the work I deliver is not my own."

She could hardly believe her ears. "Jacques, listen to yourself. You are not only completely demeaning what I do, but you are not trying to make out as if it's all a big sham to mess with your head and career. Honestly?" She felt close to tears. She wanted to tell him about her opportunity to further study. But now they were fighting, and the opportunity just didn't seem right. Daniella was 18 months away from finishing her thesis—so that would mean she would stay here for at least that long. That would allow Lauren to also finish her degree and maybe study Honors. Maybe even Masters. Possibly Ph.D. The world was her oyster too!

But he was having none of it. "I don't like her. And I don't like the influence she has on you."

"Well, you are just going to have to get over that, don't you," she said, defiantly. They glared at each other, as they have many times in the last months.

Then he shook his head as if coming out of a daze. "Yeah, I know it sounds crazy."

And suddenly, he felt like his old self. "You know what we need? To get out of this place. This weekend is the big game at Twickenham. You know I am big mates with Willie—he has arranged a couple of tickets for us."

Lauren was still angry, but she thought about it. Maybe going would be a great thing—and she could tell him about Daniella's offer when he was in a better mood. If the Springboks won, she could sell him Eskimo ice for God's sake. She knew how this went.

"Come on, pretty bird. We'll do some sightseeing... ride the London eye... go to the market... you love that stuff."

He made a compelling argument. So, she let herself be swayed. She had lost her appetite for rugby along with Jimmy's shoulder dislocation in high school—but at the end of the day, there was no getting away from it either at Stellenbosch or in South Africa. And this was the Springboks and All Blacks at the World Cup! It was a once-in-a-lifetime opportunity to witness history.

"Forgive me, buttercup?"

She kissed him on the lips. There was a lot of conversation left... but she had become good at pushing the thoughts to the back. She smiled and said, "With a bribe like that, you betcha. When do we leave?"

They caught the morning train down to London and soaked up the atmosphere. There was tight security around the Springboks hotel, but they were snuck through the fans to meet with Willie le Roux, the

Springbok fullback. He left the breakfast table where the rest of the team were sitting to come over to give them their tickets. The banter was short—The tension could be cut like a knife through hot butter.

They wished him well, and spent the rest of the morning walking on the banks of the River Thames. They visited the Burrows Market, snapped pics at Tower Bridge, and took a ride on the London Eye.

For Lauren, it was wonderful. They had spent a few days in London at the start of their adventure, but since then it has been all Oxford. It felt like an escape from the tension between them, and Jacques seemed back to his old charming self. She was afraid to break the mood by telling him about her news, knowing that it would probably not be received well. No, she would wait… but then, she realized, she was just fooling herself. The Springboks would probably lose—and then, she could definitely not broach the subject.

She didn't have to wait even that long for his mood to change.

It started when he checked his phone for messages. He had been anxious about his latest paper… and they were sitting at a bar, having a pint, when he started swearing. He was doing a lot of that lately.

"What's wrong, Jacques?"

"Faculty professor has failed me on my paper. Says I completely misread the brief!"

He shook his head, and downed his beer, signaling for another. "I lost the physical paper, so I downloaded a copy off the internet… but it looks like the question on the campus server is different… I don't understand it… this is ridiculous…"

"Jacques, you're starting to talk crazy again…"

"I'm telling you, L. I've had lots of bad luck lately. I swear they are out to get me!"

"Who? Who is out to get you?" She almost dared him to blame Daniella.

He didn't rise to the bait. He simply said, "This shit isn't right. I might get flunked out after this."

"Can you forget about it? Just for today? We can figure it out on Monday… together?"

He smiled at her—briefly. "Sure." Then he downed another beer.

On the way to the game in the subway, a snide comment ("Not

only will you lose, but you will also lose badly") by a drunk Kiwi set Jacques off, and it almost led to a physical altercation. His mood now foul, they made their way to the stadium. There was much merriment and expectation, but they made their way to the seats quite quickly.

As they watched the seats fill up, and the pitch started to get ready with the pre-match ceremonies, she said, "Jacques, thanks for bringing me along. I really, really love you for including me."

He snorted. "Yeah, well. You always said you didn't like rugby. Maybe today will prove why."

"What's wrong, honey?"

"I need a drink, that's what wrong. Spent the whole day fucking sightseeing and now I'm thirsty."

Lauren nodded and got up. This was the Jacques she had gotten used to. "Your wish is my command, sire. I will go get us some beers."

She left him staring at the pitch, and made her way to the crowded refreshment stations one level down.

She had just gotten in line when she felt a tap on her shoulder.

She turned around. "Sam!?"

She instinctively hugged him, surprising herself with how fiercely she clung to this familiar face. After a few moments, she let go. He was grinning when he saw her—but now he had a look of peculiar interest on his face.

"L? You ok?"

She felt raw emotion push up inside her. But she immediately put on a brave face. It would not be fair, in any context, to put her romantic troubles onto this boy—no, this man—who she had probably treated so badly in high school.

"I'm fine" she said, forcing a smile. "Just so happy to see you! Excited for the game?"

"Nervous. Ah, you're up." They had reached the front of the line.

She turned to the person filling up plastic cups with Heineken from the tap. "Two beers, please."

She turned back to Sam. "Yeah, it's not looking that good for us."

He nodded. "One always thinks the Springboks can pull a rabbit out of a hat. And sometimes we do. But these guys are at the top of their game, and we… Well, we lost to Japan didn't we…"

She brightened. "I'm just happy to be here, I guess. And it's so good to see you—man, you've gotten big!"

"Bulking up on Coach's instructions. I hope to make the team next year." He paused. "Your beers are ready to go."

She grabbed them and stepped out of line, and waited for Sam while he placed his order.

He came out with four beers and smiled. "For the lads. Listen, do you want to come to join us after? My dad would love to see you. We're a big tour group, lots of his buddies who are ex-Springboks."

She thought of Jacques in his foul mood. If they lost, it would get worse... but then again, maybe seeing some South African legends would cheer him up.

"Sure. Just give me the address."

She returned to her seat just in time for the national anthems. Jacques grunted thanks for the beer and drained his quickly. She hardly touched hers, so he had that as well.

The game was tight, with very little running. She, therefore, amused herself with people watching around the stadium—it was a colorful cacophony of green, Black, and white (many England supporters had held on to their tickets and came out to watch the big Southern Hemisphere show). Jacques seemed happy, he struck up a conversation based on stats and past matchups with the guy next to him.

About 30 minutes in, the beers were both drained and she went for another round. By the time the halftime whistle blew, Jacques had blown through four beers. She could tell he was starting to feel it. He excused himself to go to the loo, and she found herself sitting alone.

She reflected on that feeling. Daniella had offered her an amazing opportunity and great stimulus. But beyond that patronage and friendship, she truly felt alone here. She missed South Africa, and Stellenbosch, and her friends.

She looked around at all the Springbok fans. It was truly special to be here, in this moment. And yet, she didn't feel happy.

Jacques returned, and started on another beer he had brought. "Game is getting going again. Come on BOKKEEE!!!"

It was among the more horrible 40 minutes of Lauren's life. She

OFFSIDES

kept quiet as the game slipped away from their team. Jacques was like a different person, he was shouting obscenities at the referee, jumped up and down obstructing the view of the folks behind him and his words started slurring more and more.

As Stan Wilson slotted another penalty that put the All Black six points ahead, he finally spoke to her. "Girls love that guy. Do you think he is good-looking?"

This was dangerous ground. Jacques was pretty jealous normally, and now…

She decided to play dumb. "The flyhalf? I can't really see from this far out. Who is he?"

"Ha! Probably the man of the tournament! Just shows you—wasted a golden ticket bringing you." His bloodshot eyes challenged her to respond—he was drunk, but this was a barb designed to get a reaction.

She would be ashamed later, but she rose to the bait.

"So why did you? Bring me, I mean. Why not bring one of your fancy Rhodes Scholar buddies?"

"That lot had their noses stuck up each other's asses too much to appreciate a great game like rugby. You, at least, would look good on my arm, and maybe a shag later will help me get over another near miss."

Wow, she thought. "So, I'm here as eye candy, and your hooker for the night?"

"Whatever you want to call it, baby."

She felt a mixture of anger, resentment, and hurt swell up in her. She had given up so much to be here with this prick, and right now, he was spoiling what could be a great memory—win or lose—for both of them.

Again, she pushed it down. Keep it together. "I'm sorry the team is losing. Look, we just got another penalty. Maybe they can still pull it together and win this."

His unfocused gaze returned to the pitch, and he shrugged. "Don't think so. There's only one team in charge now."

He kept on looking at the pitch and then stood up unsteadily. "Let's go. I have had enough of this."

217

She looked up at him. "Let's stay. We might still win this. There are only 10 minutes left."

"You and your fucking optimistic attitude! Just get mad once in a while! Why do you have to be a little miss-perfect all the time! I'm the rugby fan; I got us the tickets; I say we go!"

"Jacques, lower your voice. You're making a scene…"

Behind them, a voice piped up, "Sit down or leave, mate. You're blocking my view."

"Lauren, come let's go. Don't embarrass me like this." He tugged at her arm; she shook it loose.

"I'm not leaving. I want to finish watching the game."

From behind them: "Sit down, Saffer!"

Jacques blinked. "Fuck you. I'm leaving. I've had enough of this shit."

And he left. She was trembling slightly—but at the same time, she felt, for the first time in months, a feeling of… pride? She hadn't stood up for herself like this since they arrived in England—and it felt good.

The game finished as predicted, and her surroundings reflected her mood—both sad like the SA supporters but energized and happy like the Kiwis. It was weird. Her phone started buzzing as they filed out—Jacques was sending her numerous messages, but she decided not to read them. Screw him. She had places to go that did not include his drunken, sorry ass.

Feeling liberated, she took the tube up to Hammersmith.

26

The pub was pretty full—but Lauren spotted some of the South Africans that were with Sam outside. They also recognized her and motioned her to the upstairs area. They were big men, and probably famous. There was also an air of mature resignation about them, differing from the drunken depression she saw on the faces of many of the fans. The wisdom of experience, she supposed.

She reflected on this, walking up the stairs. The thing that bothered her about Jacques was, for all his worldly knowledge, he was still a spoiled brat. Life had never been unkind to him, and now, struggling at Oxford, he was acting out at his own shortcomings. First world problems, she supposed, and…

There he was. Sam. And the person he was talking to… with his back to her… it couldn't be…

Jimmy turned around. There was the briefest moment of surprise, and then just that warm smile she remembered so well.

They looked at each other for a moment, and the spell was broken by Sam, who shoved beers in their hands. "Just in time to lighten the mood, L! I tell you this crowd needs it!"

They stood for a moment, the three players in a youthful drama now incongruently gathered in a smelly English pub.

Sam spoke first, clearly seizing the responsibility for bridging the awkward silence.

"Who would've thought hey? Here we are, together again…"

Jimmy laughed. "Sam, I don't think the three of us were ever 'together'. You were too busy hating on me, and Lauren was too busy managing the situation."

"True story. I was an idiot back then, but then so were you Jimboy."

"Touché. The only one that comes out of our teenage love triangle with her honor intact is Lauren here."

"Hey!" she finally found her voice. "It was no fun for me, either… but I think it's great that the three of us are here together, now, in our moment of great loss. Misery loves company, right."

They cheered to that, and Sam said, "Speak for yourself, L. My best days are coming, and I am just glad to be here with my old man. Hopefully next time there is a world cup, I'm with the team and in the thick of it."

"I'll drink to that, Sam," said Jimmy. "And the odds are pretty good." He turned his attention to Lauren. "Lauren, it's good to see you. What are you…? I mean, I knew you were in England, but aren't you with…"

"Jacques. Yes, I am still with Jacques. The prick."

Their eyes widened. It was not like Lauren to use such language.

"Yeah, I know. Dirty mouth, right? But I think, for the first time in my life, I just want to say: screw it. It has not been a great week or day, and somehow it feels right that I can just be here, and let my hair down with a couple of ex-boyfriends talking about the old days. Especially while my current one is throwing his toys somewhere."

"Well, ok then. You can talk about it if you want, I guess…" said Sam, but it was clear the last thing he was looking for is to hear about Lauren's love troubles. There was enough depression to go around.

"Nah," she saved them. "I'm not going to spend more energy on him tonight." She downed her beer. "Could I have another?"

"Sure. You guys catch up," and with that, Sam made his escape.

Lauren was glad she had brushed up downstairs before she ran into Jimmy. She was just conceited enough to know she looked pretty good.

But then, so did he. When she saw him in Stellenbosch, their couple of meetings were filled with raw emotion and arguments. Now he was casual and relaxed, and she noticed how he filled out his jeans and Springbok top. In a good way.

His phone beeped, and he mumbled an apology while he replied to a text.

"Lauren, I need to go."

She felt a mad rush of disappointment. She was here to spend time with Sam... but he had found a reason to get stuck at the bar. She desperately wanted to connect with Jimmy. Why? It wasn't because she wanted to get back at Jacques, or was it? Or did she want... what?

While she was mulling this over, he caught her off guard.

"I've been invited to dinner. It's with a good friend and his wife, and they would be ok if I brought a date."

"Um... well, I don't want to leave Sam hanging, I just got here..."

"Sam will be fine, promise you. Come. It would be good to catch up, I do need to go, however..."

Would it be ok? How would she feel if Jacques went out with an ex-girlfriend tonight? She wouldn't be cool. But then she had no intention of doing anything. It was dinner with friends, wasn't it?

Having convinced herself of the justification, but still not answering her texts, Lauren said, "Sure, why not. I am getting hungry. How far is this place?"

Jimmy's smile took her breath away. "20 minutes by subway, West Kensington. Come, let's say goodbye to Sam and make our way."

Five minutes later they were on the tube. The tube was even more packed than usual, and she found herself squashed against him. He felt... solid. And she could pick up his scent, which was different from what she remembered. "I like your cologne," she murmured. It was noisy in the tube, and he didn't reply. Maybe he hadn't heard her. Oh, no hold on... his body told her he did. She felt her heart rate quicken but moved slightly away, and to break the spell, she asked: "So who are we having dinner with?"

She couldn't see his face as he replied: "I don't think you would know them; they are Kiwis. Kind of like a surrogate big brother, a friend of mine from my time in France. You'll like them!" In safer territory now, the spell was broken. But she had felt him... and she felt daring. She smiled to herself. What would this night bring?

The place was called Casa Bardotti, and Jimmy's friends were waiting for them at a corner table. It was a little Italian place (of course it was) and packed with customers, both at the bar and the dozen or so tables. There was a pleasant buzz to the place, mostly Italian. In fact, they were probably the only English-speaking people there.

The other couple introduced themselves as Stan and Grace. She was slightly intimidated—they both seemed tremendously athletic and ridiculously good-looking. But they set her ease almost immediately. Red wine was poured and they were a-for-away.

It felt so comfortable. While Stan and Jimmy launched into an animated discussion (or argument) about the game, Grace immediately went to work asking Lauren questions about her life, what she was doing. Lauren felt that it was great to talk to someone. Somewhere along the line of spilling her guts about Jacques, her life choices, being here with Jimmy, she also managed to find out that Grace was a business coach. No wonder she was good at asking questions.

There were interruptions in the conversation for ordering pizza and more wine. It puzzled Lauren a little bit when the Aussie waiter asked to take a picture with Stan, but she thought little more of it. She was surprised and delighted when they delved into their spell working together in France. Grace rolled her eyes, saying: "If only he washed the dishes as much at home." But then she immediately followed up with an affectionate hug and kiss, and launched into Stan's virtues as a dad. Two little ones weren't easy.

As dinner wound down, Lauren found herself becoming quieter and more reflective. The kind of relationship Stan and Grace had seemed so... pure, and selfless. It was clear he traveled a lot for work, while she was happy to put her career on hold to focus on the kids for a while. They were also very clear that she would go back to work once they were older, and that they each needed "their own thing".

It was only toward the end of the evening when they paid their bill that she cottoned on to the inside joke. The owner came over personally and asked for a picture and autograph.

Stan said, after signing the bill: "Biggest challenge for me—for a lot of us—is when this is all over. A lot of the guys live for the adulation from the fans. I must admit, I like it, but it also gets a bit much. And when you're done, people mostly forget about you and you have to find something else." He took his wife's hand: "Tonight was such a treat—these Italians couldn't care less who I was."

He looked at Jimmy. "Do you remember our conversation that one night in Saint-Paul-de-Vence, Jimmy? About opening up our own restaurant?"

"Sure," said Jimmy. "But that was all just talk… obviously you are not going to go wash dishes once you retire…"

"Damn right," winked Stan. "But Grace and I have been talking. You remember Il Leone back home? We have an opportunity to buy it… It's no longer what it used to be. But it could be again! But I'll need someone to run it for me."

The conversation had turned serious again, and Lauren was trying to keep up.

Jimmy had an earnest look on his face, one she remembered so well. It was the look he had when he was faced with a good thing. He had so many good things taken away in his life, that he was always suspicious of good things. Silently, she willed him to not let this one slip past as well.

"Stan… I don't know. It's a dump… and mates and business…"

"Yeah, I know. But listen, I must admit, this one has always been a dream of ours. But I need someone I can trust, mate. You are that guy. You can fix it up, get quality going, I can bring the peeps, you just need to be the one that drives the service and quality. It could become the place I loved as a kid again…"

"And I would be a partner- shareholder? I Don't have much cash…"

"We'll work that part out, mate. Say yes. Think about it! I'll be able to leverage off this fame for the rest of my lifetime, and as long as I have you to do the actual work, we could have a helluva good time. The sky's the limit!"

He was getting excited. Lauren was stuck on the 'leverage off this fame' bit again. Who was he? Man, he looked familiar…

Lauren didn't want to sound stupid—again—but Jimmy, bless his soul, helped her out. "Stan, let's talk about this again. I am intrigued. You also might want to put Lauren out of her misery. I have loved this girl since high school, and the best thing about her is this: She still doesn't know, and couldn't care less, about the stars of the game."

Stan laughed. "Well, then you are just about my favorite kind of person. It was a delight hanging out with you tonight. And for reference—my surname is Wilson."

"Our surname, love," Grace reminded him, winking at Lauren.

It came to her like a ton of bricks. Mostly because she was distracted by Jimmy's presence the whole night, the stuff on her mind. "You're Stan Wilson? THAT Stan Wilson?" she spluttered.

"Afraid so. Sorry about today. Good game though," he replied, winking.

She took a moment, then started giggling a bit hysterically. "Oh, that's too much… this day…"

And then she started laughing. Deep, proper guffaws. It felt like a crazy dream—the game, her awful boyfriend, Jimmy and now having dinner with the man of the moment—and not even knowing it.

The best thing was, Jimmy also started to laugh. And then the Wilsons joined in. And then, as they couldn't stop each other, and it just kept on rolling, the table next door joined in. And suddenly she was in the middle of hysterical laughter of an entire Italian restaurant.

When it finally died down, and she wiped the tears from her eyes, Jimmy squeezed her shoulder. On impulse, she leaned over and kissed him on the cheek. "Thank you, Jimmy—this was just the best evening."

He gave her a short, earnest look, his eyes thoughtful. "My pleasure L. It was so good to see you." And they kept looking at each other, there was a clearing of the throat on the other side of the table.

Breaking the spell, they all stood up and strolled outside. It was quite chilly outside, and everyone buttoned-up, Stan pulling a beanie over his head.

"This way, I might make it all the way back to the hotel," he mused. "But listen, we're heading this way—which way are you going, Lauren?"

She realized she hadn't thought of it. It was late to catch a train back to Oxford. Jacques was somewhere out there, drunk and probably misbehaving. They hadn't even booked a hotel, there had been a vague plan to stay with his friends. She felt a mixture of anger to be pulled back to that reality, she had completely forgotten about the whole mess during dinner.

But she didn't want to bring her personal drama into this—not with Jimmy's friends, especially not now.

"I'm staying with friends," she lied. "Jimmy, could you walk me to the tube?"

"Sure." And with that, they parted ways with the Wilsons, and strolled in the opposite direction.

The subway station really wasn't far away, but it was quite nippy. On impulse, and quite naturally, she hooked her arm into Jimmy's. It felt good to be this close to him. Different emotions swept up in her. The smell of him, the feel of him… She suddenly realized she wanted him—the feel of him inside her, the way his mouth would seem to devour her when they made love.

She felt him stiffen, but not like before. Now it was his whole body as if he sensed her change in mood. Just before the entrance of the tube station, he turned to her.

"Lauren…"

She put her finger on his mouth, shushing him. "Jimmy, take me back to your hotel."

2 7

I t was one of the hardest things he had ever had to do in his life.
The person next to him was snoring up a storm. Jimmy tossed
and turned but there was no getting away from that noise. The team
physio Olson was a big man, fit and tough as nails, and everyone's least
favorite roommate due to noise factor. He therefore always had his own
room on team assignments. They had become mates during Jimmy's
time in merchandising for the All Blacks. Olson was not put out to let
Jimmy sleep in the other bed in his room.

Two floors up, Lauren was alone in Jimmy's room. Walking her
back to the hotel, he was more tempted than he ever had been in his
life... he still loved her, but he had also done some growing up in the
last few years. She was hurt, vulnerable, and needed a friend—not
someone to take advantage of her.

Although, he thought to himself, he might have permanently
ruined things between them. She was incredibly hurt when he told her
she could sleep there, but he would not be joining her. For a second,
the Lauren of old flared up—feisty, combative. But just as quickly, she
bit her tongue and accepted his offer. Maybe they had both grown a
little bit?

In the morning, after a fitful night of impressive timbering from

Olson, Jimmy made his way to his room. He had a key, but he still knocked. There was no answer, so he let himself in.

The bed was made up, and there was a note.

"Jimmy, thank you so much for what you did last night. And what you didn't do. I hope you'll stay in England for a bit, so we can have a more proper catch-up. And don't worry about me—I'll be fine. See you soon, here's my number. Lots of love, Lauren."

Would he? Should he? She was there to be with Jacques... but, things were changing for her too. Now she was asking him to stay awhile as well? Part of him thought that would be a grand idea—but there was another part that was deeply cynical of the situation. Should he stay and fight for her? And what then? What would he do? He had no working permit for England. Neither did she, for that matter. Although from what she had told him last night...

He generally didn't spend too much time thinking about these things—he was invited to stay till after the World Cup Final, which was in a week. There was also a playoff game he could watch.

He put her number into his phone, wondering if he would call her.

At breakfast, the WAGS were in full flow. Grace had already spread the word about Jimmy's delightful companion from back in the day, and he spent the next hour dodging questions about her. He left them with a vague story about it all just being platonic. Of course, no one bought that story.

Stan and the rest of the team had gone off for a captain's run. They would see their spouses intermittently over the next week as they prepared for the final challenge: the Aussies in the final. Jimmy did not think he would see much of Stan again, and he realized that hanging out with the WAGS for the whole week would get tired quickly. What could he do?

On a whim, he decided to hire a car and drive up to Scotland. He had always wanted to visit Edinburgh. His association with Max had not just taught him the value of fine wines but good whiskeys as well. He had a whole week before the final. There was a play-off game between South Africa and Argentina for the third spot during the week. As much as that would still be fun, to Jimmy that would just feel like kissing your sister.

No, he would go up to Scotland. Taste some whiskey? He didn't play golf, but maybe he could go visit the Old Course at St Andrew's? Maybe go up to Loch Ness and look for the monster.

Mind made up, he went to the reception at the hotel, and enquired about renting a car.

Lauren woke up invigorated, and somewhat clear on what had to happen next. She was incredibly angry the previous night—angry and hurt. In all the scenarios that she ran through her head, Jimmy rejecting her was never one of them.

But, tossing and turning for the first hour or so, she calmed down and realized that he was being an absolute gentleman. She was a mess, and he did exactly the right thing by not taking advantage of her.

It made her want him even more. And it put things in perspective with Jacques, who was increasingly selfish and unmindful of her.

She snuck out of his room early, after sending Jacques a text—but it was some time before he replied, she while away the time walking around the city and lost in her thoughts.

When he eventually replied, they agreed to meet at the Starbucks just off Leicester Square. He looked awful—like he hadn't slept the whole night. And he kind of smelled.

They bought cappuccinos, then went walking on the square. There were a million tourists around. They were queuing for the next West End Sunday matinee or flitting in and out of the many bars and restaurants, even at this early hour.

Jacques opened the conversation: "L, I am so sorry. Yesterday… Well, I don't know what came over me. I was just… I drank too much."

She stopped. "That's it? That's your excuse? Your validation for your behavior? Did you drink too much? For God's sake Jacques." She could feel the anger rising, and for once, she didn't want to keep it in. "You left me alone! In London!"

"I tried to call… I left you several messages…"

"Sure! But I wasn't about to answer them and take more abuse from you."

His eyes narrowed. "So where did you go? I mean... you must have slept somewhere."

"Yes. I found a perfectly nice hotel room to spend the night in. You don't look like you did as well." And the riposte gave him pause.

"Yeah. I was gonna crash at Eddie's... but he didn't answer his phone... spent the night at a cheap B&B on Earls Court, was all that I could find after the tubes closed..."

She didn't ask why he was in Earls Court. But she could imagine he went on a further drinking spree; he certainly smelled that way.

She sighed. "Look, Jacques, let's just go home. Sleep it off, sober up, and we can talk this through later."

He nodded, and they walked toward the tube. But before they went down there, she said, "Let's rather walk a bit. It will take us 20 minutes to Victoria Station, then it's a direct train from there. I don't think I could handle the stuffy old tube just now."

"You mean you can't handle being in there with me, the way I smell right now," he retorted.

She could have been kinder. But she just nodded. "That's part of it, I suppose."

They started walking, but now she could sense that he was once again gearing up for a fight.

And there it was. "So, you didn't answer my question. Where did you go last night?"

She thought for a moment and decided: screw it. Let's go with the truth. Or part of it, at least.

"I went to meet up with my old high school boyfriend Sam. He was at a bar with a bunch of the Springbok Rugby Legends with his dad. There I ran into Jimmy, my other ex-boyfriend. Then I went with Jimmy to meet up with Stan Wilson and his wife Grace for dinner at a lovely Italian restaurant in West Kensington. After dinner, I crashed at his hotel room, and when I woke up, I came straight here."

Jacques stopped and blinked. "What? You met Stan Wilson?"

She threw her head back, and she wasn't proud of the cynical laugh that escaped her lips. "And that's your chief takeaway from that conversation? Not that I slept in my ex-boyfriend's hotel room?" Her eyes challenged him, and he visibly shrunk under her gaze.

"Well, of course... that too... I mean..."

She felt incredible. She had the advantage, and now she meant to press it. Months of built-up frustration were coming to the fore for her as well, and what the hell. Let's let him have it. Right here, right now, halfway between Green Park and Victoria Station.

"Jacques Jardine, you are one of the most arrogant, self-involved, insecure pricks I have ever met. I can't believe I ever fell for all your bullshit, let alone followed you here. You might be smart—and rich—and I will concede that you know how to work hard." She breathed, as she plunged more arrows home.

"But you have no sense of self. You don't want to be a wine farmer, you don't want to be a scientist, you don't want to be anything... you just want accolades and recognition for being. And consequently, you can't stand the thought of me doing something with my life, having direction, either. And you don't even give a shit if I happened to sleep with my ex- which I didn't—when there is the bigger matter at hand of which current superstar celeb I hung out with."

"Now wait a minute..."

"No, you wait. We're going back to Oxford on the next train. You will clean up and take a shower, by the time you are done, I will have packed up all my things and I will be gone."

"Where will you go?"

She looked at him, and she could physically feel all the love and affection she ever had for him die away. In front of her was a sad, lost soul. And she was done.

"Jacques... that is, from this point exactly, none of your business."

But they both knew she would call her only friend.

Once he had his mind made up, he went into full planning mode. Sam texted him to see how things went with Lauren and if she was ok—he replied with the minimum of feedback which he was sure Sam would appreciate. Stan also called him, and was delighted that he decided to go on a road trip. In true dude style, no reference was made to who is going with him.

He jumped on his laptop and spent the morning just checking on his responsibilities back in New Zealand. Everything was under control, and the home base was still happy for him to come back after the final.

He then went to travel planning, which had become one of his favorite things in the world.

He could get a pretty nifty mini-SUV for a relatively cheap price from Avis at Euston station. If he picked it up by 1 pm, he could probably drive as far as Liverpool before finding a B&B. Rugby was his game—but he had met enough Brits while traveling to develop a love for British Football too. He did like Liverpool, partly because they had such a cool theme tune.

It seemed fitting. "You never walk alone" … but in this case, he would very much walk alone. And that would be fine.

Google maps revealed two routes up to Liverpool. The quicker route up was on the M1, but the M40 went through Birmingham, which was another English city that he had heard a lot about. And, if he had to admit it to himself, the route went right by Oxford. He still had her number…

He decided he would make that decision once he was on the road. He packed his stuff and boarded the tube.

———

They arrived at their flat in Oxford just after noon. Jacques went straight to have a shower, while Lauren started to pack her things.

It didn't take long, and by the time he came out of the bathroom, she was just about done.

"You're really going through with this?" he asked, standing half-naked in the doorway.

She considered him, and his self-conscious parading of his body. Jacques was in great shape—always had been, but she realized that she was emotionally turned off by him, and she felt nothing.

Her suitcase clicked shut as she faced him. "Yes. And you're blocking the door."

There was a momentary look of defiance, and she felt a small pang of fear. Jacques had never even been remotely violent with her—but he was a man, and she felt in control.

Mercifully, he stepped aside.

As she left, he said, "You're making a mistake, Lauren. It could have been so good."

She turned around and looked at him for the last time: "Maybe. But maybe good is not good enough. We should all be looking for great. I hope you figure it out, Jacques, I really do. I know I'm starting to."

She kissed him on the cheek, and he stepped aside. As she walked out, he couldn't resist a parting shot.

"That dyke is dangerous, Lauren. Just you wait and see. Don't say I didn't warn you."

Outside, she ordered an Uber to take her to Daniella's place. Her mentor and friend had been a godsend. She immediately offered her the spare bedroom to crash for however long she needed, and was determined to help her in any way she could. She was out of town herself for the weekend, but said Lauren must just let herself in—after all, as a research assistant, she already had a key. While she waited, she had a quick look at her WhatsApp. Horrified, she saw she had missed a few while packing.

As the Uber drew up, she looked at her phone for a long moment —then typed a quick response. Let the chips fall where they may. She loaded her suitcase in, and the car drew away.

They wound through the quiet Sunday streets to Daniella's place, on the other side of town. She almost willed her phone to life, transfixed to the small screen. Then it dutifully beeped. Slightly breathless, she looked at the message.

Then, smiling from ear to ear, she replied.

She tapped her driver on the shoulder. "Change of direction, cabby. Please go to the train station."

Jimmy made his choice while pulling out of Easton station. The Ford Escape Mini SUV was a great ride, and as he contemplated which route to put into his GPS, he received a text from Stan. It simply said, "Don't waste a moment mate. Enjoy."

He texted her on impulse, then punched in the route that skirted Oxford. Roll the dice on life, and see what happens.

It was about an hour's drive. As he started to see the turns for the exit, he still had not received a reply. In fact, she had not read his message at all. This created a bit of a quandary—but she might be busy. There was, after all, a lot going on in her life. What to do?

He pulled into a gas station and bought a cup of coffee. He would give it another five minutes… if he didn't hear from her, maybe he would call? He decided to go for it and dialed her number. It went straight to voicemail.

That was that, he supposed. And he was surprised how heavy he suddenly felt—not for the first time in his life, he cursed her for the hold she had on his emotions. "Fuck it," he thought. "Liverpool, here we come."

As he got behind the wheel, his phone buzzed. His emotions now a measure of the old anger, a new excitement, and something in between, he looked at it for a long moment.

"You never walk alone, Jimmy," he said to himself. And typed his response.

He got goosebumps and started the car.

As he pulled into Oxford Station, there she was. He felt the old familiar feelings wash over him… and as he got out of the car, she came up with her big suitcase.

They looked at each other for a moment. Her face was flushed—from the cold? Excitement? Either way, she had never looked this good.

He couldn't help himself. "Hey beautiful, going my way?"

And she flew into his arms.

They never made it to Liverpool. 30 minutes down the road, at Lauren's urging, they pulled off the highway and found a B&B in Stratford-upon-Avon, the birthplace of Shakespeare. Not that they cared.

They didn't even unpack their suitcases. The moment they closed the door, they attacked each other. It felt forever to take their clothes off, and Jimmy was pretty sure he had torn open her blouse in the process. Then he was inside her, and she was wet and ready and they clawed at each other and loved each other and it was glorious and when she came, she shouted out with an abandon that he had never experienced before. He felt like he emptied all of himself into her... and then they came down from the mountain together, blissfully entangled in each other.

The second round was gentler—as if they were now careful with each other, studying each other's bodies, exploring the changes as if anew. Jimmy remembered her to be a bit more conservative in her ways—but now she took him into her mouth, and it took all of his willpower to not come right there and then. Impressed by her evolution, he decided to return the favor, and she squealed with delight as he started to massage her with his tongue—gently at first, then with increasing urgency, as her squeals turned into slight moans, then the familiar increase in tenor as she couldn't restrain herself any longer and he felt her come. He was still rock-hard, and immediately he fell on her, she picking up his rhythm and their mutual groaning rising in pitch until they came together once more.

They lay down together, hands touching. He felt so content… and drowsy. He drifted off to sleep, and when he woke it was dark outside. He looked over to her, and she was perched on her elbows, looking at him expectantly. "Hey…" he managed.

"Hey yourself," she said and grabbed his penis. He felt himself immediately go hard again.

And so it went.

They did manage to do other things that week.

For example, they visited famous Shakespearian sites. They drove up to Liverpool and did visit the stadium and museum. They continued to Glasgow but didn't stop, keeping on to the seaside town of Oban.

They ate fish and chips at the harbor, did a whiskey tasting at the famous distillery, and walked around the quaint seaside town. Then they found a room with a view and made love. Exhausting each other in rediscovering their bodies, exulting in their newfound skills and experience, and cautious with their words but free with their affection, they woke up exhausted and refreshed. They made their way even further north and took on the full-day climb of Ben Nevis, the highest mountain in Scotland.

Jimmy mused that she looked equally good in her exercise gear. She had always been athletic, but the last few years she put on just a few pounds—which, in his mind, made her even more attractive—slightly softer, and he liked the way her body melted into his. Her breasts had filled out a bit as well, and as they summited the mountain, he observed how she filled out her sports bra… Well, suffice it to say, they barely made it down the mountain this time.

She was everything a good Afrikaans girl should be. At the same time, life had happened, and her inhibitions had also left her. It was as if she was eager to dare, enthusiastic to try new things.

Finally escaping their hotel room at Ben Nevis, they drove through spectacular countryside and awful weather across to St Andrews, the home of golf. They walked around the famous course, Jimmy recalling famous victories he had watched in documentaries with his dad. It felt like he had never really discussed his father with Lauren before.

What was great about him, and all the things that Jimmy now knew to be falsehoods. She listened, did not judge, and he felt drawn even closer to her.

Jimmy's dad played a lot of golf—he always said it was the one place he could switch off. He even tried to teach Jimmy—but it never took, Jimmy was a much bigger fan of team sports. Still, they watched a lot of golf tournaments on TV when he was growing up, and he had a high appreciation of the Home of Golf. Now, walking around the course with Lauren, he felt closer to his father's memory than he had in a long time.

That night, they ate dinner at a local pub, filled with golfers from all over the world. Many of them were also going to the game on Saturday, and Jimmy found himself in the middle of an animated discussion with a bunch of Aussies about the chances they had against the All Blacks. He was in his element, and the best part was, Lauren was too. She did not know much about the game, but she had her hands full in fending off all the uproarious men. They, despite being friendly with Jimmy, were still openly flirting with Lauren. She gave as good as she got, and Jimmy loved seeing her in action.

They were both slightly tipsy when they walked back to their hotel, the cool air doing its share to sober them up.

The moon had come up over the golf course, with the mists settling in on the famous 17th green, known as the Road Hole.

They stood still for a moment, arms interlocked, taking it all in. Jimmy sensed a shift in her mood. He waited for her to be ready.

Finally, she spoke. "All that stuff with your dad. I mean… you never really spoke about him like this before. You must miss him a lot."

"I do and I don't. He loved the game of golf—sometimes, more than he loved spending time with us. And nothing was ever enough… So yeah, I miss him, but the last few years I also had to figure out how to forgive him. After they died, you know… I was so angry. At him, for leaving me with nothing. At all of them, for leaving me behind."

She hugged him close. "Yeah, I feel horrible that I didn't... you know... show more empathy. I was dealing with my own stuff."

He kissed her cheek. "We were kids, Lauren. You had your family issues, I had mine, everybody deals with a shitshow you know. I don't think either of us were kids long enough—the home life kind of cut that short."

"True story. And now, here we are... at St Andrews..." she giggled.

"Are you thinking what I'm thinking?" she whispered, a twinkle in her eye.

He feigned shock and embarrassment. "Surely not. Defile the Home of Golf? I would love to have a go, but there are security patrols... and it's too damn cold."

"The hotel then?" and she playfully stuck her tongue in his ear, immediately arousing him.

"Yes. And let's hurry."

Their last stop was Edinburgh, the fabled Scottish city. Here, World Cup fever was still alive and well, the myriad pubs that lined famous Queen's Street, all broadcasting the Springbok/Argentina game. They did the mandatory sightseeing of the city including the fabled Castle on the hill, and also made a trip to go check out Murrayfield, another stadium Jimmy's dad had always talked about, but never had an opportunity to visit. They found an appropriately credited joint by the name of Filthy McNasty's and watched South Africa defeat Argentina for third place with a rowdy crowd of Irish and Scotsmen. Afterward, they made slow and deliberate love, somehow sensing their time together was coming to an end.

After, with the sounds from the city dying down around them, she lay perched on his chest, and the moonlight illuminated those big eyes of hers.

He was spent and half asleep when she said, "What happens tomorrow, Jimmy?"

"We drive back to London," he said sleepily.

"And then?" she pressed.

"And then..." he started to become awake, as he realized this was turning into 'the talk' territory. "Then we... we figure it out. I'll get you a ticket for the game, we go watch it, and then we..." he trailed off.

"That's it. I don't want to spoil this moment... but I plan to go back to Oxford and help Daniella with her Ph.D. And I am finally going on with my studies. I need to. And you... well, you are going back to New Zealand, I guess? Stan's offer..."

He was now fully awake. "I guess I haven't thought about it... I mean, she's going to help pay for your studies, and even beyond. But you'll be done in 18 months... we could make it work... long distance I mean..."

"Sure," she felt herself becoming emotional. "But what happens if you are phenomenally successful over there? And meanwhile, I keep on studying, and get my Ph.D. It could be years..." tears started to form, despite her best efforts. "I just found you again..."

"Hey," he said, pulling her close. "You are such a chick. Forget about all that stuff for now—let's just be in the moment. We can work all that out later... All I know is that, right here, right now, I am in love with you, and we will never have this moment again."

"I love you too, Jimmy."

She let it go, but her heart was in turmoil. There was no way they could be together without either of them sacrificing an amazing opportunity... and in her case, she knew it could not be her. The experience with Jacques had scarred her too much—she needed to get back on track, to get back to her sense of self.

After she heard him drift off to sleep, she let herself cry silent tears for what was coming, until oblivion also took her.

For Jimmy, the drive down to London had a bittersweet feel to it. They sat with their thoughts for a lot of it. On arrival in West Kensington, however, things sped up. There were no pretensions this time, much to the delight of the WAGS. With Grace leading the way, Lauren was welcomed into the fold. Saturday was a blur of champagne, excitement, and activity as the wives and girlfriends of the impending world champions laughed, danced, and joked their way to the stadium.

Grace did pull him aside at one point at the pre-party close to the stadium. Lauren was being entertained by Richie McCaw's missus.

"She is delightful, Jimmy. I now understand why you're always distant with the ladies—this one has always had your heart."

Jimmy smiled ruefully. "You got me, Grace. She is the one."

"You seem a little bit… off your best though," she remarked. The lady didn't miss a thing.

"Is Stan serious about the restaurant thing?" he asked. "I mean… I wouldn't hold him to it, it was late and we were…"

"Tipsy? Sure. But you know my husband, Jimmy. He is one of the most amazingly focused people I have ever met. He has a vision. And he sees it clearly. When he hangs up his boots, he wants to have business interests with people he trusts. We see it too often—star players lose all their gains from the gain by trusting the wrong people and making the wrong choices. Stan is determined that's not going to happen to him, or us."

"Why me? I'm still very young."

"That's for Stan to tell you, Jimmy. Why don't you ask him, when we're all back home? But trust me—the conversation, and the offer is real."

She took his face in her hands and squeezed his cheeks like he imagined a kindly grandma would do.

"We already made an offer, sweet boy. But that girl might ruin our plans. Truthfully, half of me hopes she does. You are good together." She turned serious. "But Jimmy, for the two of you to work, one of you will have to sacrifice a lot. And be ok with that sacrifice. If it were her, I don't think she would ever really forgive herself for not following through on her dreams—and by extension, that would be poison for you."

He watched Lauren laugh with the ladies, and his heart swelled with love. "Fuck it. I would just move here."

"And then, Jimmy? Find a job as a maître d while she studies at Oxford?"

He frowned. "It wouldn't matter… we are both more mature now…"

"But it would matter to you, Jimmy. What I do know about you is that you may be young, but you are destined for big things. It is time for you to evolve—and coming here would set you back."

"Grace, this conversation is depressing me."

"You're right, and I'm sorry. I don't mean to be the bearer of doom and gloom... but I truly believe that the two of you might have a chance of being together one day."

"But not now?"

She shook her head. "Now, now, Jimmy. I'm sorry. Now let's go watch some rugby!"

The game was exciting enough, if only because of the energy of the rest of the ladies. For Lauren, she had no vested interest in either team, beyond now really liking Grace and Stan. When the All Blacks won convincingly, she was pleased with the result.

But she was conscious that both she and Jimmy were horribly distracted by the deadline of choices hanging over their heads... and that night, they talked well into the early hours of the morning.

Funny enough, initially neither of them felt like making love. They just lay in each other's arms and talked about their future—how they might make it work, how they might give each other space to follow their dreams, how they might find each other again.

They argued. Then she cried. Then he demanded. Then she shouted. He apologized, she cried some more, he went cold, she begged him to say something. And so, it went... two 21-year-olds with the world on their shoulders and their whole life ahead of them. When they did make love, it felt almost desperate. They promised to work it out, fell asleep, woke up, talked some more... and dawn came...

And before they knew it, he stood at the departure gate at Heathrow Airport, and they clung to each other.

"I'm going back to Oxford for me, Jimmy. I am not going back to him." She said it as much for herself as for him.

"I know. And as I said, Lauren... I have no demands on you. We need to let each other go now. I will write to you all the time... but to insist we stay together for almost two years if we are going to be apart..."

"I don't want to break up, Jimmy. I told you. I can wait." She felt tears welling up again.

"I don't want you to wait. I want you to live, Lauren." And with that, he kissed her, and held her tight.

She clung to him fiercely. "Please, Jimmy. We could make this work. We could."

He shook his head. "Let me go, Lauren. I love you, now and forever."

And then he was gone.

She took the train back to Oxford in a daze. She let herself into Daniella's apartment, the guest room ready for her. Daniella was there —but, never the most empathetic of humans, she knew her limitations and, despite shoving a hot cup of espresso in Lauren's hands, she kept her distance.

She paged through the photos of the last week on her phone. She thought of the coming months and years, not feeling his hard body against hers, the smell of him next to her, his laughter ringing in her ears… and it was all she could do not to pick up the phone and book a ticket to New Zealand.

But help came from the most unexpected source. Her phone beeped, and it was Grace.

"Good luck, Lauren. You are going to make an amazing impact on the world. Make it for women everywhere. We will look after Jimmy for you."

There was another message on her phone, and it was from someone she had not heard from in a while.

Her mother.

29

It's a pretty long haul back to Christchurch. The international connections via Asia demand two 12-hour flights. That meant Jimmy came back to his place late Tuesday evening. And he had proper jetlag.

He crashed hard. His dreams were fitful and he wanted to check in with Lauren a dozen times as he went in and out of sleep. He didn't. He knew that if they reached out, he would lose his resolve, and go back to her.

He also didn't know if he was making the right decision. Stan and Grace were teeing up an incredible opportunity for him. To be part of a business, this time for real. He had left South Africa despondent and slightly heartbroken. This time felt different. Still heartbroken, but by choice. He had to see where the path led.

But it would be a waiting game. Stan was completely swamped by media and fan commitments after winning the game. They were on their way back in a few days to a victory parade all over the country. It would be a couple of weeks before he had a chance to talk to them. Fortunately, merchandising had spiked, and he and Mick were crazy busy in the weeks around the parades and fanfare.

When that died down, to take his mind off Lauren, he considered how he could work proactively. He was surprised—and delighted—when Robby phoned him out of the blue. His old friend had decided to come to tour New Zealand for his summer holiday. It would turn out to be the biggest stroke of luck for Jimmy.

Robby spent his first few days with Jimmy in Christchurch in early December. They went for dinner a couple of times at Il Leone. Robby insisted on paying every time. He also helped Jimmy look at the place more critically. The service was average, a function of both bad training, bad hiring, and lax management. It was clear that it was not owner-run, and he suspected the manager spent half her time in the back smoking or reading her book—sure smelled like it.

Also, the pizza was ok—but not great. Ingredients were not 100% fresh. Jimmy had to admit a weakness for avocado on pizza, a South African convention that had not quite caught on in New Zealand. They did action it on his request. But the avocado was often slightly browned, and it just wasn't up to par.

A sneak peek into the kitchen suggested that the pizza ovens and equipment might need an overhaul as well. There had not gone too much love or effort into the place for many years. When one of the owners did stop by for a chat one night, he realized that it had been a lifelong passion for old Luigi. His two sons, however, had careers in finance and law, and they had little appetite for the restaurant business.

He and Robby were walking home one night when Robby asked, "You sure seem to like that pizza joint, bud. I'm not complaining, mind you. But what gives? It's nothing like what Uncle Joe cooked up."

Jimmy decided to confide in Robby a little bit. "Well, I was just wondering? What if one could buy that place? What would you pay for it?"

Robby laughed, but then he turned serious. "Interesting question."

"Put all that education to work, Robby. Let's say I had some money and I could buy it, then fix it up and run it properly. What would that look like?"

Robby paused, thoughtful for a moment. "Look, there's more to it. Let's say the guy wanted a million dollars for it. I have no idea how much, but let's call it that. It wouldn't just be the purchase price. Then the capital cost for renovations, adhering to health and safety requirements, registering a company to run it, the audit fees, bank fees, merchant facilities… A lot of that is in place, but I also suspect a lot of it isn't."

Jimmy was surprised. "Wow. You are thinking of a lot of stuff I didn't consider."

Robby nodded. "I never filled you in on what I've been up to since the whole Ben fiasco, did I? Were you ever wondering how I paid for this trip?"

"Yep, I kind of was… usually you would be working your ass off during the summer, trying to save money for the next year's tuition."

Robby winked at Jimmy. "Remember Gretha and those earbuds, my friend? After the Ben thing, I went full tilt for it. Gretha had secured the rights from the Danish manufacturer—but we still needed working capital. You know, to do the first batch of imports and fund the marketing and distribution. Bank wouldn't give me any money without a proper business plan, though. So, I wrote one with Gretha's help."

Jimmy had been too busy with his own new life and now remembered that Robby had talked about this. "And then?"

"So, we went to some private investors in the Stellenbosch mafia. There are a few of those cats we catered for when we were with Ben—and I pitched them the plan."

"And?"

"And they fronted the money for a convertible loan with the option to convert at a share price buy-out. It was a busy time, I'll tell you. The biggest mistake I made—and which I won't make again—is underestimating the market. These things sold like crazy, Jimmy."

Jimmy stared at Robby. "So, you're the earphone king of South Africa now?"

Robby shook his head. "Not anymore. I underestimated how quickly this would work. The moment my partners knew we had something, they converted the loan and had a controlling share. They offered me a bundle to step out, they wanted only Gretha on the other side."

"So, you took the money?"

"Didn't want to. But you need to watch those contracts, Jimmy. We didn't have one with Ben—I had one with these guys, but their lawyers drew it up, and it offered me little protection. Had to cash out." He paused, then said something out of character. "Bitch sold me out. I thought…"

Robby seemed to be going darker. "Good thing too. I wasn't out for two weeks when our idiot president fired our finance minister because he wouldn't play ball. The Rand currency went for a backflip, it really hurt the business. So, I guess it worked out for me… not so much for the other guys, although they have deep pockets. And Gretha—fuck her. Women, my man. Can't trust them. As for our country, when is this dog show going to end?"

His friend sometimes went dark on South Africa like that. He was oddly broadly optimistic in life, but pessimistic about their country. And true to form, suddenly he was a ray of sunshine. "On the flip side, I can now easily pay to finish my studies without any further side hustles and go on holiday. With a bit of money left over…"

Jimmy laughed. "What's a bit of money, Robby?"

"Enough to pay for this trip. And to take you to lunch. Now, let me show you what a proper business plan looks like before I catch the bus to Lake Taupo. I'll be back just before Christmas!"

With Robby helping to crunch the numbers, he found himself coming around to Stan's way of thinking—this project might have legs, after all. He was working full days to catch up, but in the evenings, when the urge to call Lauren or just have another whiskey was too strong, he whipped open his laptop and started working. Robby turned out to be a massive help. He sent him the business plan for his earphone business. After two weeks of touring New Zealand, he came back just before Christmas. After that, he helped Jimmy with the plan for the duration of his stay.

They spent a wonderful Christmas together with Stan and Grace. It was a busy house and not much was said of the Il Leone plan. Stan promised he would come to see them in a few days to discuss, before he took the family on a short holiday.

For the next few days, with the All Black office closed and being able to focus on the business plan—they worked around the clock. What are the financial projections? He had to dust off his rusty accounting skills, and found enormous pleasure in spitballing what 1,2 and 5 years could look like.

They watched YouTube videos on how to fill out the plan. How would you do marketing? Operations? What would be the capital cost? What about uniforms? Contracts for staff? Casual or permanent, what were the labor laws? They were working magic, and the two friends had a blast.

After Christmas, Robby had spent his final days sailing on the bay islands before flying back to South Africa. He had not left before arming Jimmy for the upcoming conversation with Stan. Jimmy had also given Robby his cell phone for a few days, so they could keep in contact even if there wasn't a great signal. Cell data was great in most places.

As promised, just before they left for their New Year's holiday, Stan punched in with Jimmy, coming to the flat. They cracked open a beer and discussed the future. Jimmy kept his council, as it became clear that Stan had not done any of the detailed research. He was more in love with the romance of owning his own restaurant, without having thought through the myriad of complexities.

"Have they accepted your offer?" asked Jimmy.

"Not yet. They like the idea of selling to me—but the boys are also concerned that their dad's life work will go down the tubes. I assured them that I would keep the spirit of the place, and his, alive. They also didn't seem to trust that I knew how to run the thing," he grimaced.

Jimmy smiled and took out a folder. "Maybe I can help with that."

Stan took it from them and leafed through. "What's all this, mate?"

"I have been doing my own research, Stan. Financial projections, capital expenditure, upgrades needed, training and overheads outlay, and marketing budget. I also played around with the idea that if we pulled it off, what would additional outlets and/or franchising look like."

"Holy shit, Jimmy," murmured Stan, leafing through the thick Perspex folder. "You really put some thought into this."

Jimmy was getting excited. "I must admit, my buddy Robby has been an incredible help. He has some real game—he knows all about how to put the plan together, and the ins and outs of what a bank or investor would look for."

Stan nodded. "He's an interesting guy, from what you've said about him. Does he want to stay?"

Jimmy shook his head. "He's going home to finish university. He has a head for business though—told me to call him if we wanted to go bigger. There is a proposal for that in the second section."

Stan whistled and sat back. "Ok, clearly I am dealing with a bit of a sneaky finance mastermind here. But then I knew you had some layers, mate. So how do you see this working?"

"Well… look at the third page, Stan, at the investment required. We crunched some numbers, and they don't own the premises, just the business. So, you would take over the lease and just buy the business with all the stuff inside, including fittings. Then you would need to do a big overhaul, the place needs a lot of work. But you would keep the base character, just spruce it up. You would do this over the next month, so you are ready for the summer season by December— providing you can do the deal quick-quick."

Stan paged through. "Hmmm… so you reckon I should offer half a million dollars for the business, and put in another half to jack it up? That's a big chunk of change, mate."

"Yeah, but you would make it all back in three years if you look at the long-term plan."

Stan chuckled. "And pay you a handsome salary, plus a hefty bonus on targets achieved?"

"It's all in there. Also, you would not pay all of the bonus. I leave half of it in the business, and if we hit the target year three, that money buys me a 20% share of the restaurant. At a predetermined share price, of course. And that includes all future expansion projects."

"Gotta say, Jimmy, I'm impressed. Can I take this? Grace would also want to have a look, plus I probably should run it by my accountant… how did you know I offered half a million?"

"That's what the numbers told me, Stan."

"They want a little bit more, you know." Stan frowned. "But I'm going to stick with the offer—I'm starting to think we could probably do this without spending that money, you seem to know what you're doing."

Jimmy hesitated. "They have some good long-term client equity, Stan. That's what we're paying for. Yes, we could probably just start up a different location—but you know how you feel about this place."

Stan winked. "True story. But they don't need to know that. Leave it to me, Jimmy."

He walked out, and Jimmy immediately phoned Robby. "It's going to happen, bud! Man, this is exciting! I wish you were here to celebrate with me!"

Robby asked, on the other end. "Did you shake on a deal?"

"No, not yet, but he's looking at stuff…"

"Don't count your chickens before they're hatched bud. But hey, it's almost New Year. I'm heading back, we should celebrate in style. Here's to 2016!"

"Cool. Would also like my phone back, I want to tell some people. Umm… were there any messages for me?" Jimmy suddenly felt a strong urge to call Lauren and tell her. But he didn't know if she would receive contact well… other than polite Christmas wishes, they had not talked. Maybe if she had reached out…

There was a slight pause, and then Robby said, "Nothing important. See you tomorrow!"

In the end, six weeks later, the brothers accepted Stan's offer. They were partially swayed by his star power, and partially by Jimmy's charm. Stan also agreed to Jimmy's terms—although only 10% equity could be purchased in year 2, with a further option of 10% if he stuck around for a further two after that. Stan Wilson (or/and his wife) was no dummy.

Jimmy heeding Robby's advice about contracts, hired a top legal firm to help him with the contract side. And in March, he left the merchandising job, and a distraught Mick—to start his journey as a restaurant owner.

30

Daniella was as good as her word. She opened up the doors in terms of Lauren's further studies. Lauren was swept up in an exhausting cycle of classes, homework and assisting responsibilities with Daniella. They shared Daniella's expansive flat. Lauren could not afford her own place. She longed for some privacy though. Daniella never crossed the line, but Lauren was well aware her mentor had feelings for her.

The flat started to feel really small. The cold winter days also weighed on her mind—she started for the sunny climes of South Africa. She solved the problem with work. There were numerous places of study she could go to.

It was a good thing too. It gave her very little time to think about Jimmy—in fact, she was amazed at how her mourning was not for the loss of the connection with Jacques. Jacques went back home within weeks of their fight. She avoided the Rhodes Scholar community, leaving it to Daniella, who had a scarce interest in social activities (or friends). Truth be told, beyond her classes, Lauren found herself quite isolated.

Which was ok. She had worn the cloak of popularity easily if reluctantly at high school. Her unhappy home situation and her mother's neediness had made her unwilling to let people get too close and see her vulnerability. So being a bit socially withdrawn was actually… interesting.

She did spend a good deal crying about Jimmy, though. The phone call from her mother was at just the right time. Her mom had moved back to Cape Town, landed a job, was doing some exercise, and as far as Lauren could tell, she was having fun dating again. Lauren had expected her to be angry that she had broken up with Jacques. Her mom surprised her by being very empathetic. It was a breath of fresh air and a whole reframing of their relationship. She suddenly knew she missed her terribly, and they started to talk every day.

Her mom also had some great advice, without being too judgmental. She was adamant that she and Jimmy would end up together if the time was right. In the meantime, Jimmy was doing them both a favor by letting them follow their respective dreams and goals. She relayed to Lauren, for the first time, how her deep resentment toward Lauren's father had poisoned their relationship at an early stage. He was of course not absolved of blame for his indiscretions… but it was a weird admission of own complicity in the toxic environment, which surprised Lauren.

But it did strengthen her resolve to not waste this opportunity. Even if it was cold, and Daniella was sometimes a bit much. She was quite surprised that she had ever sacrificed so much. How easily did she allow herself to let go of her sense of self, and personal goals? Never again.

Daniella was philosophical, during one of their infrequent heart-to-hearts. Daniella did not touch alcohol, but periodically, she indulged in a bit of marijuana by way of a doctored cookie. She said it was her one vice and took the edge off. Lauren joined in with some trepidation and found the experience (in measured amounts) quite pleasant.

So, slightly stoned, they reflected on Lauren's loves and lives lost and found and lost again.

"We are all a result of our parents, Bella. You end up dating versions of your dad, you don't want to be like your mom but a part of you is drawn to repeat her mistakes- the science around this is broad and astounding, and knowing versus doing is not the same thing. I am rambling, but you catch my drift... I do not have your problems with men, my sweet. I have neither the physiology, the patience, the humility nor the need to indulge the weaker sex."

Lauren giggled at that. "Aren't we supposed to be the weaker sex?"

Daniella smiled lazily, resting her hand on Lauren's arm. "Physically, sure. If measured by strength. But if measured by tolerance to pain, longevity, and our capacity to endure God-given limitation, not even that. But I digress. More so they are the weaker sex because they have fewer thoughts, less complexity. Our neurons fire at a thousand times their quantum, our brains and chemically induced emotional velocity are on a level that no man can comprehend or process. No, they are the weaker sex because they have been designed for simplicity. We, on the other hand, are complex creatures. And as complex organisms, we are in some ways stronger."

Lauren slightly shifted, breaking physical contact. Daniella paused and sighed. "Or maybe there is strength in simplicity. For sure, I often long for less stimulation in my mind. It would make life more palatable."

Lauren was aware, even as stoned as she was, that she had once again put up the boundary that Daniella should not cross. She tried to focus on her response.

"So, we are both stronger and weaker. And we are both positively shaped by our parents' behavior, and we are shaped negatively... We want to rebel against their model. It sounds to me like a neat form of ambiguity, lacking in the courage of conviction and not giving any clear commitment to a stance."

Daniella nodded. "Quite right. I have a deep prognosis of your conundrum. I am deficient in the practical experience of love, ambivalent to the vagaries of parental neglect, and unsympathetic to your particular plight. Maybe your problem is that you keep on dating boys? What to do?"

This was dangerous ground again. Lauren tried a different tack. "Maybe you're right... maybe an older man this time... much older..."

Daniella shook her head in irritation, and got up sulkily. "Sleep on it once more. But probably the one that is here is part of your past. An important lesson, nonetheless, but I do know you would be a fool to entertain him. Do the work. Follow your bliss. Who knows where it might lead? But move forward, my Bella. And that..." she burped, "is my final wisdom."

And so it went. Study, work, evolve. Lauren occasionally gave in to the temptation to check for news of Jimmy on the internet and Facebook—but he was, as always, pretty much invisible. There was limited stuff on Stan Wilson buying the restaurant...

Jacques had gone home, and, according to Facebook, was dating a girl from his old crowd. Rich, educated, dad had a wine estate too. Lauren remembered her as not being very nice.

Lauren thought they deserved each other. Maybe even be happy together. She tried to cling to the memory of early Jacques, not the ogre she had dated in those last few months.

But it wasn't her problem, he wasn't her problem. Daniella suggested she try a dating app, but after a drunken dalliance with Tinder, she was horrified at the resulting approaches and retreated into books and movies.

She also rediscovered her love of running. At school, she had often jogged with Sally and her friends, but it was never for the sake of the sport itself, more to keep fit and lean. Now, there was something soothing about the cold chill of winter as she ran past the myriad historic buildings of Cambridge and Oxford.

As the European winter settled in, she gave in to her mom's persistence, and decided to go home for Christmas. Her mom was now in a flat in Cape Town, but she was assured there was a spare bed ready for her. Daniella was supportive. She was going back to Milan for the holidays, and then to Cortina, the fabled ski resort in the Dolomites. She had cautiously broached the subject of Lauren coming with her. This helped Lauren make up her mind to go home for a bit.

So, on the 22nd of December, she took the train to Heathrow, and onward to a flight to Cape Town. It was a two-week holiday that she suddenly knew she desperately needed.

Her mom picked her up at the airport, along with the new boyfriend Tim. First impressions revealed he was a very different character from her father. He was a bit round, but with a kind face and laughing eyes. She could immediately understand why her mom gravitated toward him.

It was also clear that she was quite welcome in her mom's flat, and for the first few days, they reconnected in the most amazing way. Her mom was a different person, she looked ten years younger. She had, with Tim's support, started her own little store specializing in boutique crafts and she was thriving.

It felt to Lauren as if she was meeting her mom for the first time. She was now the person she had been, before an unhappy married life had slowly throttled her soul. She spent a few days and a wonderful Christmas with the two of them. Pretty soon, though, Lauren had a distinct feeling that it might be good to give her mom and Tim some space. They were happy to have her—but they also wanted to spend time alone, as new couples do. She needed to reconnect with some old friends. As you do, she went to social media... and Facebook came to the rescue.

Sam, of course, was now the new rising star in the local Stormers Franchise. The handsome salary that the rugby club paid came in handy, and along with two other players, they had taken a long-term lease in the Cape Town suburb of Camps Bay. Their spot was two blocks from the beach.

Her mom lived in Gardens, a sleepy suburb in the summertime. A short Uber ride, though, revealed a whole new world in Camps Bay, the swanky neighborhood on the other side of the city bowl. Sam was holding court with a few of his mates in the notorious Café Caprice on the strip. Warm afternoon weather, craft beers were flowing and a bevy of really pretty and young girls were in attendance. They had taken residence, it seems, on the couches in the front section, and the name of the game was see and be seen.

Sam did his best to introduce her to everyone, and they did share a look where he shrugged and apologized with his eyes as if to say "This isn't really me."

But, it kind of was. He was no longer the awkward bully from high school. He was living his dream, but she did know how hard he had to work to get there. The little bit that they could chat, it was clear he was still the same guy, but the setting had changed. She retreated into the fray and, after having to fend off a few advances from the peripheral chaps in their crowd, decided to beat a hasty retreat.

She left the party to go for a walk on the beach. It had been packed during the day, but now, as the sundowner hour was kicking in, it started to thin out. And that suited her just fine! Elderly people were walking their dogs, couples holding hands and sitting down facing the ocean. Tourists had cameras out and were taking snaps, waiting for the inevitable sunset show.

She felt a pang of longing for Jimmy, and sudden flashbacks to Thailand—which now felt like a million years ago. A different beach and a different scenario completely. He had been there when she needed him then—as he had been there when she needed him in England. On impulse, she sent him a text and a selfie of her on the beach in Cape Town. Then she realized that 6 pm in Cape Town was early morning in Christchurch. He would probably only see it much later.

She had been a bit of a fool when it came to him, she knew that now. But there was nothing to be done... except, maybe if he texted back, they could at least start talking again...

She was pulled out of her thoughts by almost being run over by a small dog chasing an errant frisbee. The dog, fixated on the toy, collided with her legs, and she almost went down.

Steadying herself she patted the dog, who was panting and looking at her with what was either apology or expectation. It was a rescue dog, and a cutie at that. Impossible to identify the breed. She realized he was waiting for her to pick up the frisbee and throw it. She obliged, but before she could throw it...

The dog's owner came running up. She did a double-take—he was one of the most beautiful men she had ever seen in her life—square-jawed, with a muscled body (mostly hairless) and thick black hair and matching brown eyes.

"Sorry about that," he said. "I'm the worst frisbee thrower in the world, but Simba doesn't seem to mind. Bad for bystanders though."

She laughed. "It's ok—I think Simba likes me," and she patted him, which elicited ecstatic yelps from this bronze god's canine companion.

"I think you're right. Now... could I have that frisbee back? Or do you want to have a go?"

She realized she was still holding it. "Sure." And she surprised herself with a good effort (her netball ball skills kicking in). Simba snapped it out of the air some 10 meters further. He was delighted.

"That's pretty good," said Simba's owner. He paused. "You look like you have some ball skills. Are you here on holiday?"

She didn't see any harm in replying. She was enjoying talking to him. "Yes, I am. Staying with my mom in Gardens."

"Great. Then you can come to play in our volleyball team tomorrow. We have a standing game at 10 am before it gets crowded. We set up the net over there, right next to the boulders leading to Glen Beach." He stuck out his hand, and she realized it was massive.

"I'm Danie. But you can call me Stan."

"Lauren," she said, stifling the urge to smile. Jimmy had his Stan... was this her Stan? The universe was playing a joke? Sam and Stan? She did smile...

The volleyball game the next morning was an eye-opener. Sam joined her, and it was an interesting experience. Lauren was conscious of having filled out a little during her time away. She still had a good body, but Stan was surrounded by girls with exquisite figures in tiny bikinis. He was also, today, accompanied by an older man. The older guy, introduced as Jeff, was also in pretty good nick—and very clearly Stan and he were together.

And so, a rhythm was set for Lauren for her stay in Cape Town. Early morning runs or hikes with her mom, followed by volleyball with a collection of supermodels, beautiful gay men, and guest appearances from Sam and his entourage of rugby buddies. Then there were usually lazy afternoons hanging out at Stan's place, the beach... Sometimes Sam's place and evening cocktails, *braais* and dinners with either group or a collection of and/or. And one day, with Sam, a day trip out to the Winelands.

Driving through Stellenbosch, she thought of Lee, Jacques, and Jimmy. She realized that she did not miss her friends... Lee had unfriended her on Facebook after she broke up with Jacques, and the others had also gone quiet. She had built a life in Stellenbosch that she didn't feel like she could go back to. And then Jimmy. He never responded to her message. It hurt her, even though they had agreed to give each other some space. She had thought… she didn't know what she thought. Why send him a sexy photo of her in a bikini? She didn't know, really. She was just missing him so much in that moment.

But he had not made contact. That, in itself, was a message.

She quickly found Sam's company pleasant but tedious. He was the same wonderful guy, but his world was now focused on nutrition, training and conditioning to make the national team. And that, along with playing PlayStation and enjoying the attention of a steady stream of girls, was all that was going on in that house.

Stan's crowd was a bit more varied. They were all professionals in the creative space (Stan was a photographer, and Jeff owned a production studio). Their world consisted of lavish dress-up parties, boutique drugs, and a commensurate focus on the body beautiful. They were more focused on aesthetic than actual fitness.

And so, she found herself drifting in between both. She missed Oxford, with its intellectual bias and chilly weather. She was, by all accounts, a girl of the hot Karoo sun and enjoyed the Cape Town summer weather. However, she now realized that things had shifted materially for her, and she was quite eager to get back. She loved the time spent with her mom too. But Stellenbosch was no longer home— and neither was Cape Town or Oudtshoorn, for that matter. Where was home? She wasn't quite sure.

Still, it was two weeks of rest. She could leave the parties early, avoid the serious drugs, and with Sam's guarding eye, most of the men left her alone.

Still, it was lonely. She had no desire to engage in a one-night stand. Yet, she was aware that, having discovered the depths of sexual joy with Jimmy, she had a bit of an itch she needed to scratch.

Her penultimate night in Cape Town provided an interesting opportunity.

She was chatting with Jeff at the bar at Café Caprice as day turned to evening. An equally attractive older man, with a completely shaved head and clear blue eyes, came to join them.

"Lauren, please meet my friend Edward. Visiting, like you, from the Isle. In fact, somewhat surprising that you don't know each other, seeing as you are both attached to that venerable institution of Oxford College."

Edward laughed. "Jeff, if you ever came to visit, you would find it is a big place. Lots of hidey-holes for attractive young women and boring professors to hide out in." His eyes sparkled with humor, and Lauren noticed he had a lean body. She judged him to be in his late forties early fifties, but it was hard to tell.

She took his outstretched hand in greeting, but instead of shaking it, he turned it over and kissed it gently, keeping eye contact. She felt a sudden thrill course through her. This was the epitome of a cheesy move, but somehow, he had made it feel intimate and daring.

Gathering herself, she said, "And where would a boring professor be hiding out?"

"Mostly in the literature department, trying to educate the modern youth on their lack of originality."

Jeff snorted. "Young lady, watch out for this one. My oldest, bestest straight friend, far too cultured to not be one of us. Been trying to convert him for years, but like a true stereotype, he prefers to sleep with his adoring female students. Mind you don't become his latest conquest." And with that, he fluttered off.

Edward, not missing a beat, had not let go of her hand yet, and said, "And where would an attractive young woman hide out? And am I to assume you are a student?"

She pulled back her hand. "Buy me a drink first, and I'll tell you my life story."

She found him fascinating. He skirted the subject of his relationship status and steered conversation mostly to her work and studies. He was knowledgeable on the genetics component of her work with Daniella, but also deeply interested in her trajectory and what thesis she would pursue if she did so.

She had missed the intellectual conversations and environment of Oxford. Even though a part of her was always guarded with Daniella, she realized that she now needed—craved—that level of interaction. And Edward was all that, and more.

The hours flew by, and they went for a stroll on the beach after midnight. He entertained her with tales of his early days as a news-paper reporter. He had been the Times of London's front-man in South Africa during the fall of Apartheid and had met Mandela, De Klerk, and Tutu- among others. He had fallen in love with the country during that time, and now came back annually. Always at the invitation of many good friends like Jeff.

He was accomplished. He had written several acclaimed and successful novels, both fiction and non-fiction. He had ghost-written the memoirs of some of Mandela's prison guards, and one had even been made into a moderately successful Hollywood biopic.

He was also, clearly, a womanizer. He was effortlessly charming, complimentary without being overt and she felt powerfully drawn to his unapologetic sensuality. But he was also old enough to be her father, and anyway, there was still Jimmy in her thoughts and heart.

Incredibly, they were still talking on the beach when the sun came up. With several other couples scattered around the beach, they lapsed into silence to appreciate the timeless spectacle of nature in all its glory.

He had given her his jacket, like a proper English gentleman. She rested her head on his shoulders, and felt the strength there. She waited for him to make his move.

Only he didn't. When the moment came, and he took her face gently in his hands, he studied her with those clear blue eyes. He planted a gentle kiss on her forehead, even though she had her lips slightly parted.

"Let's get you an Uber."

Her last night was, predictably, spent with her mom and Tim. It was a pleasant goodbye, but she surprised herself at how much her thoughts lingered on Edward. He was not there for her lunch send-off with the rest of the gang (from both groups of friends, surprisingly easily intermingling on the strip at the Bungalow). But she was delighted to get a call from him just before she boarded her flight. And a promise to catch up "On the other side".

Lauren headed back to Oxford with a tinge of excitement. She was pretty sure she was about to do something really stupid and quite naughty. And she couldn't wait.

The restaurant business is not for the faint-hearted. Jimmy had always excelled in his various roles. He had never before had to deal with the background issues though. There were labor relations, health and safety requirements, liquor licenses, and—most infuriating of all—partners.

Stan was a professional rugby player. But he caught on quickly, and Grace had a mind like a razor. They wanted frequent updates and management reports as things progressed, and Jimmy quickly realized that to maintain the friendship, he needed to be on top of everything.

So, he worked like a trojan. He set up the systems, hired trained staff, worked most of the initial shifts himself, doing everything from front-of-house management to flipping pizzas and cleaning the shop at the end of the day. It was a funny thing about the business. He was getting a negotiated salary, but the profit share meant that every extra person he hired took money out of his pocket.

And it paid off. They renovated Il Leone to a superficial degree. Stan was adamant that the character needed not to be adjusted too much, so cleaning it up, redoing the toilets, and refurbishing the furniture and kitchen equipment was all necessary. The memorabilia, however, was mostly left by the brothers at Stan's request. It was augmented by stuff from the Wilson collection, mostly round awards, rugby jerseys and trophies from the All Black days.

Stan committed to eating there twice a week (something he just about did anyway)—and his celebrity pull helped bring back the numbers. Jimmy figured out social media and launched Facebook and Instagram campaigns ("Dinner with Stan Wilson!"). Jimmy scoured the local markets and suppliers for the best ingredients. They raised the prices slightly but also ensured that their ingredients were pumped up. The wine list was revamped and deals were done with a local craft beer manufacturer for a good deal on beer on tap.

A combination of star power, service and quality quickly made a hit, and before they knew it, Il Leone was packed every single night. They immediately showed great numbers. Being a small, intimate pizza joint, they found that winter was good for them too. June, July and August met and exceeded expectations.

Possibly because of the hours he worked, possibly because of specifically Grace's watchful influence, Jimmy found he started drinking a lot less. He enjoyed early morning runs around his neigh-borhood in Christchurch. The only way he found he could do them and work the crazy hours in the restaurant was to stay mostly sober. It felt good. Running—and the occasional weekend to go for a hiking trip —kept him in relative balance. And not thinking of Lauren.

By September, they had smashed their targets, and, as agreed, half his bonus went back into the pot, and he took a nice paycheck home. Jimmy had had a few meaningless one-night stands in the last year… but truthfully, he had hoped that Lauren would reach out. She didn't, though, and the Wilsons kept on trying to introduce him to "nice Kiwi girls". Those he always treated with respect. None of them interested him.

So, in October, he used his bonus to treat himself to a one-week hike in world-famous Milford Sound. On the walk, he met quite a few other folks from all over the world. It brought home to him how much he had missed the international interaction he had in France and Kitzbuehel. Il Leone was great—but the client base was mostly locals.

He also used the time to figure out his next move. The restaurant was thriving, but he thought it was time to hire a manager. He would need to motivate this to the Wilsons, though…

Stan had decided to go play rugby in Japan, and now wanted monthly management reports. Jimmy missed him at the restaurant, but the place now had enough traction that he didn't always need to be there. A bunch of his mates from the team, including Richie McCaw, were happy to pop in frequently. Jimmy made a deal with them that they could come to eat for free once a week except for weekends, and the regular flow of celeb All Blacks ensured continuously packed week-nights as well.

Jimmy decided to go spend Christmas and New Years with Uncle Joe and Melissa back in South Africa. Robby was wrapping up his studies and they would also be able to catch up. And maybe even Lauren would be home, visiting her mom?

He booked a flight mid-December and did a video conference call with the Wilsons before he headed out.

"The numbers are sensational, Jimmy. You've been knocking it out of the park. Slight increase in personnel costs, though."

"Nothing gets past you guys. I recently promoted Sydney to assistant manager, and I must admit I have been taking a few nights off a week—but all went well, I think we might have a keeper there."

Stan arched an eyebrow. "If Sydney is running the place now, what are you doing?"

"Looking for new outlets."

He could see both of them take pause. Finally, Grace said, "We planned to run this for a year or so first—then start looking at expansion."

Jimmy had his answers ready. "Time flies when you're having fun, guys. In less than three months it will have been a year. Our cash position is strong, the business is working well without Stan there, and I have been actively stepping back mentoring Sydney into the management role. I'm ready."

They digested it. Then Stan asked, "Where did you have in mind?"

December back in South Africa was bittersweet. There was no Lauren—but there were many other old, familiar faces. And some new ones! Jimmy spent the first week in Oudtshoorn. He was immediately smitten with their new-born arrivals, twin girls called Julie and Sarah. They were six months old. It made Jimmy realize that he never had cousins.

An extended family was not something he was used to. It made for a glorious and happy Christmas celebration. As a couple, Uncle Joe and Melissa were firmly entrenched in the Oudtshoorn business community. Uncle Joe was super proud of Jimmy's success, especially when Jimmy told him what he was up to in terms of expansion of the restaurants into a chain.

It mirrored what Uncle Joe and Melissa had been busy with. They had both roused themselves out of their self-imposed "go slow" and had started to take over, buy, and operate several guest houses and restaurants in the town.

It was pretty mad. The restaurant in town was where Uncle Joe spent his evenings, but they had purchased a small farm outside of town too. They were busy turning it into a 10-bedroom guest house with a restaurant. The girls, according to their vision, would grow up on a farm—but they would also be close enough to town to enjoy all the conveniences thereof.

It was perfect. He loved bouncing his ideas off them, they had so many good learnings to share of their expansion journey. In New Zealand, he had met many expat South Africans that were hugely pessimistic about their old country. As far as Uncle Joe and Melissa were concerned, there was no place better in the world. And they should know—they had literally lived everywhere else.

Robby felt a bit different. He had passed his exams, and they celebrated at the old joint. It was great to see him, and swap stories over pizza almost as good as the fare Jimmy was now cooking up in Christchurch. He resisted the urge to go back there and give them some pointers—and focused on the conversation with his old mate.

"So, Rob, no new headphone projects to report?"

"Jimmy my boy, there are always new projects. No headphones, though." He frowned. "Truth be told, I lost my mojo a bit this year. All the political crap gets me down. Our country is in such a mess, even after what Zuma did last year, they are still holding on to him. And people hope that Cyril will take over... but Zuma, and these Gupta gangsters of his, are already maneuvering his ex-wife into this job. I tell you, you are a wise man, leaving this country..."

Jimmy hated it when Robby went dark. He loved his friend... but this side of him always bothered him. "Hold on Rob. I haven't left. I'm just... on an adventure, I guess."

"You've been on an adventure for a while, my friend."

"True. But I suppose I always think I'll come back... I mean look at all this. It's magic."

Robby looked around, then smiled. "True that. Ok, so why are you building yourself a business empire if you plan to come back here? Why come back?"

Jimmy shifted in his seat. "I guess... maybe one day, I'll sell my share of that business. Come here with lots of capital, start something. And maybe..."

"Lauren?" prodded Robby.

"Yeah," admitted Jimmy.

"My friend, I tried a full-time romance this year. All women are a bit crazy, in my opinion. This last one screwed with my head... It was all I could do to get through finals after she broke up with me. That's two for two on psycho bitches after Gretha. So, trust me, you're better off alone."

"Robby, you're such a ray of sunshine. What happened to you? And for the record, Lauren and I broke up by mutual consent."

"Sure." Robby shrugged and asked for another beer. It felt like old times, getting pissed in Stellenbosch after a gig. Jimmy gestured at the waiter. "Make it two."

The next day, they decided to do a road trip. Sam, now a famous Springbok, had rented a house in Knysna on the lagoon. They crashed there for a couple of days. It was a great spot, and Robby became his old self again. With the exception that he was now the one laying into the drinks, and Jimmy found himself to be the more reserved one. Jimmy felt sympathy for it though—a broken heart is no joke. And party Robby was a lot of fun, leaving his negativity mostly behind.

Sam updated Jimmy on Lauren. She had come back for holidays the previous year, and they chatted frequently. She was doing amazingly well. She was going into her last six months, and by all accounts, she was slaying it. Her mentor, Daniella's Doctoral Thesis had been published, and in the field of bio-genetics was making waves in the scientific community. It was all very positive, and there was one overriding message: Lauren was not coming back to South Africa any time soon. She had even elected to spend Christmas and the holidays with friends in the UK.

Sam said he hoped to see her in June. She would be graduating, and he had accepted a contract to go play with Saracen's rugby club in England. Jimmy felt an unreasonable pang of jealousy at that, as if Sam was going to rekindle old flames.

It was as if Sam read his mind. "It's nothing she said exactly, bud. But I get the feeling she's not available. To me... or you..."

Which sat interestingly for Jimmy. He was 22, and he knew he was still young. He also felt like he had piled on a lot of miles in the last few years. He was, in his mind, way too young to think about settling down and having a family. On the other hand, the joy Uncle Joe and Melissa were having with their girls was something he wanted. One day. But he was, somewhere, clinging on to the idea that one day would be with Lauren. What if she had met someone?

And for Jimmy, he started to seriously contemplate the question. What was home? It was not Cape Town anymore. When his world crashed with his parents, and he left for Oudtshoorn, it was like he also severed ties with his old self and environment.

It was not Oudtshoorn. He had lived there less than a year, and although Uncle Joe felt like his real family now, the house felt more like a favorite place to visit.

Maybe he needed to face the fact that he had, by default, become a bit of a nomad. And as such, Christchurch was as much a home as he ever had. He had friends, purpose, and now business interests.

So, the answer, he supposed, was yes. It's great over there, and he would stay for the foreseeable future. Which begged the question—who would he share his life with?

Lots of time, he told himself. For someone.... But not necessarily Lauren?

Before they knew it, it was time for him to fly back in time for New Years, always a big night at Il Leone. Robby drove him to the airport and raised an interesting topic.

"Jimmy, what if I came to New Zealand? To help you?"

"Umm... Robby, sure... but you would need a work permit. I suppose we could sponsor you... but I would need to check with my partners first." Truth be told, he wasn't sure it was a good idea. Robby had amazing ideas and entrepreneurial flair... but he was in a bit of a bad space, and Jimmy didn't think his reasons were right for wanting to come.

On the other hand, they had a lot of history. Maybe changing location would lift him out of his current funk.

It was as if Robby sensed his thoughts. "You do that bud. Either way, I'm coming over. I'm sick of this country—time for a fresh start."

Lauren woke up to the familiar sound of coffee grinding. She kept her eyes shut, and just listened to him move around the kitchen. It was one of her favorite parts of the day—waiting for a freshly brewed cup. Edward was, among many other things, a true coffee snob. Most Englishmen were very much inclined toward tea. Edward, however, had spent time covering the second wave of socialism in South America. It had given him an unforgettable taste for "the good stuff".

She wrapped the sheets around her. Only the finest cotton for Edward, and it was another reason she loved to share his bed. She was aware that she was not the first to enjoy the feel of this high-quality linen. Probably not the last, either.

Was this what it meant to be wanton? Now, warm in the apartment, the cold winter from the window blowing lightly on her face, the smell of his sex still on her, she was deeply present. And contented.

She watched him move with easy grace around his kitchen. She did not love him. She was clear on that. She was still—and would always be—hopelessly in love with Jimmy. But Edward was... primal. He kept her very much in the present, challenging her, taking her at will, and also allowing her to spend herself on him. It was passionate and oh so secret and the clandestine nature of their affair added only to the spice.

No, she thought, as he handed her a steaming espresso- it was not love. But deep mutual affection, with a powerful slice of sexual compatibility.

She sat up, nursing the coffee. Edward was sophisticated and worldly. Where Jacques had "breeding" in the South African sense and moved in elevated circles there, he had been lost in the evolved academic competition of Oxford. Not so with Edward. It was, she admitted, an unfair comparison due to their differentials in age. In time, she mused, Jacques might outgrow his petulant insecurities. Her current lover had no such hang-ups.

Comparing him to Jimmy was more difficult. They were worlds apart. And she chose not to dwell there.

Still, self-awareness did not lead to alternative action. Jimmy was, for the time being, maybe forever, lost to her. Jacques was in the past, and this man... this gloriously weathered and sophisticated intellectual, was her present.

His fussing in the kitchen concluded and with his iPad in hand, he climbed back into bed with her. He popped open the news feed and raised his eyebrows. "Idiots," he muttered under his breath. As often happened when he became agitated, he took a few breaths with his asthma pump. It was a curious physical debilitation in otherwise robust physiology.

"What now?" She knew that look on his face. He was a model of British restraint, but occasionally a darker temper took hold of him. It never manifested as physical violence—but rather in a brief but powerful audible utterance, such as now. "Idiots" was very much in the zone of something big had happened.

"This last year has challenged my faith in humanity. Trump, Brexit... I maintain, if people still maintained their faith in the written word by quality authors, instead of this current disaster of social media, the world would not be in such a stupid place."

She liked him this way. He did not while away his time obsessing with things beyond his control, he had too much of a stoic mindset for that. Oh, she had also learned that from him. They spent many cold evenings strolling on the river, where he had expanded on the virtuous thinking of Marcus Aurelius, Benjamin Franklin, and Epictetus. She was fascinated by this "lost" philosophy so misappropriated in modern times, and eagerly lapped up his teachings. It was damn sexy too, and a spirited discussion around stoicism would usually lead to multiple orgasms in bed later. But sometimes he got his back up...

So, she was doubly interested and decided to poke the bear a little.

"I thought you detested the EU's undue influence on British sovereignty? Did you not, just last week, put that poor Ph.D. graduate in his place for daring to suggest that a more integrated UK would be good for all?"

"Quite right, young lady. You do pay attention. I am not in favor of further throwing in with the European cause, especially not currency adoption. But to go completely the other way, which is what would happen if they pulled this thing through..." he frowned once more. "I suppose it is time to face the truth? After all, the young are apathetic, and the old uninformed. By God, it could happen."

She put her hand under the blankets and was pleased with what she found. One more push...

"Maybe it would be a good thing? Great Britain, back to complete self-determination, free from the shackles of Brussels and—gasp—the Krautish influence of Angela Merkel?"

He turned to her; his pupils dilated in concordance with his pulsing erection.

"I know that you are simply seeking a reaction from me, you minx. Well, you have succeeded, and now you will receive your punishment."

"Be gentle!" She squealed, as he fell upon her.

Later, she rushed to the faculty office for the usual 10 am meeting with Daniella. She was slightly disheveled, and she felt the smell of him must be on her. Of course, her mentor noticed. Over the last 10 months, she had made her disapproval of the relationship abundantly clear.

Lauren knew she had cause. Edward was wildly inappropriate, both because of his age and the relationship with her (he was a professor at the uni, if not hers). On the other hand, he challenged her mentally, satisfied her sexually... and since they had consummated their flirting at Valentine's Day, he had supported her in other ways.

The flat was his. But he traveled often, and she could use it when she wanted. The escape from the confines of Daniella's place was always welcome.

She knew she was a total cliché. You didn't need to be a shrink to know that at some level her daddy issues were playing out as well. But hey... it was almost New Years', she was getting closer to the incredible reality of being an Oxford Graduate, and she was sleeping with a rogue. Even if she did not love him. she did, however, adore him.

Daniella snapped her back to the present. It was their last meeting of the year before they broke for the holidays. She was doing her annual pilgrimage back to Italy... while Lauren would go and spend it in a French ski resort with Edward. She was excited—she had not had a white Christmas before.

"It is either good news or bad news, Bella. Depending on your perspective."

Lauren hesitated. "Are we talking about Brexit, or..."

"Good heavens no. I do not concern myself with the economic or political flows or our leaders in this regard. Except to ponder how the shift in Europe will be affected by a deeper crisis..."

Lauren was a bit lost, but pressed on; "Ok, so what is good news or bad news?"

"Ah, yes. Our paper has been published, and people are taking notice. The field of virology is exploding—and the theorem around a flu pandemic, while not exactly new, is attracting new attention. None other than the Gates Foundation have reached out to us for further grant support."

Lauren's eyes widened. "Bill Gates!?"

"None other. And while I detest the strategies that made him the leader of information technology as we know it, there is no denying that through his foundation and the efforts of his wife Melinda, they have been a significant force for good in recent years. It is an intriguing offer, to be sure." Daniella smiled a rare smile.

"The offer is..."

"We would transfer to his alma mater at Harvard. He would fully sanction further research, to be published through Harvard, and our stipend would be infinitely more generous than what I receive now through Rhodes and the current administration here."

Lauren's mind reeled. "You are considering it?"

"I am. Of course, you would come with me." It was a statement as much as a question.

Lauren tried to process this. First Oxford… then Harvard? She had a good chance at qualifying for further study here, but she had thought she would throw in with Daniella's research anyway, there was enough congruence with her ambitions. Harvard?

And then she thought of Edward. She always knew that this affair had a sell-by date—but it suddenly loomed large.

"If we did go… when would we?"

"We would be expected to be settled by the end of July. Their academic year kicks off in early August. You would, of course, be fully credited for your work here, and would be free to pursue your Honors and Masters accreditations with me as your study leader."

Lauren stood up. "So, I could finish my degree here? Then go for a Masters there? Maybe even a Ph.D.? That sounds amazing, Daniella. This is a massive opportunity. I mean… Bill Gates. Harvard."

Daniella waved her down. "It might seem like a… how do the Americans put it? A 'no-brainer'. I suspect there is more to this story. My Ph.D. thesis gained attention—but they are asking for a more specific brief."

"What do you mean?"

"Remember our research participation in project Cygnus?"

She nodded. "The National Health Service simulation on readiness for a viral flu pandemic. We were asked to sign a quite comprehensive non-disclosure to that effect just for the initial workshops."

"The report will not be published. A storm is coming, and the authorities are keeping the research under wraps while they try to prepare," said Daniella.

Lauren was not quite sure where this was going. "How is this linked to the Gates grant?"

"There is a high level of cooperation between the UK and US governments. They want us to run the simulations in the US as well."

"Daniella, this is huge." She hugged her friend, knowing that this rare show of affection would be received with great pleasure.

Daniella smiled. "Once in a lifetime, Bella."

Later, Lauren would go sit on the banks of the River Cherwell and pen down her thoughts in her journal. She had great affection for Edward, and would be loath to once again face an empty bed in Boston—but there were six months left before she needed to go.

She immediately told Edward. She was delighted when he did not take the news well. She sometimes wanted him to show her in a deeper way that he cared for her... even though they had agreed on the terms of their dalliance long ago.

His reasons, however, were not what she expected.

"I don't like it, my dear." They were in an off-campus coffee shop, their favorite place to not be seen. They were to depart for France the next day.

"I know this means the end of us, Edward... but we have six months..."

"Oh, hush. We both know that our relationship was of finite length. It's an amazing opportunity. You do know, however, that with your academic momentum, you could probably apply for further study here?"

She bit her lip. "Sure. But there are two problems. I can't afford to study without Daniella's support... and I mean. It's Harvard. Bill Gates. Come on! Are you not excited?"

He sipped his tea, smiling ruefully. "She has presented you with another carrot, I'll give her that. But it ties you to her even further."

"I know. I know." She did not like that he saw the truth this clearly, sometimes.

He took her hand. "There are six months until your graduation, and first we must go on holiday. When we come back, permit me to help you navigate the Oxford grant system. You should at least know what your further options are."

She nodded. It made sense. She had said yes to Daniella... but, if

Edward could help her gain her independence as a scholar, she had to look at it. Even if it meant missing Harvard.

Daniella would not like it. Lauren decided she would not tell her until she had more information.

She would come to regret that decision.

32

As promised, Robby turned up on Jimmy's doorstep. He immediately went to work charming the Wilsons. There was no trace of the negative person Jimmy had encountered in South Africa. He was like the old Robby, and he was brimming with ideas.

The first thing Robby brought to the party was a take-out service. He volunteered to run it as a profitable stand-alone division. He then set to work getting some mopeds, training up delivery staff, and putting in place (by trial and error, to be sure) a slick ordering and payment system.

Pretty soon it was working like a charm. Which tied in with their next project: opening up a second Il Leone. Robby helped him look for a location in a different neighborhood of Christchurch. Their search was so successful they found two prime spots.

Over dinner with the Wilsons, they hotly debated the opportunity. They had neither the capital nor the management capacity, Grace argued. Robby shot back; "Not true. There's Jimmy and there's me. And we'll find good managers. Come on guys, think big."

Stan shook his head. "Slow and steady wins the race, Robby."

"Sure. But when a golden opportunity presents itself, one should take a close look before passing it up."

Jimmy decided to weigh in. "It's a moot point, Robby. We crunched the numbers. We can fund another location, we have about that available in cash. But we would need to borrow money for a third one, and we don't want to do that."

"So let me put up the cash."

This took them all by surprise. "It's a million dollars, Robby," said Grace, carefully.

"I have it. Come on! We change Il Leone into a holding company, we build another 'owner' store and you franchise out a third location to me."

"This all feels very familiar," said Stan, looking at Jimmy. "And it's too quick. I don't like it. Besides, it will take a big investment. Do you have that kind of cash?"

Robby was a bundle of energy. "I have investors lined up to come in with me. Look, I can't do it by myself this quickly. We need the corporate entity and your sign-offs as citizens. All the paperwork will take time anyway. But we have to sign a Memorandum of Agreement with the sites in the meantime."

"I don't think so, Robby," said Grace.

He tried one last time. "Do you guys trust Jimmy?"

They looked at each other. "Sure. But, like you, he is young. And none of us have a lot of experience in the restaurant chains/franchising business. Better to tread carefully."

"Ok. What if we found the best lawyer on this stuff money can buy? And I paid for an airtight contract that set up the structure and fully protected your current investment. I would take all the risk for the third location, but I would have a controlling interest in the franchise operation. You would have all the upside, and none of the downside."

Stan looked at Jimmy. He knew about this plan. "Robby, as I said to you before—you can go ahead and explore this, but it will be expensive to prepare a legal structure. And there's no guarantee we'll sign off on it."

Robby grinned. "That is absolutely fine…"

The bigger surprise, to Jimmy, was that the very next day, they were sitting on the top floor of a massive legal practice.

"Robby, how far down this road are you?"

"After we scouted the second location last week, I immediately phoned these guys. I pretended to be an irate customer and threatened legal action to a couple of other bigger restaurant franchises here. They all referred me back to this firm. They are the best. And this woman… the word is, she is dynamite."

They were ushered into a plush office. Massive desk, leather chairs, expensive artwork. Meant to intimidate and impress.

Jimmy wasn't looking at any of that. The lawyer stood up from behind her desk and moved to greet them.

Robby was right. She was something.

The skirt covered her knees—but her ankles were exquisite. In that incredible way that women did, her breasts slightly strained against her cashmere blouse. Her skin was a flawless bronze. Her eyes were slightly slanted, her lips full, her lustrous black hair falling to her shoulders.

He took her hand in greeting and realized he towered over her. She looked from him to Robby—who was equally mesmerized. Her eyes locked back onto his. It was then he knew he was in trouble. Then she broke the spell, a slight smile on her lips and reaching her eyes. She had the slightest of laugh lines. How old was she? Late twenties? Early thirties? Impossible to know.

"My, my," she murmured. "A visit from giants today." She gestured at them to sit down.

"My name is Anna. I am a senior associate at the firm of Young, McDonald & Yao. You gentlemen are here to talk to me about assistance with franchise agreements. You came to the right place."

Robby took the lead. Jimmy was still looking for his ability to speak.

"That's right Anna. My colleague Jimmy and I… Well, we wish to expand our single location to a national chain. We want to do the legal paperwork right from the start."

She raised an eyebrow. And said nothing.

In the ensuing silence, Robby shouldered on. "Well, what I meant to say is, I am here to help Jimmy and his partners… senior partners… to put in place the structures."

She stayed silent. Robby was now visibly starting to perspire.

"Ok, look," he said. "Jimmy has a good thing going, his partners don't want rapid expansion. I want in, I have some capital and investors. I need to put their mind at ease with regards to their legal liability first."

She smiled. "Now we're getting somewhere."

They walked out of the building and looked at each other.

"Wow," said Jimmy.

"I know right?" Robby frowned. "Right bitch, that one. But I suppose that's what we need here."

"Don't call her that," said Jimmy, surprising himself.

"Ah..." grinned Robby. "So finally... a woman that can make Jimmy forget about the exalted Lauren... if I recall your French stories, you do like them slightly older, don't you?"

Jimmy punched him in the arm. "Bugger off, Rob. But man... what a woman. She's like... Eurasian or something, right?"

"Don't know what she is bud... but the only thing more appealing about her than the sexiness is her reputation for getting good deals done. And that's what I care about—and what you should care about." Robby sounded sensible again. "Plus, my little sister Jess is going to be devastated all over. With Lauren gone, she was still hoping you would one day see her..."

"Ha-ha. High schoolers are not my style, Rob. And I can keep it professional here, don't you worry."

They walked off. Robby muttered, "We'll see. Still, if she's better at her job than she is sexy, she must be insanely good."

For a few months, Lauren felt that nothing changed. She was stressed, Daniella was edgy, Edward was helpful. In the sense that he presented her with possible alternatives to study at Oxford. All of the grant applications, however, required her to submit recommendation letters. She just knew Daniella would not give her one.

Then, inexplicably, two months before they were to leave, he broke up with her. He allowed her to keep on staying in his flat, but he had to "go to the country" for a while.

She was perplexed. She was, as always, studying incredibly hard for finals, as well as wrapping up admin for Daniella and doing paperwork for Harvard -which now was a fait accompli.

When he finally came back into town, she cornered him in the flat. After a mildly polite meeting (kiss on the cheek), he proceeded to make them tea.

She stared at the back of him—he felt like a stranger to her. Finally, he turned, handed her some tea, and motioned for her to sit down.

She gathered herself, and dove in; "What happened with us? I never made any demands on you… and yet the last few months…"

He played with a spoon in his tea. "Honestly, people at the faculty started to ask questions. Something they had never done before."

"What do you mean?"

"Technically, I am in breach of professional conduct by dating a student. Even a student in a completely different department."

"So? Never much bothered you before."

"Neither did it bother anyone else. But there is a particularly pious administrator that has always had it in for me—and God knows how she found out as she is a social recluse—but she did, and I was forced to terminate things with you. And they asked me to go work on my next paper for a while… somewhere far away. I shouldn't be here now."

Lauren sensed there was more. "That explains things… but still."

He looked her in the eyes. "Someone went to a lot of trouble to make sure we could not continue dating, Lauren. That sounds to me like a jealous lover."

Lauren shook her head. "You can't mean…"

"We both know that what I am saying is plausible."

She still hesitated. "To accuse Daniella? I mean, she is strange, but…"

His gaze kept her transfixed. "And she is in love with you. Always has been. From what you told me, you accepted her affections, if only tacitly. And in exchange, you are following your dreams."

"Are you implying…"

"No. I think you have always kept her at a distance sexually. But she sees you as her partner, I am sure of it."

He played with his tea. "I did some subtle inquiries, Lauren. Your ex, Jacques. He seems to have also been the subject of some unfounded rumors and rampant innuendo within the department. It feels like a very similar strategy to what I endured. Now, who would have the cause of benefit to try to eliminate the men from your life?"

Lauren felt a great weight coming down on her. "Jacques always said that. I was sure it was just his insecurities…"

"Maybe. But even so, someone manipulated things."

"I mean… if what you say is true…"

"You are making a deal with the Devil, Lauren. She is giving you your education… and with that, maybe one day your independence from men, which is what you always claim to want. But are you not tethering yourself to a proxy right now? And in a more destructive way?"

Lauren grasped for the right words to respond; "I… I need to confront her."

He gave her a direct look. "If you do, she could also manipulate your results. Delay your graduation. Be very careful."

Lauren felt her throat constrict. "Then I will wait till after the results are out… and then simply not go to Harvard with her."

Edward nodded. "You could do that, I suppose. I would still worry. The physical ceremony will happen long after you are gone, and until you have that piece of paper in your hands, the results are simply numbers in a database. Which can be altered."

"Edward…" she felt like crying.

He leaned over, and took her hands in his. "My advice? Work hard. Do nothing. There will come a day when you are free of her influence… but just know, in the meantime, that any man in your life… you put them at risk too."

Edward did not stay the night. In the morning, she went back to Daniella.

She was torn. She did not want to believe that her mentor could be behind both things… but how could she find proof? She decided to follow Edward's council and put on a brave face. At least until she could somehow find a way out of this mess.

Daniella was in a great mood. "Focused today, are we? So, let's get to work, my dear."

The second location for Il Leone was a roaring success. Jimmy had planned for it to be a slightly bigger restaurant. While they did try to maintain the charm of the original, it made sense to try a couple of small innovations. One of those was a couple of big-screen TVs for big sports events—and it worked a treat. They expanded the menu to allow for more bar snack-type food for the pre-dinner sports crowd.

It all worked, and with some sponsored All Blacks adding to star power, it was also immediately profitable. Robby was running an efficient home delivery operation. Overall, the vibe was great.

Opening night drew a big crowd. But the most exciting thing was toward the end of the evening, when Grace, Robby, Jimmy and Stan were toasting their success.

"We had a look at the franchise agreement you cooked up," said Grace, with Stan nodding.

"And?" asked Robby and Jimmy, holding their breath.

"More importantly, our lawyer had an independent look. It's airtight, protects everyone… we're ready to push play."

"Yes!" Jimmy and Robby high fived.

Grace wagged a finger at them as they left. "We'll talk in the morning, and sign off on this. Now behave yourself, boys."

But Jimmy and Robby were as drunk on the excitement of their possible future as they were on the beers and tequilas. It was a big night.

At some point in the evening, Jimmy felt a tap on his shoulder. He turned around, and he was surprised to see Anna. She was dressed more casually, in a beige sweater and jeans. Impossibly, she looked even hotter. He was slightly tipsy already but tried to keep his cool.

"Anna! So glad you could make it!"

"What a great turnout. So glad for you guys. Where's your partner?"

"Around… oh here he is, watch out!" But it was too late, as Robby lifted her in a bear hug.

"We are doing it, Anna! Franchises are happening! You are just so awesome!"

"That's wonderful news Robby… but could you please put me down?" Jimmy grinned, she handled it well—although he would have to talk with his buddy about that sort of thing.

"Anyway," she said, lightly brushing her hair back, "I am delighted for the two of you. Let me know when all signatures have been collected, and I'll send someone to collect the original."

"Nah," said Jimmy. "I'll come to drop it off myself."

"I'd like that," she said. She gave him a pointed look and left the restaurant.

"Dude!" said Jimmy, punching Jimmy lightly in the shoulder. "Did you catch that? She wants you."

"A woman like that? I don't think so, my friend. Come, we have work to do."

In the morning, though, they got down to brass tacks. They still had a conditional offer on the new lease, so Robby would immediately take ownership of opening that location. The Wilsons were not interested in running more locations. They did want Jimmy to oversee the two current owner stores, and the franchise operation.

"Think of it, Jimmy! With the Wilson star power pull, your executive ability, and my nose for a deal… man, we can take over the world!"

Once all documents were signed, he found himself excited to see Anna again. And disappointed when she didn't come down to collect them in person. He just left it with reception. Robby just laughed and told him not to punch above his weight.

He didn't spend much time moping though. More locations were coming... and they would need more help.

It was bittersweet. They left for Harvard before Lauren could attend her graduation. Lauren received her degree in absentia. Daniella did try to make a fuss—but given the ongoing doubts that she now had about her mentor, it was hard to put on a happy face.

She felt completely trapped.

On the one hand, the academic environment offered by Harvard was one of the most vibrant in the world. The competitive excellence that prevailed meant that Lauren, in pursuit of her own Masters Accreditation, was doing cutting-edge work. And with some of the most brilliant minds in the field.

But, as her personal contribution and network grew, Daniella's resentment also grew.

It had been only a few months after they had arrived there, and now, Daniella was quite overt with her efforts to isolate her socially.

This realization started to erode things between them. Lauren had, with Daniella's support, been accepted into the Master's program at Harvard. One of the conditions was that she would have an external moderator with no prior relationship. Meanwhile, her work with Daniella on virology would continue.

This did not sit well with Daniella. She would have preferred to be in complete control of Lauren's academic environment. But the rules were clear.

Consequently, old patterns seemed to repeat themselves.

Because she had been accepted into the Master's program on scholarship, she received an independently funded grant that allowed her a greater degree of financial independence. Daniella was, obviously, not pleased when she insisted on independent accommodations and a structured work schedule.

Lauren was still conflicted. Daniella guarded her files and computer codes zealously, even from Lauren. She had done what digging she could, but there was no proof to be found of nefarious behavior. And Daniella had opened incredible doors for her. Their work of late had centered around virology modeling, with a focus on social and economic consequences of global pandemics. Lauren had decided to be more focused on the analysis of conditions that would be conducive to accelerated viral spread.

Or more in layman's terms, Daniella was focused on consequences and control, while Lauren was more interested in cause and underlying environment.

An uneasy rhythm therefore developed. She found a wonderful mentor and promoter in Professor Higgins, who was close to retirement. He could be mistaken for a grouchy grandfather if he did not still possess one of the pre-eminent minds in the field.

She did it because he was brilliant, of course. But also, because, at his age and temperament, he could never be seen as a legitimate threat for her affections. She split her time between her own work and assisting Daniella. The last thing she wanted was for another man's life and career to be affected because of her jealous mentor.

As before, she threw herself into the work. She made no friends, and definitely was not dating. She was extremely cautious about collateral damage. She convinced herself that the work they were doing for the Gates foundation was of supreme importance. Additionally, the research and access for her own Masters was a dream come true.

She often wondered at Daniella's acceptance of their uneasy friendship. How could this possibly be enough for her? A part of her wanted to shake her mentor and encourage her to go find love somewhere else... that the situation was doing an injustice to them both. But she had neither the conviction of proof nor the courage to take that step. And, truthfully, she understood the power of love.

Harvard comforted her. The world-famous campus proceeded with the glorious show that signaled the coming of winter. The fall was a kaleidoscope of glorious color that persisted into early November 2017. It felt like a metaphor for her soul: glorious, beautiful fleeting moments, but the constant knowledge that a cold hard winter was soon upon her.

Sitting with these melancholic thoughts, she received a message that threw her emotions into even more turmoil.

It was a wild ride. Robby and Jimmy once again put in crazy hours, just like before. Their third location in Christchurch, which was now a franchise Il Leone owned by Robby, was as great a success as the others.

They opened in August of 2017. They timed it to coincide with the classic rugby match-up South Africa vs the All Blacks. It was a horrible day for South Africa, their beloved Springboks thrashed in record fashion 57-0. What was even worse was the condescending remarks from their Kiwi patrons. But the pain was lessened by extraordinary sales. And once again, Anna came to congratulate them. This time, she was by herself. She took great care to chat to both of them—but she reserved most of her attention for Jimmy.

They sat down at the corner of the bar. Anna was wearing a tight-fitting black dress this time, with a gold necklace and her hair tied back. She seemed impossibly glamorous among the rest of their patrons. Jimmy could sense the jealous looks from all the other men in the room, as he sat and chatted to her in a corner.

She languidly sipped her cocktail, her eyes locked onto his. "And now? Have you had more offers for franchises?"

"To be honest, we haven't marketed the concept at all. We have been completely absorbed with opening up these two locations. Not to mention putting in the delivery component across all three suburbs, and figuring out what the management and supply side should look like." He liked that she was completely focused on him. He could feel himself wondering what her lips would feel like. She was leaning in close to him.

He struggled to keep a hold of himself. "We need to work on our roll-out plan for more outlets now. I'm trying to get a handle on what that should look like. We don't want to grow too fast, and the Wilsons are desperate that we don't dilute the brand they've attached their name to." He could smell her perfume... it was musky, and it drove him crazy. Concentrate, idiot.

"For someone so young, you have a really good grasp on the challenges of this situation."

This cooled him down a bit. He still did not know how old she was. She could be five or six years older, maybe even 10. He decided to find out. "I could say the same about you."

She laughed. "You never ask a woman her age, Jimmy."

"I didn't ask," he smiled back.

She put her hand on his knee, electrifying him. "Come closer."

He leaned in, and she whispered in his ear, "Someday I might tell you."

Then she took her hand away, and sipped her cocktail. He, of course, felt shaken and stirred. But she surprised him with her next words.

"While flirting with you is a lot of fun, Jimmy, I came here with an offer."

He was intrigued. "An offer?"

She nodded. "Every year, we send a handful of our premium clients to an entrepreneurial executive course at Harvard. It is a four-day seminar and very expensive. We do it because we have found that we see an exponential return in work for us. The knowledge gleaned there helps these clients to scale."

"Harvard? I don't even have a base degree. You must be kidding." But he found himself getting excited.

She shook her head. "It does not matter. All that matters is a proven track record and a valid sponsor. With us, you have both. The partners in my firm approved that Il Leone should be represented—and they were particularly excited about sending Stan Wilson associated with our brand."

Jimmy's face fell. "Oh. So, you want me to let Stan know about this opportunity."

She smiled mischievously. She was toying with his emotions, he knew it. "I convinced them that Stan was merely the figurehead. The real brain of the operation is a 22-year-old South African."

"And they believed you?"

"They trust my judgment." She finished her drink and grabbed her purse. "Walk me out, please."

He passed a boisterous Robby surrounded by pretty girls. His buddy gave him a wink and a thumbs up. Jimmy tried to ignore it, but he knew Anna noticed.

It was chilly outside, and she put on her shawl.

"Why not Robby? He was the one that drove the relationship with you—and your firm."

She took a moment to answer. "The truth? He is also dynamic—but we will see more benefit for you to go. And besides..." She stood on tiptoe and kissed him lightly on the lips.

"I'll be hosting the trip."

33

It was a brutal trip from Christchurch to Boston. Three flights in total taking a whole day. The blow was softened by his first flight in business class.

Anna, now hosting not just him, but a half dozen other clients, had dialed down the flirting. She deftly rebuffed the clumsy attempts from the mostly middle-aged other men. Jimmy found himself slightly irritated. But mostly he was impressed by the way she handled herself.

And she was great at facilitating introductions for him. They were from technology, media, food and liquor companies. They were all at least 10 years older than him. They dismissed him until they learned his partner was Stan Wilson. Ah, the magic Wilson name did the trick every time. By the time they touched down in Boston, he felt he had somewhat earned their respect in his own right.

He was excited. He had never been to the US before. He wished there was time to go visit New York. But their purpose here was clear: An intense four days of case studies focused on entrepreneurs from all over the world. Jimmy was sure he would get the ideas he needed for the next steps with their restaurant business. After all, this was the world's most famous university. He could pinch himself.

What he didn't tell Anna, was that he had reached out to Lauren.

He had heard she was here, still working with her Italian mentor. She had quickly—if coolly—replied to his text message, and they had agreed to meet at the first available opportunity. Given that they were in class all day and then hosted dinners, he knew that the first after-noon was his only chance.

After they had put down their suitcases, Anna arranged a minivan to take the group for a sightseeing tour of Boston. They had a few hours of daylight left before the welcome dinner. He declined, citing fatigue from the trip, to jeers from the rest of the guys.

Then he hailed a cab, and made his way to the Boston downtown area.

She met him in Boston Central Park.

He recognized her from afar. She still cut an imposing figure, the winter jacket and scarf not able to completely conceal her athletic build. The woolly beanie didn't quite cover her blonde hair.

She turned to face him. His heart stopped. It was still Lauren—his Lauren. But something was different about her.

"Hi," he said.

"Hi back." And she moved into his arms to embrace him. She clung to him for a second. It was not a hug of romantic intent—more like desperation. He was confused… and worried.

"Lauren?"

"Come sit." She gestured to a bench.

"Nah, it's cold. Could we rather walk a bit?"

There was that nervous look again, but she nodded. "Let's go down here…. Through the park."

It was a clear day… The crisp cold air was something he had gotten used to in Christchurch, and he felt at ease. He was glad to finally see her, but he tried to keep a check on his emotions.

"So… I hear you graduated from Oxford, and now are well on your way to a Masters in Virology at Harvard." He shook his head. "I'm so proud of you, Lauren."

"Thank you," she murmured. "I hear you followed through with the restaurant. According to my mom, you are about to go even bigger."

He smiled. "Robby likes to exaggerate, and the moms like to brag.

But yeah… we're getting there. It's crazy, right? Who would've thought?"

They stopped by the pond and watched the ducks for a bit. Her cheeks were flushed, and he thought she looked as beautiful as ever.

"I miss you, Jimmy. I wish we had kept contact."

He started. "I wanted to… but I was worried about breaking our deal. You also never did, so I tried to stay strong and leave well enough alone. Didn't want to get in the way of your dreams, right?"

She turned to him, a twinkle in her eye. "Some self-control. I sent you my sexiest picture."

He was confused. "You did? When was this?"

"Christmas, a few years ago. You ignored it… so I thought that was it."

Jimmy couldn't work it out for a second. Then it clicked. "Robby. The bastard had my phone. Probably thought he was doing me a favor by deleting the message. My head was still in a mess about you then."

"And now?" They started walking again, passing the dog park.

He thought about it. "My head is no longer in a mess. Too busy I guess."

"Is there… someone…?" The question was hesitant. He quickly said, "No." But in saying it, he knew he was lying. "You?"

"There is no man in my life. Hasn't been for a while." The way she said it sounded strange to him. There was a story there… but he didn't press.

As they came to the end of the park, they turned around and retraced their steps. There were now many other walkers enjoying the dusky twilight.

"So… will you stay here, once you complete your studies?" He had wondered what her end game was.

"For what I want to do… the kind of work… This is the epicenter. Our models predict that we are at huge risk of a major pandemic… so I do think I might stay for a while. Be part of the first line of defense, you know."

"Still want to save the world. You haven't fundamentally changed, Lauren. As I said… proud of you."

"And you? Any plans to expand your restaurant business… this way?" A hopeful tone.

"Not anytime soon. We're just getting going." But then they stopped, and he turned to face her. "So, nothing has changed... except now you're even further away."

"A lot has changed, Jimmy. There is a big part of me that wants to just come with you."

That surprised him. "What's wrong, L?"

She shook her head. "My problems. And I have to find my own solutions. But I'm in no place for dating right now. The work is too important."

They stared at each other for a long time. They could both feel the love... and the gulf between them even wider. Something was weighing her down, and that now also stood between them.

"So, what now?" he asked.

She gently touched his cheek and pulled him toward her. Her lips were soft... and he could taste salty tears on them. The kiss lingered, then she pulled away. "Now we say goodbye again. And this time, for good."

When he arrived back at the hotel, he had a message from Anna.

He took a shower, suited up, and went downstairs to meet the group. They went to a lovely restaurant in Boston—Anna picked up the tab, of course, and they came home at a reasonable hour with not an excess of alcohol in them. Tomorrow was day one, of course.

Anna had been courteous as usual to all of them, and he was disappointed she didn't give him more personalized attention. The encounter with Lauren had him all churned up... and he could have used a bit of validation.

He had hardly entered his room when the phone rang. "Hello?"

"Room 318." And the light went dead. He stared at the phone only for a second, then he rushed one floor up. After a couple of knocks, she let him in. She was half undressed.

She ushered him in, then turned around. "Unzip me, will you?"

He duly did so, noticing her skin. Lauren was blonde, tall, and had fair skin. This woman was the complete opposite—her skin glowed with exotic vitality. And once again, that perfume.

She wriggled out of the dress, and turned around... and now he could fully appreciate her perfect petite figure, splendorous in black, lace underwear. "Here," she tilted his chin to look her in the eyes.

"Did you have a nice rest?" Something in the way she said it made him believe that she knew he had gone out. And he instinctively knew he shouldn't lie to her.

"I went out. To meet an old friend. We had... unfinished business."

She took out her earrings, her gaze never leaving his. She put them down on the dresser with slow, deliberate movements.

"And now? Did you finish it?"

He had thought about the question. And now, more than ever, he thought he knew the answer. "Yes. It's finally finished."

"Good." She unclipped her bra, and then, she took his hand and put it on one of her perfectly formed breasts. "Welcome to your future."

Then she bent his head down to hers, and her tongue slipped into his mouth. It was exquisite. After some moments, they broke, and she said,

"Tomorrow, you will be in a room with some of the sharpest minds on the planet."

She took him by the hand, and they walked to the bed. She started to undo his trousers.

"But tonight... you are mine."

She undressed him, and as she released his manhood, a smile crossed her lips. She bent down, and her mouth closed over him. He groaned with pleasure. After some moments, she pulled away. "No, no... not too quickly. Control... we must teach you control..."

He was beside himself. But she clearly planned to prolong the experience. "Don't stop!"

"Say please, Jimmy."

"Please don't stop."

She smiled. "Good boy." And as she bent down again, she said, almost too softly to hear, "I will make you forget all about her."

And she wasn't lying.

3 4

It was early April 2018, and Lauren had just finished a large piece of her research. Things were starting to take shape. The last months' worth of work was going to turn the dial forward for her in a big way. She was just about to turn her laptop off, it was already 10 pm. She was dead tired, but then an email from Jimmy popped up.

She had not heard from him for a long time—they agreed to not have contact. She also suspected there was someone new in his life—she did stalk him on social media, and there was no indication of such, but she had a feeling about these things that she trusted.

So, she was delighted to see his name, and the message "Happy Birthday!".

She realized that she had forgotten that it was the next day—and he, being on the other side of the world, was early with a message.

She opened up the attachment without checking that the underlying email address was his—and her screen suddenly went blank.

She frowned. This was strange. She restarted her computer; it must be a glitch. When it had booted back up, a message started up on her screen, filling her with horror.

"Your files have been locked by Ransomware. Please pay 2000 USD to unlock it. Do not alert the authorities."

Shit! She thought. There was a lot of confidential research on there, as well as her work, which she now realized—she hadn't backed up in over a month. Stupid stupid stupid! She always backed up to a Dropbox folder. For some reason, she had forgotten to do it this time.

2000 USD wasn't that much—but what guarantee did she have that they would follow through. She needed to talk to someone about this. Who? Professor Higgins might know what to do. He wasn't that tech-savvy, but he would know what to do about the research... Daniella also knew a lot about this stuff, but she didn't want to involve her. Who knows, it might even BE HER. As the thought crossed her mind and she had the phone pressed to her ear, a further horror occurred:

The number on the screen doubled to 4000 USD. And a message appeared: "Put the phone down or it doubles again."

Horrified, she put down the phone just as Professor Higgins answered.

"What do you want?!!" she shouted at the screen, feeling slightly silly."

A robotic voice came out of her screen. "I would like to talk."

"I'm going to report you to the police!" she shouted. "You can't do this!"

"Yes, I can," droned the voice. "I have. Your research, the confidential files for both your sponsor and promoter... If I released this, it would mean Professor Higgins's career and the end of your time in Harvard. They take breach of intellectual property very seriously around here."

"You're bluffing! This is not my fault!" But she wasn't sure. Things were hectic in the US, and it did feel like this disembodied threat might have a point.

"Doesn't matter. You opened a non-professional email on a work server—letting me into the system. Grounds for all grants and commitments to be terminated."

She sank in her chair. "I don't have 4000 dollars..."

"I know. I also can see your bank accounts. Maybe we can make a deal..."

She had heard of perverts trying to extract all kinds of nasty things over the internet. She suddenly imagined some fat pimply nerd some-where salivating over the prospect of making her take her clothes off.

"Fuck you." She said, and she slammed down the screen.

She immediately regretted it. He could no longer see her, but maybe he could see her WhatsApp messages? She didn't know how smart these hackers were, but she had to go speak to someone.

She left the apartment and walked over to Professor Higgins, leaving her phone behind.

Halfway there, she thought it through. How would they find this guy? The professor would just encourage her to go to the authorities. It would compromise her momentum, create an unease between them in terms of the relationship, and trust in her judgment. Dammit, she should rather try to still fix this herself.

But she was not going to take her clothes off or do anything weird.

She turned around and went back to her apartment.

When she flipped open her laptop, the number was now 8000 USD.

"Ready to make a deal?" came the voice.

She sat back. She was so pissed off! But she tried to remain calm. "What do you want? I'm not doing anything illegal—or taking my clothes off."

There was a pause. Then there was a burst of weird laughter. "No, nothing like that. Can we meet?"

She considered. "Tell me what you want."

"I'll tell you in person. And come alone. The coffee shop across from the bus station, tomorrow 11 am. Don't tell anyone, I will know and then all your files are gone—and so am I."

It was a public place, at a time when the station would be packed. She thought about it. She couldn't, at this time, think of a better play.

"Ok."

She arrived 15 minutes early and sat down. She looked around. A few other people were sitting on their laptops. Any one of them could be her assailant. It was difficult to tell these days.

When he suddenly sat down in front of her, she was surprised.

He was a massive guy—she judged him to be late twenties early thirties, even though he was completely bald. He had deep brown eyes and a strong chin. He was not unattractive, except for the fact that his head seemed slightly too small for the massive arms and chest. He actually looked slightly comical in that tight black t-shirt.

He gave her an akward smile. "I'm sorry about all this."

She had had an initial pang of fear at the sheer size of him. They were in a public place, though, so she felt no immediate physical threat. It was still disconcerting.

"Not as sorry as I am. What is your deal? Why are you doing this to me?"

He was about to answer when the waitress came over. "Can I have a cappuccino, please? And for the lady…"

Lauren looked at the waitress. "Just a skinny latte, please." As she walked away, Lauren said, "Thought you would also know my coffee type, since you are my cyber-terrorist."

He shrugged. "Easy enough to find out, sure. But I didn't dig that deep. A girl needs her privacy."

"Hmpf!" she snorted. "You just violated me in cyberspace. Kind of hypocritical for you to speak about violating privacy."

"You have a right to be pissed. I would be too," he said, as their coffees arrived. "But I have a problem only you can solve."

"I doubt it. I'm a virologist on a study visa, and you… well, I don't know what your deal is."

He put his hand in his pocket and pushed a photo across to her. It was of a very skinny teenager, standing awkwardly next to an… ahem… a very large girl with long blonde hair. In the photo, they were hugging very comfortably.

"What am I looking at?" she asked.

"This is Britney. We were best buds in school, we were both sort of social outcasts… and we had a shared love for computers." He paused. "I never told her I loved her."

Despite herself, Lauren felt a twang of sympathy for the large man in front of her, who was suddenly speaking with a very tiny voice. "Go on."

"It's our 10th high school anniversary coming up next week. She will be there—and I don't want to go alone. I need a date, and I need a date that will make her see me in a different light. I have one shot at finally winning her heart—and I mean to make it count."

"You want me to be your date?" It was quite sweet, in a fucked-up blackmail kind of way. It almost reminded her of an old Patrick Dempsey movie she saw.

As if reading her mind, he said, "Can't buy me, love? Yes, I saw that too. And I'm not looking for popularity—I have no desire to impress all the idiot jocks or other hot girls from high school. I just want her to think that… well… that I have a girlfriend, and someone likes me in that way."

"Why don't you just hire an escort for the evening? That's a design shirt, and your shoes also tell me that you're doing ok. Never mind your side gig as a cyber-terrorist."

"She is also in the IT space. She will find out info on whoever I bring. If they are not legit, she will see through it. You're legit. Ph.D. virologist, smart, attractive, and I have been watching you for a while… you also have a kind heart."

She was flattered. But it still felt offside. "It's not my style… What is your name?"

"Todd," he replied. "I know. That's why it's got to be you. You're sincere. You don't need to lie for me… you just tell people we recently met, and I convinced you to come with me to the reunion. You tell them at first you didn't like me, but now I've kind of grown on you, like a bad rash. And you tell them that even if there could be something deeper, you're probably going home after your studies so you're afraid to get your heart broken again."

She laughed. "All true, I suppose. And what do you mean, again?"

"I conducted a cross-index on old correspondence. This Jimmy character, by my algorithm, is your weak spot. Worked, didn't it." He wasn't smug about it—he was still giving her that same sincere look.

She bit her lip. "Scary what our computers know about us. Ok, and that's it? Go to the reunion, be your date, and that's it?"

"That's it. I unlock your computer; we go our separate ways."

"How can I trust you? On that night, and that you'll do what you say?" This childlike brute was quite something. He seemed, funny enough, quite sincere—and sort of harmless. She was still pissed off, but the romantic inside of her also now wanted to help him.

"You can meet me there. And the plan is that you leave earlier because you have a submission deadline. Hopefully, that allows me to talk to her. The venue is not far if you travel by Uber."

She nodded, making her mind up. "Ok then. You have a deal. Only, your plan doesn't quite work. Here's what we need to do…"

It was the nature of their agreement that Lauren committed almost all of her Saturdays to Daniella's work. Her mentor was taken aback when Lauren packed up early—she usually worked late with Daniella.

"We are not finished yet!" she exclaimed.

"I know. I know what needs to be done. I will finish up at home tomorrow."

"You are… going out!?"

"Just a guy I met online. Figured it would be ok to start meeting some people."

Daniella frowned. "There are a lot of creeps out there. What is his name?"

For some reason, Lauren went with a white lie. "His online handle simply says 'Tommy'. Don't worry—we already met for coffee; he is ok."

This did not appease Daniella. "Can you show me a picture?"

Lauren looked at her phone—and faked a frown. "Phone is dead. Need to recharge before I go out. Will show you later if it works out. Call you tomorrow!"

And she was out the door before Daniella could further object.

Todd was waiting for her in the foyer of the Boston Park Plaza. It was quite a magnificent hotel, in the middle of the Boston downtown area and, as promised, a short Uber ride from her apartment.

She had to admit it was fun. He had even given her a generous allowance to splurge out on a gorgeous black dress, and she had her hair properly done for the first time in over a year. It felt good to dolly up. The appreciative look he gave her was nice too. Even though it was a blackmail date.

He had also cleaned up well. He filled out his tux with his muscular frame and, even with her heels on, they stood toe to toe height-wise.

He smiled. "I was worried you wouldn't show. Seeing as I already unlocked your set."

She winked at him. "You're still an asshole, Todd. But now, you're kinda my asshole. Plus, I figure if you did it once you could do it again. Let's go get your girl."

She hooked in, and they went up to the main ballroom.

Their target was difficult to find, initially. The ballroom was already packed with the class of 2009. They were a collection of people slightly older than her, who had all entered the university system during a horrible economic downturn, but with the enthusiasm that came from the Obama administration.

The looks they received told her that their height, his physique, and (she had to admit) her knockout figure in this dress, it all made them stand out. But few people approached them. It was affirmed to her that Todd had not been one of the popular kids by a long shot.

They finally found their "crowd"—Todd's school buddies, an assortment of young men and women (some still single, some with partners) that probably made up the computer club. Britney, the object of his affections, had not yet arrived. They were all slightly socially awkward—but Lauren rolled with it, and followed the brief.

She was enjoying herself.

The best friend from school; "So how did you meet?"

"Online. He friended me on Instagram... and initially, I wasn't interested, but he finally won me over with his cool posts."

"Ooh—that sounds like the Todd we remember. He was always a bit of a stalker!"

"Nah. It was kind of sweet. And I think persistence is sexy. Makes a girl feel special, you know?"

OR the girls:

"Wow, he looks so different!"

"Yeah. We like to go work out. And we follow a strict vegan diet, you know."

"He's changed so much! He used to eat junk food, hence the bad skin. But now…"

"It's all about nutrition, you know."

"How did you meet?"

"First time was when he helped me with an IT problem at work—I am busy with a Virology Ph.D. at Harvard, and Todd has been great at solving some problems for us. He finally got me to agree to go on a date—and here we are."

He whispered in her ear, "Maybe just keep the story straight… but you're doing brilliantly."

She giggled. Don't get carried away here… but she was enjoying the masquerade.

Suddenly, he squeezed her hand. "Britney's just arrived."

She looked in the direction of his gaze. A statuesque woman was standing in the doorway—and the only resemblance between her and the overweight teenager in the photo was the long blonde hair. Like Todd, she had transformed since high school. This Amazon, who had arrived by herself, was making her way across the room. And her gaze was locked in on their group.

She turned to him. "Ok let's go. They are playing Summer of 69, time to dance."

He gulped. "I did the lessons as you instructed… but still, I don't know if…"

"Trust me, Todd. Let's go."

Part of the plan was for him to go for some ballroom dancing lessons. Focusing on the basic moves of the salsa, they locked in and started to move together on the dancefloor. It had been years since Lauren had herself, danced at Stellenbosch—but Todd, after a few initial missteps, got into the rhythm, as did she. They were surprisingly good. She was not surprised. From what she already knew of him, he was focused and disciplined. He had applied himself to the craft of dancing, and it showed.

He spun her around a few times, even a couple of dips. His arms were strong and he grew in confidence, and a small crowd was forming around them. She was loving it! They were now showing off—and then the song ended.

Slightly breathless, she kissed him on the cheek. Over his shoulder, she spotted Britney looking at them. She had a quizzical look on her face… as if she was trying to make up her mind how to feel about what she was seeing.

"She's watching us, Todd. Lead me off the dancefloor in the direction of the bar."

Turning their back on Britney, he led her in the opposite direction. "Are you sure about this?"

"She doesn't know that you've seen her yet. She'll go to the others. Let her do some inquiries on us first. We'll do a couple more dances before we move in."

"Are you sure?"

"Todd, I don't know computers… but I know girls. She's interested right now… let's let her work up eagerness a bit."

She calmed down her nervous date as they got a drink, chatting now to some people that seemed like the jocks and beauty queens of yesteryear… who were all suddenly very interested in him, and her. She reflected that Todd would enjoy this attention more if he wasn't distracted and kept on sneaking glances back at the "nerd" crowd, where Britney was.

"I Gotta Feeling" from the Black-Eyed Peas came on—and suddenly everyone was on the dance floor going nuts. It was great fun. In the melee, they worked their way back to his crowd. They were all singing "and tonight's gonna be a good night" when Todd and Britney were suddenly face to face. They both paused for a moment, then he hugged her spontaneously, even as the chorus got into full swing and the whole place was heaving.

It was great—the joy of the moment swept them away, and when the song finished, it went immediately to Lady Gaga's "Poker Face". Todd, taking Lauren by the arm, steered her off the dance floor, with Britney closely following.

They all walked outside to the terrace area, and Britney and Todd started talking at the same time, then laughed.

"Brit—it's so amazing to see you. You look great!"

"And you Toddy. It's been… wow, how did we not keep in touch?"

"You went off to join the peace corps after med school, remember. I always admired you for that…"

She smiled, and Lauren noticed how she lightly took his arm. "Todd… introduce me to your friend?" And her eyes moved to Lauren.

"Ah, yeah where are my manners? Lauren, this is Britney… the girl from high school I told you about. Britney, this is Lauren…"

Good, Todd. She is still unsure what I am in your life, thought Lauren. Let's just keep the mystery going a while longer…

She hugged Britney, surprising the other woman. "Todd has spoken about you so much! It's so great to finally meet you!"

Britney looked a little off-balance. "Thanks. Your accent… Australian?"

Lauren laughed. "No, South African. Lots of people make that mistake. Babe, could you grab me a drink? Let the girls chat for a second? Britney, can he get you something…?"

Britney nodded absently at Todd. "I'd love a margarita, Todd." Lauren felt a bit ashamed—the 'babe' comment was calculated, intimating that they were more than just friends.

As Todd walked away, Britney stared after him pensively for a second. And Lauren went into ultimate wing-woman mode.

"He was so excited to see you here, you know."

Britney turned to her, an immediate flash of pleasure spreading across her face.

"So was I. I mean… I only recently got back from Africa, and I wanted to reach out sooner, but things have been mad…"

"What did you do over there?" asked Lauren.

"Worked with water projects in Rwanda and Gabon. It's an outfit called Charity: Water, based in New York. Amazing stuff—but I felt I wanted to come home now, you know?"

"We have been following your updates. Kind of makes what Todd and I have been doing seem kind of mundane, right?"

Britney started. "Oh no! Todd's business has been flying, especially since the IPO. And he gives so much to charity. I know, from some of the people in the office in New York, that he's given a ton to Charity: Water as well."

Good, thought Lauren. She has been keeping track of him as well.

"But I didn't know he had… I mean…" Britney probed.

"What are we, you mean? I suppose I am his girlfriend. In the sense that we spend quite a bit of time together, and I adore him. I wish we could take it to the next level… but I am wrapping up at Harvard at the end of the year, and then I don't know…"

She let it hang, and Britney took the bait. "Harvard?"

"Yep, I am finishing up my Ph.D. in virology. After that, I think it's time to go home to give back, you know? Lots of work to be done in Africa still. You would know all about that from your time there."

Britney brightened. "That's amazing! Wow. We have so much to talk about. But then if you go back… Todd's whole business is here, and he's just getting going…"

"Yeah," said Lauren, as Todd came up with the drinks. "He truly is amazing. I wish…" and then she let it go. She had let enough sink in.

The next day, they met for coffee.

"And?" she asked, but he need not have answered. He was grinning from ear to ear.

"You were amazing last night! At some point I felt like the third wheel. The two of you were just totally vibing around the virology and water stuff."

She leaned over and squeezed his hand. "I really like her, Todd. Smart lady, pretty too. And I think she's come home to hit her roots again. Pretty sure you are part of that plan. I'm not sure this whole production was needed."

"Maybe not," he mused. "But I didn't get to where I am by leaving things to chance. You were great, Lauren. As per the plan, now we do a couple of coffees… and then we fake break up?"

"I have a Facebook profile, Todd. You're like someone else I care about—invisible on social media, mostly. Drives me nuts. I'm not super active there… but I've already sent her a friend request, and in a week or so time, I'll just post something vaguely around "Endings and beginnings… sad but also excited about going home next year".

He laughed. "You are good at this!"

"Yeah," she frowned. "I rock fake relationships. Wish I could do the same for real ones."

"Hey, look at what just happened. Don't give up on Jimmy just yet..."

"Thanks, stalker. Ok, pay for my coffee and see you in a few days. Stay disciplined. Reach out to her but don't be too eager, keep it friendzone until we 'fake' break up. Then let her come to you..."

"Lauren, I'm going to owe you. Forever. Anytime you need help... at all. Let me know."

Lauren stood up. "Thanks, Todd. But I should be ok, I don't foresee needing an uber hacker any time soon."

She walked home, and her thoughts turned to Professor Higgins. He had said something that excited her. A lot. But she didn't want to think about it just yet...

Wellington was Jimmy's favorite city. But this was the first time he could call it home. On the 1st of August 2018, he took possession of his own property, and moved into a three-bedroom townhouse in the hills overlooking the harbor.

He had packed up his stuff from his flat in Christchurch and sent it by freight. Why? Because he decided to cruise up at high speed in his brand-new BMW X3 convertible. Anna joined him for the ride, and he felt like the king of the world.

The timing was brilliant. Stan had wrapped up his rugby career and they jointly opened the flagship Il Leone on Dixon Street. It was in early June, in time for the Football World Cup: A 100-seater with sports screens everywhere. It was a massive departure from where they had started. As always, he and Stan were convinced by Robby's enthusiasm. It was the 14th Il Leone franchise, outside of the original restaurant in Christchurch. They were now in every major city in New Zealand, with a few smaller towns too.

The chickens had come home to roost. And in a good way. Jimmy's buy-in had matured in March, and with Anna's council, he took out a loan for the difference, and he was now the proud owner of 15% of the mother company. They were confident he could liquidate the loan in less than two years with dividend proceeds. Robby owned four fran-

chises and was making a killing. The delivery business had its challenges, but Robby was working hard to make it work.

But the big news was, the Wilsons were out. Stan and Grace
wanted to slow things down and refocus on just the original small place.
So, they sold the business as a whole to an outside investor. They did
keep the original outlet, which they would run as a franchisee. It was a
great deal for them. But outside of mandatory appearances here and
there by Stan, they were no longer involved. The new investor was an
overenthusiastic Japanese tech mogul. He liked Robby's vision of going
for sports bars, and he was throwing even more cash into expansion.

Anna had brought the deal to them. As she represented both
clients, she regretfully terminated her professional relationship with Il
Leone. They were referred to another reputable firm. She was tough to
negotiate with on the other side of the table. It did make their sex
afterward even more exciting. And they eventually agreed, to his
surprise, to a price of 10 million New Zealand Dollars. It was crazy
money, and the current numbers didn't support it. But their new boss,
Mr. Masataka, had major plans. And it meant Jimmy was now, at least
on paper, a millionaire. He was rich.

Or was he?

He would've preferred to get a partial cash deal like the Wilsons.
They took half upfront; two million of the price went to the buy-back
of the original Il Leone... and the rest was profit guarantees. Mr.
Masataka made sure Stan and his celebrity buddies would keep on
showing up to drive feet. Jimmy received no cash, but his shareholding
remained in place.

He actually had to take out a small loan to do the buy-in of the
extra shares... his bonuses didn't quite cover the amount. So, he was
actually in debt for the first time in his life, instead of sitting on cash.

The banks treated him like he was the man, though. And the
media had started to notice him too. He enjoyed the attention—and
the sex with the super-hot lawyer. It was easy to buy the sports car on
credit, now that he was somebody. Even easier to buy the apartment
with almost no money down.

The Wilsons cautioned him to slow it down a bit. To be more careful. But Masa wanted the CEO to be in the same city as their biggest outlet, so he moved to Wellington. After that, he didn't see a lot of them. Robby moved in later in August, promising to find his own place. But he didn't. He knew about Anna, though… and he knew how to keep his mouth shut.

On the 8th of September 2018, he was sitting down with Robby and a few of the lads for an early evening rugby game. His beloved Springboks were playing the Australian Wallabies. There were big screens everywhere, but as it was early and New Zealand was not playing, the place had only a few patrons at that hour. That would change later when a local derby came on, and the live band got kicking. Oh, and there was still pizza. Kind of.

"They are taking a beating, bud," said Robby.

"Yeah. Rassie is canny, but it's not looking good. Mind you they look better organized than last year."

"Ha. Could hardly look worse, could they?"

It was true. The relative mediocrity of 2015 was followed by two years of absolute horror. It was probably the worst time in history to be a South African living in New Zealand. The Springboks succumbed to successive record defeats crowned by a 57-0 drubbing… at home! It all finished with the Springboks losing to such minor nations as Italy, and the coach resigning in absolute disgrace. An SOS was sent out to Rassie Erasmus, the man who should have had the job in the first place, were it not for political considerations. So far, he had not showered himself in glory either.

Admittedly, there were signs of light. But here they were, the familiar sight of the Springboks losing to Australia in an away game, and with the mighty All Blacks looming in Wellington the following week.

As if reading his thoughts, Robby said, "Yeah, I must tell you, I'm getting over it. These Kiwis are relentless at taking the piss. Never thought I'd say it, but I miss home."

"That's new. But we're doing so well here, Rob. No reason to go home."

Robby ordered another round, keeping an eye on the delivery guys rushing in and out. "Your woman presented me with a new service contract with the takeaway business, bud."

"Yeah. Masa Corp wants it that way. They wanted to be sure we're doing a market-related deal with you—so they went out and tested."

"It shaves away a lot of my profit, you know."

Jimmy didn't want to get into it with Robby. He tried to change the subject. "Yeah. Man, things have changed so quickly bud. Who would've thought, hey? Here we are… on top of the world, two kids from South Africa running a Kiwi Restaurant chain."

"You're running the business. I'm just a franchisee. And the delivery boy."

"What's wrong, Robby?" Jimmy knew his friend by now. Something was up.

"Jimmy, I need a new challenge. I realized I'm a bit of a cowboy. This stuff is fun… but man, I think I don't want to be in the hospitality business. The delivery side is more fun for me. I want to focus there; it feels like the wild west of new opportunity. But being so busy with running the restaurants, I'm not doing that side justice."

"You always do this, Rob. Too much hay on the fork."

Robby took a big swig. "Damn right. The entrepreneurial curse. Anyway…" he paused.

"I have an offer for my franchises."

This was big news. "You do? From who?"

"Consortium of ex-All Blacks players. The original investors. They want to buy me out. Offering me a good price too."

"That's great Rob. Wow. You sure have the Midas touch. Are you going to do it?"

Robby toyed with his beer. "I think so. I have a new business idea… and I kind of want to see where it goes."

"Man." Jimmy finished his beer. "How is it we keep on doing business together—and you keep on walking away with bags of cash, and I am even deeper in debt."

"Hey, no fair. You are a major shareholder of the company, and the CEO… the 'Young Gun to watch' as the newspapers here call you."

"Yeah. Lots of attention, but my shareholder's agreement dictates I can only sell the shares at market value two years from now. Until then, Masa can buy them back at the same price as I bought them."

"Yeah, I remember. We put in that clause, remember?"

Jimmy sighed. "When my partners were the Wilsons. They're out now. Anyway, it is what it is. Two years from now, I could offer it back at value at the time... and if we keep on growing as we do now, they might be worth even more."

"True story." Robby gave Jimmy a look. "Just don't go crazy in the meantime, Jimmy."

"What do you mean?"

"The car... the flat...the expensive gifts for Anna..."

"So?"

"Hey, I think you deserve it. But leave some money over for me."

"Why?"

Robby winked. "I'll tell you when I'm sure. But after this, I'm going back to South Africa. And I might need investors. Now let's watch the game."

The Springboks did end up losing. It was not a capacity crowd for the game.

Jimmy mused, "This place will be packed next week, though. With the actual game at the stadium, the bars will all be full too. And if Stan does decide to come make an appearance after the game, we will do record sales I think."

Robby licked his lips. "The new boss is quite something. And I hear Anna will be there too. From what I hear, he's as fond of her as all the rest of us. Will you be able to play it cool?"

"I was born cool, Robby." But he had hit a nerve.

The following Thursday was a big night of specials at the bar. Once again, they were sitting at their usual corner... but tonight would be different. It happened when Stan Wilson walked in. "Boys!" And felt like old times. They were two beers in when his phone rang.

"Yep?"

"Am I speaking to the hottest thing in Italian cuisine since pizza? The main man almost on the cover of every single minor local teen mag?"

Jimmy laughed. "Sammy! Of course! You are touring with the squad, right?"

"You got that right, Jimmy boy. Might even get a run on the day after tomorrow. Listen, we just finished training, and we want to go for a beer. Do you know a place? Want to bring a few of the lads for a quick meal, Rassie is pretty good about treating us like adults but we still have a curfew, so won't be a late one."

"Do I know a place? Texting you the address right now."

"See you in half an hour."

"Sam?" asked Robby. Jimmy smiled and turned to Stan. "This is going to be fun."

Sam, of course, was even bigger than the last time he had seen him. He had added a bit more bulk, but his face was also... Well, let's just say it was clear he did his dirty work in the depths of the scrum. It showed.

The rest of the crew was the "dirt trackers". They were the members of the touring squad that would not be starting on Saturday. They all settled in for a beer and catch up. Jimmy, of course, recognized all of them. After a moment of suspicion at his "defection" to New Zealand, they thawed when he made it clear his blood still ran pure with the green and gold.

And they were all awestruck by Stan. It was quite funny. He had only stopped playing international rugby a few years before, but these guys were massive fans. Stan put them at ease, and story sharing and autographing were in the order of the day.

The food out of the kitchen was pretty good, although Jimmy thought he might need to go do some more training on details. The place was heaving, and they were just coping. It wasn't Il Leone—the original—standards. He and Robby, in a side conversation, decided to put some work in the following week.

The conversation stayed with rugby though. There was a lot of enthusiasm from Sam and the team members on their chances on Saturday.

Stan needled them a bit. "We beat you chaps the last 11 games in a row. You have to go back to that game when Pollard stuck it to us in 2014 to remember the last time you guys gave us a run."

Sam nodded. "Sure. But since then, we had to deal with a politically appointed coach. Things are different now with Rassie." The others nodded.

"It was impressive the way you took down the English earlier this year. We love anyone who beats those bastards. But then the last two games..."

Jimmy chimed in. "Away losses. Still, you make a good point Stan. We don't really win over here. A South African will always believe we could, and you never know hey. This year might be different."

Having established his allegiance, the conversation turned to other things. The place got jammed up, and Jimmy could see some of the waiters starting to spin. He and Robby decided to get stuck in and helped out behind the bar or bussing meals. This was something that they often did. It showed the troops leadership by example, and it took them back to their roots.

Sam and his mates eventually had to leave, but not before Sam came up to Jimmy. They shook hands, and Sam said, "You did well, bud."

"We both did, I think," smiled Jimmy.

"Yet neither of us got the girl."

They laughed, and Sam was gone. But he had not thought of Lauren in a while. He wondered how she was doing.

The restaurant business had consumed his time over the last two years, and he had crisscrossed the country to open, support and cross-market the various outlets. Often, Anna would come with him, as their legal representative.

She had him completely under her spell from day one. She was both sexy and demure, vulnerable and confident, outgoing and shy. He was fascinated by her, but because of their professional relationship, total discretion was required at day time. But at night time...

The Wellington opening night, in early June, was a grand affair. The 2015 World Cup Champions were in robust attendance (those who were in New Zealand and not playing somewhere else) and it was topped off by receiving the first payment on the deal with Mr. Masataka for the sale of the business. It was heady stuff, but the best part of it was not the money (which was nice) ...

It was when Anna took him, late that night, to the flat she thought he should buy. And then proceeded to jump him and break in the place —and him—in the most comprehensive way.

Before she had brought the Masa Corp to the table, she had insisted on total discretion. She was a professional, and she couldn't afford sniggers or aspersions to her credentials. She was happy to go out with him in public if they left town… but in Christchurch, she would only meet him at his or her flat.

After the deal, she was no longer his lawyer. He thought things would ease up. Unfortunately, she now represented the boss. And she became even more cautious. He hated it. And he suspected that she used her flirty behavior on Mr. Masataka as well. But he agreed… in private, she told him she adored him. She made him feel like a king. She was like a drug, sex with her was like a ridiculous rollercoaster every time, and he just could not get enough.

He never told the Wilsons. And, he supposed, that contributed to a widening rift between them. They knew he was keeping something from them. Bit by bit, their trust relationship started to change. He was sure it was part of the reason they decided to sell.

The annual Springbok-All Black showdown was two days later, on 15 September at Westpac stadium. Mr. Masataka was jetting in with his entourage to watch his two favorite teams slug it out. "Springboks good Jimmy. Come back they will!" he had said on their first meeting, in a very Yoda-ish backward English. His company was heavily involved in the Japanese bid for the Rugby World Cup in 2019. He had already promised them tickets to the main fixtures.

So, he found himself in a private box with his two best buddies. And his girlfriend, who was ignoring him, as usual. There was expensive whiskey and Champagne, some of the top wheeler-dealers from Japan and New Zealand in the box. Grace had elected not to come down for the game. Jimmy was glad. He was sure she suspected something with Anna, and he didn't feel like getting interrogated.

Jimmy's problem was legitimate. He had just moved to Wellington a few months ago. He was newly financially comfortable, still only 23 years old, getting his brains screwed out by a half Asian nymphomaniac and starting to gain attention in the local media. He had even been interviewed on television earlier in the week!

Why wasn't he happy? He had spent the last five years trying to prove something to the world. He wanted to prove he wasn't a loser like his father, that going to university was unimportant, that he wasn't defined by his given identity. Whether it was Bishops Boys, South African, poor kid rich kid… he just wanted to make his mark in the world, and now it felt like he did.

Only, he had no one to share it with. And by no one he meant Lauren. Stan and Robby were his best friends here, and they shared in the joys of expansion—but he still missed that deep connection of having a proper partner. Stan was now pulling away… and Robby was making the same noises. But there was Anna, right?

It wasn't enough. He and Lauren had only had conflicted tormented spells of mismatched togetherness, or wild short periods of travel romance. But he missed the open-ness. They were crazy about each other… and never afraid to show it.

And yet, she had never tried to hide their relationship. Although Anna clearly defined the reasons why, and the sex clouded his judgment, he was uneasy with the skulking around.

3 5

J immy and Robby were outnumbered. There were a few Japanese guests in the box—and they were vocally supportive of the Kiwis. Mr. Masataka was, graciously, decked out in Springbok colors. Jimmy thought it was a classy move from their boss. Anna looked good, even in an All Black jersey. He was conflicted about her being there. Since she took on Masa Corp as a client, things had shifted, and she seemed to take on an ever-increasing role beyond legal counsel.

It was quite a game, the old rivals squaring up like in the old days. The Springboks had a goal, and it was a glorious afternoon for South African rugby. After two seasons of record defeats against the old enemy, the first 20 minutes of the game signaled more pain for Jimmy. The All Blacks ran in two slick tries to lead 12-0, and Jimmy was once again dealing with condescending comments from the Kiwis. The Japanese, who would never say a disparaging thing contrary to their code of honor, were also visibly avoiding eye contact.

But things turned around. The Springboks ran in two of their own tries of their own accord, and then took control of the game. By half-time, they were leading! Jimmy and Robby were aware that there was a pattern of the All Blacks coming back in the last quarter, so they tempered their excitement… but still. There were a couple of ex-All

Blacks in the box too—and Jimmy assumed these were Robby's potential buyers. They were good value for comments.

For example, Beauden Barrett did a shocker of a pass that led to the second try.

One of them said to Jimmy, "That chap is like an Alfa Romeo. Pretty, handles well, it's a sexy car. But when it breaks down it's a bitch to get going again."

Or: "That Malcolm Marx of yours is the real deal, mate. Reminds me of a chap I used to know when I was a bachelor in Dubai. Bloody chap kept on popping up at parties and poaching my mate's girl. Nuisance."

Jimmy was enjoying himself. And the drinks kept on coming. Robby was deep in conversation with a Kiwi chap Jimmy didn't recognize. The talk seemed to be all about e-commerce. He halfway listened to their conversation.

"You see, Robby, it's become a whole industry. You make the food, right. But you only have a certain number of covers you can do a night. You need to have waiters, cleaners, all that stuff. Doing your own take-out service is a pain in the ass, because it's a whole different business. You need drivers, logistics, all that."

Jimmy kept an eye on the game. The Springboks had a good lead, but the All Blacks were fighting back. He heard Robby say to the chap, "It's worked for us. But only because I ran it as a separate business."

The guy snorted. "Sure. But you need economies of scale to make it work. Service customers beyond your operation."

"I've seen some movement around this already, Mike."

"Sure, but…. Whoa! Ioane, you beauty! There you go, mate! We are clawing it back on you bastards. Watch the second half."

It was true. The All Blacks scored just before halftime, but the Springboks still had a decent lead. The whistle blew, and they all got up for some lunch.

Anna drifted in among the conversation. She focused on Mr. Masataka and his Japanese friends, who were quite courteous, but also engaged in their own conversation. They crowded around the bar where she held court. They were quite jovial, slugging back Saki and whiskey brought in from Japan.

Jimmy joined Robby and Kiwi Mike, and listened to their conversation as they helped themselves to the generous buffet for a quick bite during the 15-minute break. "Sure, it's a crowded market, Robby, but it's still early days. The trick is in making it easy."

"You sound like you have an idea around all this, Mike."

"I do. I've been kind of obsessed since I saw what's happening in South Africa. You guys are ahead of the curve down there. There's a massive opportunity here to do the same thing."

"Which is?"

"Create the platform for home delivery. There are guys already doing it. But they ain't doing it well. It's all in the tech, and focusing on a specific part of the process."

"What do you mean?"

"Well, there's the tech to talk to the restaurant to put in the order. There's the software to talk to the customer. You need apps for Android and OS, as well the back-end encryption to safeguard customer credit card information."

"Ok..."

Mike became aware that Jimmy was part of their conversation. "Robby, let's do this another time. But let's talk soon."

"I have your number. Call you next week and we can talk about it some more."

That done, the game kicked off again. The Japanese contingent had loosened up considerably, and were now starting to ask all kinds of questions in broken English. Jimmy found himself explaining a bunch of the moves as the game progressed. Right after half time, an intercept by replacement Cheslin Kolbe led to a big lead for the Boks. As always, the All Blacks fought back, with the same Kolbe not getting a tackle in and Ioane scoring another soft try.

Mr. Masataka said, "I like that Kolbe! Good player. Fast! Small like Japanese!"

"Yeah, but he doesn't do that well in defense. Our winger just swatted him off like a fly," said Mike.

"It doesn't matter! He scores tries. You see—next year's World Cup, he is a key player for you!"

Jimmy sure hoped so. The next move saw the Springboks extend their lead with a great try in the left corner. Unfortunately, they missed the conversion.

Robby muttered, "Hope that doesn't bite us in the ass."

And like so many times before, the script seemed to be pre-set. The All Blacks fought back with successive tries. Barrett, however, missed the conversion on the first one. They kept on the pressure, and inexorably moved forward. At the 74th minute, they scored again.

Jimmy felt a familiar despair settle over him. Barrett lined up the conversion kick—and it rebounded off the posts! He had missed two in a row, and the Springboks still clung to a heroic two-point lead with five minutes to go.

What followed was the stuff of legends. The All Blacks camped out on the Springboks goal line. Wave after wave of attack was repelled by what can only be described as heroic defense. As the clock wore down and went past full-time, they kept on coming, trying to force an error that would give them a penalty shot and the game.

But at 82.5 minutes, the All Blacks made an error, the Springboks got the ball, and the game was over. A famous victory over the old enemy, and Robby, Jimmy, and even the Japanese (who had, up to that point, been pretty favorable toward the All Blacks) celebrated with high fives, hugs and clinking of glasses. It was pandemonium in their box. There was mostly dead silence everywhere else in the stadium.

Mike was magnanimous. "Great for the game, guys. We didn't like it when the Springboks were pushovers these last few years. We never like losing either, but to have a true contest is always the best outcome."

One of the ex-All Blacks put it more succinctly; "We're here to be entertained, Jimmy. We love the jersey... but a good South African side was something we missed the last few years. And boy, were we entertained! This is great stuff. I can't wait to kick your ass in a couple of weeks in South Africa, though. This is another step to your redemption —but you boys also got lucky..."

And Mr. Masataka: "AH! The Springboks are back! Japan beat Springboks last time World Cup. Now, Springboks beat New Zealand. Means we also can beat New Zealand! Great day for rugby!"

Even Anna swayed in for a hug and a celebration. There was no kiss though. There were too many eyes watching for that. But there was a quick spoken word in his ear; "Tonight, a winner needs to be rewarded suitably…"

The revelry in the box continued. The next thing they knew, the Jägermeister and Tequila came out. Anna stuck around as the only woman there as the men got drunker and drunker. Jimmy tried to not participate, but their Japanese friends were insistent. Most of the Kiwis left, dejected.

One or two of the Japanese guests started to get "handsy" with Anna. They were still quite respectful, as was their culture. But this was the thing that drove him nuts. She couldn't help oozing sex the way she does, and other men reacted to it. He never wanted to be jealous, but he had had a few, and he started to feel his mood darken.

The stadium started to empty. It was now well past 8 pm. One of the Japanese guys was all over Anna, and Jimmy had had enough. Jimmy started to move toward him, but Anna flashed him a look. And then Robby put his hand on Jimmy's shoulder, and piped up;

"Ok gentlemen! We have a table waiting for us at Il Leone! Stan has already gone ahead, and he is waiting there for us with… wait for it… Richie McCaw! Who is coming with me?!"

There was an immediate buzz of excitement and the prospect of meeting the former captain and legend, and they all grabbed their jackets.

"Thanks, Robby," said Jimmy.

"As I said, play it cool. She can handle herself. Let's just hope Masataka didn't notice how you feel either. There's something weird there."

As they filed out following Robby to the waiting cars, Mr. Masataka turned to Jimmy; "Congratulations Jimmy. Everything is ready at the restaurant?"

"Yes, sir. Robby is going to make sure there are no hiccups."

"Then I see you tomorrow morning at 10 at the restaurant, yes? Tonight, you must celebrate. Great victory."

"Yes sir." Jimmy bowed, and Mr. Masataka returned it. He nodded at Anna, and he was gone.

Anna went across to the door and peeped out. Then, assured they were gone, she locked it.

She walked across to him; he was putting some more glasses away.

She put his arms around him. Jimmy was slightly drunk… but his body immediately reacted to her, like it always does.

"Here. Now." She said, urgency in her voice.

And she pulled him down toward the couch.

They eventually made their way back to his flat. But, as she lay in his arms just before dawn, in the afterglow of the fourth round of love-making… he aired something that bothered him.

"You never talk about your family, Anna."

He felt her stiffen. "Not much to tell. My mom lives in China… my dad, I never knew him. I came here as an exchange student and made my own way. So, I don't really see them."

"Do you want a family of your own one day?"

She sat up, abruptly, and turned on the light. "Where is this coming from, Jimmy?"

"I just… Well, I just felt like we've been seeing each other for a year. Don't you ever want to make plans?"

She touched his face gently. "My beautiful man. I always make plans."

The answer didn't satisfy him. But she put her hand on his penis, and he forgot more questions…

In the morning, when he woke up, she was gone. But she left a note: "See you at 10" with a little heart next to it. He realized it was the first time she had also done that. Maybe they could finally start entering into a real relationship, with real conversation.

He got dressed and made his way down to his new office on top of the restaurant by 8.30 am. The cleaning crews were already mopping up the revelry for the previous night. A quick look at the cash ups revealed that they had indeed done record sales, despite the All Black loss. The presence of some of the greats including Richie McCaw clearly had an impact. Robby turned up by 9.30 am. It was clear that he was slightly worse for wear after a big night.

"Hey, Jimmy boy. Those Japanese buggers know how to party. Had me up till 4 am, and we had to go hit the club after we closed here. Don't have the stamina I used to; I tell ya."

"How is Mr. Masataka?"

"Good. He was jovial the whole time—but I swear he either has a bull's constitution or he wasn't taking his share of the shots. By the end of the night, he was still dead sober, as far as I could tell."

This theory was supported when Mr. Masataka arrived promptly at 9:50 am, flanked by his assistant and Anna. He, in contrast to Robby, seemed to carry no after-effects. He walked around the restaurant, scanning everything with laser-like eyes before they all settled in for the meeting.

Jimmy found himself immediately challenged to keep up with Mr. Masataka. His mind was razor-sharp. Thankfully Jimmy was prepared. They worked through the current financials, the performance of the flagship site and the legacy restaurants around the country. They looked at projections, new sites and expansion plans. It all took a couple of hours, and at the end, it felt like they had passed the test.

Mr. Masataka leaned back.

"Company looks healthy. If you continue like this, your buy-in will be worth even more. You are gaining much face, Jimmy-san."

Jimmy bowed slightly. "We are happy with the partnership, honorable Masataka-san." From the corner of his eye, he could see Anna's lips slightly curve upward. She gave very little away, but her coaching on protocol was paying off.

"Good." Mr. Masataka gave him a steely glare. "We will capitalize further. Open in Auckland, Christchurch next."

"There are already Il Leone's in both cities, Masataka-san. In Auckland we have two, one in North Auckland."

"We upgrade these locations. Now we change the business model to a sports bar."

Jimmy frowned slightly. Anna shot him a warning glance, but he ignored it. "Should we not wait and see if this location is viable? Large sports bars need a lot more revenue to be viable. The small restaurants we have been working well with a lower cost base."

"Hai!" exclaimed Mr. Masataka. "Concept go to Tokyo, Singapore, Hong Kong! First, we experiment here. Then global. No time to lose. Rugby World Cup next year, Olympics 2020 in Japan. We need to go strong! Bold like tigers!"

Jimmy and Robby exchanged a glance. They had known that Mr.

Masataka had international plans, but this was the first time he had shared them. Robby, while not a shareholder, was the largest franchisee and ran the delivery side of the business. But Jimmy still wasn't sure where the meeting was going.

Mr. Masataka turned to Anna. "Please give them lease agreements for new sites."

Anna proceeded to hand them signed and sealed lease agreements for three new sites. The agreements were to commence on 1 October.

They looked at each other, astonished. He was also slightly perturbed. Anna had mentioned nothing of this to him. And he had just bought a place in Wellington? Were they now required to go to these other cities to open these branches? And Stan, who was now a franchisee, would not be happy if they replaced the original with this monstrosity in Christchurch.

Mr. Masataka, anticipating the questions, said, "I will talk to Stan Wilson. The original site stays. New site: different animal. Room for both."

Jimmy scratched his head. He supposed... but it felt like they would be very different beasts, and the quality would not be the same.

Mr. Masataka continued; "You are the opening team. You, Robert, Anna. You open branches, manage operations. Now that Robert is leaving, so we need a new team. You, Jimmy, CEO. Anna COO. I am Chairman."

Jimmy's head was reeling. There was a lot to absorb here. "Masataka-san, Robby..."

"Robby is selling his interests. We like new shareholders. We buy the delivery side of the business."

Jimmy realized that Robby and Mr. Masataka must have finalized this deal at the bar last night. But what about Anna... she hadn't said a thing. He looked at her questioningly.

She held his gaze. "Mr. Masataka asked me to join the firm, Jimmy. But not before you gave your approval. I plan to tender my resignation at the practice next month, and come on board to help."

Jimmy felt blindsided. He didn't like it. But at the same time, he would lose face if he resisted this move. Mr. Masataka should not be aware that he and Anna had a private relationship. And, disregarding that, this move made total sense.

He turned to Mr. Masataka. "This is a good idea, Masataka-san."

Mr. Masataka beamed. "Hai! And we save a fortune in legal fees!"

The meeting adjourned, and Jimmy and Robby found themselves alone as the others had left.

Jimmy frowned. "It's all happening very quickly. I mean…"

Robby nodded. "I know. Too quick, in my opinion. And it looks like Masataka is formalizing the structure. And don't be fooled—Anna has been working this angle for a while."

"What do you mean?"

"I wondered why she was doing so much beyond the normal legal brief. Now we know. She's got you wrapped around her little finger, bud. I'm sure the sex is amazing… hey, hey, don't get mad… I'm almost jealous. But remember what I said when we met her? She is a force to be reckoned with. But I think, with her, ambition comes first. Her first loyalty is with Masataka—never forget that. He is her meal ticket."

"You're full of shit, Robby. You also didn't tell me your talks were this advanced."

"Good point. Didn't want to say anything. But I'm out bud. And so are the Wilsons. From where I'm sitting, you don't have anyone watching your back. Just be careful."

Jimmy grinned. "Noted. But in the meantime… Hell, I like what he said about other countries. I reckon the ride is just starting. I'm up for building an empire!"

"Sure," Robby muttered. "As long as there are sports and people can go to bars, things should be fine…"

Jimmy's life became a succession of hotel rooms and late-night bars. For scouting international locations and then making the deals, it was at least three trips. And he and Anna would go as a team, business class. It was glorious. She remained a closed book. It still bothered him… but the absence of good conversation was smoothed over by an excess of alcohol and sex. And eventually, designer drugs.

He was cautious at first. But she introduced him to ecstasy during sex one night. Thereafter, it became their drug of choice.

Anna liked a variety of hallucinogens when she let her hair down. When they went location scouting in Singapore and Hong Kong, she took him to the most glamorous clubs. They were always invited to the VIP suites, and the drugs loosened him up to the music. He normally didn't like the DJs in those places. Mushrooms, Cocaine, designer weed… Anna opened up his world to a whole new menu of experiences, and he would dance the night away.

A part of him told him he was on a slippery slope. But he was young, uber-successful. He was screwing the most gorgeous woman in the world. And she expected nothing from him but pleasure.

One night in Kuala Lumpur, Anna invited the drop-dead gorgeous waitress to their room. A threesome was every man's fantasy… Jimmy was as high as a kite, and he enjoyed it immensely. But deep down, he felt troubled. It still didn't match the honesty of the true love connection he had felt with Lauren.

The months passed. He spent Christmas in Bali with Anna, but they were both bored and cut the holiday short to get back to the thrill of work. It was going to be a big year for sport in 2019, with the anchor being the World Cup in Japan. And Il Leone sports bars, with locations in five countries, would be there to cash in.

Jimmy was going over the numbers for their Singapore opening in early January, when Robby called. And he was up to his old tricks…

36

The message from Robby was simple: "I'm in town, and I need to speak to you."

Robby had sold out, and gone back to South Africa. Jimmy missed him badly. From their conversations, however, it seemed like Robby was running with a new idea around e-commerce. He had gone full circle—he had, once again, made out like a bandit from selling the franchises and the delivery business. He had gone from Mr. Negative to Mr. Positive about SA and kept urging Jimmy to come back. Jimmy had to admit he missed SA… but he had now been away most of his adult life, would he still belong there?

So, they met at a small dive bar off the main drag in Wellington. And Robby, true to form, was overcome with excitement!

"Jimmy, I'm ready to press play, bud! There's a great piece of tech I'm going to bring into New Zealand from SA—and once we register the intellectual property here, we can start rolling it out globally!"

"Robby, slow down. I don't know what you are talking about."

"I am talking about home delivery of food, Jimmy. But bigger than you've ever seen before. Lightning fast responses at the touch of a button, seamless chat between all the different players—this is great stuff. And we can be at the forefront of it!"

Jimmy took a swig of his beer. "You've been developing this tech in South Africa? I thought you said it was time to leave."

"Yes. But now Cyril's in charge. He's going to clean up the town, like a brand-new sheriff. There's lots of positive flow in the tech space. I put in some of my cash, found some investors… and I think we're onto something."

Jimmy laughed. Robby. Hot and cold. "So, what do you want from me?"

Robby smiled. "You, my friend, are what we call smart money. I see you operate. You are in with all the restaurant chains now, with that Japanese cash you are playing in the big leagues. Not just with Il Leone… I don't like that lady of yours, but she is effective. I'm sure you know all the big players in the various markets by now. You already have a lot of the contacts that I need for this. Plus… I want you to have a piece."

Jimmy frowned. "I have a job. And it's full-on. I couldn't market your… tech…"

"No, no… You misunderstand me. You wouldn't market it. You would just sit on the board, advise us how to proceed, who to contact. Now and again, you would make an introduction, and always in a way that there is no conflict with Il Leone."

It sounded like a good deal to Jimmy. There had to be a catch, and here it came.

"I want you to buy a stake in the business," announced Robby.

Jimmy smiled. "Yeah? How much?"

"5%. And I'll give it to you at a 50% discount."

Jimmy enjoyed this game. "So, what is the company worth now, Robby?"

Robby wasn't about to be drawn into that game.

"Jimmy, I am not full of shit. It's start-up stuff, so valuations are tough. I put in a couple of bars of my own money, I have some other investors… We have enough capital. And I have sold them on the idea of bringing you in. They would need you to have some skin in the game. And it can't be at no cost."

Jimmy laughed. "So, you are selling 5% of nothing for a couple of million dollars?"

PG GELDENHUYS

"No. Told you. I'm giving you a deal, cause you are going to open some doors for us. I want 1,000,000 USD for a 5% stake—but I will let you have it for 500,000 USD, as long as you agree to get involved."

Jimmy shook his head. A couple of years ago, that was more money than he could even imagine. And even now…

"Robby, you are overestimating my cash position. And my influence, for that matter."

"No, I'm not, bud. And remember, I know you. You're earning a fat salary, but you're also living large. And you have a big shareholding in a reputable company. You could easily raise the money for this from the bank, putting up your stake as collateral."

Jimmy thought about it. His stake in Il Leone would take another year to be liquid… he could free up some cash now for another investment, sure. But did he want to risk it on one of Robby's schemes? On the other hand, from what he had seen so far, Robby had the Midas touch… well except for the fiasco with Ben.

"Ok, let's say I'm interested…"

Robby beamed. "Fabulous! Once you sign a NDA, I can show you what I'm talking about. And you'll be in!"

"What's a NDA?"

A non-disclosure agreement was something Jimmy had not come across so far in his business career—but Robby had done his homework, and it was quite a hefty document. He presented it to his lawyer (Anna was adamant that she no longer fulfilled that role) and once he had gone over it with a fine comb, Jimmy signed off to see the business plan.

The presentation blew him away. Robby wowed him with an audio-visual presentation on a home shopping utopia, where everything was a click away. The secret, as Robby put it, was solving a global problem. It was an easy solution that was secure for user information; did not cost a fortune to implement for suppliers, and could integrate into different settings.

He was carried away by Robby's excitement, but he needed to get a

322

second opinion. The NDA, however, restricted his ability to bounce the opportunity off someone.

Robby understood his dilemma—and even had a solution for this. It was, at the end of the day, an obvious choice.

Jimmy went to visit the Wilsons.

He walked into Stan and Grace's beautiful home. She came up to him and kissed his cheek. She studied him. "Are you ok, Jimmy?"

He had taken a quick hit before he got there, just to take the edge off. "I'm brilliant. Things have gone amazingly well. We're expanding…"

She shook her head. "I know you are making headlines with the business. My question was: Are you ok? You look a bit… unsettled…"

He wanted to tell her. How he felt a bit out of control sometimes. How Anna kept him at a distance, and he felt a longing for more. How he seemingly had everything he ever wanted… and he felt empty.

But he didn't.

"Let's go sit down. I want to bounce something off you."

They reluctantly signed the NDAs at Jimmy's assurance, and then he told them all about Robby's proposal. There was a lot of technical stuff that he also didn't understand… but he thought he relayed the gist of it.

"What do you think, Hon?" asked Stan.

Grace shrugged. "I wouldn't bet the farm on it—don't know this stuff well enough. I want to do some more homework on what products are already out there. What he says makes sense to me, especially if he can make it super-efficient. That's the piece that's currently missing—people are doing it, but they're not doing it well. And there's a lot of grumbling around identity privacy right now. Companies are scared to lose client info and get sued."

Jimmy chimed in. "And that is where Robby and his team are focusing. The more efficient tech that can communicate with a variety of systems… and protect the client info."

Stan nodded. "I do like it. The problem we always had is outsourcing delivery and not losing the relationship… he is suggesting that he could do that for smaller boutique restaurants that don't have the infrastructure for home delivery. Places like Il Leone… or at least the Il Leone we used to know."

Jimmy felt the jab. "Yeah, Stan, about the Christchurch location…"

Stan stopped him. "Jimmy, it's all good. Water under the bridge. Masataka's buy-out meant we've all done extremely well—and we get to still retain the original under the deal, which is kinda what we wanted to in the first place."

"I'm glad to hear it. The bigger restaurants are not quite the same, I know."

Grace chimed in. "It's all good. We get that we're following a bigger trend. I do think it is a riskier volume game. As long as there are frequent live sports games, people will come to restaurants like those to watch, drink and be merry. It is a very different business though." She paused. "As is this. Robby wants you to put in a big chunk of money."

She observed Jimmy. "You brought him to us, Jimmy? Does he want us to invest too?"

"He's open to it. But he doesn't need your money. He wants to tie me in. I get to buy my stake at a 50% discount. The catch is he wants me to serve on the board and open some doors like this one."

She looked at Stan. "I like it. We've signed the NDA—we'd be happy to match your investment."

He started. "You wouldn't get the same deal. Remember, he's offering me a discount."

She smiled sweetly. "Tell Robby we insist."

He wanted to discuss it with Anna—but Robby cautioned against it. She was his lover, but neither she nor Mr. Masataka would like it. They wanted his full attention on the Il Leone business. He decided to go ahead and disclose it when the time was right. There was, as far as he was concerned, no conflict at this point.

And that was also part of the problem. The corporate gears had started to come into play. He was still having fun, but it wasn't the entrepreneurial joyride that he had with Stan and Robby in the first two years. They now had reports to fill in, there were aggressive completion targets and the pressure was building. He was exhausted all the time.

And part of it was Anna. She was insatiable.

They got together at his place at 7 pm. She always went off to do yoga in the evenings—and then she would come to drop in at his place in time for a take-out dinner. Sometimes they would make love even before dinner—and tonight was such a night. She attacked him the moment she flew through the door, hungrily sticking her tongue in his mouth and undoing his pants. Tonight, she slipped him a pill with her tongue. He didn't even know what it was... He often felt at these times that she wasn't even seeing him. It was like he was just at hand to fulfill her need for sex. He reflected that he might have treated a couple of women like that in the past. It was not a nice feeling.

It didn't bother him enough to stop. She came multiple times when she did this, and he was always exhausted afterward.

They lay sweaty on the kitchen floor for a while. Then she hopped off, pulled him up, and dragged him into the shower.

He was scrubbing her back, marveling at the tight smoothness of her muscles, when she asked, without looking at him; "Tell me about your dinner with the Wilsons."

He was caught off guard, he couldn't remember telling her he had gone to Christchurch. Doing it naked, semi-erect in the shower was not how he thought it would play out. The pill—whatever it was—started to kick in, and he felt slower on his mental faculties.

"It was... hmmm... it was great."

"Are they well?"

"Sure." He felt slightly irritated. It was an old argument between them. He was sure the Wilsons suspected his relationship with Anna, but she insisted that they pretend there was nothing. And so, she would never join for dinner.

She turned around, her nipples fully erect—and THAT was enormously distracting.

She put her arms around him and locked him with those big eyes of hers. "And? Anything interesting?"

"We were just discussing... an opportunity...oh God..." She had put her tongue in his ear, gently flicking. He was erect again, and her hard, soapy body was rubbing against his.

"What kind of opportunity?"

"Just something... Robby came up with... but they need to do more research..."

She slipped her hand down to his cock, and he felt he might lose control right there. Then she pulled herself up onto him standing, and slid into her...

"I heard Robby is back in town," she murmured. "Looking for investors..."

"Hmmm... I... oh man..."

"Anything else, Jimmy?" she was starting to gyrate on top of him. He was again ready to climax, man this chick... his head was swimming.

"He... he wants me to be part of it... and they... they also want in..."

"In what... oh that's good right there... in what way?"

Her pupils were dilating, even as he was going faster and faster. He didn't want to talk anymore... he just wanted to fuck her... like this... over and over...

"In what... oooh... in what way Jimmy?"

"He... he wants me to serve on his board!" As he said it, he felt himself release even as she cried out.

She patted him on the back and whispered in his ear. "Good that you told me, love. Very good..."

And she slid off him and pushed him out of the shower.

Later, they sat down with a cup of tea and she teased the rest out of him.

He realized that there was no way he could keep secrets from her—in fact, by the questions she asked, it was as if she already knew.

"How do you see this playing out, Jimmy? Your first responsibility is to Masa Corp and Il Leone."

"Yes, I know… but I won't take an active role with Robby's venture. He only wants me to grease some wheels, open some doors."

She shook her head. "Mr. Masataka wants your full focus here. This does feel like… a distraction." She handed him his tea, and watched him over the rim of her cup, thoughtfully.

"Unless…"

"What?"

"Unless he got involved too."

3 7

Lauren spoke to her mom regularly. They had a rhythm over Lauren's lunchtime, which was usually just before dinner in South Africa. Today she was excited to share big news.

"Harvard has contracted with a leading viral research institute in Wuhan, China. As part of the agreement, a task team will be sent over to Wuhan in September 2019," said Lauren.

"That's three months away!" exclaimed her mom. "What about your Ph.D. research?"

"Well, Professor Higgins thinks it would be a perfect extension of the current research—if we get really good data, I might even be able to round it off there. The initial contract engagement is just for three months, and it is specifically to study viral transmission from animals, consistent with the SARS outbreak of 2003."

"Wow. What an exciting prospect. But… that would now mean that you would completely break with Daniella in a professional capacity?"

Lauren bit her lip. "Yep. And I don't know how she's going to take it."

"Good luck, my love. Listen… Do you think you could come to

visit for a bit? Before you go there? You haven't been home in so long, and I miss you…"

"I want to, Mom. I miss you too." Lauren felt a pang of uneasiness. "Everything ok?"

"Yep, no, everything is fine. I find I'm lonely sometimes, Tim was so much fun, and I miss the company…"

"He was also a freeloader, mom. You did well to break up with him."

"Yep, I know. Funny. Your dad always took care of me, then the first real relationship after him, I chose a guy who needs me to take care of him."

Lauren laughed. "Such a cliché. You'll find someone else. Listen, Mom…"

"You have to go. I know. So proud of you, my angel. Before you go… anyone in your life? Anyone… special…?"

Luckily, this was not a regular interrogation from Lauren's mom. She was acting a little weird. "Nope, no change. Happily single. Why?"

"Such a pity it never worked out with Jimmy. I hear he is doing so well in New Zealand."

"Ok, mom. Now that he's like a tycoon, is he suddenly acceptable?" This conversation was going in the wrong direction, time to end it.

"No, no… I just… Well, life is short, you know? Anyway, talk to you soon. Good luck with that hard conversation, my love."

Her mom wasn't telling her everything. She would have to call Uncle Joe and get to the bottom of things. In the meantime, she had to work out how to break the news…

She knew Daniella would not be happy. She was also concerned that she would deploy dirty tricks to stop her. At the same time, she deluded herself into thinking that Daniella had her best interests at heart. After quite a bit of obsessing, she finally mustered the courage on a hot July afternoon to talk to her. They were wrapping up the day's work.

"Daniella, I have been offered an amazing opportunity."

Daniella arched an eyebrow, a familiar trait that showed she was expecting bad news.

Lauren plowed on. "Professor Higgins wants me to round off my research as part of a Virology task team going to Wuhan, China."

Daniella pursed her lips. "And you want to go?"

"It is a perfect fit. It would mean, though…"

"That you can no longer help me here? If you go, how long do I have to find a replacement assistant?"

It was not what Lauren had expected. She was being incredibly calm and factual about the whole thing.

"Well, we would leave at the end of August. So over two months? You can easily find someone for the new academic cycle?"

"Yes, easily. The work is not that difficult. I will find someone." Daniella was stone-faced.

The insult was not unexpected, and Lauren knew it not to be true. She had done exceptional work. At the same time, Daniella was probably right—there were lots of extremely talented people around who would jump at the opportunity. She was perplexed at Daniella not putting up a fight. It was too… easy?

Relieved, she said, "Thank you so much, Daniella. I am so extremely thankful for all the doors you opened for me, and all the opportunities you created."

But Daniella only turned away.

Initially relieved, Lauren found that the next month was extremely frosty in terms of working conditions. By the end of July, Daniella had found a replacement (Sandy, a bright and intelligent sophomore) and Lauren started to hand over her duties. She didn't mind. She was now also ready to leave, relieved even. She wanted to focus on the new opportunity.

The first setback came in early August, just a week or so after Lauren had officially given her notice to Daniella. She arrived at Professor Higgins to see him slumped behind his desk.

"What's wrong, Professor?"

"It's the strangest thing. I just received a letter from the Chinese Consulate. My travel visa has been denied. They wouldn't give me any explanation. This means I won't be able to travel to China."

"What does this mean for the cooperation agreement?"

"We could still send a task team, but I would need to check with Wuhan. They were quite insistent that my participation was key."

Lauren went to check on her visa. The Chinese visa had been approved. However, she also received a letter from the US Home office, denying her re-entry to the US if she were to go to China. So, she would not be able to go, at risk of throwing away the opportunity to graduate.

She called to ask what the problem was, and the answer was telling: "Your sponsor is listed as Daniella Liprini, and therefore you need to have her do the necessary paperwork."

"I have a new sponsor, Professor Higgins. He had filled out the necessary paperwork."

"There was a problem on our side, I cannot disclose what it was. You have to please get approval processes ratified by the original sponsor."

Lauren felt a cold chill going down the back of her spine. She would not be finished with her work by December. Now her extension seemed to be dependent on Daniella. This seemed completely unnecessary. As before, the "other" person in her life seemed to be falling victim to some unfortunate bad luck.

This was all the proof Lauren needed. And now she also knew the lengths Daniella would go to. Even when the other person was not even a lover, he or she would still be eliminated. She would never let her go… and Lauren felt the stirrings of that part of her that had been buried too long.

The fighter.

And if there were any doubts left, in the following days, more disaster followed.

Trump America was engaged in highly controversial relations with China, and there were rumblings from the Harvard fraternity that the project might be politically tricky. Professor Higgins started having personal problems too. Out of nowhere, an old article he had submitted was cited for plagiarism, and an official inquiry was launched. Harvard was ruthless to cull any such aspersions to the name of the institute. Lauren suddenly found her mentor suspended pending the outcome of the inquiry.

From flying high, she was about to be kicked out of the country unable to finish off all her hard work. Unless she went back to Daniella. Her respect—and love, as it was—for her mentor and friend was now completely gone. For the first time since Jimmy, she cried herself to sleep one night, more out of frustration and anger than sadness.

But when she woke up in the morning, she was clear. Another good man was going to be destroyed. And it was time for her to draw the line.

It was time to fight fire with fire.

The Boston Public Garden was picture perfect—and they had a ready-made frame up to prove it for tourists taking a snap. It was also right across from the famous Cheers bar, from the TV show… but now, in the late autumn afternoon, there was not a lot of activity around.

The last man Lauren had come to meet in the Boston Public Garden was Jimmy. She reflected how coldly she had treated him… but she didn't have a choice. Daniella would have found a way to also screw with his life. But this time, she felt different. She had had enough.

She had brought along some breadcrumbs for the ducks. She sat on a bench feeding them when the hulking figure walked up.

She jumped up and embraced him. She was quite taken aback at how much she needed the strong arms around her, just to feel safe for a second. But it was more like a big brotherly thing now…

"Ok, your message felt urgent. What's up? You ok?" asked Todd.

"I'll tell you in a second… but first, how are things? How's Britney?"

He grinned. "Amazing. She moved in last week."

"Wow. That was quick!"

"Yeah… but when you know, you know you know. I know it's cheesy. I think we both waited so long to press play, you know. But we are both there now, and it just feels right."

"I'm so happy for you Todd. Really."

"Thanks. I'm looking at a ring. We'll be engaged before the end of the year."

"Wow." She sat back down. "Respect, dude."

He laughed. "Your coaching helped in the early stages. Above and beyond, considering how I got you to go with me in the first place."

Her face darkened. "I suppose that brings me to the reason for this meeting. I need your help... my life is being fucked with, and I now think the best defense is an offense."

Todd rubbed his hands together. "That kind of talk from you? Must be serious."

"It is. Will you help me?"

He smiled a wicked smile. "They messed with the wrong girl. Tell me everything."

———

He called her two days later.

"Your friend is quite something, Lauren."

"Not quite sure if she is my friend anymore. Go on."

"Well, first and foremost, she's pretty good at covering her tracks. And her encryptions are legendary. But if I wasn't the rock star that I was..."

She sighed. "Yes, Todd. You are a rock star. Now tell me!"

"Ok. Yes, she is the one that's been screwing with your life. She uses a quite famous Filipino hacker, I can respect that. His handle is Yoda—yeah, cheesy, I know—but he can get in almost anywhere I can. He's been putting obstacles in your way to get free of her ever since you were dating that guy in Oxford."

Even though she expected as much, she still needed to hear it. She had one concern though.

"This Filipino... once you start doing what you do, could he..."

"Undo it? Nah. He's one of the best—but I'm better. Plus, I'm going to distract him for a while. His famous thing in the hacking world is to rig new online games that come out with back doors for him to do funny stuff. It's part of his rep."

"So, what are you going to do?"

"I'm going to create a back door for him in the new iteration of Fortnite. But it will be incomplete… and he'll take a while to figure it out. In the meantime, he'll not be available for your girl."

She nodded. "Ok then. What else have you got?"

A lot of it was useful, but almost nothing that gave her permanent leverage. One thing did surface, but they agreed that it was too flimsy to serve their purposes. Daniella has been using the dark web for untoward purposes for a long time—but she was also very, very careful.

"Not careful enough though," she said.

"You can use this, but it's only circumstantial. If we can catch her in a further act of fraud, that would seal the deal for you."

Lauren bit her lip and transferred the phone to her other hand. "How do we do that?"

She could hear him smiling. "As it happens, I've thought of that as well. And Britney fakes a mean British accent."

The phone rang with an unknown number. Daniella usually ignored such calls, but today she felt uneasy. She trusted her intuition; it had helped her evade some awful traps in the past. She picked up.

"Miss Daniella Liprini?" asked a female voice in a clipped British accent.

"Yes? Who is this?"

"Miss Lancaster, with the Rhodes Scholarship fund. We are just updating our database, and a discrepancy in your records has cropped up. We were wondering if you could help us clear it up by supplying original documentation."

She suddenly felt herself breaking out into a cold sweat.

"What… what is it you require?"

"Well, as you know, your scholarship was awarded based on several criteria, including academic record at your university. We recently upgraded our system, and we now have a live feed with feeder institutions. Your transcript at Milan university does not match our records. Could you please forward your original transcript so we can fix it please?"

"Uh… sure… no problem…"

"Thank you so much. I know it's still early there, but I'm about to clock off its almost 5 pm here in England. So, no rush—I'll check my mail in the morning. Your Gmail account still the same?"

"Yes, it is."

"Perfect. I'll send you an email now so you have my address. We can resolve this asap."

Daniella put the phone down and cursed. Her inbox pinged with a new message. She immediately forwarded it to an account that she used for just these purposes. From that account, she forwarded the email to a familiar address, with the message:

"Need to fix asap. Adjust transcript in original Milan records to modified transcript (copy attached). Also, verify this email is legitimate."

It took five minutes for a message to beep back: "Email legitimate. University database is more secure than Fund Recordkeeping. Will cost more."

"Cost is not important. Time-sensitive, must be done within next 10 hours. Please amend records to reflect qualifying grades as before and that records match between systems."

A few seconds passed. "Will action. Stand by."

He came through, as usual. The message simply read: "Transcript modified. Charge 5000 USD into a new account—details below."

It was an extortionate amount—more than five times his usual fee. But she did the wire right away, then fired off an email to Miss Lancaster, muttering to herself.

"Enclosed copy of the transcript as requested. Have also contacted the university, they have corrected a mistake that side- records should now match up."

She closed her laptop, breathing a sigh of relief. "Madre Mia."

She was about to pour herself a stiff shot of Bourbon (her favorite since moving to the US) when there was a knock on her door.

It was Lauren. Despite the girl's recent disloyal behaviors, Daniella felt the familiar pang of affection. She was in equal parts proud and jealous of her protégé. She was under no illusion that their relationship could ever go to the level that Daniella wanted. But she did know that she could keep her close. All she needed to do was sabotage the pesky men that came on the scene from time to time.

Only now, Lauren looked... different? Agitated? Daniella smiled to herself. *She is probably here to ask me to write the sponsor's letter. Good. She is crawling back to me. This day is getting better...*

"May I come in?" Lauren asked.

Daniella smiled and waved her in. "You know you never need to ask, Bella. Come, have a drink."

Lauren came in, but remained standing and turned down the proffered drink. Daniella flopped down into her couch, taking a deep sip, and waited. She was sure she knew what the visit was about.

She couldn't have been more wrong.

"Daniella, you have been so good to me over the years."

"Ah, it was nothing my sweet. Anything I can do for you, I will do."

"I have always been grateful. But now it is time for me to spread my wings. I have the opportunity to go to China."

"So, you said, but the professor..."

It was Lauren's turn to smile. "Oh, he had some trouble. A simple misunderstanding, though. Turns out someone was sabotaging his records. The Harvard internal audit committee has been notified of new evidence pointing to a Filipino Hacker. It turns out it was he who has been messing with Professor Higgins."

Daniella sat bolt upright. "A hacker? Surely not? Why would they..."

"Oh, I don't know. Why do people do things? A sick individual probably hired him to mess with Professor Higgins. Luckily I think it's being cleared up."

"Will be hard to get some answers out of this hacker, I presume."

"Almost impossible. The guy is a ghost. But luckily there are physical backups of all records kept, so the damage can be undone. It will take a bit of work, but I'm sure we can sort it out. Also, even hackers leave a trail of their dirty work."

"They do?" said Daniella.

"Yes. All you need is a better hacker," Lauren said the last bit with emphasis, then went in for the kill.

"Like, for example: If someone decided to hack into university records and tamper with a transcript. There is always a trail of that, you just need to be able to dig deep enough."

Daniella stared at her, and she went on; "These hackers are amazing. They can intercept email correspondence, create fake IP addresses and get into your whole cyberworld. Pretty scary stuff, if you ask me."

Dry-mouthed, Daniella could only venture, "What... what do you...?"

"What do I want? Oh, I want to know what would it take for an evil person, like the person that has been fucking with my promoter's records—what would it take for such a person to back the fuck out of my life?

If I had written proof that this person was tampering with records, wired money for the transaction? And it was all to defraud one of the world's most prestigious scholarships. Would I need to share it and destroy them? Or would they crawl back into their hole, and never come out again? If I showed mercy?"

Daniella licked her lips again. "If you destroy them, the people they work with might be affected too."

"Yeah," Lauren nodded. "I thought of that. Probably better for all concerned if this nasty evidence just went away. Don't you agree?"

"Yes... yes, I fully agree."

Lauren turned around, but before she left, with her hand on the doorknob, she said, "And it would be worth it to consider this. The evidence is out there now. If anything... anything... further happened to people like Professor Higgins, it would be sure to surface."

And she walked out of Daniella's apartment for the very last time.

38

Hong Kong's Il Leone was a smashing success from the very start. They held their grand opening on April Fool's Day 2019. The crowds streamed in. Sports fever had once again gripped Hong Kong in the lead-up to the famous Sevens tournament. Jimmy worked round the clock as Masa Corp pressed play on international expansion. He was now the one on the road most of the time. It was hard work and long nights.

Anna remained in Wellington, managing things on an operational level. But she, along with the Masataka C-suite, had jetted in for the opening, and it was a grand affair.

Jimmy would usually take the stage. But this time, Mr. Masataka asked that Anna be the spokesperson. And she dazzled them. An excited and full house of media, influencers, and sports celebrities hung on her lips as she announced the Tokyo and Singapore bars. The opening dates were set for July and August.

It was smart, Jimmy mused. The timing was always to coincide with important sports events. Each new opening came with spectacular press and fanfare. As he watched her, it occurred to Jimmy that of late, in New Zealand, the press had favored pictures of the highly photogenic Anna instead of him. They called her for quotes. He suddenly felt enormously resentful of her. He was still CEO…but she would jet in just for the opening, and then receive all the acclaim and attention.

Mr. Masataka had invested quite a bit in Robby's new venture, as did the Wilsons. Jimmy had borrowed money to buy his stake. He had needed to put up his shares in Masa Corp as surety with the bank to release the funds. So far, he wasn't 100% happy with what the company was producing. Robby assured him he should just keep the faith.

He was stretched pretty thin with how busy work was. He also wasn't looking after himself physically. He was now using uppers daily, and when on the road, drank half a bottle of whiskey a night before stumbling to bed. Especially if he was alone, which was most of the time. It wasn't even if he could indulge in one-night stands. Anna seemed to always know where he had been and who had been with. She was jealous, and possessive.

The slide had been slow, but noticeable. Jimmy started to hang out more and more in their bars, especially when on the road. The pressure was intense, and he needed to unwind. He was also the recipient of lots of attention, expected to be present, and he did enjoy the good time. When he did stop to think, he would plan how to break up with Anna. He knew she was no good for him. He even worked up the courage to do so a couple of times, knowing there would be unpleasant repercussions at work. But they would have some wine, take some drugs, and she would take him into her bed. And he lost his resolve.

Almost like a pet, given the occasional treat to keep them loyal.

As agreed, he helped to introduce Robby to a lot of people in his restaurant networks. The online delivery business had gone operational early 2019 in New Zealand. There were technical bugs and limited uptake, but overall, Robby again told Jimmy not to worry, as these things take time. Masa Corp had agreed to a six-month pilot phase, then review. Robby was confident.

But the drinking and the pills were out of hand. He had dinner with the Wilsons one evening in Christchurch, and Grace brought it up, even as he was on his third bottle of wine. Jimmy was quite defensive. After all, he knew that he could take his booze, and it didn't interfere with his work. Grace and Stan were worried, but they didn't push. They didn't see each other after that, either.

Now, Mr. Masataka and his entourage were fawning over Anna. And Jimmy was set aside. Or at least, it felt like it.

When Mr. Masataka finally turned his attention to him, it was with great deference. "You have done an amazing job here, Jimmy-san."

"Thank you, Masataka-san." Maybe it was all in his head.

"Our business is growing. You have gained much face these last years."

"Hai," he agreed. "It has been my pleasure." This was great. He started to feel better.

"We are looking forward to Singapore and especially Tokyo."

Jimmy bowed in acknowledgment.

"We are excited about what this team can do going forward," concluded Mr. Masataka.

And with that, the night continued on its merry way.

Anna did not come to his room that night. But she did ask him to have breakfast with her in the morning.

He felt worse for wear. She looked perfect, as ever. He still found her irresistibly sexy, but he didn't quite trust her anymore. He couldn't quite figure out why.

She buttered her toast, as the waiter poured some coffee.

"Jimmy, Masa Corp is really happy with your performance."

He shrugged. "Sure. We are killing it; the numbers look amazing."

"But there are concerns."

She was speaking to him like she was his boss, about to deliver bad news. And, suddenly, it dawned on him that she was. Despite their titles, their roles had imperceptibly switched in the last few months...

"What concerns?" he asked, carefully.

She sipped her coffee, her eyes on him.

"Mr. Masataka was reminded that you are still quite young... and the pressure is intense. He suggests we bring in someone with some experience to help you."

"Who?"

"We don't know yet. But you can't deny that you are not at your best. The company wants to help you." She delivered this in a calm, soothing voice. But he wasn't fooled.

Were they looking to replace him? They couldn't do that. He was a founder and a major shareholder.

Or could they? They were not a public company. There was no board of directors.

It was, once again, as if she read his thoughts. "It's the next step, Jimmy. Mr. Masataka wants us to form a formal board of directors."

"And my role as CEO?"

"Stays the same. But we just have a bigger team to support us."

He didn't believe her.

As April melded into May and May became June, with openings in Singapore, Tokyo, and Osaka, Jimmy found he struggled to sleep. Anna would continue to come for the openings. She was now clearly in charge, even though he was still the CEO in name.

His visits to her bed became more infrequent, as well. He started to wonder if she had found someone new. A new toy boy? It drove him crazy wondering. There was little he could do about it, being on the road all the time. But, when it suited her, she ruthlessly slept with him. It was no longer as good as it had been… and it all came to a head in Osaka, middle of May.

Mr. Masataka and his entourage were there for their Tokyo opening. As if by conscious design, they hardly spoke to him. Anna addressed the guests as usual. It was a boisterous affair, with lots of Saki and Japanese whiskey flowing.

He had been accompanied by Anna for most of it. It was as if she was keeping an eye on him, and he resented it. So, he did not take any substances. But, that night, he hit the whiskey pretty hard, and he was not as sharp as he once was. He was supposed to stay in the background, making sure ops ran smoothly. But he missed a few things. And, as a result, there were a few complaints about the food and service. It was sloppy stuff. And people noticed.

End of June, she called a meeting with him. Sitting in her office, Jimmy found it hard to focus. The pills had now become a necessity. And he needed them to calm down, he was a bundle of nerves.

Anna got straight to the point. "You need to clean up, Jimmy."

"What are you talking about?"

"Don't be a fool. People are talking. The drugs. The drinking. You're becoming erratic. Making mistakes. Mr. Masataka is very worried." She changed tack and took his hand. "I'm worried."

God, he needed a drink. He didn't feel like she was sincere.

"I've produced the results, haven't I? We're on schedule."

She betrayed a slight flash of annoyance. "Yes, but I have had to save your bacon a few times. And I am getting tired of covering for you."

"Liar. You love the spotlight." He took away his hand. She frowned.

"This is exactly what I'm talking about. You're aggressive and irrational. You need to clean up. Or you need to leave."

"I bet that's what you want."

She regarded him coldly. "It's not. But it doesn't matter if you believe me. I'm the messenger, and this is an ultimatum. Go clean up, or you're fired."

"You can't fire me. I'm a shareholder."

"I can. I have been empowered to do so by Mr. Masataka. You would keep your shares, but you would lose your position and salary. There are grounds. You would fail a drug test if we did one today, grounds for dismissal. Go clean up, Jimmy."

"You would do that? To me?"

She shrugged her shoulders. "We have had good times, Jimmy. And maybe we can have them again. But for now, we need to keep things professional."

"So, we're over?"

She nodded. "You and me, yes. For now..." She again lightly touched his leg. "But come back strong? Who knows?"

He felt cornered. He also knew that he would need to dig himself out. Maybe a break would not be a bad idea after all.

"What do you have in mind?" he asked.

"There's a place Mr. Masataka went to as a young man... in Guatemala..."

It was humiliating. He had been flying high: the golden boy of the hospitality press in New Zealand. The parties, the acclaim, the unlimited bar tab... and now he found himself on a small boat in the middle of bumfuck nowhere in Guatemala, Central America.

The message had been quite explicit. Go clean up, or just go.

Jimmy was no longer enjoying the work, but he wasn't ready to give it up, either. And truth be told, he had gotten used to the attention and the acclaim. After years of feeling slightly inferior, he was somebody again. He wasn't exactly proud of the way he had been behaving... but it also felt good to be out of control again.

What the hell was he doing here? A private car had transported him here from the airport in Guatemala City. Here being Panajachel, a medium-sized town on the shores of Lake Atitlan. And he was immediately put on a speedboat across the massive lake, to the town of San Marcos.

Now, Jimmy didn't speak a word of Spanish. This was the first problem. Secondly, the place was poor. The kind of poor that you saw a lot in South Africa, but after living in New Zealand for so long, it was a bit of a shock. But it was also beautiful. The water surface is unbelievably serene, with four majestic volcanic peaks surrounding the massive lake. There were a smattering of fishermen and scattered settlements, only reachable by boat.

On arrival at the very basic wooden dock at San Marcos, he was escorted up about 300 meters on a wooden walkway to the meditation center. It was called Las Piramides.

Jimmy had no wallet, no money—and his passport had been kept by his local minder. He was checked into the center and shown to a very basic hut. Then he was left alone.

He would be here for a month.

It had been two weeks since his last hit. After his talk with Anna, they put him in a rehab facility first. Withdrawal had been tough, but it felt like he turned the corner. Now he needed to be somewhere where access to stuff would be tough.

Saint Marcos fitted the bill. There were no ATMs, no banks, no access. He needed to walk around the lake to Panajachel to access any of such—and he had no identification with him, or money.

He was isolated, sober and miserable. But he made a decision to lean into the experience. He had learned long ago that sometimes you go with the flow. He didn't really have much of a choice, it was the base of his deal with Anna.

Leaning into it meant a morning swim in the ice-cold waters of the lake. That was followed by yoga, daily meditation, a lesson in some form of alternative spirituality, more yoga. There was lots of sitting around eating vegan food, and having the locals practice their Reiki on you.

Initially, Jimmy was bored out of his mind. And irritated. There was no proper food, not even a fridge. It was all freshly cooked veg in a basic dirty kitchen. The emaciated half-breed hound Flaco slept on the stove more often than not. It was all pretty rank if you compared it with his spotless apartment in Christchurch.

But by the third week, he started to feel… different. No one drank here—and drugs were, strangely, not part of the setup. It was all fruit juice and veggies, and he started, despite himself, to feel good.

There was also lots of time to think. He found himself thinking about his choices, his place in the world, about Anna, his job… and often—oh so often—about Lauren.

It was in the third week where they did the regression therapy. Along with 10 or so other retreat attendees, Jimmy attended the afternoon session in the temple. It was all pretty much out there. The spiritual leader of the place, Santi, instructed all of them to lie down and relax. Then she took them, by way of mantra and the natural energy of her voice, into a journey back in time. Go back 2 years, 5 years, 10 years, 15 years, 20 years… and she anchored for that date, 15 August 2019, memories.

Jimmy went with it… and as her voice droned on, he found himself going deeper and deeper into parts of his memory that he had thought he had long since left behind.

15 August 2017… he was in Auckland, opening the third Il Leone restaurant…

15 August 2014… he was wrapping up in France, on his way to Austria…

15 August 2011… he was 16 years old, and his father and mother

just had a fight in the kitchen, and he knew his dad was going to go for a trip again, and not watch him play for the first time for the first team...

15 August 2006... he was 11, and he failed a test at school, and his mom said it's ok, but his dad said it's not ok you had to do well at school to get money and you had to have money to get respect...

15 August 2001... he was six years old, and he loved school. The school was where he could go to learn about things, and school was where he could hide from the bad thoughts because daddy was being mean to mommy again...

He came out of the regression treatment and surprised himself with tears streaming down his face. They sat up in a circle and debriefed with quiet respect. With the others there, he had built such a rapport of trust and respect that he felt completely at ease to share his truth.

"I never... I never realized how much my dad shaped my thinking. I had such a tough relationship with him, and I was always determined to be different. But now... it looks like I am just repeating his mistakes..."

Santi nodded. "You can never judge them too harshly, although the spirits know we all do. They did their best with what they were given. Now it is your task to take the lessons from them and make your life better in the process."

"I feel... quite resentful toward him. I mean, I felt it before... but that was mostly because they died and left me with nothing. That feels stupid and selfish now... it's more to do with the fact that I needed a father to guide me, and he was never around. In the meantime, I developed into a proper little bastard in high school."

"Self-awareness comes to each of us through different channels. Maybe you had to live this experience to truly be free of the shackles of your past."

Jimmy still struggled to buy into the totality of the hippy speak. He had to admit though: She might have a point.

In the following weeks, Jimmy had much more time for introspection.

The month-long full moon to full moon program concluded with a week of silent contemplation and fasting.

He thought of the work. He had loved the wild ride... but his relationship with Anna had left him lonelier than ever. He had bought the car, had a nice flat, people fussed over him, he was even relatively famous in his part of the world.

But in the last few years, he had spoken less with the important people. Rarely with Uncle Joe. With Robby, only about the business. And never with Lauren. The voices in his ear were Anna, and a few superficial friendships built around sex, drugs, and rock n roll. Man, it felt so unoriginal.

The absence of food meant his body felt... different. There was no physical distraction, and the total lack of electronics and outside stimuli felt great. He was in the optimal place to explore with his mind and body. So, he sat in meditative contemplation on earth, fire, water, and air. He meditated in the garden, on the dock on the lake, in the temple, and in his quarters. He meditated on his core, and his core purpose, and by the full moon, he felt tremendously liberated.

For Jimmy, it was the perfect solution. He journaled like crazy, and at the very end, he succeeded in penning down what was important to him. Where did he want to go, and what was he willing to do to get there?

And at the center of it was Lauren.

The course finished, and when the small boat propelled away from San Marcos, Jimmy could not help feeling a strong pang of whimsical regret... it had been an enormously enriching experience, and he now knew what he needed to do. Would he ever go back here, though? Doubtful. But he hoped so.

On the other side, his minder stuck his cell phone into his hand, which immediately started buzzing.

"Oh, well. Zenful state completed," he sighed and answered the phone.

"Jimmy. How are you?" It was Anna. Hearing her voice, he felt nothing. No joy, no anger... just a weird dissonance. He would need to reflect on that on his flight.

"Anna? Thank Mr. Masataka for me. This was, indeed, just what I needed. I am looking forward to coming back and being 100% there for the company."

"I'm glad to hear that. We'll arrange..."

"My flight is home via New York. I'm going to stay over a few nights... last time we were in Boston, I didn't get to see New York, remember?"

A pause. "You might find a city like New York a shock after the month of isolation you had."

"I know. But I will be in transit through there. Who knows when I will have the chance again? Thanks for your understanding."

And with that, he terminated the call.

He was sure Anna suspected his real motives. He would deal with that when he got back to Wellington. In the meantime, he had his phone back.

The first thing he did was to book an onward flight to Boston.

———

He missed her by a day.

He had clarity on the ways that he had always sabotaged the good things in his life. And he was clear that he needed to anchor a future with Lauren. No time to waste...

Only she wasn't there. He arrived late in the evening. He tried her last known address first. No answer there.

Her business address was a no-go as well. The assistant advised that she, along with her thesis advisor, had left the previous day. It was a Hong Kong three-month research assignment, and they were due back in early December. She couldn't give him details without permission, though.

Deflated, he decided to WhatsApp Lauren. This also received no response. She had gone quiet on social media as well, which was unlike her. Her American number no longer worked.

He had an old Gmail account for her, and he popped her an email there.

In the meantime, he walked around the Harvard campus for the rest of the day... and he didn't quite know what to do. He had always just assumed he could get a hold of Lauren easily off her social media and online tools. Only now she had become like a ghost. He couldn't understand it.

In a flash of inspiration, he tracked down Daniella. She should know, right?

She was sitting alone at her desk, frowning at a textbook. And she was not what he had expected. When Lauren had talked of her, back in 2015, she had described this incredible friend.

This woman seemed neither friendly nor a friend.

She looked up. "Who are you? I am very busy here."

"My name is Jimmy Barnes. I… I am looking for Lauren…"

Her eyes narrowed. "The boy from South Africa. Ah yes, she has talked about you." She sat back. "She no longer works for me. As far as I know, she is concluding her Ph.D. with a research project abroad."

"Surely you can tell me more than that. They say she's gone to Hong Kong… don't you have a way to contact her?"

"I don't…" and then a sly smile crossed her lips. Jimmy thought it made her look even more unattractive. There was something… quite off about her.

"If she does not want to be found, Jimmy, there is a reason."

"It's not like her? What do you think might be her reason for going off the grid?" he heard himself asking, and he wasn't sure he would like the reason.

"Maybe she is ashamed? She doesn't want people to know what she is doing, or who she is doing it with?" The suggestion hung in the air.

"She has gone abroad with a professor… but he is close to retirement…"

Daniella stood up. "I need to work. But she does have a history of bad decisions about men. Especially older men. That fool Jacques, the rake Edward…" Daniella scowled. "But her Ph.D. is now her primary concern. And she will do anything to get it. It is no longer my problem; I have tried to warn her off in the past."

As she took his elbow, leading him to the door, she concluded; "My suggestion to you—stay away. She has… changed. Ambition has become her sole reason for living. For your own good, go on with your life."

And she shut him out of her office.

Jimmy felt disconsolate as he took a cab back to the airport. He couldn't change his flight again. He spent the next day walking around New York by himself. He found the city all he thought it would be. It was the epitome of material hustle and bustle, the ultimate sign of success.

Was she really sleeping with her promoter for the sake of her Ph.D.? He didn't want to believe it. He refused to believe it. It weighed on him as he walked around Central Park, young couples and moms with strollers everywhere.

For him, Central Park was the best part of the city. He liked Wellington for that reason—it was, like Cape Town, a gloriously green city surrounded by hills and facing the ocean. He was excited to go back there. But thinking of Cape Town, he was struck by an even stronger longing to go home.

He stopped in the middle of the park. Home? Was Cape Town home? Surely Wellington was his home now. Or was it?

This question occupied his thoughts back to New Zealand...

39

It was a whole new chapter for Lauren.

Todd had worked his magic. Her application issues and Professor Higgins's visa issues had all disappeared. A few weeks later, they were on a plane to Hong Kong.

The contract to work with the center in Wuhan was withdrawn. They cited the visa issues faced by Lauren and the professor, but he was not so sure. Professor Higgins had his own theories around the research facility in Wuhan. In academic circles, it was suspected that the Chinese Government used the data for their own purposes and did not do full disclosure.

The good news was a sister facility in Hong Kong would extend them the opportunity. This still fit their brief, and for Lauren, Hong Kong was a much more attractive option. It was an incredible city!

She had also put herself on a digital detox. She had, following Todd's advice, terminated all her legacy email accounts. She activated a new one that had quite a few additional security protocols on it. She also abstained from social media and WhatsApp comms. "Daniella might now not do anything, but she is probably still able to watch you if you use these channels," he said.

The thought creeped her out too much. So, she went back to traditional ways. Physical letters to her mom and friends, phone calls from her new number, and the occasional Zoom call. She always changed the meeting IDs, just because she was slightly paranoid.

Professor Higgins, of course, thought it all a bit odd. He had never really adapted to the "New-fangled ways of the youngsters". He was quite oblivious to her lack of Facebook and Instagram.

And there was, of course, the work. Professor Higgins came alive on the subject of infectious disease. He was convinced, as was she, that the world at large was particularly vulnerable at this point. Given the callous handling of specifically animal products and the high mobility and population densities of the time, the risk factors were exponential.

It was both scary and heady. And she was getting quite close to finalizing her thesis. This would mean, by mid-2020, she could even be Dr. Kinsman. What a thought!

But there was lots of work to be done in the meantime. They found extracting relevant information from the Chinese difficult. A lot of what they were doing was "state classified". It was understandable given the strained relations between the US and China.

They refocused their efforts on greater cooperation with the World Health Organization. She was a little bit frustrated. The work was meaningful, but she needed a lot more data analysis to round off her research.

She was so preoccupied with the work that she almost missed the fact that South Africa was once again playing in a World Cup. It was only a regular weekly call with her mom that alerted her.

They usually chatted on Sunday mornings, which was the evening in South Africa.

Lauren was worried about her mom. She had lost a lot of weight in the last few months, and her complexion wasn't great either.

But her mom always reassured her. "Honey, it's all good here. We had a great winter. The dam levels are back up to a reasonable level, so the drought in Cape Town is over. It's been pretty horrible, but now at least I can tend a garden again."

"I'm glad, mom. Any other news?" Tell me what's wrong with you, she thought.

"Same old same old… government not doing enough, none of

these crooks from the old guard have gone to jail yet, and Cyril is hanging on…"

Cyril Ramaphosa, the South African President, had failed to deliver on the early promise to root out corruption. Lauren, from a distance, thought it was funny how people obsessed about this stuff. In Hong Kong, they had their own problems with civil unrest, and in the US… Well, that was the Trump dog show. She was glad she spent less time plugging into the internet.

"Mom? How's your health?"

"Getting better, I think. Had an awful tummy bug for a while there, as you know. But I think I am on the mend… summer is coming, it always lifts my spirits." She paused. "I have been wrestling with my conscience over this… but now I feel like I need to come clean."

Lauren felt a cold chill. She knew her mom was hiding something. "What is it, mom?"

"Almost a month ago, Jimmy called. He was looking for your number. I said I would ask you if I could give it to him first. He understood, and followed up a few times. I blocked his calls."

"Why did you do that, mom?"

"Because… because I didn't want him distracting you from your dream. You're so close Lauren. And I…" her mom sniffed, but her eyes remained irresolute. "I thought it could wait."

Her mom. Interfering again. "Maybe I'm old enough by now to make those calls, mom?" She suppressed her anger.

"I'm still your mother. And I want what's best for you."

"So why tell me now?"

Her mom snorted into the hanky. "Life is short. And you've always loved him. Who am I to stand in the way of that? Plus, you would never forgive me."

The thought shook Lauren's mind. Something was up. "Forgive you for what?"

"He got hold of me through Joe. Said he wanted to invite you to a party. The Springboks are playing the All Blacks in the World Cup this weekend, and he will be in Hong Kong, at a place called… Let me look now…"

"Is it Il Leone?"

"Why yes, that sounds like it. He will be there this weekend. He wanted to get in touch to ask you to come to the party. Do you, Lauren?"

Did she? Hell yes.

She never really went out. There was no one to go with. But she knew about Il Leone. She had kept track of Jimmy's business successes on the web, and the few expats that she had met and made friends with in Kowloon all loved to go there. The place was packed with supporters of both teams, and she was immediately transported back to that fateful day four years ago. South Africa, brutally knocked out in England by the All Blacks.

She had not had the guts to call Jimmy. She didn't quite know what to say to him after all this time. But she did send him a text to let him know she was coming. She received a big smiley face in reply.

She arrived at the pub in her skinny jeans and Springbok shirt, and was gratified to immediately be enfolded into the melee of green, gold, and black and white shirts. The game had started, and there were cheers and groans every few seconds from the crowd. She made her way to the bar, and asked the barman, "Do you know where I can find Jimmy?"

The barman gave her a look. "You must be Lauren."

She started. "Yes, that's me."

The dude grinned and stuck out his hand. "I'm Doug. Also, a Saffer, was working in a dive downtown when Jimmy found me this gig. Will let the boss know you're here. Come with me!"

He took her behind the bar, and then they walked through the kitchen and up some stairs. The place was abuzz with activity. Dozens of different waiters, kitchen staff and cleaners working in a well-oiled machine swinging out pizzas and plates of pasta. Meat dishes were served alongside more traditional bar food like Burgers and Wings. She thought the food choices were not all consistent with the seeming Italian vibe. Then again, it did seem to work.

At the top of the stairs, they went through a thick wood-paneled door. Suddenly, they were in a more sedate lounge. Here, the vibe was markedly different. The men wore suits, the women were dressed in chic evening outfits, and the barman was doing some kind of cocktail producing show. The game was on, but on mute.

Doug ushered her to the bar, and left her there to order a cocktail.

It was only a moment before all the old feelings rushed back.

"Hello, Lauren."

―――――

They stared at each other—then she was in his arms.

"I'm so glad you called!" she said into his shoulder.

"I'm so glad you got my message," he murmured. "What happened to you? You went off the grid."

She stepped back, she had so much to say just then. She didn't get the chance. They were interrupted by an explosion of noise as a bunch of Kiwis entered.

"Excuse me for a second," and he disappeared. She got a drink and watched him work. He was older. He looked fit and healthy, but his face also had some lines on it that weren't there before. The result was not unattractive.

And he was clearly in his element. Everyone in the place deferred to him and treated her like a queen. The game itself was another New Zealand beating South Africa showpiece, as far as she could tell. As she watched him, old feelings stirred.

She needed some alone time.

40

Jimmy managed to divert the group of rowdy Kiwis. They had already pulled well ahead in the game, and Jimmy was already resigned to another defeat. He settled them down, took the jeers, and made his escape. All he wanted was to not let Lauren slip away again.

He had a lot to ask her. He didn't want to believe Daniella about Lauren's affair with her professor. He wanted to know about her work. What had really been going on in Harvard when he had seen her the last time. So many questions…

Jimmy had, since Guatemala, developed the habit of drinking virgin Mojitos. The barmen all knew, and it helped him avoid the incessant pressure to drink with clients. He was therefore crystal clear on how he wanted the encounter with Lauren to go.

They danced around the big questions for a bit. When the final whistle blew and the Springboks had officially lost the game, Jimmy said, "Let's go take a walk. I don't want to fend off these Kiwis in my own bar the rest of the night."

"Yeah, you go Saffer! You owe me a hundred bucks!" shouted one of the Kiwis. They all left through a different entrance.

The Hong Kong streets didn't seem to care about rugby that much. And that suited the two of them just fine.

There was a particular vibe in Kowloon, the mainland part of Hong Kong. They delighted in the bustle of the night markets, the noise, food, people and energy. Lauren had spent a fair amount of time exploring a lot of it by herself, and now she had a lot of fun showing off in front of Jimmy.

She was so glad to have someone other than her mother or Professor Higgins to talk to. They talked about Daniella. She confessed about Edward, the move to Harvard, the episode with Todd and her cyber antics. Eventually, they dwelled on the more serious matter of her current work in infectious disease. It now made sense to Jimmy why Daniella would have said what she did to discourage him. It was one last, cheap shot.

"She said you are sleeping with your professor."

She burst out laughing. "She would say that. He is old enough to be my grandfather, Jimmy. He does have some moves on the dance-floor, though."

"Yeah, I also learned how to dance these last few years. Mostly drug-fueled boogies, to be fair."

"Funny. Now that we've cleared my name, tell me about you."

He decided to be blatantly honest. About his drinking and fall from grace, the drugs, the success they had enjoyed, and the clean-up he did in Guatemala. And he told her about Anna.

When he arrived back in New Zealand, Anna immediately tried to take him to bed. He was, as always, very tempted. But things were different. His kind but firm rebuttal was not well received. And things had quickly become untenable at work. Anna was, in the end, also a woman. She was not happy to be rejected, an experience he was sure she was not overly familiar with.

Luckily, he had an intense travel schedule during the World Cup supervising major party events in all the international outlets. He was glad to be away from her and the drama. Wellington still didn't quite feel like home, even after a few years.

"So…" Lauren asked, as they sat down to dinner at a small little family place. The authentic Filipino cooking here was, in her opinion, best of breed. "You are clean, the business is booming, and are working with your ex…"

"Yes," he said, and helped himself to some noodles. "The fact that my ex is also my boss makes it complicated. I mean, on paper I am the boss. But after I came back from Guatemala, there had been more subtle shifts. I have very little authority left."

She nodded. "Power games. It took me a long time to untangle from Daniella. Not the same thing, I know, but she was in love with me. I know that now." She changed tack. "So how long will you still stay with this company?"

"I can't sell my shares until March next year. If I leave before then, they can buy them back at a discounted rate. That would be a silly mistake. So, I will stay at least until then. It's a lot of money."

He could tell she didn't like that. "Money. It's still that important to you, Jimmy?"

"Not as much as it used to be. But sure. I now know you shouldn't be a slave to it. I also don't want to make hasty decisions. My skin is thick enough to hang on for a while longer." He didn't want to seem defensive. But it felt like she was judging him. "And you? Close to getting your Ph.D.? After your time in Hong Kong ends, going back to Harvard?"

"Well, yes, I suppose. Our research institute is there, and they do insist you complete the work on campus." She looked away. "It's all I have ever dreamed of."

"All?" he asked.

"Not all," she smiled. They sat in silence for a moment.

"So here we are," she said. Her cheeks were flushed.

He signalled a waiter. "The bill, please. Quickly."

Their lovemaking was, in a way, as if they had never done it before. It was the rediscovering of their more mature bodies, the delight of reconnecting. But as they found their rhythm once more, they easily scaled the same heights. And more.

After the second round, she lay back, exhausted. "Being completely sober has done a bit for your stamina, Jimmy."

"True story. I miss having a drink, though. But I found I am better without it—Guatemala was great that way."

"Someday you must take me there," she smiled, tracing a hairline on his stomach downwards.

"I will," he sighed, as her hand came to rest a bit lower.

"Really?" she asked. "So soon? My my…"

Even later, after they had both slept for a bit, they ordered some burgers and milkshakes from room service. And they sat by the window, looking at the Hong Kong skyline.

"Where is home for you, Jimmy? Is it Wellington now?" she asked.

He finished chewing a French fry. "For the moment. But by mid next year… who knows?"

"You could come to Boston," she ventured, holding her breath.

"I could. In time for your graduation as a doctor." The answer pleased her no end.

"But afterward, Lauren…"

Oh-oh. His tone has changed.

"I think I'll go back to South Africa. I miss home. And I want you to come with me."

"Jimmy. The world is a strange place right now. Harvard is at the very front of what I'm doing. I don't think I'm ready to…"

"To downgrade to a place like Cape Town?" There was a challenge in his voice.

"Well, it wouldn't be at the same level at all. What would I do? Lecture at UCT? Consult with a local pharma?" She heard herself talking. She wanted to go back someday. Or did she? Definitely not yet.

"We would be together." His tone was relaxed again. But he seemed anxious. Maybe try a different tack?

"Yes… but I don't want to be resentful that I gave up my career, Jimmy. Why couldn't you come to Boston and start something there, as you did in New Zealand?"

"No Stan Wilson, for one. There, I would always be the non-graduate boyfriend/partner of a Harvard Professor. I know what that looks like from my Stellenbosch days. No thank you."

"Jimmy. It wouldn't be like that... and besides, you would also have to start over in Cape Town if you moved there."

"Not exactly."

He told her about Quick Meals, the delivery business Robby was building.

"Robby wants me to come home. Help him build out the business. He is signing up clients left right and center... It has the potential to be a great business!"

"Potential? Robby hits the jackpot sometimes, but he also..." she didn't have to finish the sentence.

"Talks a big game? Yeah, I know. Look, it's an exciting area. They are burning through cash. But that's what tech businesses look like. There should be a tipping point soon, and then..." he shrugged. "I have a small stake because I got in early, and the tech seems to work. We are piloting it in all of our outlets in New Zealand, and Robby had a pretty good footprint in SA as well." Jimmy sat up, and their eyes locked.

"I want to go home. Soon."

"Jimmy..." she wanted to assure him. Some kind of promise that she would come with him. But she couldn't. She looked away.

He didn't say anything. She pulled him back down, and they lay in each other's arms till daybreak.

After she had left, he checked his messages. There were quite a few from HQ, the normal stuff. None from Anna. Good, he didn't feel like talking to her. Especially with his head in turmoil, as it was right now.

He showered, ordered some breakfast, and headed to work.

He needed to work on his integration proposal for Quick Meals for the Asian outlets. It worked relatively well in New Zealand. The tech was pretty good, but he was worried about competition. Uber Eats was going strong into that market, built on existing transport infrastructure and deep pockets.

As he was plowing through it, he received a call from Robby. It was the middle of the night in South Africa, but he knew his buddy was a night owl most days because of the international operations.

"Jimmy? Everything ok?" There was an edge to Robby's voice.

"All good." He immediately wanted to tell his best friend about Lauren—but something stopped him. "Wrapping up in Hong Kong, flying back to New Zealand tomorrow."

"Anything you want to tell me?" Robby's tone of voice…

"Launch went well, numbers are good. Think we're back on track here, and I am looking at the business case for bringing in Quick Meals. Why?"

"Dude, it's me. You saw Lauren, didn't you?"

"Whoa, Robby." What was going on? "How did you know that?"

Robby sighed on the other end; "Sometimes you're not that smart, bud. My phone has been going nuts. Ever since about 10 hours ago, I have received a ton of discrepancy inquiries from your accountants. Small stuff that we can explain easily, but I've seen this before since starting this business. This is what companies start with when they want to exit their agreement with us."

"That's pretty strange, Rob. I mean, I know it hasn't exactly taken off yet. At the same time, Masa Corp and I are personally invested in the business, so it serves us to ride it out for a bit."

"If logic was in charge, sure. But I called some old friends. That bitch Anna instigated all of these investigations earlier today. She has been in the foul mood of the century, and we are the target." Robby paused. "And apparently, everyone is chatting about how the boss left the party in Hong Kong early." He paused. "After his old girlfriend showed up."

"Robby, honestly, Anna has been off after we broke up. This is a bit extreme; don't you think?"

"I'm telling you what I know, my friend. True, she might not give a shit about you. She does care about how your behavior makes her look. If she is like any other woman that I know, this will hurt. And it feels public. You made a mistake."

"I'm flying back tomorrow. I'll fix it."

Robby shook his head. "I hope so bud. Otherwise, we are both screwed."

41

W hen he did call, Anna simply wanted to know if he needed a car from the airport. They had a board meeting coming up and they needed to prepare. She was always professional over the phone. But Jimmy knew there would be trouble.

He was uneasy on the flight back. Excited about the prospect of picking up with Lauren, but still confused about how they could possibly make it work. He was equally apprehensive about Anna's sudden animosity toward Quick Meals. The story that he had told himself all these years was that Anna didn't care. He could break it off at any time, right? That theory suddenly felt naïve.

On arrival, 12 hours later, this was supported. There was a board briefing pack in his email inbox. One item caught his attention: "Executive Role Review".

Uh oh.

The quarterly planning day was attended by everyone in upper management. Mr. Masataka did not attend all of them—but today he, too, was present. He was flanked by his usual entourage. Anna barely acknowledged him as he entered. He was also introduced to Ray Booth, an American gent he judged to be mid-forties. Jimmy recognized the name, and the face seemed vaguely familiar.

Jimmy had gone over his presentations in detail during the previous week in Hong Kong. Now that he was no longer boozing, his ability to focus had improved dramatically.

The format was a snapshot of current numbers and initiatives, presented by each of the regional managers. Anna was responsible for the New Zealand main business, and Jimmy was running Tokyo, Hong Kong, and Singapore.

The numbers were ok. But his heart wasn't in it, and he barely made it through his presentation.

When all the divisional heads had wrapped up, Jimmy took the stage. His job was to outline a vision and strategy for the next year. And he had done his homework.

"We currently are operating 20 'legacy' restaurants in New Zealand. These will continue to operate under the Il Leone brand, we might sell off or close one or two. The seven outlets we now run as bigger sports bars will be rebranded in the new year to "Wilson Action Sports Bar". focus groups have taken well to the name, and Stan has agreed to a licensing deal.

We are not planning further expansion in New Zealand. We are just consolidating operations under the two brands and expanding local volume through strong brand positioning and additional services, like home delivery through Quick Meals."

The room temperature plummeted when he mentioned Quick Meals. Now really concerned, he finished his presentation and sat down.

You could cut the tension with a knife when the company secretary said, "Next item on the agenda: Executive Role Review".

Mr. Masataka stood up. "Thank you, Jimmy-san. We like plan. But we also believe that new initiatives needed. I give to Anna to explain." And he sat down.

He turned to her. Anna looked around the room, only briefly holding his gaze. When she spoke, her tone was level. There was not a trace of anger or remorse... no emotion.

"Masa Corp has, for some time now, felt that the management team for Il Leone needs a reshuffle. It is generally accepted that we have done an amazing job bringing the company to this point." Polite applause.

She continued, "We now need a more experienced CEO to take the reins for our further expansion."

At this, Anna gestured to the middle-aged man. The one Jimmy had not recognized when he came in.

"Ray Booth comes with incredible experience in running multinational restaurant chains. He has assisted with the expansion of Buffalo Wild Wings and Five Guys into Asian markets."

That's it, Jimmy thought. He's the American Five Guys guy. Walked away with a bunch of industry accolades for the successful market entry into Dubai and China.

"Ray will take over the role of CEO of Il Leone, effective immediately. Reporting directly to him, Jimmy Barnes and I will be joint COO's responsible for different geographic divisions."

So not fired. Demoted. He shook his head, and replied to her; "We were not consulted as shareholders on these decisions."

She held his gaze, and now he detected that slight arrogant-even vengeful- glint that he knew so well. "As majority shareholder, Masa Corp has full autonomy for this decision. Your remuneration package with associated increments remains intact."

She had thought through all the answers.

"So, I will continue to look after international expansion as my primary focus?" he finally asked.

She smiled that evil smile. "No. You will, going forward, be in charge of the consolidation of local operations. I will take over the international expansion portfolio."

Dead silence. Even Mr. Masataka and co sat completely still, stoically avoiding his gaze. He had no friends here. And now he understood. The money and opportunity would be in the global portfolio. There would be no more growth in New Zealand. They knew that it was not his preference. They were shifting him into a job that they knew he would hate. They were effectively forcing him to resign earlier rather than later.

Ray Booth stood up, expressing his appreciation for the warm welcome into Masa Corp. He had a pronounced Southern drawl, and immediately started to charm the Japanese.

Why do this? Anna might be pissed that he had reconnected with his ex-girlfriend. Surely that wasn't enough reason. But suddenly, things made sense. They didn't send him to Guatemala to get him better. They sent him to get him out of the way, so they could start paving the way for this guy. And what was in it for Anna? She had always been ambitious, but there was nothing in this for her.

He thought it through. The only thing he could think of was that, in a patriarchal society like Japan, Mr. Masataka still didn't trust Anna to run the company. That was what she really wanted. So, what was the play with Ray Booth? He needed to figure this out. In the meantime, legally challenging it wouldn't work. Masa Corp was not touching his benefits, they were simply changing his management position.

But he wasn't born yesterday. This was the beginning of the end.

The meeting ended, and the Japanese filed out. Mr. Masataka gave Jimmy a curt nod on the way out. How quickly things changed…

He was alone in the boardroom with his new boss. Ray Booth stood up, and walked over to him, finally settling in on the chair opposite.

"Look, Jimmy, I know this is not the way to kick things off. I would like us to start fresh—you have been an amazing asset to this business, and I would love to continue working well with you." The older man had a favorite-uncle way about him. Likable, seemed authentic. Jimmy thought this was what Colonel Sanders, founder of KFC, must have been like. Jimmy was so angry. At the same time, he realized his anger was not best directed here.

"Ray, what if I didn't want that job? What if I resigned?"

The question was not unexpected; "You are of course free to do as you wish. In terms of your contract, we would buy out your shares at the original valuation price." That warm all-American smile.

"But that's peanuts! We have grown exponentially since then; the shares must be worth a hundred times that by now!"

"That is correct. But you have six months to go on your contract agreement for that value to realize. If you leave the business before then, you will forfeit the gains." He talked in measured tones as he delivered the bad news.

"Wouldn't make sense." Once Jimmy said it, the favorite uncle put a warm hand on his shoulder.

"Glad to hear it, sport. I need you to help me get this ship back on track. Bygones are bygones. Now, is everything cool between you and Anna? She is a key member of the team, and I have a sense of these things. Is there history there? Can we work together effectively?"

Jimmy nodded. "We'll work it out." But he knew it was a lie.

His next stop was Anna's office. It had a beautiful view of the Wellington harbor and incorporated a huge desk and low chairs. It was intended to intimidate. She now ushered him to sit there.

"You are angry," she said, as she closed the door. She sat down next to him, as her skirt rode up, once again showcasing her magnificent legs. He knew it was intentional. It was one of the games she played. He kept his gaze on her face.

"Yes, I'm angry. This was an ambush!"

"It's just business, Jimmy. You have done an amazing job. In every way," she said, with a hint of a smile. "But your problems… we needed to make a change. I warned you."

"How does this serve you, Anna? You were practically running things while I had my issues. Now you once again report to someone else?"

She stood up, walked to the blinds—and closed them. She turned back to him and poured herself a whiskey from the crystal tumbler on the desk. It was probably a Glenmorangie 21-year-old…. One of their favorites when he was still hitting the sauce. She looked at him with a question in her eyes. He shook his head, and she poured him some water instead.

As she sat back down, she replied, "Mr. Masataka is not ready just yet to appoint a woman. But he will… if I prove myself."

"And what does that look like, Anna? Did you orchestrate all this to get me out of the way? Man, sometimes I wonder if any part of us was real?"

Her eyes flashed. "You insult me, Jimmy. But I will forgive you. You are the one that broke with me, remember? But I can move past that." She put her hand on his leg.

He detested her. But his body betrayed him.

"There's my old friend... We were a great team... we can be again..." and he felt her deft fingers undoing his trousers, that perfume of hers...

With a supreme effort of will, he jumped up and away from her.

She was caught off guard and sat sprawled on the couch. She was breathing heavily. He had never seen her off balance like that. It helped break the spell.

"No more games, Anna. You don't care about me. You care about power. Let's keep it civil. We can work together for the next six months, and then you will be rid of me for good.

He was taken aback by her look of pure hatred. Man. This was going to be a hard few months.

He turned to leave, but she said:

"You are making a big mistake, Jimmy. Come back here. Or you will regret it."

He was sure he would. But he didn't care.

He walked out, and felt a burden fall from his shoulders.

It took less than a week.

He was called back to Ray Booth's office. Ray Booth's tone was still warm and engaging—but the instruction he had was less so.

"Jimmy, I have made a proposal to Masa Corp based on my analysis of the numbers. They agree with my recommendation and have given me the green light to execute."

Jimmy knew he wasn't going to like it. "And the proposal is...?"

"We could immediately claw back five base points of profit if we terminated the contract with Quick Meals and outsourced all deliveries to Uber Eats. They are so eager for our business they will do a preferable profit share. The numbers don't lie. We should do it."

"We have a significant investment in Quick Meals, Ray. And they are only now coming out of the start-up phase... Loss of this contract could severely damage their operating cash position. We would get pennies of the dollar on our shares if we pulled the plug." As he said it, Jimmy knew his plea would fall on deaf ears.

"I worry that you have a conflict of interest there, as you are also a shareholder in that business on a personal level. As such, I have been authorized to buy out your stake at the contract price, and have prepared a document as such. We would then hold the entire interest —and you would be absolved."

"But we would still terminate their service contract with us," Jimmy stated.

"Yes. We would, as you say, lose quite a bit. But it's the right move strategically."

Jimmy was fuming. This man was a fool, he hadn't been here five minutes and he was making really bad decisions already. "Did Anna put you up to this?"

For the first time, the smile on Ray's face slightly faded. "No one put me up to anything, Jimmy. I have a job to do. And so do you."

"Ray, you do know that Robby could face financial ruin. If that happens, my friends, the Wilsons would also lose a lot of money. I couldn't take this offer. I would be selling them out."

Ray nodded, sympathetically. "You'll learn this about business, sport. It's tough to be a leader, sometimes you just need to make hard decisions." He moved a document across the desk. "It's show business, not show friends."

Jimmy couldn't believe what he was hearing, and didn't look at the document. "If you piss off Stan Wilson, he will stop making appearances. He wouldn't want anything to do with us, and he has wide influence. It would be disastrous for our sales…"

"People like him, sure. But I have never heard of him before taking this job. Celebrity status wears off quickly after you hang up your boots. I don't think the impact is as much as you think it is."

"Ray, with all due respect, New Zealand isn't the US. People here think he is a god, it would be a massive mistake to do this. Please listen to me…"

Ray Booth nodded, and the tension eased. "Ok, let me look at this again. But in the meantime, this is the offer for your shares." He tapped on the document.

"Ray, I won't sell my shares to Masa Corp. End of discussion."

"I understand that. But you need to look at this contract, at least. And, to make sure we are clear from my side, you need to sign this other acknowledgment," and he grabbed another piece of paper, "that you are refusing our offer of fair value."

In hindsight, Jimmy should not have done it. He should have let his lawyers look at it. He should have thought it through. But he was too worried about Robby, too angry at Anna, too disappointed in Ray. Hindsight.

The refusal document was straightforward. He read through it, and signed.

He walked out, in search of Anna.

She was not in her office. Her secretary advised that she was on a trip to Japan, to spend the week overseeing the Tokyo launch. She would stay on and watch the World Cup Final with Mr. Masataka in their suite. South Africa was very much in contention with a semi-final against Wales coming up. The fact that Mr. Masataka had not invited Jimmy as their South African connection was a telling slap in the face. The writing was on the wall...

But, as before, history would repeat itself. Sort of.

New Zealand had a bad week. They had suffered a humiliating defeat to a visibly arrogant England in the World Cup Semi-final. The Kiwis were gutted, the Brits in the bar elated. In such instances, the majority of the patrons would not stick around and it would be a bad night at the till. Which suited Jimmy. He had to head to the airport to pick up Robby. His friend had flown over immediately after Jimmy's disastrous meeting with Ray.

"I have a meeting with Ray on Monday, bud. And I'm dead worried. When you left it with him, what was his vibe?"

"Robby, it's a mess. This guy is a horrible leader. I get the sense

Anna hand-picked him because she can manipulate him. God knows it worked for how long on me."

"True that. So do you think he'll jerk the contract?"

"I tried to talk him out of it. But he wouldn't hear of it. I think the writing is on the wall."

They threw down their bags at Jimmy's flat, and Robby poured himself a drink.

Robby looked around. "Still, you're doing ok my friend. This pad is pretty nice, and in five months or so, your share option with Masa Corp will mature."

Jimmy smiled. "Thanks. I paid too much for this at the height of the market. If I sold it now, I would just about repay the outstanding loan with the bank."

Robby laughed. "Sex, drugs and rock and roll bud. But you had a good time for a lot of it, as I recall."

Jimmy had to agree. "Some of it. But a lot of it was just Anna driving me to a dark part of myself. I know, in the end, it's all on me. I was really lost there for a while, though. The company you keep, right?"

"Let's change the subject," his friend replied. "Remember, your deal with me is different from the Wilsons. They gave us a convertible loan at the current share value. And they can pull it at any time. If Masa Corp pulls the contract, you need to convince them to take the shares not pull the loan, otherwise, we are truly dead."

"He's still in Japan, doing promo there. But I'll talk to him when he gets back."

Three things happened over the following few days. South Africa beat Wales to make it to the World Cup Final. Stan Wilson flew back to New Zealand instead of staying in Japan. And Jimmy received a call from Lauren.

The match between South Africa and Wales was a typically robust affair, with South Africa just marginally pulling ahead. For Jimmy, it was especially gratifying, as Sam was instrumental in a final move that helped them win the game. He was happy for his erstwhile rival—and suddenly he was also a bit irritated not being invited by Mr. Masataka. He was delighted, though, when Lauren called him right after the game. She had also watched it. More importantly, she had an indecent proposal for him.

"Sam called me, Jimmy. He had heard I was in Hong Kong, and he wanted to invite me to come watch the games. I told him it was too short notice, last week was hectic... but I did say I might be able to break away this week."

Jimmy snorted. "I bet he was delighted. I thought he was engaged?"

"He is! He was inviting us, silly. Not just me."

"Really? That's gracious."

"We've all grown up a bit, Jimmy. Will you come with me? Once in a lifetime..."

"When did you become such a big rugby fan?" he responded, playing with her.

"I'm not. But... Jimmy, we chatted for a while. He said... Well, he said that this team is something special. He's pretty sure they're going to win."

"You do know that the English completely dominated the All Blacks yesterday, while we barely scraped through against the Welsh. No one is giving us a chance."

Lauren sniffed. "Jimmy. Do you want to debate rugby with me, of all people? Or do you want to jump on a plane, meet me in Tokyo, where we can eat sushi, go sightseeing, watch the World Cup...?"

He laughed. "It's a big offer. I have a bit of a situation on my hands over here, though."

She lowered her voice. "Jimmy, do you remember the last time there was a World Cup? And the two of us together? What were we doing? All the time?"

He did remember. Oh boy.

"Meet you on Wednesday in Tokyo."

Meanwhile, Stan was released from his appearance commitments once New Zealand were knocked out. He decided to go home early, and he also wanted to urgently speak with Jimmy. Jimmy elected to go meet him in Christchurch to update him on developments with Mr. Masataka.

Jimmy booked his flight for Tuesday morning, to arrive in Christchurch more or less at the same time as Stan. Afterward, there would be a direct overnight to Tokyo, so the logistics worked out.

Lauren's offer delighted him. Another World Cup. Another week or so together. Maybe... just maybe... they could find a direction. But he needed some clarity on Ray Booth and the Robby issue first, so he could jump on the plane clear of baggage.

The meeting was set for 10 am Monday. Ray, Anna, Robby, and Jimmy were present.

And it was not a great meeting.

After the initial overbearing American greeting from Ray, they all sat down.

"Robby, I want to start by telling you what a terrific job you've done building Quick Meals. Terrific, simply terrific." Ray was buttering them up. Both Jimmy and Robby waited for the but.

"But Il Leone is going to go back to basics. Focus on being an in-store dining and entertainment experience. And leave the home delivery stuff to the big boys."

There it was. Robby was irritably shifting in his seat, as Ray continued; "Jimmy will be in charge of the logistics of it. We want to transition to an outsource to Uber Eats within the next month, to be ready for the December/January holiday period. One month's notice, as per contract."

"As an investor in the business, you must know this means a setback for equity growth. Plus, reputational damage in this market," noted Robby. Jimmy was impressed by how calm he was.

"Understood. But we have to protect our core brand. Sport, I appreciate your drive and creativity—but this ride is over. Masa Corp is prepared with the downside of their investment to right the ship." With that, he stood up. "I will let you and Jimmy work out the transition details. Thanks for coming in."

Anna also stood up, and Ray walked out. She was about to go, when Jimmy said, "Anna, you do know he is making a mistake. You are making a mistake. The Wilsons..."

"We have considered it, Jimmy. Sometimes you have to break some eggs to make an omelet." She smiled sweetly and turned to Robby. "It was good to see you, Robby. I have the paperwork with me, I will wait for you in my office?"

As she walked away, Robby whispered under his breath, "Bitch."

Then he turned to Jimmy. "Pity you ain't drinking, bud. But after I sign her damn termination contract, I'm going to go have me a morning beer. Coming?"

"So, what happens now, Jimmy?" asked Stan Wilson.

They were having coffee in the airport, and Jimmy was glad Grace wasn't there. She would have probably ripped him a new asshole for all this. As it was, Stan was surprisingly sympathetic.

"I am working with Robby to close down operations here for Quick Meals. All the deals in the pipeline will also disappear, probably. Uber Eats is a monster competitor, and no one will invest in working with us on this after Il Leone pulled out."

"What about other markets? Hong Kong? Tokyo? All that?"

"Stan, we never got that far. Right now, there was only a footprint in South Africa and here in New Zealand. South Africa is limited— they have a gorilla competitor there too in the form of the Naspers group."

"So, this business is…"

"Pretty screwed. Robby is struggling to onboard further investors; operations will now go cash flow negative. Look, the tech will be great once we iron out the bugs. But it's taking a while."

Stan finished his cappuccino. "Mate, you win some, you lose some. I'm not going to call in my loan. That will really finish this thing."

Robby felt the tension ease from him. "That was my biggest concern. You have been such an incredible mentor to me. It would be awful if you lost all that money."

Stan smiled. "Look, not all your bets pay off right? We made a killing on Il Leone off your hard graft. And Robby has always been a mover and shaker. What I'm going to do, to help him and you, is exercise the option to convert the loan to shares."

Jimmy couldn't believe it. "You sure? You could lose everything—with the loan you at least are in the front of the line if it folds."

Stan laughed. "Yeah, but at that point, it wouldn't matter. Nah, let me keep a piece. I believe in you, Jimmy. And let's not count Robby out just yet."

"Dude, I am so so grateful." Jimmy once again reflected how lucky he was to have had this guy in his life. But there was more.

"Jimmy, I'm glad that's out of the way. But that's not why I wanted to meet you." He dug into his pocket and brought out an envelope. Jimmy's interest was piqued.

Stan could be a trifle dramatic. "Now, before I give you what's in this envelope… tell me what the next six months of your life look like."

Mysterious. But Jimmy had thought about it. "31 March 2020 is when my contract finishes. After that, I can sell my shares in Il Leone at market evaluation whether I work there or not. So, 1 April, I plan to be on a plane back to South Africa."

"What about your apartment here?"

"I will sell it. At a loss, but enough to cover the bond. I also have the loan outstanding I used to pay for my shares in Quick Meals."

Stan nodded. "So, you are carrying a lot of debt there, mate?"

Jimmy smiled. "Despite all my best efforts to not turn out like my father, yeah. Lots of toys, no money. The upside is, selling my Masa Corp shares back to them in April should give me enough to pay off all my debt… and still be a millionaire with what's left."

"Don't count all your chickens before they're hatched, Jimmy. Ok, so tough it out a bit longer then leave our fair shores. You sure you don't want to stay?"

Jimmy had worked through it, and was certain. "If I do, I can't go and try to help save Quick Meals. I need to be back there to save this thing. More importantly, I love it here. But South Africa is my home. After school, I've been away more than I've been there. I miss the people, I miss the… the soil, I guess."

He wanted Stan to understand. "Don't get me wrong, New Zealand has been amazing to me. And France. And Austria. I do think, however, I could take what I have learned, go back there, and make a difference."

Stan nodded his head and waved for the bill. "And are you going back alone?"

He knew all about Jimmy's convoluted history with Lauren.

"I wish she would also come back. She is close to finishing her Ph.D., and she is doing all this amazing work with Harvard. It's what she always wanted—saving the world and making her mark as a woman. South Africa doesn't fit into that plan." Jimmy frowned. "She did ask me to come back with her to the USA. I suppose that is an option. We're going to discuss it in the next few days."

"If you really want to be with her, you should consider it. Love of your life or going back home. It's tough stuff, my friend." The starstruck waiter swiped Stan's credit card, and they stood up to leave.

"You're going to have a great time in Tokyo. Go do the go-kart-ing... it's insane." With that, he handed over the envelope. Jimmy opened it, and an electronic key card and a page with an address on it came out.

"An access card to a flat in downtown Tokyo. The flat is paid for by my old club, they said I could use it for the duration of the Cup. It's an amazing spot. Also, I have VIP access to a few things. My guy there will hook you up."

"Stan... you just did it again. I mean... this is too generous..."

Stan Wilson hugged him. "And this time, it's not even a bribe to try to get you to work for me. I have a good feeling about the Boks for this one, Jimmy. Go watch them make history. Go get your girl. You deserve it."

"This is the most fun I've ever had in my life!!!" screamed Lauren, as they sped through Shibuya Crossing, thousands of Japanese gaping at them.

She was wearing a Minion suit, and Jimmy was dressed as Spider-Man. They were in go-karts, hurtling around the world's most insane track... the streets of Tokyo.

They slowed down at a traffic light. Immediately tourists started to take snaps of them, and she found herself giggling hysterically as Jimmy pulled up next to her. "This is insane!" she screamed, leaning over to kiss him. He returned the kiss with meaning, then the light turned green again. They sped away, narrowly avoiding a massive 45-seater tour bus.

Some 30 minutes later their wild ride had ended, and they pulled back into the head office of Shibuya Go-Kart. Their guide nodded appreciatively of their driving skills, and gave them directions to a cool area for eating.

They finally found a little mock American Burger joint, complete with a vintage jukebox. A few other tourists were milling around, mostly Englishmen. They sat down in a corner and ordered large colas and burgers with fries.

They had been in Tokyo for two days. The apartment Stan had organized was incredible—a spacious, 20th story modern furnished flat with a view over the Rainbow Bridge. They took a hot second to appreciate the opulence of it. Then they tore each other's clothes off. They would only surface for food 24 hours later.

Their next mission was exploration. They crisscrossed Tokyo, taking in all the amazing sights and sounds. The Light Museum, the Whiskey Library, Shibuya Crossing, and the insane markets, varieties of foods, and cosplay. It was wild.

Sam had joined them for the Friday afternoon and introduced them to his fiancée. He had not made the matchday squad and could therefore take some time to himself. It was amazing walking around the city with them.

"I'm surprised you are not more bummed not playing tomorrow, bud," said Jimmy. "I mean… you did nothing wrong in the last game, some might say you helped win it."

Sam shrugged. "This team is something special, Jimmy. I did my part, but our coach Rassie is amazing about telling everyone where they stand. I know I am good. Francois Louw is a little bit more experienced and does what I do. He is better, I hate to say it. I had my chance last week because one of the other guys had a niggle. Everyone is in full fitness now. And it's about the team, not a person."

His fiancée, Julie, also put in her two cents; "Sam will get his chance, I'm sure of it. In the meantime, I'm just happy he now has a bit of time for us to walk around. And for me to meet the famous Lauren and Jimmy." Lauren had liked her immediately, she seemed to have her feet squarely on the ground. And Sam seemed to have grown even further as a person with her.

"Famous?" asked Jimmy.

"Oh, the two of you with your star-crossed lovers' story is still the talk of the town in Oudtshoorn. It's all your mom talks about."

"You met my mom in Oudtshoorn?" said Lauren. "Was she visiting? How is she?"

Julie and Sam shared a look, then Sam said. "She's good, you know. She misses you."

It felt to Lauren like there was more there. And they didn't answer her question. Her mom hardly ever went back after she had moved to Cape Town. She would need to check in on that.

But then they stopped at a pedestrian crossing, waiting for the light to change. "People are so obedient here!" remarked Jimmy.

"Yeah, we would just walk back home, right?" Sam shook his head. "I was away in the UK for a year playing for Saracens. Man, I just missed home too much. Truth be told, I don't know how you do it. Living abroad for so long."

The question hung in the air for a second. "Busy chasing our dreams, I suppose," replied Jimmy.

"And now you're together!" squealed Julie. "Dreams do come true!"

Later, after they had said goodbye to Sam and Julie, they stood pressed close on the subway back home. It reminded them of another tube, another city, another tournament.

They had both tried to not bring their issues along. But it was hard. She pried the truth about the horrible situation at Il Leone and Quick Meals out of him. She could tell he was relieved to finally talk about it with her, and in turn, she offloaded her concerns with him.

"The data doesn't lie, Jimmy. We have the perfect incubation environment for the next super-flu pandemic. It's just a matter of time."

He held her tighter. "Your modeling of the possible scenarios sounds like it could have a real impact."

"Yes. We have presented it to multiple audiences in the last year. Professor Higgins is a leading expert in the field. People are not listening. The message is just too inconvenient for current business practices."

"What would need to change for people to pay attention?"

"I'm sorry to say so, but an actual threat would change everything. But by then it might also be too late." She decided to change the subject. She felt a naughty smile form on her lips.

"Babe, seeing as we're in Tokyo, and cosplay is all the rage here, I thought we could go to that market close to our hotel and pick up some costumes."

He lifted her chin, kissed her lightly on the lips. "Are we going to a party that I don't know about? I thought we just did the costume thing in those go-karts."

"Yep. And I'm feeling inspired. I think a nurse's outfit for me… and maybe you could get an aviator suit." Oh, she felt wicked, and she put her mouth to his ear.

"And it will be just a party of two."

The day of the Rugby World Cup Final would remain forever etched in their minds.

The tickets Sam had supplied were magnificent seats, right on the halfway line. The energy in the stadium was electric. The Japanese had put on an incredible show of hospitality for the world, this was the climax. A stadium filled with English, Springboks, and other fans. But it was the Japanese fans that had fully embraced one side or the other, and had come out in force. It was magical.

The game itself did not disappoint.

The English had been hyped up to be the hot favorites. Their canny coach, Eddie Jones, had been unusually quiet the whole week.

Jimmy had loved getting the inside scoop from Sam the previous day. The Springboks were super motivated. They never needed much to bring their 110% against the English, who everyone loved to hate in the sporting world. And the team was in a great space. Rassie had created a transparent, inclusive, and accountable team culture.

In contrast, the word from the other camp was about unhappy players. They were being treated like schoolboys by their coach. Also, they were the hot favorites, while the Springboks could go into the match as firm underdogs. It was a label they relished.

And Sam had told them about a secret weapon.

The "Move" came in the 55th minute of the game. Things were still ridiculously tight. Suddenly the backs were in the maul and the forwards were out in the line, roles reversed. The forwards formed a sudden pack and drove hard for the line with the ball. The English backs, smaller and caught off guard, couldn't stop them. They were forced to commit a foul to collapse the movement. Penalty. Points. And suddenly the Springboks were 6 points ahead.

Shortly thereafter, the stadium erupted when black winger Makozolo Mapimpi scored the first try of the match. It was the Springboks' first ever try in a World Cup Final. And by a black player who had overcome all obstacles to claim his place in the team. It was the stuff of fairy tales. The game had a history of being linked to Apartheid practice and exclusion in South Africa. This felt like a beautiful closing of an arc.

The game was closed out by a spectacular last try by diminutive Cheslin Kolbe. Also, a player of color, but in his case, oft-derided because he was small by rugby standards. But he was fast—and he had heart. The English hung their heads, defeated. Jimmy and Lauren were laughing and jumping up and down in delirious joy, caught up in the moment. The final whistle blew, and history was made.

The whole stadium stayed for the awards ceremony, gracious Siya Kolisi accepting the Cup on behalf of an ecstatic team. And when the festivities were over, the teams had done their laps of honor and the crowds began to file out, Lauren grabbed Jimmy's hand. She gave it a big squeeze, and said, "Come. One last surprise for you."

She took him down to a security door, and he suddenly felt himself in a corridor jammed with officials and press. She led him through the throng, to be met by Sam, grinning from ear to ear. Jimmy and Sam hugged, and then he said, "Come."

They went through a further security checkpoint and came to the last door. It opened from the other side, and someone came through moving in the other direction, trailed by a few men in suits. Jimmy could just clock a familiar face, and the tall ginger man smiled at him and extended his hand. "Well done, your team was amazing today."

Jimmy shook his hand, slightly bewildered. The man turned to Lauren, also shaking hers. She, like Jimmy, was lost for words. Then the man walked briskly in the other direction. Jimmy turned to Sam, who just laughed.

"It's a big day for you guys. You just shook hands with royalty, and now you are about to go celebrate with the World Cup Winners. Now forget about Prince Harry. Let's step inside guys… you are going to love meeting Siya."

They didn't stay long. The team was amazingly hospitable, but they had final rituals to perform. So, after a short chat with Siya and some of the other players, they made their excuses and went in search of a late-night seafood spot to celebrate.

The joyous energy of the final was everywhere. The South Africans in the stadium and on the surrounding streets were elated. As they moved further away, Tokyo swept them up in a different kind of magic. Bright lights and constant movement. It helped to divert their thoughts.

But later that night, after they made love, the thoughts kept her awake. She realized she loved him, and she couldn't be without him. They were going back the next day. She to Hong Kong, he to Wellington. But she also was so close to finishing her studies. And the opportunity to make an impact on the world was too important. For that, she needed to go back to Harvard soon.

And after that? They had not circled back to it. He was determined to go back to South Africa and try to help rescue Robby's business. Professor Higgins had assured her that once she finished her Ph.D., Harvard and the US government would probably extend their research grant. The impact she could make! It was mind-boggling. But she would need to decide to live permanently in Boston.

She needed to find a way to convince him to join her. But she also knew him. He was in his element among the South Africans, he thrived in the changeroom and in the crowds, excited to be among his own. He was going home, she knew it. He would not be swayed.

And she had no plan to go back anytime soon. It was impossible.

She eventually fell into a fitful sleep.

When she awoke, he was gone. She felt a moment of panicked abandon. But then she grabbed her phone, and he had left her a WhatsApp note.

"Gone for coffee and bagels for breakfast. Starbucks, the great equalizer. Be back in a bit."

There was also a message from Sam. It was a voice note, and he asked her to call him. It had been sent 30 minutes before, so he must be up.

Jimmy not being back yet, she decided to take the gap.

Sam picked up almost immediately.

"L? Thanks for calling me back…"

"Sam, again congratulations. So proud of the team. Of all you guys."

"Thanks. Yeah, it's magic. But listen, the reason I called you…" he hesitated. "Lauren, Julie's been pestering me since Friday to tell you. There's something you need to know."

The line at Starbucks was longer than Jimmy had expected. It gave him time to think about the next steps. Only five months more, and then he would have the financial freedom to step away and do whatever he wanted to do. And he wanted to be with Lauren.

He smiled at the thought. With the proceeds from his stake in Il Leone, he would probably be able to afford an education at Harvard. Wouldn't that be an absolute gas?

Robby would need him too—but again, maybe there was a way to take the product stateside instead. Who knew? He wanted to go home so badly. But being with Lauren? He was ready to make sacrifices.

He finally got his order, excited by the possibilities. But the moment he stepped through the door; he knew something was up with her. She was out of bed, fully dressed, and quite agitated.

He put the coffee down. "L? What's wrong?"

She looked at him, in a daze. "I… I'm looking for my shoes… Jimmy…"

He stepped in closer and enfolded her in his arms. "Babe. What is it?"

She was sobbing, tears running into his shoulder.

"Jimmy, it's my mom. She's sick."

"She's moved back to Oudtshoorn. She has a lot of friends there, and she was all alone in Cape Town. Sam says... he says she is getting medical opinions on what to do, but it is serious." Lauren had finally stopped crying. It was the middle of the night in South Africa, so she would need to wait to speak to her mother.

Jimmy sat with her on the bed, holding her hand.

"What can I do?" he asked.

She hugged him and said, "Just don't disappear from my life again, Jimmy. I know we haven't talked about how, what and where... but I just don't want to go radio silence again. Promise me. Promise me we will figure it out."

"I promise," he said. He paused.

"Lauren, do you want me to go back with you? To support you?"

"Go back? Oh... to South Africa?" she had not quite thought it through. "I need to go see her... I also need to take leave from the project for a while. I need to figure all of it out..."

He nodded. "Just let me know what you need. I also need to go home and navigate the mess at work. Like I said, just let me know what you need."

She felt like there was something else he had wanted to say to her. But she wasn't quite sure what. "Jimmy... six months from now..."

"I'll be able to go wherever I want to, do what I want. Let's not worry about that now. Let's focus on what is important. Come, we need to start packing anyway- our time here is up."

They spent a sad hour together at the airport, over coffees. They avoided their usual conversation about the future—and she was glad Jimmy was rather trying to cheer her up with more stories of the weird characters he had met in Guatemala.

Before they knew it, they parted ways, their interlude over.

Sometime later, after the plane landed in Hong Kong and she was in the taxi on the way home, she called her mom.

The hesitant speech and the excuses about bad signal so no video started to make more sense.

"Mom, why didn't you tell me?" Lauren choked back the tears.

"Darling, I am so proud of you. And you are so close to fulfilling your goals. I couldn't let this weak wasted body of mine distract you."

Her voice was still strong. But Lauren knew her mother, and she could sense the effort it took to speak.

"It's not your choice to make, Mom. Of course, I want to know what's going on with you. Who's looking after you?"

"I moved back to Oudtshoorn two months ago, when I received the diagnosis. I have many friends here. Joe and Melissa have been my rock. We agreed that we wouldn't tell you."

Lauren shook her head, as the taxi turned into the street where she lived.

"Mom, what is the diagnosis? What do the doctors say?"

"Well, I'm doing chemo again… hair has already fallen out, so you see I have this sexy wig again…" It was a feeble joke, and neither of them laughed.

"You're not answering my question. How long."

"Who's to say? If the chemo works, we will beat the breast cancer into remission. They are monitoring it. I would probably need to go for a double mastectomy… but we are trying to shrink the tumors first."

Lauren took a deep breath.

"I'm coming home. I just need to clear things with Professor Higgins, then I'm coming to be with you."

But it wasn't that simple.

The next day, she was met by an agitated Professor Higgins.

He sat her down, even as she noticed a flurry of activity in their office.

"What's going on, professor?"

"Read this." He handed her a folder, which she flipped open. She took a moment to scan the contents, her brow furrowing.

She looked up, alarmed. "Is this…"

"Yes. The Chinese government is keeping a lid on it and our friends at the World Health Organization have not yet put a priority on it." He shook his head in frustration. "We ran these reports through our algorithmic simulator, and it might be very bad."

"What do we know?"

"It's being reported as a strain of viral pneumonia centralized in Wuhan Province in China. We think it's a variation of SARS, but we haven't been able to get any clinical reports from them for our testing. Our US government affiliation is the block." He shook his head. "Damn politics."

"We have alerted our friends in the US foreign office?"

"They are aware. They have asked for daily updates, but there are also a lot of territories they are monitoring." Proessorf Higgins grimaced. "Unfortunately, they won't move until it is a real thing, despite our best science."

She nodded, then put the folder aside.

"Professor, I need to take some leave."

He raised his eyebrows. "I thought you just did."

"I know… but I will need a couple of weeks this time. My mother is very sick. I need to go home to be with her for a bit." The words rushed out; she wasn't sure what he would say.

He drummed his fingers on the table. "I can't give you full leave for two weeks. We are at an inflection point; I need your input." Her face fell in disappointment.

"But," he said. "I also believe we are not fully utilizing technology in the way we work. If you promise me you will stay online, take your laptop, and keep on working while you are there, I have no problem with you going."

"Really?" She almost hugged him. "Thank you so much…"

He gave a slight smile. "I was afraid you were going to leave to chase after that man of yours. I'm still afraid you'll leave to go after him."

She shook her head. "The work is important, professor. And I will never leave you in the middle of it, especially now. You have my word. I'll be back in a couple of weeks, and in the meantime, I will work as hard there as I have been here."

He nodded and turned back to his computer. "Make arrangements, let me know when your flight is."

43

They spoke every day. They had fallen into a routine while she was in South Africa: 9 pm for her was 7 am for him, and he liked it.

"So, what are you up to today?" she asked, knowing each day brought him a new challenge.

"Same-same. We are almost done with the transition to Uber Eats. I must admit, it just works better. The tech with Quick Meals just had too many bugs. Robby is back home, trying to iron it out. As I understand it, he's had to fire his lead developer and go back to the drawing board. They are bleeding clients over there as well. It's messy."

"You don't think your shares will ever be worth anything," she stated.

"And neither will the Wilsons. Or Masa Corp, they have an even bigger stake than I do. No, I think this time Robby has bitten off more than he could chew. Still, if the company is still around in April, I'll go back there and see what I can do to help." He paused. "I put my apartment on the market, Lauren."

"You did?" Lauren was pleased. He was starting to cut ties in New Zealand. "How long do you think before you sell it?"

"The market is pretty good right now—the estate agent thinks it will be about a month before I have a firm offer, and then another two to make a transfer. So, I should be done by the end of Feb."

"The timing works. How are things with... Anna..."

"I have tendered my formal resignation. I've given them five months' notice. I consulted with my lawyer and I am within the boundaries of our deal. On 1 April, I can freely sell my shares in a third-party transaction unless they buy it. The proceeds of those sales will help me clear my loan with the bank for the shares and have plenty left over."

"How does it feel, Jimmy? You might finally have all that money you always talked about." She immediately regretted saying it.

But he didn't seem to mind; "I know. Strange, though. Now I'm just glad I have a cushion. You know, so that I can make a new start somewhere else. South Africa..." he paused... "The US maybe..."

"Don't jerk me around Jimmy. Are you serious?"

"Let's see what happens. In the meantime, how was your day?"

She let it go. He had skillfully changed the subject, but for the first time in weeks, she felt herself smile at the possibilities.

"My mom is tired. The chemo is tough. But the doctors insist this is the best way to go. It will reduce the tumors, and they will still need to operate. This will decrease the risk for her associated with a full double mastectomy."

"Sounds painful."

"It's not fun," she agreed. "But it's been so cool being back here. All our school friends are gone, but the oldies are all still here. Robby's folks, Uncle Joe and Melissa. It's been nice. And they all want to see you."

"I want to see them. How're Robby's folks?"

"Worried about him. He is taking some strain with the company, and he's always been so happy-go-lucky. I spoke to his little sister—Jess. She said she might go help him for a while."

"Jess? Man, that's a blast from the blast. How's the little squirt doing?"

"Not so little anymore, Jimmy. She's quite something. Became an Ace coder these last few years. Even has a tattoo!" She giggled. "Would you like it if I got a tattoo?"

"Depends where..." he hesitated. "Lauren, what's going on with the virus? The China thing? I haven't seen anything in the news..."

"They're still keeping a lid on it, Jimmy. We're being blocked from full access. We are working with the State Department, and what we do know is that it's worse than the Chinese are telling us. Our models of the spread predict that they need to do full disclosure soon, or all hell could break loose."

"Couldn't you push that along? Tell the press or something?"

"I work with Professor Higgins online every day on this. We would probably lose our funding because of the political fallout if we cut channels. He is still tempted to do it, though. But he is worried more about what the Chinese would do if we forced their hand."

"Sounds complicated. When are you heading back there?"

"Just before the American Thanksgiving. It's worked pretty well with me here, except for the time zone difference. But I can tell he is struggling with me, not physically being there. It's ok... My mom's treatment will continue right through to February, hopefully, she doesn't need the op. The doctors are being vague."

"So, Hong Kong until then? Maybe I'll come to visit for Christmas..."

"Maybe you should, mister. Maybe you should..."

"It's called COVID-19. It's what we've feared all along. A highly contagious, airborne pathogen. And it stays active on surfaces, and is transmitted in various ways. The scariest thing: It kills." Professor Higgins was not prone to exaggeration or drama, so Lauren knew he was very concerned.

"It's our worst nightmare, Professor," replied Lauren. It was the Monday after Thanksgiving weekend, and she celebrated with the professor and his wife Lucy. It was not that hard to find a decent turkey in Hong Kong, and Lauren had helped Lucy with preparing the meal. She loved this tradition of gratitude.

"Right now, they claim it's still localized in Wuhan. It's been transmitted from one of their local live animal markets—and the government is going hard lockdown to try to curb the spread. The World Health Organization is about to announce it." He took another bite of turkey and patted his wife's knee affectionately. "You are a magician, my dear. Tastes just like home." She beamed in appreciation. Lauren liked her. She was also super smart. The two of them had met when she was his teaching assistant many, many years ago.

She was smart, but content with the role life had cast her in, that of the dutiful housewife and the person that raised their girls. When she spoke, like now, it was always measured and thoughtful questions: "Do you think the lockdown will be effective?"

He shook his head. "They wasted too much time trying to not face the problem. Wuhan is an industrial hub with many exporting factories. I suspect the virus is already out."

Lauren added; "They are researching this strain as fast as they can. Our colleagues in that field are of two minds. The virus is unpredictable, we don't know how antibodies are created, and a vaccine might take as long as 12 months to develop. In the meantime, depending on how fast governments react, the spread could be brutal."

They sat in somber silence for a while.

"What about Jimmy, Lauren? Give us an update on your boyfriend? I'm sure I can call him that now, can't I?" said Lucy, and Lauren giggled. "I suppose you can. We talk daily now—and he is starting to say the right things…"

"Which are?" persisted Lucy. She lived vicariously through Lauren's love life.

"That coming to Harvard is not out of the question…"

"Well, that is jolly good news, now isn't it," exclaimed Professor Higgins. He put some more potatoes on his plate. "Which reminds me, I have news."

The women both turned to him.

"Our time in Hong Kong is coming to a rapid end, ladies. I've gotten through to someone at home. They are starting an accelerated conversation with big pharma to investigate the viral effects and possible countermeasures. They want us back asap to be part of the conversation. Also, the University is worried about the continued demonstrations here. They feel that the compounded risk is too much. They want us to go home."

"That's great news, Professor!" said Lauren. "When?" In the back of her mind, she thought of Christmas with Jimmy…

"We leave in two weeks."

The paperwork was nearly done. Jimmy had received a decent price for the apartment, and he ended up with a bit of money in pocket.

But Jimmy had other debts to pay. The fancy SUV needed to be sold and the bank owned most of that car. And the credit card debt. Man, how did he get here? He would walk away with a fortune if he was just patient. There was also the outstanding loan on the Quick Meals share purchase. He would be able to liquidate that with proceeds from his Il Leone shares, and have quite a handsome sum left over. The idea of this perked him up considerably.

It was mid-December, and he was gearing up for a big summer at the chain of restaurants. The problem was, his heart wasn't in it. He loved the action of expansion and scouting locations. Running the numbers, far from the coalface, on an existing business was not his style. He did not want to let the company down, even though his relationship with Anna was now untenable. But he had to admit he wasn't doing the best job possible.

When Lauren called him and told him she was going back to Harvard, it crushed him a little bit further. Hong Kong was so much closer… Harvard was the other end of the world, and would take more than a day to travel to.

He had said he wanted to go. But it also was a place where he started with Anna. Where the Italian that had made Lauren so unhappy lurked. He struggled to build up enthusiasm for it.

Mr. Masataka did not fly down for the pre-season planning meeting. He cited poor health as a reason. Jimmy wasn't so sure. It was out of character for him to not get involved.

Robby and Quick Meals were gone. Quick Meals had, as a result, completely left the New Zealand market. The shares they held were now in a purely South African-based entity.

He spoke with Robby often. His friend remained positive.

"Jimmy, the concept works. We just need to iron out the technical snags."

"That's your old story, Rob. When am I going to hear a new one? You want me to come over there and help you revive this thing, but I just don't know…"

"Bud, you have a right to be cautious. But I have an ace in the hole now. A killer coder that replaced the useless guy I had that brought it to life. And she is going to help us turn this ship around, I promise you!"

"Oh, yea. Little Jess. Lauren told me she is in the mix now… your sister was always the brains in the family."

"No joke. I would agree, only she's always had a thing for you, which makes her not that smart. But I promise you, Jimmy, we have a new vision. 2020 is going to be an epic year! Just come and see!"

Robby was serious. He was going to save the company by employing his kid sister. It was ludicrous. Jimmy feared that his friend was going off the rails. He had to get back there, to see if anything could be saved. In the meantime, Jimmy decided to go face the music at the board meeting. Just a few more months, then he would be joining Robby. He hoped he would be in time to make a difference…

———

Ray Booth was in top form at the meeting.

The numbers exceeded expectations. The new outlets had opened well in different country locations. Anna received warm applause from him for her hard work there. Domestic performance was brilliant, particularly so in the last three months since Ray took over. It was attributed more to the smart move of selling off the non-performing delivery business assets than actual operational profit. In other words: Selling Quick Meals had been a good financial move. It made Jimmy look like a fool for fighting it.

He tried to fight back. "We have needed to up our local marketing spends at the insistence of some of our key franchisees. This has cut into our profits, but resulted in happier franchisees and will reward us in the long term." He ran through the numbers, but he felt a stony silence from the room. When he sat down, you could hear a pin drop.

Finally, Ray Booth resumed his presentation. He flicked a cold glance at Jimmy, then said, "We have, of course, come up with a solution. We are planning an aggressive expansion into this market by way of acquisition."

This was the first Jimmy had heard of this. Ray proceeded to whip up a chart highlighting the locations of their biggest competitor.

"We are in advanced discussions with Action Sports Bar. They have a bigger footprint than we have in the bigger metropolitan areas, but the owners are looking to limit their risk. They have been amicable to an offer of us comprising mostly shares in Il Leone with a 30% cash component."

He paused. Jimmy processed this new information. He was completely blindsided. Ray Booth continued smoothly; "They, of course, run a company-owned model, where traditionally we have followed a franchisee model. It will require us to also onboard their management team to run these outlets. We have cracked the numbers, and the efficiencies we will unlock are undeniable."

"Their culture." Said Jimmy.

Ray Booth looked at him, irritated. "What was that, Jimmy?"

"Their culture. It's completely different from ours. I know those guys. The way they treat their staff, the way they handle food quality. It's a total mismatch. It will be a big mistake, and it will also cost us the trust of our biggest franchisees. We can't do it." Taking on Ray Booth like this was a mistake. But he couldn't stop himself. And no one in the room met his eyes. He had no support.

Except for Anna. She was smirking as if she had just won the lottery.

After the meeting, it was not unexpected for him to be called into Ray Booth's office.

The jovial American's façade had slipped. "Unacceptable, Jimmy! Unacceptable! How dare you contradict me in front of our team!"

Jimmy wasn't having it. "Ray, if you want just yes-men, I'm the wrong guy. Plus, how dare you hold these kinds of talks without my knowledge? I am in charge of the domestic business; this is my area! And you're making a massive strategic mistake going down this road!"

"No, he's not," said Anna. Jimmy hadn't even seen her, sitting quietly in the corner. "The deal makes sense. We'll lose some of the franchisees, but we'll be able to convert those outlets to owner-run businesses. The Action Sports Bar team can handle it. Higher profit, higher control, no more bitching from ex-All Black Prima Donnas."

"You know how they deal with people, Anna. They are famous for their bad practices! It's not who we are…" He was beyond furious. "And who's going to have to deal with them? Me? Who's going to have to appease all the franchisees, people I made promises to, people that trust me, who I am now stabbing in the back? Me!" He couldn't help the next words that came out of his mouth; "If we do this, I am out! I'm not doing it you hear? Out!"

Ray Booth sighed and gestured for him to sit down. "I'm so glad you said that, Jimmy. We agree. You are no longer a good fit for this business, and it would be good if you left early."

He sat down, and Ray gestured at a folder on the desk. "Read through it. Fair value for your Il Leone shares, calculated at current market value. And a decent separation package."

He suspected a rat. He looked at the document, scanning the headlines. He tried to quiet his thoughts. And then he saw it.

"What is this, Ray?" he pointed to a whole section from page 4 to 7 of the lengthy contract.

"Oh, that? It means we have the right to effect payment in cash or shares in related third parties. In our case, we both hold shares in Quick Meals, so our shares there will serve as partial payment of your share sale."

"So… let me get this straight. You are selling me your shares in Quick Meals, and taking my shares in Il Leone as payment?"

She smiled that evil smile again. "That is correct. Part-payment. There should be a little bit of cash in there to soften the blow. It is completely fair and legal, feel free to go consult with your lawyer. Your shares in Masa Corp have been priced at fair value."

"Yes, but the Quick Meals shares are nowhere near this value after you pulled the deal! I don't need to consult with my lawyer to know that this is a screw over of majestic proportions!"

Ray Booth put a hand on his shoulder. "Sport, you have a lot to learn about business. When you turned down my offer to buy your Quick Meals shares, a minimum fair value between related parties was fixed. It was in our original Quick Meals agreement." He smiled a condescending smile. "Go talk to your lawyer. In the meantime, clean out your desk. You are suspended pending the outcome of a disciplinary hearing."

His lawyer took less than a day to get back to him with the analysis.

David Adams was not a big man, but he looked... solid. And he was worth the fees Jimmy had paid for him.

The feedback was not encouraging.

"Look, they have started a disciplinary process based on insubordination, repeated misconduct, and even incapacity. If they fire you on this basis, you won't get any severance either. And what with going off to rehab, jetting off to Tokyo without permission from the CEO, and the performance at the board meeting... it's not looking good Jimmy. They have cause."

"Dave, I've straightened out. And the board meeting? That show was intended to entice a reaction. I can't believe..."

Dave Adams put up his hand. "Better believe it. You should have let them buy your shares in Quick Meals, or at least run the sale refusal doc past me first. As it stands, the original agreements do refer to subsequent evaluations. When you originally signed the new share agreement with Masa Corp, this exact situation was made provision for."

He sat back. "Look, it's legally correct. It's a helluva way to exploit the legal situation, and we could fight it. Would cost you a bundle. And I can't guarantee we'll win." He shook his head. "She is quite something, Jimmy. That woman... she knows her way around a contract."

"Dave, this is not helping."

"You don't hire me to blow smoke up your ass, Jimmy. You wanted to get out anyway. This way, you get some money out, and you can go do your next thing. Plus, you'll be a major shareholder in Quick Meals."

"Dave, that business is practically worthless right now. Robby insists he can save it, but I just don't know…"

"Irrelevant to this deal. They will tie you up in court for a while, it will take you years to get the money out of them."

"But they are firing me. That means I can sell the Il Leone shares to anyone I want to, can't I?"

"No one will buy it from you, Jimmy. They can contest any sale because you are not accepting their contractually correct offer. They've got you by the balls." David Adams stood up. "Take the deal. Move on."

44

He handed over the keys to the Beemer and said to the buyer, "Merry Christmas. She's a beauty, enjoy her."

He walked back up to his apartment. It was nearly empty now. A few cardboard boxes left, most of the furniture sold. The apartment itself held memories of Anna and not much else. He realized Lauren had never seen it. So much time wasted.

He reflected that, for all his ability to do the numbers, he had not done a good job of it the last few years. The trappings of showing off success. Taking on further debt to invest in Robby's wild scheme. The wild need for bigger, faster.

And now? He was sitting on a pile of semi-worthless shares in a tech start-up run by his best friend and his kid sister. His ex managed to fire him from the company he had co-founded. He had barely received enough severance to pay off the banks and clear his debts. He was practically flat broke.

And the woman he loved was halfway across the world.

Despite all that, he was surprised at how he felt. Free. The world was alive with possibilities.

He had enough cash for a ticket home. But first, he had a couple of stops to make.

The first one was to Christchurch. It was the 20th of December 2019, and the Wilsons had arranged a big party for him at their house. A farewell party of sorts. There was the staff from the original Il Leone, Mick from merchandising, and some of the Il Leone franchisees had even made the trip. Jimmy felt overwhelmed by their kindness, and generosity. He apologized to the franchisees for what was happening, reminiscing with the old Il Leone staff. No one blamed him, they were all angry too. But not at him. He was grateful, and felt honored. At the end of the evening after everyone had gone home, he had a final hot chocolate with Stan and Grace.

"I can't tell you how grateful I am to you," he said.

Grace replied, "We are to you, Jimmy. It's been fun being part of your story."

"And for me to get to know you. But I mean it. So many good people here tonight... It's been such an amazing experience, such a rollercoaster. And no one is angry at me. I mean, I really fucked this up." He felt quite emotional. "I betrayed the trust everyone put in me."

Stan walked over to him and put his hand on his shoulder.

"Jimmy, we're all adults. We all decided to sell the business. We all took the risks, knowing that things wouldn't always turn out as we planned. You're still super young, by business standards. I promise you; you'll bounce back from this."

"I appreciate that, Stan."

"Besides," said Grace: "After your rendezvous with Lauren, you're going back to South Africa to breathe life back into Quick Meals, aren't you?"

He nodded. After tonight...after this send-off? He couldn't ever let these two people down again.

"I promise you, Grace, after everything you've done for me? That investment is going to be worth something one day. I won't stop until it is."

Lauren always felt that Christmas was supposed to be a magical time.

She picked Jimmy up at the airport, but she was filled with anxiety.

She so wanted him to see Boston in all its glory. It wasn't to be. The weather prediction was pretty dire for that week. They would be faced with a few days of constant rain and sleet with near-zero temperatures. Not ideal to convince someone to make a life there.

He got off the airplane tired. It was over a day of traveling from Christchurch, and she immediately took him to her small flat for a shower.

He did look better once he got out and kissed her. He looked so good, just in his robe, and she so wanted to… but…

"Jimmy. Stop. We're going to have to wait a few days…"

"What? Why? I…" then he saw the look on her face and couldn't hide his disappointment. She wanted her monthly period to not be a big deal—but she felt too self-conscious for intimacy.

He sat down. Then made a manly effort. "Well, we can just cuddle then, right?"

They spent the rest of the week mostly indoors. Coffee shops and cozy restaurants, and one clear day for sightseeing the historic downtown of Boston. Christmas day just the two of them. Professor Higgins and Lucy had invited them to spend it with their busy family, but she wanted Jimmy all to herself. It was a mistake.

They had a video call with Joe, Melissa and the girls at a traditional Oudtshoorn Christmas party. The family were all in swimwear, outdoors by the pool on a super-hot Christmas day in South Africa, surrounded by family and friends. It drove home that Harvard just was not home. Afterward, they tried to cheer up, but the cold and dark pressed on their mood. She wished she had rather taken up the Higgins's on their offer.

She tried hard. But Jimmy seemed to have lost his mojo along with his fortune. She wanted to scream at him that she didn't care. But she also knew that he had planned to come to join her with enough money to start something in Boston. Maybe even further his studies himself. Now that was unaffordable for him.

They did not make love. He was jetlagged, and would get up in the middle of the night and go stare out the window. She pretended to sleep, but couldn't. Unsaid words hung between them.

On his last night in Boston, she decided to treat him to a meal in a nice restaurant. It backfired—he was fidgety from the word go.

He was looking at the menu when he said, "I want to come here, Lauren. But it's just not possible. Financially. And in terms of promises I made. If I care about my integrity, and the Wilsons, I need to go and try to help save Robby's business."

"But how long will that take, Jimmy?"

"I don't know. But I have to try."

"I'll wait for you. As long as I have to."

He frowned. "Or you could come to South Africa. Help me make a new start there."

Dangerous territory. "We've been over this. I am needed here. Especially now... with the bad news from the East."

"It's a localized problem, Lauren. No one is taking it seriously—just like SARS or Ebola, they'll contain it, it'll blow over, and life will go on. No, you are just doing what you always do... putting your career first." This was not her Jimmy talking. He was trying to start a fight.

Don't... lose... your... temper... "How can you say that? Have you been listening to a word I have been saying? The world is about to become a very different place, and right now, here is where I can make the biggest difference."

"Don't you think you're overstating your importance in all this? I mean, you act as if the whole thing depends on your presence." He was being mean, and this was her weak button. She was also tired, and disappointed, and she lost control.

"Look who's talking. Jimmy, you always put your career first. You haven't heard me bitch about your quest for money and status in New Zealand these last few years. You could have made a plan to come study at Stellenbosch. You could have stayed with me in England five years ago. But you didn't. You also chose your path first. You're just not happy where it led you!" It felt good to let it out, finally.

He had calmed down, and said, "So nothing has changed. I have not achieved anything. And you are on top of the world."

"That's not fair." She felt tears welling up. "Don't you read all those fancy business books? Don't you see? Failure is just a step on the way to success. You'll bounce back. Come do it with me here. We could be so good for each other... help each other..."

"But on your terms, Lauren. Have you noticed it's always me flying halfway around the world looking for you? I walked out of my apartment—my first apartment ever—having sold it, and realized you had never even seen it. You have never come to New Zealand to be with me. Why would you change that behavior for South Africa?"

"Jimmy, that's not fair. Right now... the pandemic..."

He sighed. "I know. I know it's important. And we're back to square one, Lauren. I have made promises, I have to keep them. You need to be there where you are most needed. And it sounds like that is here. I get it."

The waiter came to get their order, and they ate in silence. When the bill came, she reached for it, but Jimmy took it.

"I still have some dignity left, Lauren. Let me pay for this. And then let's go home and say goodbye."

They clung to each other that night. But there was nothing more to say.

The next day, he flew back to South Africa.

45

The Quick Meals office was in a shared workspace called Work & Co, on the 7th floor of a building on Bree Street in Cape Town. Robby walked Jimmy around the floor, saying hi to a collection of hipsters and designer types.

After ushering in 2020 in Oudtshoorn with the family, Jimmy had done the road trip down. He borrowed Uncle Joe's car—they had a couple, and he couldn't afford to buy his own. Robby had not gone back to Oudtshoorn for the holidays. Too busy at work, he claimed.

They stopped at a corner office with four desks. It was a tiny office, with a lone plant in the corner. The walls were covered in pieces of paper depicting formulas that were beyond him. And on the desks were four Mac workstations, two of which were occupied.

One was an Indian guy of indeterminable age with thick spectacles and a t-shirt depicting a stoned Stormtrooper. The other one was a girl. He was prepared, but he was still taken aback when she leaped on him screaming "Jimmy!"

Little Jess had certainly grown up. Once he untangled himself, aware of a not unpleasant smell from her… he had always been aware of the way women smelled, from the natural soapy fragrance Lauren had in Thailand, the overpowering floral scents of Chetaine, or the musky aggressive perfume of Anna. This was different. Before he could think of it more, a torrent of words came out of her; "Oh my God can't believe you're finally back we have so much to tell you it's crazy what a catch up let's do lunch but first I need to finish this piece of work then go to kickboxing but maybe later ok?"

He took in how she was tall—not as tall as Lauren, but tall, nonetheless. Her black hair was in a ponytail and she wore a black tank top and cut-off jeans. And there was a sexy navel ring drawing attention to her trim midsection. It was distracting.

"Promise me we can catch up later so I can tell you all about Dubai and Ukraine and those fuckers at Boolies but later ok I gotta work I'm on a mission!"

She sat back down, flat ignored him, and started to type away with animal ferocity.

"Ok then," he said as he turned to Robby.

Robby laughed. "You'll get used to it bud. This is your workstation. Let me bring you back up to speed."

Robby was still single, and he had a two-bedroom flat in Gardens in the High Cape Complex. He gave Jimmy the spare room for indefinite use. He didn't push wine or beer on Jimmy when they went for pizza at the local joint Carlyle's. And he didn't pry about Lauren.

What they did talk about were lessons learned in New Zealand. Jimmy told him the whole story, and Robby just shook his head. "I know this might sound crazy to you now, Jimmy, but you made the right move not selling your shares to those guys. They're going to be sorry they kicked us to the curb, just wait and see."

"Robby, I love you man, but isn't it time to face the music. I've seen the books. We're down to our last few hundred thousand Rands in cash. The software and hardware leasing fees to run the back-end processes will burn through that in the next few months, never mind paying the office, rental, marketing. This list goes on. How are we going to dig ourselves out of this hole?"

"I have a plan, my friend. But rather than me telling you... here she is."

Jess plopped down next to them. She had changed into leggings and a long sleeve blue top. She had also let her hair down, and it fell to her shoulder. Once again, he was struck by how grown up she was.

She snapped her fingers to the waiter, who rushed over with a draft Heineken.

"Thanks, Tommy," she said and downed half the drink. "He knows I arrive thirsty." She looked at their plates and grabbed a slice of pizza off Jimmy's. "Do you mind? Starving. Will share my own when it comes."

Once again, the whirlwind that was Jess had him slightly off balance. This was what everyone was talking about, he supposed. Time to take back a bit of control.

"Jess, Robby tells me you have an idea how to save the company."

"Not an idea, handsome," she said between mouthfuls. "A fucking inspiration. A pivot like you never saw before in your life. We are going to dominate!"

"Ok then. You don't hear the word 'pivot' that often," he replied. "Tell me more."

4 6

Lauren hated Valentine's Day. The only time she could remember where it was a memorable day, was when she was with Jimmy in Thailand, and they were still discovering each other. How young they were.

Since then, it was always a substandard affair. Jacques would take her to a fancy restaurant in Stellenbosch, which was always spectacular, but it often felt more like it was about them being seen by the who's who than about a romantic gesture. Edward intellectualized the ritual and refused to participate in the time they were together. And the other times, she was just by herself... like now.

She sat by herself in a coffee shop. To further punish herself, she scoured the internet for some news of Jimmy. They had once again stopped speaking. Their last conversation had left nothing resolved. She wanted nothing more than to tell him what he wanted to hear: That she was coming home to him, that she wanted to make a new start with him in South Africa.

It didn't help that the US had lost its sheen for her. After spending time in Tokyo and Hong Kong, she had realized how vibrant diversity could be. Harvard and Boston, despite legitimate claims to a culture of high diversity and inclusivity, were still a world away from where she had come from. Problem was, she felt a little the same of South Africa. Oudtshoorn and Stellenbosch were secular places, just like Oxford and Harvard.

But she was also aware Harvard wasn't New York. And Stellenbosch wasn't Cape Town. And the little that she could find out about what Jimmy was up to, it seemed that he was fully embracing the challenges back home. He was throwing himself into networking for Quick Meals.

He might not be much on social media, but someone at that company was sure working hard to put his handsome face on their Instagram, LinkedIn, and Twitter feeds. Jimmy meeting the Industrial Development Corporation. Jimmy attending a founders' conference. Jimmy engaging with the Black Management Forum. It did all look very exciting for him.

She would be done with her Ph.D. in a few months. But if the pandemic spread according to their models, it would be years before the world returned to normal. And she was needed here, working with the best minds on the planet. She needed to resolve the coming crisis.

The bad news kept coming from Asia as the virus spread. The World Health Organization still had their heads stuck in the sand, and refused to acknowledge the danger. Harvard, at least, was taking it seriously—even if the US government wasn't. Of all the things that she did not like about the US, the idiocy of their electoral process was the thing that most offended her. But she tried to not get into Trumpian conversation. It was the dominant topic for most of her liberally minded peers.

She finished her dinner and trudged home to her empty apartment. Yep, Valentine's Day did suck. When your only friend in town is a guy that used to stalk you, now spending it with the woman you helped him find... What was she doing with her life? And was Jimmy right? Was she overstating her importance in all this? No. She was doing important research. Living a life of purpose. He was wrong.

During the next week, the irony of ironies, they had been thrown back into working with Daniella. Harvard required all of their top guns on the project of anticipating Stateside infection.

Professor Higgins, bless him, didn't hold grudges.

"Lauren, she has always loved you. While I don't approve of her devious methods, a woman in love will go to extraordinary lengths to protect their relationship."

"But Professor, Daniella and I were never lovers."

"We know that. But you were her de facto life partner for several years, even though it wasn't anything more than a working relationship." He had paused. "Go see her. You can forgive her without forgetting. There is a bigger problem that we all have to face."

They agreed to meet at Sweetgreen in Back Bay, a favorite of Daniella's. After both ordering one of the delicious juices, they sat down in awkward silence. It was still freezing cold outside in late February Boston, and the place was packed inside.

"Daniella…"

But her erstwhile mentor put up her hand. "No, Bella, let me start. This is also difficult for me." She hesitated, studying her juice with intensity. Then she shook her head and locked eyes with Lauren. "You know, by now, that I have always loved you. To the degree of insanity. All the more for knowing that you would never be able to return my affection. A part of me always hoped."

She loved ruefully. "The great life irony. Genius IQ, but no EQ. I thought, foolishly, if I could put all the men in your life in a bad light, I would have a chance."

Lauren, despite herself, felt empathy. And pity, more than anger, funny enough. "Daniella, I have thought about this long and hard. And…" she smiled, "It also takes two to tango. I knew. I always knew, on some level. And even after the evidence started piling up… I ignored it, for my ambition. And I think, at some level, I gave you enough reason to believe that I might come around." She paused. "It does not absolve your behavior. What you did was reprehensible."

Daniella nodded. "I now know. I am seeing a therapist. After your warning, it was a wake-up call. I no longer do those things."

Lauren appreciated the words. "So here we are. Two women, in a world where no man is listening to us about the chaos coming our way. It's time to put the past behind us. I am sorry for… stringing you along, I suppose?" There, she said it.

But Daniella visibly relaxed and said, "I appreciate your apology more than you know, Bella. It just proves that you have come out of this the bigger person. I also apologize, and if I could do so on a much greater scale, I would. And now I have a confession to make."

"Yes?"

"That boy... Jimmy... he came looking for you last year. I might have given him the impression that you were... with Professor Higgins?"

Lauren paused, then burst out laughing. "I do know about that, Daniella. And I forgive you. Anyway, it made no difference. For now, he stays in my past."

She pushed thoughts of Jimmy aside and extended her hand.

"Now, can we proceed? If not as friends, then as colleagues, determined to fight the greater challenge ahead?"

"Yes," said the woman that had done so much to shape her life.

On her way back to her office on campus, her cellphone rang. It was her mom, and it was not their usual time to talk—too early.

"Lauren?"

"Hi, mom? Everything ok?"

"I wasn't going to say anything, but Joe forced my hand. The chemo was only partially successful. They are moving my op forward." She heard her mom pause on the other side, and then she said what Lauren knew was coming; "They are doing a double mastectomy."

"I'm coming home."

"Don't be ridiculous. I have Joe and Melissa to look after me, you have too much to do. You need to finish your Ph.D., and all this story of Coronavirus..."

"When and where is the operation, mother?"

"They are doing it at the Mediclinic in George. The day after tomorrow."

"I'll be there."

J immy was in the zone.

He had never actually lived in Cape Town since school. It was funny. The friends he had had in high school had mostly moved abroad. If they still lived in Cape Town, it was as if they had not moved on from the southern suburbs bubble. Same friends, same places, same neighborhood. Older but no evolution. They now were married, had started having kids, and had no interest in expanding their circles or horizons.

By contrast, Robby was part of a different Cape Town. A Cape Town of Atlantic seaboard and city bowl techies, hipsters, and hustlers. No one seemed to have an actual office, degrees and diplomas seemed irrelevant. What mattered was big ideas, "disrupting the norm", and integrating into the virtual world.

They fitted right in. The money was running out and they lived off half-price specials and home-cooked meals. Robby and Jimmy hustled to find clients to onboard them for demos, Jess and Ravi wrote code and fixed bugs 24/7, and all four of them ran support for client issues. And there were many issues.

He found himself liking Jess more and more. She dressed provocatively half the time with heavy make-up, and like she was at home in her pajamas the rest of the time. He got to see another side of her in the mornings, as they went for a few morning runs on Table Mountain together. She would turn up in hot pants and tank tops for the walks, and without make-up. He found her to not only be high energy and super interesting, but also observed a caring side to her. The little pavement special hound that she was fostering was a regular feature at the office—and on their walks.

After a while, Robby stopped coming on the walks and it was just the two of them. They talked of their lives, they shared travel stories. They had followed different paths, but also very similar. Out of school she did a Microsoft Coding course and went straight into an internship in Dubai. From there she had launched into gigs in India, China, and even a stint in Australia. They found they had a ton to talk about, everything from the culture in the antipodeans to taking time out to go meditate.

And they passionately talked about the business. Jess was invested in helping Robby get it going. She didn't need the money, so she was doing it practically free, only taking some of the worthless shares as payment. But she wanted them to turn it around. When it was done, she would evaluate her options.

The business had been built to facilitate home delivery for smaller restaurants. They had been squeezed out of that business by bigger players with deeper pockets, so a hard rethinking of their core customer was needed.

They had decided to target the "partially prepared" market. It was a growing segment, occupied by a few niche players, of sending high-end client's meals that were partially cooked. Then people finished the job at home. There were a few small players in South Africa that were doing it, but the lead times were too long according to Robby.

Jess explained to him one day during a walk on the mountain.

"I did a stint at Boolies, you know. They are the reason I came back to SA. They offered me a solid opportunity to help lead their home delivery team."

"Boolies? The upmarket food store? I heard you talk about them—you really hate them."

She nodded. "They hired me to help them get their back-end fixed.

I figured out where they were going wrong, but they wouldn't invest the money. Drove me nuts."

"Not enough to be this angry about, though," he commented, slightly out of breath. She was hard to keep up with.

"Project was almost done, and I had another gig lined up with a rival company, based on my experience there. And they badmouthed me, costing me the job. My senior manager didn't want me to take the idea I had to the competition. He even told me so on my way out."

"Hey, you could take them to court for that, I'm sure."

She stopped and turned to him. "I could. Much more fun to create a product that will eat massively into their market share. That's part of the reason I decided to come to help my brother." She smiled. "There were other reasons too."

He flushed, and thought to himself how pretty she was when she smiled. "Let's keep on going."

The team was sitting down at Carlyle's for their regular Friday night pizza. The place was packed with cyclists who had come down to Cape Town for the annual Cycle Tour, which took place the second Sunday of March every year.

"I have an announcement, guys," announced Robby. They were just about done with their pizzas, and Ravi never lingered. He liked to go home to his wife early, and these evenings were an indulgence.

"But first, I want to acknowledge the difference Robby has made to our public profile since he came back two months ago. We now have good leads into several different new funding channels. Although nothing has landed yet, I know it's only a matter of time." He clapped his friend on the back. Jimmy smiled. They were a poor start-up. And he was loving the hustle.

"But my announcement concerns Ravi, our solid never-give-up backbone of the primary code. And Jess, who, against all odds, has turned into an invaluable asset in bringing this puppy home." Jimmy looked at the unassuming developer. He was beaming with pleasure at the recognition. Robby continued; "My announcement is that we finally fixed our stock level integration issue. Jess, this is huge. I'm going to give you the floor." And he sat back down.

Jess kept her seat but leaned forward. "Ravi and I pulled an all-nighter, but we got it done. As you know, we've been limited in terms of our market to the meals segment. But now that we have a functional API to incorporate central stock systems, we can offer our product to the big boys."

She looked around, fixing those intense peepers on Jimmy. "I know it sounds technical. Just trust me, this is a game-changer. Jimmy, when I was with Boolies, we could never fix this. They did home deliveries. But they sucked at it. They could never reconcile their stock levels with client demand. I argued with them that the answer was to allow for an alternative product in the code. But they never got around to my way of thinking." She sat back and chomped into another slice of pizza. "We are going to kill them with this," she smirked.

"Are we ready to pitch to Price Right?" asked Jimmy. Price Right was the big fish in town. They were launching a home delivery service soon, and everyone was pitching to them. They were interested in the Quick Meals tech, but Robby had been holding them off. Until now.

"We are seeing them on Monday, my friend. You got them talking to us, and Jess has now got our tech ready. We are going to hit a home run on this one!"

"Yeah!" said Ravi, and raised his glass. "I know I don't talk much guys, but I'm excited for this. I think it's finally going to happen." He finished his wine. "Now excuse me—the wife is waiting."

But Robby got up with him. "I also need to go. Jimmy, Jess, could you finish up and get the check, please? I have a hot date..."

Jimmy and Jess watched the other two depart. They were sitting in a corner booth, and as it was noisy, Jess moved across to sit quite close to Jimmy.

"Can't hear you from over there. What was that?" she asked.

"I said—Robby has been on a few hot dates this last month, but he is being tight-lipped about with who...."

Jess laughed. She had a deep, throaty laugh—Jimmy found he liked it. "Yeah. I haven't seen him like this since university. I think he really likes this one." She gave him one of those direct looks of hers. "What about you, sport? Haven't seen you date since you got back. Or is it still…"

"Lauren?" he finished the sentence. Then he sighed. "I should get out there, shouldn't I? Lauren and I are not technically together. I'm not even sure if we ever were since we broke up after school. But…" He was unsure on how to continue.

"You still love her."

Jimmy was uncomfortable talking to her about this. "I do. But we are just in such a different place in our lives. Like always. I don't know Jess. it just feels like we always want different things."

"What do you want, Jimmy?" She asked. She had moved slightly closer, and he could again smell that faint perfume of hers. It always drove him to distraction.

"I want… I used to want money. And recognition. A big place, a big car, a hot wife, and lots of people kissing my ass because I was important."

He gestured to the waiter and ordered another bottle of wine.

Jess frowned. "Are you sure, Jimmy? I know you had a glass of champagne with us to celebrate tonight, but you don't usually…"

"Drink? Nah, not my thing anymore. But it's a special night, and I know you enjoy a good Cabernet. So, I'll join you for one last glass. Then we'll call it a night."

"If you're sure. But now, you were talking about what you used to want. And if you don't mind me saying so, it sounds pretty superficial."

Jimmy grimaced. "Caught me there, kid. I used to. Had it, too. But now I don't. And you know what, that's ok. I'm poor again, no one thinks I matter… but I am loving it."

The wine arrived, and he poured them two glasses. "To loving what you do," she said, and they had a sip. "What do you want now, Jimmy?"

"I want to make this company work. Not because I want to protect my investment. Because I can see how much of himself Robby has put into it. And you. And Ravi. I want it to work for you guys. And for the Wilsons, if I'm honest. I made them a promise."

She shifted closer. "Sure. But beyond the company? What do you want out of life?"

He took another sip of his wine. He pondered the question. The wine was lovely, and went straight to his head.

"I want… I want to settle down here. Build a life. Do something that will help people. I want a partner that shares the same values, who wants to build something with me. And kids. I want kids. And maybe a dog…" He looked at her face. She was definitely not a kid anymore…

"What do you want, Jess?"

She kissed him lightly on the lips. "The same things, silly."

L auren rented a small guest house in George for the few days before and after the operation, with decent Wi-Fi. That way, she could be close to her mom but keep working. She felt guilty that she was distracted. Especially because the world was going exponentially crazy.

The virus started to hit different countries. Italy had gone into a full lockdown with people—especially the elderly—dying in their thousands. The rest of Europe was running scared. In the US, cases were increasing daily. And on the 5th of March 2020, South Africa had its first case diagnosed.

The operation, luckily, was a success. She was grateful that she had made the trip. Stuff like this really gives one pause to think, and she had fretted all the way on the long flight over.

She was only dimly aware of the happenings in South Africa, largely because she was working 18-hour days. Professor Higgins had been incredibly understanding, and she owed it to him and the team to not drop the ball, especially now.

With great fiber internet speed and her faculty-issued laptop, she was able to do a lot of the work and correspondence remotely. It was frustrating not being in the room with her colleagues. When she took a day to get her mom settled back home in Oudtshoorn on the 10th of March, things had shifted again. Professor Higgins, all of their support staff, and most of the faculty had also gone into work-from-home mode.

Every day brought a ton of new data, and they were constantly adjusting their predictions. Lauren found herself torn between caring for her mother, who would need at least two weeks to recover from the op, and going back to Harvard.

The conversation took place on the 13th of March, on her customary 4 pm check-in with Professor Higgins. It was 10 am in the US, and they had quickly gotten into a rhythm of daily check-ins via videoconferencing.

"Professor, I think my mother is going to be ok, according to the doctors. But they do want another two weeks before they give her the all-clear. I am theoretically able to come back to assist the team."

He must have heard the hesitation in her voice, because he said, "Theoretically?"

"But… well, I suppose, there is a chance that she's not clear. All indications are of a hard lockdown to curb the virus. Our models predict they will ground airlines soon; quarantine measures are already being implemented…"

"Lauren, are you asking me if you are needed here?"

She bit her lip. "Professor, if I don't come now… I might not be able to come for months and months. You know how this could play out. If they lock everything down…"

He nodded. He looked tired too, she noticed. Then he said something surprising. "We are in for a horrible time, Lauren. But we are seeing rapid development in the way we work, too. We are all working remotely now. Things that we took as standard six months ago no longer apply. In terms of the virus research, I don't think you physically need to be here."

She had to ask the question. "And my Ph.D?"

"Ah…" he sighed. "Harvard has a very strict protocol around this, I am afraid. So, in terms of your contribution to the greater good—you can work from there, and we can keep you on your grant stipend. Nothing needs to change. But in terms of finishing your dissertation… that would have to wait until this is all over. It could be years."

"And if I come back?"

"Well, then there wouldn't be a problem, of course. At worst you would be done by September."

They finished their meeting, and she logged off the call. Then she went to her mother's room. She was surprisingly awake. She was still quite weakened by the trauma of the op. However, if there was one thing that her mom had shown her these last 10 years, was that she was a fighter. This was no different.

Her mom gestured for Lauren to come closer.

"What did he say, Lauren?"

She sat down. "I can do the work from here for the time being. So, I don't need to go back for that."

Her mom smiled. "You can never hide anything from me, my dear. What else?"

So, she told her mom about the Ph.D. How she was so close, had worked so hard, and that she would not be able to finish if she didn't go back.

"What are you afraid of, Lauren?" asked her mom. "It seems to me like you can be here—at home—and still do the work. But you have to finish what you started, right? You don't need to stay here for your old weak mother."

"Mom, rest. We don't need to talk about it now."

Her mom put her head back on the pillows. "You don't need to stay here for me, you know. But I'm glad you are here, nonetheless." And she drifted off to sleep once more.

Lauren tidied up around the house for a bit. She had a ton of work to do. But she also felt paralyzed by the choices in front of her. Her mind was spinning in a thousand different directions.

She tried to work but gave up after a couple of hours. Her mom is now sitting up and reading, so she decided to go for a run, to try to clear her head.

It wasn't very different from her old route as a schoolgirl. The house her mom now rented was just a few blocks down from the place she grew up in. She slowed down as she passed it… and happy memories mingled with sad ones. She never thought much about her father. He was not present most of her life, and when he left, there was no need to further stay in touch. She sped up again, pushing him out of her mind.

She ran past Uncle Joe's place. She thought of Jimmy, as she had every time these last two weeks when she ran past here. He was in Cape Town. She should call him. But she didn't. He had his life, she had hers. And if she went back to Harvard, there would be no point. But…

She ran through the dip, up on Baron van Rheede, all the way to the Cango Wildlife Ranch. It felt like old times—this was her old turn-around point.

She checked her watch and started to run back to town. She was breathing evenly, she still felt strong.

But her mom wasn't. The virus was about to be a big problem. Recovery from the surgery would leave her mom vulnerable for weeks still. She couldn't go back.

But if she didn't, she might never finish her studies. She understood, by now, the way things were. Better than most people. The world was about to shut down. When they got to the other side, there might be no place for her in the US anymore. She could secure her future by going back now.

She decided to do the final loop through town. Down to the town hall, right up Voortrekker, and then right up Jan van Riebeek again… names that harkened back to Dutch heroes of the Apartheid era, she wondered how the black residents of Oudtshoorn felt about them. She wondered if anyone cared?

And if she stayed? Her feet now in a rhythm, speeding up for the final bit…

If she stayed here… To look after her mom. And work remotely. Try to make a difference. But with no certainty. No security. They could cut her off any moment. Africa was a long way away from the US…

She did a final sprint up to her driveway. Out of breath, she didn't notice that someone was sitting in a car in front of her house.

PG GELDENHUYS

She was busy with a backstretch when she noticed him walking toward her.

"Jimmy?"

"Hi L," he smiled. "You're looking well."

She was aware that she must look horrible. Sweaty, wearing her old exercise clothes, a mess. She mumbled a greeting, then ran inside. He couldn't see her like this!

Over her shoulder, she shouted, "Make yourself at home! I just need to freshen up!

He didn't care. But Jimmy knew how women were.

She finally came out of the bathroom, dressed in shorts and a blue t-shirt, but with her wet hair tied back. She still took his breath away. But then again, she did that even looking sweaty in the driveway.

He had been chatting to her mom, something that he hadn't done a lot of in the past. He had always known how important she was to Lauren. She had, in those early days, not warmed to him. And in later years, well... she only recently moved back to Oudtshoorn.

So he found her delightful. Interested in all that they had been doing with Quick Meals, his time in New Zealand, he was surprised how much she knew about rugby. This was very different from Lauren.

"I see you too have been catching up," said Lauren, after they exchanged an awkward hug.

"We sure have," grinned Jimmy. "Your mom is quite something."

Lauren glanced at her mother, who also smiled and said, "I was telling Jimmy how I always had a crush on Richie McCaw. Most of the girls liked Stan Wilson, but I always liked Richie. Part of it was to piss your dad off, I suppose. Those final years together, he would get so angry when the All Blacks beat us, which they usually did... and I took perverse pleasure in telling him how much I liked that guy." She coughed. "The difference was, eventually, even when he wasn't here, I would watch their games. Got me a genuine appreciation for the game."

"Why didn't that rub off on you, Lauren?" asked Jimmy.

"She was too busy studying, our Lauren," smiled her mom. "Couldn't care less about watching those sports. Paid off right? Oxford... Harvard..."

Jimmy smiled. "She has enough degrees for the two of us, that's for sure."

"Oh, shush Jimmy," exclaimed her mom. "You studied at the university of life, from what I hear. Don't think that that experience isn't worth as much, you hear?"

"Ok you two," said Lauren, wanting to break up this line of chatter. Although Jimmy seemed more at ease with the subject than the last time they spoke.

"Mom, can I take him away? I'll be back in a bit to help you with your bath."

"Take your time, my dear," said her mom, picking up a trashy magazine.

She took his arm and steered him toward the front door.

He didn't mind. It was that glorious autumn twilight hour in Oudtshoorn that he remembered so well from his last year of high school. They walked in silence for a bit, her arm linked through his.

"You know what, Lauren? It's been eight years since I came here—but doesn't it feel like a lifetime ago? I mean... man, we have lived, haven't we?"

She smiled. "We have, haven't we?" She felt distracted. Why was he here?

As if reading her thoughts, he said, "I've come back for the weekend to visit Uncle Joe and Melissa—and the kids—but that's not the only reason."

"What's the other reason?"

"Your mom called me. Told me to come. Says you are heading back to the US soon. And..." he stopped, unlinking his arm from her. They stood, facing each other. "And that I needed to come to say goodbye to you. For the last time."

She searched for any of the old anger, the resentment. But there was nothing in his eyes.

"That sounds so final," Lauren finally said.

"It needs to be. We can't keep on doing this, Lauren. I'm in an extremely good place right now... even though I've lost it all in New Zealand, I feel like I've regained myself. Robby, the company, Jess..."

"Jess?" She raised her eyebrows.

"Yes." He looked away. "Nothing's happened between us, if that's what you're wondering."

"But something could happen?" She had to ask the question.

He started walking again. "It could. But I told her I needed to come here first. Finish things, we left too many things unsaid in Boston."

She felt a sudden massive sense of loss. Somehow, even though there had been other women in Jimmy's life, she had always thought he might wait for her. That they were destined to be together. And now...

She steeled herself; "So let's talk, Jimmy. Let's finish it, so we can both make the right decision for what we want in life."

"I'm glad you said that," he replied. "But let's get away. Let's really talk."

"What do you have in mind?" she asked.

49

The Otter Trail is South Africa's most popular hiking trail. Fully booked a year in advance, with a maximum of 12 people staying in the two 6-sleeper huts over five days on the trail, it is impossible to walk it at the last minute. In March, it is still mild weather on the southern coast of South Africa. The thick coastal foliage and spectacular vistas made it an irresistible experience.

And for Jimmy and Lauren, they had the trail all to themselves. Officially closed as the pandemic panic spread and institutions shut down, they snuck into the park the day before they closed the gates and walked it.

Just the two of them.

Lauren had too much work to do. There was a worldwide pandemic brewing, for God's sake. But she was also mentally, physically, and emotionally exhausted. But between her mom and Jimmy, she had relented. A few days off. To think. To take stock. She had a condition: They would do double time and walk the five-day trail in three. Uncle Joe and Melissa took them to the start, and took their mobile phones.

"We'll be waiting for you at the restaurant in Natures Valley in three days. Now go rest, relax and spend some time together. You both need it." Said Joe, and left them with their two backpacks, moderate food supplies, and borrowed sleeping bags.

Lauren also knew that, by agreeing to the few days, she was increasing her chances of being cut off. Flights might be halted at any time. But, for once, she did not obsess over it. Let it Be, as the Beatles said…

The first section was relatively short. They arrived at the empty huts in the early afternoon after a late start. They had not spoken much. Lauren had to keep all her concentration on the rocky coastal path, she was afraid that her physical exhaustion would make her trip up. But they navigated it without incident.

Jimmy went off to light a fire and cook them an early dinner. She took a shower and went for a quick nap. It was dead quiet, the two huts completely isolated in a pristine setting, close to a rocky beach.

She woke up from her not-so-quick nap at 6 am the next morning. And she was starving.

There was no sign of Jimmy in the hut. She went outside, to see him sitting by a small fire, boiling water. He heard her and stood to face her, a big smile on his face.

"Ah, she wakes at last."

"I'm so sorry, Jimmy. I…."

"You needed some proper sleep. I get it. Now give me a second, and I'll fix us some coffee… and some of Melissa's famous *beskuit*."

"Yum. Ok, let me go wash the sleep out of my face, and I'll be right back."

They sat huddled together, the sleeping bag draped over them as they watched the ocean. The coffee was strong and the rusks sweet. She still felt so tired… but the sugar started to kick in, and she got up to stretch.

He busied himself with preparing some porridge while she loosened her limbs. "Today and tomorrow are normally tough days by themselves. Lots of up and down, if your body isn't used to it, it can be quite hard. Still game to fast track this walk?"

"Sure. I've been keeping fit. You?" She felt tired—but her old competitive instincts kicked in.

"Definitely."

And so it was. They walked hard. The scenery was breathtaking. The undulating hills revealed new treasures all the time. The elusive Knysna Loerie bird. Sheer cliffs and gorgeous bays, sweeping vistas and exotic rock formations. It was a metaphor for their conversation, which was both lively and comfortable.

They reminisced over school days. They talked about their time traveling in Thailand, Scotland, and Japan. About meeting up in Hong Kong, London, and Boston.

They talked about Daniella. And Anna. Edward, Chetaine, Robby, Max, Jacques, Todd, the Wilsons, Mr. Masataka.

And as they arrived at the huts just before sunset, they moved to talk about the present. Jimmy cooked them another early dinner, just pasta, and sauce. He had brought some red wine for them. They each had a glass out of a steel coffee cup. It was delicious.

"I thought you had stopped drinking, Jimmy," she ventured.

"I did for a while there. But now… well, I guess, I enjoy a glass of wine or whiskey sometimes. Even a beer. But it feels different now. I was trying to use alcohol to compensate for stuff before. Now it's just something else that I enjoy occasionally."

"You don't feel like you need to compensate anymore?" she asked, looking at the fire.

"Lauren, I turn 25 next month. I feel like so much has happened to me in the last seven years.

I had just turned 18 when I lost my family, you know. I have lived and worked all over the world. Just over a year ago, I was on top of the world in terms of material things." He ladled out more pasta for them. The sound of the ocean was soothing, and the moon had started to come out.

"And it didn't make me happy. I thought I was just missing you. But that wasn't it, either. I love you—and I want to be with you—but I can't look at you to complete me. I had to figure myself out first. And I realized that no person, no amount of recognition, no amount of money would fill the hole." He put his hand on hers. She didn't seem to mind.

"And you know what I figured out? I'm still young. I've lived big. There is loads of time to work toward what I truly want. And right now, it's to be in Cape Town, enjoy the most awesome city on earth, and work like a demon to try to save our start-up company."

She nodded. He wanted to share more, she sensed. "We pitched our tech to a big potential partner last week. They were interested… but in the end, they turned us down. Not enough consumer movement. So, we're not out of the woods yet… but who knows, if we keep on banging down doors, we might be able to get some new investors. Win or lose, this chapter will also be done in a year. But we will win. I'm sure of it."

He looked into her eyes. "And when I have done that and fulfilled my obligations? Well… then I'll come to find you."

She felt a lump in her throat, and her eyes started to mist over. "And Jess?"

"Jess ticks all the boxes. Except one." He leaned over and kissed her. "She's not the one."

They made love that night, under the stars, just the two of them.

The next day, it was a late start. They walked hard to catch the river crossing at Bloukrans at low tide—but still missed it. It was therefore still a slog to get through—the treacherous river crossing left most walkers soaking wet, including their gear. But it was also exhilarating, as if they were fighting the elements and their demons at the same time. The waves beat at them, and they shouted defiance as they paddled their way through to the other side.

Wet but happy, they reached the fourth hut as the sun was setting. They could not reach Uncle Joe to let him know they wouldn't make it. And they both let it go. Uncle Joe would understand.

On the last day, they walked slowly toward the end, neither wanting to go back to reality. The weather was gloomy with the threat of rain, reflecting their mood.

As they crested the last hill, they were presented with the beautiful hamlet of Natures Valley. The glorious beach that fronted the town was bookended by tropical forest and a river in flow. They stared at it for a bit, holding hands.

Lauren turned to Jimmy. She took his face in her hands, and said, "I'm staying."

He looked at her, not speaking. Then, finally, he said, "You don't know how long it will be before you can go back. If your predictions are true."

"It doesn't matter. What I realized these past few days…" she hesitated, and her gaze went far across the ocean. "I've also been chasing independence. But I have it. Given my credentials, and especially with what's going on now, I can work anywhere in the world. Why not here?"

"What about your Doctorate? I mean… you have put so much into it…"

She looked at him. Saw him. "I have. But the work we do over the next few years will completely change the content of it. This Coronavirus pandemic is a whole new set of data. I could publish it. I could get it done. But it would simply be for the recognition. If I am serious about the work, then I should also take a breather. Trust the process."

"What are you saying, Lauren?" His voice had dropped to a whisper, as if he was holding his breath.

"I'm saying, Mr. Barnes, that I am not much unlike you. I've been chasing the recognition, and completely lost sight of what was important. And it's time to stop all that. It's time for a whole new chapter. Our chapter."

The sun broke through the clouds, and she kissed him.

EPILOGUE

Lauren's mom made a full recovery from her surgery. She went back to work helping Joe and Melissa in their ever-expanding hotel and restaurant business. The best part of the job was occasionally babysitting their twin girls. She told them bedtime stories of powerful women doing great things. They wanted to grow up to be scientists, like Auntie Lauren.

Daniella and Professor Higgins were co-opted into a task force to combat the spread of the virus in the United States. The response was too slow, and the virus would claim over a half-million lives in the next year. The body of research generated, however, helped to prepare protocols and vaccine readiness systems for future events. Lauren's two mentors were never friendly, but the crisis forged a resilient respect and collaboration between them.

Il Leone in New Zealand never bought Action Sports Bar, the deal was scuppered by the lockdown. When the country went back to normal operations but without international tourists, Masa Corp accepted a reversed offer and sold it to Action Sports Bar. Anna moved to Tokyo. Her career floundered due to dismal performance of large restaurants, and sports bars in particular.

Quick Meals received a 30% equity investment from Price Right in

April 2020. Overnight, consumers switched to home delivery instead of in-person dining. Jimmy and Robby helped organize the implementation of the technology in 200 locations countrywide. They both contracted COVID-19 in the process, but luckily only with mild symptoms.

A year later, Quick Meals listed as a public company in order to raise funds for global expansion. The listing made Jimmy, Robby, and the Wilsons multi-millionaires.

Jess stayed with Quick Meals until the skies opened again in September 2020. She took a contract at a top development company in the Ukraine, and started a serious relationship with a business analyst named Igor.

Harvard decided it was, after all, permissible for Lauren to finish her Ph.D. remotely. She would become a world-renowned expert in the field of virology and a sought-after speaker. But, over time, she limited her travel and professional output. She had other priorities.

After the listing, Robby immediately became bored. He decided to chase some new projects with his model girlfriend, who had some big ideas around fashion. So far, their ventures have had various degrees of success. But their tempestuous relationship makes them tabloid favorites.

The board asked Jimmy to head up Quick Meals when Robby resigned. Jimmy declined the offer. After a successful handover to a hand-picked new CEO, he disappeared from the limelight for a while.

Lauren and Jimmy bought a smallholding outside Oudtshoorn. They took all their wedding guests—10 people—on the Otter Trail for their honeymoon.

In a rare interview with Forbes Africa, many years later, Jimmy would say, "The meaning of true wealth? The love and respect of my wife and kids. And a treasure chest full of travel memories. What more could we ask for?"

ACKNOWLEDGMENTS

I have been trying to write a novel my whole life. This Number 1 bucket list item would not have been possible without the help and support of a number of people.

A special thanks to Dustin, Bill, Evan, Amelia and Sunny from my RLA Forum. You served as my lockdown accountability framework, and that helped me punch out that 20,000 words a month.

On that note, the culture of mindfulness and personal work fostered by the Entrepeneurs' Organization has been key for me. Thanks to all the amazing people that have been part of this journey, with special reference to Nicola Nel, Phoenix Forum and Rich Mulholland.

I have a great many wonderful friends who encouraged me along the way, and acted as my cheerleaders for this project. You know who you are. Particularly, it feels like my regular check-ins with Clive has not only kept me sane, but kept me focused. Thanks bud. I owe you.

I want to thank Dave and my publishing team. A big thanks goes to Abby Saayman for background support, proofreading and taking care of other things while I did this.

I want to thank the women in my life. Many of the characters here are inspired by strong women from my past and my present. Particularly I want to thank my sister Karla for doing double time in reading this, and the first edit. You know me best, and your input has been invaluable.

My "work wife", Yolanda Bekker Colman, did the final edit. After she signed off, I could send it off in peace. To show your "baby" to people is quite daunting. Thanks for liking it, fixing it and helping me to let it go.

My mother Benny was also one of my early proofreaders. I owe her -and my late father Matie – a debt of gratitude for instilling in me love of reading, traveling and writing. Love you Mom. Miss you Dad.

My darling Caroline gave me so much joy in my life, and two beautiful baby boys. During Lockdown and the 2020 chaos, her unwavering support, endless suggestions and emotional affirmation kept me going. Writing a novel is like giving birth, I think. At the end of term, I just wanted it to be done. Thanks for also finally giving me the name of the book, babe. It only took a year to name this baby.

Although many of the characters in this book are inspired by real life, none of them are based on an actual person. Those that know me would say it reads like a bit of an autobiography. I find that very flattering – Jimmy is much cooler than I ever was.

Also, I am lucky to be surrounded by storytellers and adventurers, inspiring business people and charismatic leaders. As such, a few people might think I actually wrote this about them.

Maybe Jimmy has some of the best and the worst in all of us. If you contributed to the inspiration for some of the wilder stories, I hope I did it justice.

PG, July 2021

ABOUT THE AUTHOR

PG Geldenhuys has spent a lifetime exploring the world, hiking beautiful parks and meeting interesting people. His luxury safaris business and his retreat planning businesses focus on connection through nature. As a keynote speaker and global facilitator, he loves to work with business owners on realising their personal and professional goals.

When he isn't teaching or spending time with Caroline and the boys, you can find him doing personal work on the world's epic trails. Offsides is his first novel.

Find PG at www.shoshinwalks.com